A dragon, tw...
of a horse, s...
into the brightness...

Its scales flashed brightly, and when its spike-filled mouth gaped, ragged plumes of fire shone out. Arkady yearned for a horse to ride against such a monster, for surely he could not face it on foot.

"Make it a good horse, Arkady my champion," Surata told him, her voice ringing in his flesh, moving up his arm like the strength of his muscles.

Arkady tried to imagine all the attributes he could wish for in a warhorse. He felt himself rise, his legs bowed out by the enormous red-sorrel with flaxen mane and tail formed out of nothing. He was the most perfect warhorse.

The dragon roared and half-rose on its hind legs, extending its talons toward Arkady, seeking to grasp and rend him.

"He is your dragon, Arkady my champion. You have the right to defeat him."

"Then I will," Arkady promised, gathering up his warhorse's reins and riding forth to meet his fate...

*   *   *

"A compelling and finely crafted novel of a faraway place and time...a searing, climactic journey into deep truth. I was sorry when it was over. This is grand entertainment indeed!"

—Whitley Strieber, co-author of *Warday*

TO THE HIGH REDOUBT

CHELSEA QUINN YARBRO

POPULAR LIBRARY

An Imprint of Warner Books, Inc.

A Warner Communications Company

POPULAR LIBRARY EDITION

Copyright © 1985 by Chelsea Quinn Yarbro
All rights reserved.

Popular Library® and Questar® are registered trademarks of
Warner Books, Inc.

Cover art by Rowena Morrill

Popular Library books are published by
Warner Books, Inc.
666 Fifth Avenue
New York, N.Y. 10103

Ⓦ A Warner Communications Company

Printed in the United States of America

First Printing: October, 1985

10 9 8 7 6 5 4 3 2 1

for
SEVEN
from
SIX

redoubt: from the Old French *reboubte*: nest, niche. Hence, a breastwork fortress, especially one located on the crests of mountains or above passes.

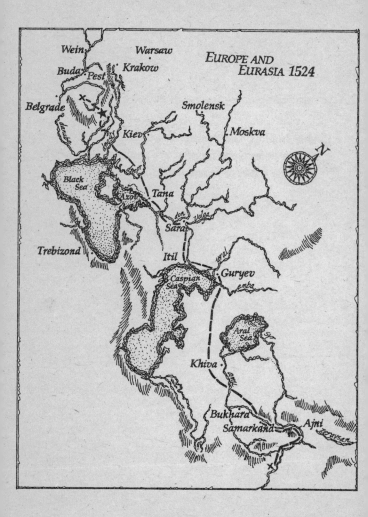

EUROPE AND
EURASIA 1524

Wein
Warsaw
Buda
Krakow
Pest
Belgrade
Kiev
Smolensk
Moskva
Black
Sea
Lvov
Tana
don
Volga
Sarai
Trebizond
Itil
itil
Caspian
Sea
Guryev
emba
Aral
Sea
Khiva
Bukhara
Samarkand
Ajni
zerevscan

Chapter 1

Afternoon was fading into evening when the Margrave finally summoned Arkady Sól to his headquarters. The herald who brought the cordial message delivered the words so woodenly that Arkady felt dread go through him in spite of the flowery references to "our most-favored captain" and "your loyal and devoted leadership in the presence of the enemy."

"Very well," he said to the herald as he shoved his straight brown hair out of his eyes. "I am almost finished with mending this hilt. It will be an honor to go to the Margrave within the hour."

The herald cleared his throat. "Captain Sól, the Margrave is waiting for you now. He would not . . . look kindly on a delay. He is going to hear Mass shortly."

Arkady sighed and got up from the three-legged campstool he had been perching on. "All right. Let it be now." He stared at the herald. "Do you accompany me, or am I to go alone?"

"I have other messages," the herald said, his eyes firmly fixed on some distant spot over Arkady's left shoulder.

"Then I am not under arrest," Arkady said, not making it

a question. He forced his lips to smile. "The Margrave is gracious."

"Your years of service stand for much," the herald mumbled, then turned away before he could embarrass himself and Captain Sól any further. He fingered his tabard. "Other messages."

"Deliver them," Arkady said lightly. "Don't let me detain you." He offered the man a half-salute before he turned away, not permitting himself to walk slowly no matter how much he desired to postpone the confrontation. He carried only one weapon, his cinquedea tucked into his belt and lying now horizontally along his back, as its Luccan smith had intended. So used was he to carrying it that he almost forgot he had it with him now.

Three officers guarded the entrance to the mill where the Margrave had established his headquarters. They raised lanthorns to see Arkady's face, though all three knew him well and recognized his voice.

"For the love of God, Vencel," Arcady protested to the nearest. "Must you do this?"

Vencel had the grace to cough before he replied. "You are under orders, Sól. We are under orders as well." He looked away. "The Margrave is in the main room."

"Yes, I assumed that. Why are you pretending that I know nothing of this because of . . . what happened?" He did not bother to wait for an answer—there would be none given, he was certain—but permitted Vencel to open the door for him. "Thank you," he remembered to say before the door closed behind him.

The servants inside the mill came to escort Arkady into the main room of the mill, where once the family of the miller had gathered to eat and talk in happier times. One of the servants could not resist looking at Arkady as he indicated the open door. "It's a shame, Captain Sól."

"Yes, it is," Arkady said, trying not to reveal how bitter he felt at that moment. "Thank you for escorting me." He could see the distress in the servant's eyes and could not bring himself to make it worse.

2

"I will pray for you," the servant promised him as he turned away.

The Margrave Fadey sat with one leg propped up on a stool, his arm resting on the table, a document beneath it. "Captain Sól," he said with distaste as Arkady came into the light.

"You wanted to see me," Arkady said, because he felt he must say something. "I've come."

"Yes," the Margrave said quietly. "I assume you know why you are here."

What possessed the man to draw this out so much? Arkady asked himself. Why would he not simply inform him that he was discharged and in disgrace. "I know."

"And you have no sense of shame for what you did?" the Margrave demanded. "You do not cringe at the sight of men of honor."

"There is no honor in riding into an ambush. I told Captain Kamenetz that at the time." He said this wearily, having repeated it more often than he could bear in the last few days. "I did not want my men to be killed."

"You admit to your own cowardice," the Margrave Fadey accused him, his moustaches quivering more than his indignant voice.

"If refusing to permit my men to be massacred is cowardice, then I own it freely." He folded his arms. "I will take the writ and I will leave. That is what you want me to do, isn't it?"

"What I would *want*, Captain Sól, is for you to have followed orders. None of this would be necessary now." The Margrave Fadey glared his disapproval.

"Only a Requiem for all of my men," Arkady said as gently as he could. "I'll take the writ, Margrave, and I will leave you."

The Margrave kept his arm on the parchment. "You must also sign an oath, very binding, on the graves of your parents and your hope of salvation." He took a deep breath. "You are to vow that you will never, for any reason whatsoever, aid our enemies, the Turks, or give council, advice or instruction to them."

"I doubt they'd have me," Arkady said lightly. "A Pole fighting with a company of Polish and Ukrainian soldiers? They'd be more apt to kill me than seek my advice."

The Margrave folded his arms. "You may jest if you wish, but you will sign the oath."

"Gladly," Arkady said at once. "Then you will be rid of me and you can go back to your battles for glory." He had not wanted to sound bitter, but he could hear his own words and they shocked him.

"You are still under my command, I will not tolerate your insolence. It is sufficient that you are a coward." He held out a quill. "The ink is there. Read this and sign it."

Arkady sighed. He had the rudiments of letters, but it was always a chore to go over documents. He came and leaned over the table, staring down. He pieced the words together, grateful that the Margrave had not insisted in writing in Latin or Russian or Greek. The intent was clear and not even the courtly language could disguise the severity of the vow. He reached for the quill and dipped it in the ink. *Arkady Todor Sól, from Sól, on the Feast of Saint Stanislas* he scribbled, not caring if the ink spattered. "There." He gave the quill back to the Margrave Fadey.

"This will be sent to Sól and entered in the roles of your church." The message was plain: everyone would know of his disgrace and he would not be permitted to return home.

"If that is necessary, by all means," Arkady said. "I will not argue with you." He felt more weary than before. "What else? Do you give me the writ, or is there more?"

"The company will watch you leave camp. You will be allowed to take your weapons and your horse. The rest remains here." He paused. "You have some prize money. If it were up to me, I would claim it, but I have been told that I am not empowered to do so. You may take it with you." This last certainly galled him.

"Do my weapons include my armor?" He had paid a high price for the armor and hated the thought of leaving it behind.

"You may take the steel-studded leather, but the rest is

4

forfeit," the Margrave told him, knowing that this would distress Arkady.

"If you insist," Arkady said. He would not give the man the satisfaction of losing his temper.

The Margrave rose slowly. He was over forty and battle had taken a toll on him: he moved like an old man. "Here is the writ. It is signed by me and both our priests, as witnesses. You will be expected to leave here before sunset tomorrow."

"So long," Arkady marvelled. "A pity that you could not require me to leave tonight."

"Yes," the Margrave agreed, not aware of the irony in Arkady's tone. "Your men will be given disciplinary action and a reduction in prize mon—"

Arkady faced the Margrave Fadey, making an effort to contain his fury. "My men only did what good soldiers must do, and followed my orders. They accepted my judgment. If I had ordered them into action and they had not gone, you would punish them. But they did not go because I would not permit it. If there is to be any more punishment, it should not fall on my men." His head ached as he spoke and he could feel the blood pound in his neck. He was able to keep a reasonable level to his speech, but he could not disguise his feelings completely. "You are concerned about the morale of the other men, those who fared so badly in the last fight. Their morale would be much worse if a third of your forces had been hacked to bits and what was left of them hung out on hooks for trophies."

"They should have fought," the Margrave persisted, his hands trembling.

"Yes, they should," Arkady said unexpectedly. "They were eager to fight, and I was proud of our chance to face the Turks. But what were we to do in the face of certain ambush? The defile was narrower than the scouts told us at first, and the walls of it too sheer for men in armor to climb. The Turks were waiting around the rim, with others to close in behind us. What chance would any of us had?"

"There is a Turkish fortress above that defile. Until we take it, we are held back from our advance. The Turks have come too far as it is, and they are not being rebuffed as they should be." The Margrave wore a large crucifix on a thick chain around his neck. "Ever since Constantinople fell, God has seemed to turn His back on us for that failure. If we are to redeem our faith as well as our souls, we must turn these despicable heathens back into their own lands and purge our soil of their presence."

"You and the Archbishops are agreed on that," Arkady said quietly. "Most of the men in my unit fear for their homes and their families. They do not want to return to find burned-out ruins and scattered crops, with no way to learn if their wives and parents and children have been taken as slaves or killed. You and the Archbishops may not think highly of such reasons, but I would pledge my honor—if I had any to pledge—on such men."

The Margrave Fadey sighed. "You are not the sort of soldier who can understand what is at stake here." He leaned back. "Very well. Be gone with you. The entire camp will be told of my action against you, and there will be a formal escort of disgrace when you leave the camp."

Arkady sighed and saluted. "It will have to be as you wish."

"You are a disappointment to me, Captain Sól. You were sent here with such high praise and recommendations for your valor and your tenacity."

"It is good to know that my former lord thought well of me," Arkady said, his attitude suddenly gentler.

"He will also be informed of your disgrace." The Margrave sat back with a sour expression of satisfaction on his old features. "You will not be able to find honorable employment in Poland anywhere."

'Of course," Arkady said. He stood quietly, wishing the Margrave would finish it.

"Here is your writ," he said, handing a smaller piece of parchment to Arkady. "You are no longer a part of this or any other Polish or Ukrainian force of Christians opposing the advance of the Turks."

Now that the thing was in front of him, it was almost

impossible for Arkady to take it. Fierce resentment against this stupid, vainglorious nobleman welled up in him, making his head hurt more than before. "Honor and glory to the defenders of the Church of Our Lord Jesus Christ," he mumbled as he took the document and crossed himself.

"You may leave me, Captain Sól. If it were for me to decide, you would lose your rank, as well, but only your lord may do that." Clearly this irritated the Margrave. "Inform the bailiff of the camp when you are ready to leave."

Arkady did not trust himself to speak; he saluted and turned on his heel. He was out of the room quickly, brushing past the two men who guarded the door.

Night had come, bringing its own rustlings. The camp was quieter now, with most of the men tending to their gear, for in two days they would all be on the march again. Many fires glowed, and where they burned, men gathered around them, some silent, some talking, some singing, a few throwing dice, though such activities were forbidden. Arkady walked back to his tent through the familiar huddle and clutter, missing it already.

"How bad was it?" Hedeon asked as Arkady appeared in the flap of the door.

"I can keep the leather armor, but I have to leave the steel. I can keep my weapons and my horse." He held out the crumpled writ. "This declares me coward, Hedeon, for trying to save my men from destruction. The Margrave Fadey wants someone to blame for the way the battle went." He kicked his saddle in anger. "He's an old fool, and dangerous. Take care he doesn't get you all killed."

"He wishes to save us from the Turks," Hedeon said, his voice cracking, for although he had been serving as an aide for more than a year, he was just twelve years old.

"At this rate, he will save us by sending us all to Heaven or Hell, to save the Turks the trouble." As soon as these words were out, he lifted his finger. "No. Do not repeat that. You would be cast out, too, if you did, and you have less chance of making your way in the world than I do, and that is little enough for me." He stared at the lanthorn, which was the only

7

light in the tent. "Is there any wine left? I'd like to get roaring drunk tonight."

"One skin," the lad said apologetically. "You didn't ask for it, and so—"

Arkady waved him to silence. "Probably just as well. My head is bad enough now; tomorrow it would be intolerable if I drink." He looked at his gear. "Do you think they'll let me take the helmet if I leave the helm?"

Hedeon did not venture an opinion, but he winked.

"Well, pack it for me in any case. I may need to sell it one day, to buy food."

"It won't come to that," Hedeon said with false certainty. "You will find another unit to take you on."

"I will?" Arkady said bleakly. "Who will take me? What for? Contract soldiers might let me sign on, perhaps. Then it will be take any man's battle if he has enough gold. Or I could do what many another man in my position has done, and turn robber. Until they caught me and cut off my hands, or blinded me, or hanged me, I would live adequately, I suppose." Abruptly he flung the writ away from him. "Thorns of God! What right has the Margrave to do this?" He went on without allowing Hedeon to speak. "Yes, I know, rank and place and all the rest of it. He believes he must make an example and I am it." He dropped down onto the pile of blankets that served him as a bed. "What sorrows me the most is knowing that he will try and try to take that Turkish redoubt until every single soldier in his forces is dead. And what is the worst aspect to all of this is that it doesn't matter. That breastwork fortress means almost nothing to the Turks. Taking it would change very little."

Hedeon listened nervously. "You're not being cautious, Captain Sól," he warned. "There are those who can hear you."

"What difference?" Arkady asked, then relented. "Very well. I don't want to see you compromised. If you have good sense, you will go to Captain Pliecs when I'm . . . not here. He is a good and sensible man and he will not abuse you."

"Captain Tworek already has asked that I serve for him," Hedeon said, trying to sound pleased.

Arkady shrugged. "He's a sensible man. He won't treat you badly. He's got more fleas on him than a heartsick camel, but there's nothing new in that." No soldier was free of them, and if one officer attracted more than another, what did it matter?

"I'll take care," Hedeon said, relieved that this was the only comment that Arkady made.

"And God guard you," Arkady added as an afterthought. "You will need His protection, I am afraid." He started to lean back. "See that my leather armor is packed, and my weapons." He drew the cinquedea out of his belt and handed it to Hedeon. "I'll want to carry this with me, but the two swords and the maul . . . pack them as usual." With that he leaned back and closed his eyes.

By morning, Hedeon had attended to his chores and had brought Arkady's horse around to the tent, where he waited now, bridled but not saddled, while Arkady went about the rough business of shaving with a knife edge. "There is food, Captain, if you want it," the boy called out.

"Cheese will do. See if you can swipe a few extra rounds for me, so I'll have something to eat on the road. Don't get caught at it, or the Margrave will see you flogged for helping me." He kept up his chore, dragging the blade over his wet face, wincing every now and then at the little cuts he gave himself.

"The priest has come to hear your confession," Hedeon added a moment later.

"I will be ready shortly." Why did he wish to go to such trouble to make himself a respectable figure, he wondered, when his departure was intended to disgrace him? It might be that he would not permit the Margrave to dictate everything to him. "Ask the priest to step inside."

The tent flap was drawn back and a small, bent man came through the opening. He made a blessing in Arkady's general direction, then said, "It is unfortunate that you must leave us, my son."

"Yes, it is, isn't it?" Arkady said with a lightness that he did not feel. "I will be with you in a moment, Father."

The priest took his place on the three-legged campstool.

"Sometimes it is in distress that we glimpse the Face of God," he remarked, then waited for a response.

"I haven't seen Him so far," Arkady said, nicking himself one last time. He blotted his face with the same rag he had used to clean his swords, then turned to the priest. "I appreciate your coming, Father, and I know that it is expected of us both for me to make some sort of accounting to you as my excuse for my actions. But I still believe that it was right to stay out of the defile, and I cannot apologize for helping my men live."

"God is merciful," the priest said quietly.

Arkady knelt and crossed himself. "I admit that I swear— all soldiers swear. I admit that I wench when I have the opportunity. I admit that I hanker after gold. I admit that I have killed men in battle. I admit that I have been drunk and made a great fool of myself over dice and women. All that is so. But I have never knowingly exposed my men to any more danger than is a soldier's due. That is why I refused to fight, and why the Margrave is sending me away."

"Is this a confession, my son?" the priest asked, a bit bewildered in spite of years of experience listening to soldiers.

"No. I do not think this is a sin. I cannot confess it, Father. It would be a greater sin if I did." He crossed himself again.

"I cannot offer you absolution without confession," the priest reminded him.

"Then let me confess to drinking or wenching or gambling or stealing ducks from the Margrave's larder—it's all one to me." He was ready to get to his feet but paused out of respect to the old man.

"I will give you a provisional absolution, my son, and that is all that I may do, properly. This is not what will please the Margrave, for it will be learned in the camp and questions will be asked."

"As well they should be," Arkady said brusquely, rising without the priest's permission. "But in a day or two it will all be forgot, and there will be another battle." He looked at the neatly tied bundles that Hedeon had set out. "By tonight, some of the men will have put up a different tent here, and I will be nothing more than another officer who left."

The priest got slowly to his feet. "I hope you will think about what I said. There are times when God is seen from the depth of the abyss."

"Thank you, Father. I will remember it," he said, doubting it would ever occur to him again.

Outside, Hedeon stood, the reins of Arkady's horse clutched in his hands. "I will pack the saddle," he offered.

"I'd be grateful," Arkady said, proffering one of the two bundles he carried. He made a studied effort not to look around him, for he knew that half the men in camp had been alerted that he was about to leave. *If only I do not have to look at them, I can bear it,* he thought as he went through the familiar motions of lugging the bundles of his belongings. "Make sure you tie that bag on well; that's food for me and the horse."

Hedeon blinked back tears and did as he was told.

"We hate to see you go, Captain Sól," one of the men said in an undervoice. He was standing not far away, and at these words, Arkady looked up, taken unaware. His eyes met the soldier's.

"I . . ." He shook his head, unable to risk saying more. His eyes stung.

There were other words he heard, whispered among the men as they stood, watching him prepare to leave them. Pride and grief almost overwhelmed him as Arkady listened, incapable of ignoring the approval of the soldiers. He tried to convince himself that this alone was enough and that because of it his leaving would not be as bitter as it had been.

"It's ready, Captain Sól," Hedeon announced, no matter how obvious this was. "The saddle is—"

"I know, Hedeon." He reached into his wallet, which was tied to belt, and tossed two silver coins to the lad. "Take care you don't lose them foolishly."

Hedeon caught the coins and gave half a salute, then turned and ran away into the crowd.

The herald appeared and looked squarely at Arkady. "You must understand me: if it were up to me—"

"I realize that," Arkady interrupted him, getting into the

11

saddle as he spoke. "Let's get it over with. I don't fault you, man. Just don't take longer than you must."

The herald nodded as he took his place ahead of Arkady's horse and raised his staff so that the men would clear a way for them, which eventually would lead to the edge of the camp. "This is Captain Arkady Todor Sól, from Sól, who has brought shame upon himself and disgrace upon his lord. He has refused to act in the face of the enemy and has shown himself to be unworthy of the rank he holds. May his name be vilified by every one of you for his cowardice and his insubordination." The herald had repeated this more than seventeen times by the time the edge of the camp was reached, and his voice was growing worn.

"It is not on your head, herald," Arkady told him as he leaned down and gave the man a silver coin. "Take care. Your master will bring you to ruin if you do not check him."

The herald took the coin. "It is not right that I should listen to you."

"No, it's not," Arkady said. "But you are in danger if you do not: Well, I've said more than I ought and you have been patient with me. I am grateful to you for being so calm."

"It was not I. The men were silent, that's all." He looked back. "You need not tell me this, but which way will you go?"

"How should I know?" Arkady answered, more testily than before.

"As you wish," the herald said, nodding. At last he stepped aside, permitting Arkady to go.

Chapter 2

Two days outside of camp, Arkady came to a main trade route. He looked at the road, weighing his choices. Westward was all of Europe, and the center of his faith, but westward also lay the fruits of his dishonor and the life of an outcast. "If I am truly exiled," he said to his horse, "then let it be on my terms." With that he turned east.

At the end of the third day, he came to a market town, a squalid, hot gathering of mud-covered buildings and old, crowded wells, where men, camels, horses, mules and goats congregated, all of them determined to make more noise than the other. Toward the center of the houses there was a large open square, and in this place a good number of merchants set up their awninged tents to show their wares. Many of the farmers brought produce to sell to the merchants, and the most enterprising of the villagers made food to sell to both merchants and farmers.

Arkady dismounted and led his horse toward the market square, smiling a bit at the bustle. He knew that as a soldier he attracted some attention, but as he was alone, most of the others avoided him, fearing that he was one of those men turned rogue who was not safe to deal with. He made his way to one of the food booths, and since he did not know the language the woman spoke, he did his best to make himself understood in mime. The woman accepted two copper coins in return for two puffs of bread filled with a highly spiced mixture of lamb and onions. Arkady smiled widely at her and gave her another coin for a third helping.

The woman returned his grin and said something in a friendly tone of voice, then scowled in the direction of a platform on the other side of the market square. She shook her head in disapproval and made another incomprehensible remark before giving her attention to a new customer.

Arkady munched at his food and led his horse toward the well where other horses were tied up. He looked around in the hope of finding a farmer selling grain, since he was low on food for his animal. "I'll try to find you some apples or dates, fellow," he promised the horse.

A turbaned merchant in hodgepodge of clothes had climbed up on the platform and had started to harangue the crowd in a high, metallic voice. The attention he attracted was not entirely favorable, for some of the villagers whistled through their fingers at him in a derisive way. Others approached the platform, some of them holding wallets ready in their hands. Whatever he was selling, those merchants were interested in buying.

His curiosity piqued, Arkady strolled toward the platform, nibbling on the last of his food. He hoped to find out what it was the turbaned merchant had to offer.

An assistant was summoned, and he mounted the platform, pulling two large chains with him. Fifteen men and women, all shackled, stumbled up onto the platform. Most of them were dragged down by hunger, fatigue and the enervating weight of their wretchedness.

Arkady looked at the slaves in a little surprise, for although he had heard of open slave markets, he had never before seen one. He looked over the men and women offered for sale, wondering who they were and where they came from, that they should be where they were now. He had never seen clothes like they wore, or faces quite like theirs. He wished he knew enough of the local tongue to ask who the slaves were. He moved closer, as if proximity would explain matters to him. Once again he looked over the slaves as the turbaned merchant began to point out the various qualities of the first few men on the chain.

The woman next to last was the one who held Arkady's interest. She was young, certainly not yet twenty, with a strong and lithe body under the swathes of stained silk she wore. Her skin was a light shade of bronze and her hair was black as onyx, without a trace of red or blue in its shine. Her face was unusually tranquil, and a moment later Arkady realized why: she turned toward him, and he saw that her eyes were a strange, light shade, like frost-blighted leaves. The dark blue mark in the center of her forehead seemed more truly an eye.

Arkady was not aware that he had come to the foot of the platform and was staring up at the woman, but the little slaver was, and he hurried over to the soldier, a fawning grin on his grizzled features. He bowed ingratiatingly and began to say something that Arkady could not understand.

"Be quiet, you," Arkady snapped, his eyes fastened on the young woman. He had the oddest feeling that blind as she was, the woman was *looking at* him. "How much?" he asked the slaver.

Although the slaver did not understand Arkady's words, he had been a merchant long enough to know when someone wanted to buy. He held up both hands and flashed his fingers twice, then touched the gold earrings he wore.

Arkady shook his head, and held up all the fingers on one hand and two of the other, thinking as he did it that he was being incredibly foolish. He was a soldier without employment. To buy a slave was a ridiculous extravagance, and when that slave was a blind girl . . .

They compromised at fifteen gold coins, and Arkady gave

them to the merchant with an expression of distaste, and watched
while the woman was unfastened from the chain. The assistant
started to drag her forward; she missed her footing and almost
dropped to her knees.

"No!" Arkady ordered in the same tone of voice that he
used with his troops. He clambered onto the platform and took
the chain, shoving the assistant aside. The merchant and some
of the men in the crowd laughed; Arkady ignored them.

The young woman turned her face toward Arkady and said
something in a low, musical voice, extending her hand.

As Arkady closed his fingers around hers, he had the oddest
sense that a current had run down his arm, and he looked at
her, startled. He still did not know why he had brought her
and, now that he had her, what he would do with her. He
decided that he was mad. He said to the young woman, "Come
with me. This way." Gently he led her toward the stairs, then
checked her. "You have to step down here." He knew that she
did not have the words, but he felt her hand tighten, and she
went down the stairs carefully, feeling her way with her slip-
pered feet.

At the foot of the steps, she faced him again and murmured
something more, touching his arm uncertainly. There was a
question in the words she spoke.

"Take my arm; it's all right," he assured her as he went
back toward his horse. What on earth was he doing, he asked
himself as he guided her to his mount. What possessed him to
purchase a slave like this one? "Stay with my horse," he said
to her, feeling helpless to make himself understood.

"N'yeh," the young woman said, taking hold of the stirrup
as soon as Arkady put her hand there.

"Uh . . . good," he said, having no idea what she meant.
"You . . . stay here . . . I . . . *I*"—he pointed to himself and spoke
very slowly, finding the whole situation too absurd to deal
with—"have . . . to get food."

The young woman nodded, taking hold of the stirrup with
both hands. She said something more that sounded like "sim-
bruk" to Arkady and made an attempt at a smile.

"I'll . . . be back . . . shortly. Shortly." He took a few steps away from her, half expecting to see her run off or be taken by one of the other men in the crowd. He looked around and decided that she might not be safe, even if she remained where he had told her. He went back to her side and said. "Look, I'm going to take you and the horse with me."

She ducked her head, but whether it was a nod or a bow, Arkady had no way of knowing, and this was more frustrating than complete and stoic silence would have been.

One of the men in the crowd pointed at Arkady, laughing and saying something to the men around him. The others glanced toward the two strangers—not only different from the people in the market square, but different from each other as well—and joined the first man in laughter.

"Don't mind them," Arkady said grimly as he led both the horse and the young woman through the crowd toward the farmers' stalls. "We'll be out of here in a little while."

"N'yeh," she said with great serenity.

"Right," he agreed, still trying to figure out why he had let himself become caught by her and her plight. He might as well have joined forces with the soldiers of the Chinese for all the good he was doing, and now to have this slave as well!

She touched his arm. "Tara manidatta." She moved after him with unusual confidence, for although he chose their way carefully, she did not appear to falter as he led her. There was an odd half-smile on her full mouth.

Arkady found a seller of grain and had much to do to keep his horse from helping himself to the farmer's produce while he bargained for a price. At last he was satisfied that he had got the price as low as the farmer was willing to go for a stranger, and paid out the money. He noticed that his supply of coins had become dangerously low, and again he cursed the impulse that had caused him to buy the slave. Yet now that he had her, he could not stand to part with her. He gave her a puzzled look, then accepted the two bags of barley and oats the farmer held out to him.

Near the market two men in foreign dress stood, one of

them holding a long staff of bamboo. They watched Arkady and his slave as they made their way through the crowd. Although they did not speak to each other, there was an air of communication about them, as if they had no need for words. One of them frowned, but the other wore an expression of satisfaction, if not pleasure; his bamboo staff seemed to twitch in his hands.

"The Bundhi will be satisfied," the frowning one said at last, staring hard toward Arkady. "He is nothing."

"Yes; he will be pleased," the man with the staff said. He nodded to himself. "A mercenary soldier. I could almost feel sympathy for the girl if she were not so dangerous."

The other laughed. "We need not concern our master about that now." He stepped back, making a strange gesture before starting through the crowd.

Beside Arkady, his slave turned suddenly, as if she had heard something.

"What is it?" Arkady asked, cursing himself for not knowing how to speak even two words of her language. He felt more foolish than ever.

She shook her head slightly, motioning him to silence, and once again he had the eerie feeling that she was actually watching for . . . he could not guess what.

In the crowd, the two strangers halted. "We should not get closer," the one with the staff told his companion.

"True," the other whispered. "Move back. We must not let her know we are here."

"What does it matter? That lout who bought her cannot understand a word she says, and if he did, he would do nothing. No more than a dozen men in this marketplace know our tongue, and they would not listen to her if she complained." He folded his arms, holding his staff with care. "The Bundhi will want to be certain that the soldier will take care of her for us." He sniggered, making a disgusting face. "If he knew what he had, I wonder what he would do with her?"

"Be cautious!" the other said sharply. "She might overhear."

"Not in this confusion," the first declared. "Still, no harm in watching at a distance. We've done it this far."

Arkady's slave continued to stare, one hand raised to her mouth, and alarm in her large, clouded eyes.

They had reached two stalls where food-sellers had travellers' meats set out. Arkady, who had been trying to decide if he wanted goat cheese or a crude lamb sausage to take with him, noticed that his slave was still distracted and staring. "Is there something wrong, girl?" he asked, touching her elbow in the hope that he would not frighten her more.

"Salghi," she told him, tears of vexation coming into her eyes. She shrugged, sighing. "Salghi, immai."

The vendor in the nearer stall laughed and pointed derisively at Arkady, then pursed his lips toward the slave and laughed more loudly.

"Stop!" Arkady turned on him. "By Saint Michael, you will not—"

His slave took his hand and shook her head. "Vret, immai."

Arkady listened closely to the words she spoke, knowing it was absurd to try, but hoping that if he gave her his full attention, he might yet come to understand what she was saying. "I did not buy you for that," he protested. "This man is lying." But what *did* he buy her for? he asked himself. Blind as she was, what other use might he have for her?

The vendor continued to laugh, and several of those around him joined him. They hooted and guffawed.

"Monsters," Arkady muttered, turning away. "We'll get our food elsewhere," he grumbled to his slave. He took her arm roughly and propelled her through the gathering crowd, away from the stalls and the mirth of the men there.

The stranger with the staff watched them go. "You see? He is not going to bother us."

"Apparently not," the other responded. "The Bundhi will be relieved."

"Yes." He touched his staff with respect but not affection. "We may start back today."

"It would be best," the other agreed, shuddering as the staff in his companion's hand moved slightly. "That . . . bamboo will need—"

"—Food," the first man finished. "And soon."

The second man shook his head. "It may be a mark of advancement, but . . ."

The first man nodded, patting the long, enveloping robes he wore. "It would not reach me easily, Mayon."

"Still," Mayon warned him, not quite concealing a shudder.

"The Bundhi carries a staff much more potent than this one," the first reminded Mayon.

"I am aware of that," Mayon said, plucking nervously at the patterned silk of his robe.

"It will be good to return to the Bundhi," the first said, nodding to himself. "We have done the task he set for us. We will be able to tell him that his orders have been carried out as he wished them to be. That will bring us rewards."

Mayon could not bring himself to be as pleased about the prospect as the other was. "I will settle for an uneventful journey and a return to my studies."

"You're too cautious, Mayon, that's your trouble. You do not take advantage when it is offered to you." He grinned. "I am not so reluctant. When the Bundhi tells me that he will give me what I ask for, I will speak of my desires." He touched his staff again. "You could carry one of these, but you have not asked for it. The Bundhi does not give what is not sought."

"Perhaps I do not seek that," Mayon evaded. "You have what you want, Vadin. Be content with it." He started away through the crowd. "I will arrange for mules."

"Excellent. But choose them carefully. Not all of those animals can tolerate this staff." Vadin took a last glance toward Arkady and his slave. "I trust that Surata is happy in her master."

"It does not matter what she is," Mayon snapped, ignoring the young blind woman. "She was the Bundhi's enemy and now she is a soldier's slave. That is sufficient."

On the other side of the market, Surata made a strange, disturbing cry, gripping Arkady's arm with her free hand.

He stopped at once. "What is it?" he asked, startled at the strength she revealed. "Is something the matter?"

She stood still, her head slightly cocked, her blind eyes

moving as if she could will herself to see. "Rillemata," she said with urgency, making the sounds roll in ways he had never heard before.

"Do you have to stop? Is there something wrong?" It was fruitless to speak to her, but he could not stop himself. "Tell me, woman!"

She released his arm and touched her brow, a puzzled expression coming over her face. "N'yeh." Her step faltered and she blundered into him.

Arkady took her by the shoulder. "Steady," he said to her in the same quiet way he used to talk to his troops before a battle. "Calm down. There."

Embarrassed, she tried to step back from him, but he would not release her. She lifted her head. "Toressu, immai."

"That's better," Arkady said. "You're proud enough, girl. That's good." He drew them to the side of the broad road that led to the market square, slapping the horse close to the building to be out of the way of any travellers or merchants. "I don't know what I'm going to do with you, but don't worry that I might treat you badly. I still have a little honor left to me. I won't harm you while you are in my care." He knew she could not understand him, that his reassurances meant nothing, but he went on, as if to convince himself that his disgrace had not ruined him completely. "I don't know what made me buy you, but now that I have you, I will use you well. I won't take you by force, or let you starve. I'm not so low as that."

"Cherut, immai," she said gently. Her eyes were lowered, but there was no shame about her.

He shook his head unhappily. "One of us is going to have to learn a few words from the other." If he could not learn something from her, he supposed that he would have to sell her in time, and that realization made him cringe. It would be one more damning indictment against him if he removed his protection from this blind, foreign girl.

"N'yeh, immai," she said, this time more confidently.

A party of men on stinking, mangy camels came by. Arkady looked at them in disgust while his slave simply held her nose.

"You'd think they'd do something about such animals. Horses and mules can smell pretty bad, but nothing like those beasts." He sneezed. "Well, we should be away." It did him no good to stand here trying to get her to comprehend his words. It was better that they go on, he knew that. "I'll get a hare for us, or some game birds. I can spare a few arrows for that." He touched the small unstrung hunting bow that hung from his saddle. "I bought it yesterday, from a Turk with an eyepatch. I chose a dozen of his straightest arrows, so one or two for dinner won't trouble me." That was not quite the truth, but he wanted to reassure his slave as well as himself. He took hold of her arm with one hand and the reins of his horse with the other, then led them both out of the market town on the smaller of two roads stretching out to east-northeast. "Once we're out of the town, we'll ride. By Saint Michael, I hope you can ride, girl."

"N'yeh, immai," she said softly.

Arkady shook his head. "You've said those words before. I only wish I knew what they meant."

There were beggars along the road, a few with criminal brands on their arms and faces. Most of them held out their bowls with pitiful cries, but some were silent, either from apathy or the loss of tongues. Arkady had never gotten used to beggars, not even those who waited around the church in Sól, and these seemed worse to him because they were more miserable and more vicious than those he had seen in Poland. He thought, as he walked, that perhaps the reason he had bought the slave was that he could not permit her to end this way, another discarded and sightless derelict with a bowl and nothing else.

Finally the huts and beggars became more infrequent, and there were fewer travellers jostling toward the market village. Arkady halted the horse and brought the reins over the head. "I'm going to mount, and then I'll pull you up behind me. You'll have to sit on the blanket roll." He took one of her hands and wrapped it around the stirrup. "Hang on for a bit." With that, he vaulted into the saddle, keeping his boot out of the stirrup until he leaned down and took her hand. "Come up, then," he said sharply, as he would have to another soldier.

The slave did not respond quite as he had expected, and he had to haul her onto his mount, trying to settle her while he struggled with his horse. The bay gelding snorted and shook his head at this treatment, sidling and scampering while Arkady attempted to balance his slave on the bedroll behind the saddle. Finally, flushed and breathing deeply, he satisfied himself that the girl would not slip off. "You've . . . you've got to put your arms around my waist and hang on. We're not going to go much faster than a trot, but for the most part, we'll be walking. The horse has too much of a load with both of us for me to run him very far."

"Cherut, immai," she said, the hitch in her voice betraying her nervousness more than her expression.

"Fine. That's fine," he said a bit inanely. "Here we go, girl." He loosened his hold on the reins and nudged his mount with his heels. Relieved, the bay gelding broke into a trot, jarring both riders with his abrupt movement. "Hold on!" Arkady barked, turning slightly in order to be sure his slave heard him. "You've got to hold on."

The slave said nothing; she put her arms around Arkady's waist and clung to him while she bounced on the bay's rump, only partly protected by the bedroll.

The horse soon slowed to a walk, but in the time it took the bay to calm down, Arkady thought he would be deprived of breath by the grip of his slave. He tried to pry her fingers loose but found that he could not. Once he started to shout at her but realized that was a foolish thing to do. She could not understand him no matter how loudly he spoke. He resigned himself to her strangling embrace until the gelding dropped back to a walk. When that finally happened, he felt her arms relax a bit, and he took advantage of this.

"If you don't hang on that way, it's easier for me," he said very slowly and precisely. "Remember that, will you?"

Behind him, she said something he could not make out, then sank her fingers into his belt, which permitted him to breathe more freely.

"Right. That's better." He decided that she was a sensible girl, for all her foreignness and her blindness. "You probably don't know what's going on. I wish I could explain it to you." He would have to find a way to talk with her soon or their travels would be impossibly difficult. He tried to think of a way to start as they made their way across the flat valley toward the first rising hills in the distance.

By evening they had begun to climb, and Arkady was secretly pleased that they had made such good progress. He decided not to press on too far that day and began to search for a place they might be able to camp; in a while he found a small glen a short distance off the road. A stream ran down the far side of the glen, and there was enough shelter to give them some protection during the night.

"This will do it, I think," Arkady said aloud. "We can lay out the bedroll and make a fire. I've got a pot for cooking, and if I can bring down a rabbit or a bird, that should give us a fairly good meal." It would be little enough for two, but he decided that he would not suggest that, and not simply because his slave would not understand him. He swung the bay off the road and brought him to a halt in the glen. "This is where we stop tonight, girl."

"Immai?" she asked, her expression puzzled as he dismounted.

"Give me your hand," he told her, taking hers before she could become frightened. "I'll help you down. Just lean and I'll catch you." He tugged gently on her arm, and as she shrieked, he caught her and helped her to the ground. "There. All fine."

She put her hand to her head, shaking it a little. "Verrek, immai?"

"Sure," he answered, having no idea what she might have said. "I'm going to gather wood for a fire and get my saddle off the horse. I want you to sit down. Sit down." He pressed her shoulders and found that she was willing to do it, although she moved stiffly from her hours on horseback. He sighed a little as he untied the bow from his saddle and strung it. "I'll have to do a little hunting. I won't be long." He was already reaching for the hobbles to secure the bay. Once the hobbles were in place, he unbuckled the girths and tugged the high-fronted, straight-canteled saddle off his gelding's back, putting it on a clear space of ground. "You can lean against this while I'm gone," he said to his slave.

"Cherut, immai," she answered, sounding tired. Obligingly she braced her elbows against the saddle and half leaned against it.

"I'm taking one of my swords, but you can have the other," he said, bending down and taking one of her hands and laying it on the hilt of his shorter sword. "Just don't take out after the horse with it, will you?" He smiled at her as he would have smiled at green troops, but the sight of her eyes froze the expression in a rictus grin. "I won't be long. I'll call out when I come back."

"N'yeh, immai." She held the sword more firmly.

"That's right," he said, not with much certainty. "Hang on to it." He stepped away from her, fixing an arrow in place as he went. If he had not shot something for their supper by dusk, he would go back and they would have to make do with what he had in his saddlebags. He decided not to waste time searching for arrows that went wide of the mark. He did his best to keep his thoughts on small game instead of the slave he had bought.

To his surprise, by the time he returned with two small rabbits, his slave had found a way to gather wood and lay a fire, and she sat by it patiently, her hand not far from the sword he had left for her.

"You've done well," he called out as he started across the glen toward her. "Next time I'll leave the flint and steel with you so you can light it as well."

She had turned toward his footsteps and the sound of his voice. "Selleh, immai," she called out, lifting one hand in greeting.

Arkady paused to pat his horse and to replace the bay's bridle with a halter. "There you are, boy," he said to the horse. "You can graze awhile. How's that?"

The bay nuzzled his arm, whickering softly.

"Good boy," Arkady said, patting the gelding's neck once more before continuing across the glen toward his slave. "I've gutted the rabbits already. They'll cook nicely on a spit, and I'll make some gruel." He flung down the rabbits not far from his slave and saw her draw back in alarm. "They're just rabbits, and dead ones at that," he explained as he set about flaying them. The soft pelts were matted with blood by the time he was through, and he tossed them away with some regret, since he knew that when winter came, he might want a few soft rabbit pelts to line his one cloak.

When he finally struck a spark for the fire, his slave was the one who made a nest of dry twigs and leaves for it and blew on it gently until flames appeared. She stayed close to it, and Arkady decided that she must be chilly, for night was coming on and she had fairly light garments—he had not seen such clothes before—and of course had not been given anything heavier.

Once the rabbits were on the spit, Arkady went through the gloom to the stream and filled his single pot with water. Then he tossed some grain into the water and set it against the burning, dry branches.

"Durran jamni, immai," she said to him while he turned the rabbits on the spit.

"Whatever that means," he said, shaking his head. "What can have possessed me? You'd think you'd worked some sorcery on me, girl. But what would you want someone like me for? Tell me that." He chuckled. "I suppose this is as bad as talking to myself." He had a short, stiff twig and he used it to stir the gruel.

The slave sat very still, then touched his arm so softly that he was not certain she had actually done it. She waited, then put her hand over her breast. "Surata. Surata."

"What?" He looked at her closely. "Surata?"

"N'yeh, immai," she said enthusiastically and repeated the gesture. "Surata." Then she put her hand on his chest. "Immai?"

"Arkady Sól," he answered, hoping that was what she wanted to know. He pointed his finger at her, letting her hold his hand as he did. "Surata." He turned his hand back to himself. "Arkady."

"Arkady," she said, actually smiling. "Arkady."

"Right." He could feel himself grin at this. It was not much, he had to admit, but it was better than nothing. At least his slave had a name and he could call her something other than girl now. "Well, Surata, it's about time we had a bite to eat."

"N'yeh, Arkady-immai," she said.

"Not Arkady-immai, just Arkady. Arkady Sól." He was worried that she might have misunderstood him after all. "Arkady."

"Arkady-immai," she corrected him, pointing to herself again. "Surata." She put her hand on his chest once more. "Arkady-immai," she said serenely.

"Fine. Arkady-immai, whatever that means," he grumbled.

Surata began to hum, plainly very happy. She swayed where she sat, her movements so beautiful that she seemed almost to be dancing.

Arkady watched her for a little while, enchanted with what he saw. He realized with sudden irritation that his resolve to treat her with courtesy might be more difficult that he had first assumed. She was blind, but there was a fascination about her that Arkady felt as keenly as he felt the shame of his dishonor. He put his mind on stirring the gruel and turning the spit, so he would not dwell on the opulence of her body.

After a time, she was still again. "Arkady-immai?"

"Here," he said shortly. "The food's almost ready. You can have gruel now and the rabbit in a bit."

She nearly burned her hands on the side of the pot; she would have done so if Arkady had not restrained her. She made a strange exclamation, then drew back, blowing on her fingers and trying to keep the tears from her eyes.

Arkady handed her his one spoon. "Use this," he suggested, pressing it into her hand so that she could feel it. "And give it a moment to cool."

Surata must have heard how irked he was, because she sighed and gave a contrite smile. "Poehl, immai."

"Fine. Don't do it again," he responded, then came very

27

close to burning his own hands as he started to reach for the spit. He swore loudly, then started to laugh.

It was a little time before Surata started to laugh with him, and as she did, he found that his vexation had faded completely.

Chapter 3

By midnight all that remained of the fire were a few glowing embers, and the air was colder. Arkady had pulled his saddle closer to the ashes, doing his best to wrap his blanket around both himself and Surata. He had thought at first that he was tired enough not to be disturbed by her nearness, but after a short, deep sleep, he became aware of the curve of her leg against his and the steady rhythm of her breathing. Still somewhat asleep, he let himself drift with his dreams, hoping that he would be forgiven for the lusts they revealed. In time he became lost in them, letting his imagination take him to the forbidden places where he could revel in Surata's flesh. He would confess these lusts the next time he found a priest to hear him.

"Arkady-immai," Surata whispered a bit more loudly. "Arkady-immai!" She shoved his arm. "Emtahli."

Her reality vied with his dream; Arkady hung in the confusion between, not wanting to relinquish the dream for the stern world. He mumbled and tried to turn over.

Surata shook him with force. "Arkady-immai!"

He opened his eyes and looked at her, seeing little of her in the darkness. "Wha..."

"Emtahli!" Her voice was still low, but the urgency in her tone communicated her fear through the foreign word.

The last of his dream faded and he came fully awake. "What is it?"

She poured forth a hurried message while she mimed several men on horseback, riding hard and brandishing weapons. She then pointed to his two swords and his maul, indicating that he should arm himself.

"How close?" he asked, not pausing to wonder how he knew this. He had been a soldier far too long to discount such presentiments. "How many?"

Surata said several words, then held up her hand opened. She pushed him again, clearly hurrying him.

Arkady scrambled to his feet, reaching for his metal-studded leather brigandine, bending to reach the buckles under the arms. It was long enough that he had no need of the corselet, and for that he was grateful. He fumbled for his helmet and his boots, cursing as he shook the boots to dislodge anything that might have crawled into them during the night. He hopped as he pulled each boot on, hearing the tinned steel clink and jangle. "My swords! Where in the name of Saint Michael are my swords. And keep the maul handy—I may need it."

"N'yeh, Arkady-immai," Surata said, drawing the cover close around her.

"Take this and hide under it," he ordered, kicking his shield in her direction, then pausing to show her how to do it. "And stay there until I tell you to come out. Keep the blanket tight around you. It will protect you a little where the shield does not." He straightened up, a sword in each hand, turning slowly in a circle and listening with such concentration that he could hear the breathing of his horse.

It was not long before he heard the approach of muffled hooves and the soft slap of saddle leather. Whoever was coming was using stealth. The horses were pulled up just off the road in the low trees and brush that screened the glen from travellers.

"Hold steady, Surata," Arkady said in an undervoice just before he moved to a more shadowed part of the glen. He knew he would require every advantage if the intruders were to be held off. His gauntlets, stiff from cold, did not yet afford him a firm grip on his sword hilts. The longer weapon, in his right hand, had been sharpened less than a week ago and would cut with ease; but the shorter had not been honed or sharpened for more than a month, and its edge was not as keen. Arkady shook his head at his own negligence. If he came through the night, he would have to do something about his short sword.

On the other side of the glen, two men emerged from the brush, both carrying axes and wearing short mail cuirasses, the standard gear of bandits. One of the two made a gesture, and three more men joined them, the last pointing to Arkady's horse and gesturing his approval of the gelding.

Arkady glared at them. It was bad enough that these five wanted to rob, capture, perhaps kill them, but that they should also plan to take his horse infuriated him. He flexed his fingers in his gauntlets. He was entirely awake now and ready to fight.

The bandits were striding toward the fire, moving swiftly but with practiced silence. They fanned out, making a half-circle that would be closed quickly once they reached the dying fire.

As soon as the bandits were past his hiding place, Arkady stepped out behind them, matching his pace to theirs so that they would not hear him move. He kept with them for a dozen strides, then chose the man on the end of the crescent and moved behind him, raising his sword as he did.

The man on the end shrieked as Arkady's sword bit deeply into his shoulder. He fell to his knees and then to his side, clutching the wound and howling from the pain.

"Ah!" Arkady burst out, spinning toward the next man in line, his long sword held low and straight. The blade caught the next man on the side of his thigh, lifting him up with the blow. As he pulled the long sword free, Arkady thrust out with his short sword, catching the man on the chest and knocking the air out of him.

The other three had recovered from this surprise attack and

were bringing their axes up to the ready, the bandit in the steel helmet bellowing to the others as he began to swing his axe in a lethal pattern before him.

Arkady dropped back, working carefully. He was confident that he could defeat two men armed with axes, but three changed the odds too much. He moved quickly, not wanting to give one of the men the opportunity to get behind him, or to let two of them outflank him. He made two quick passes with his long sword, just enough to make the bandits keep their distance. "Not yet, not yet," he breathed as he sought for the best footing.

The leader of the bandits began to press his advance, swinging his axe more quickly and forcing Arkady to give ground as he and his men closed on him.

The leader drew a poignard from his belt, making an unpleasant sound as he did. His two men followed suit, pressing closer to Arkady.

With a swift change of stance, Arkady lunged at the man on his right, nicking his leg before the bandit's axe clanged down, deflecting the sword. Arkady moved quickly, driving his short sword at the belly of the man on his right. This time he had the satisfaction of seeing the bandit double over, retching violently. In the next instant, he almost dropped his short sword as the leader's axe cut into his forearm.

There were two bandits still on their feet, and one of them was limping. That might be enough, Arkady thought, as he tested the grip on his left hand. It was weak but he could still hold the weapon for a little while. He had received worse and continued to fight. He hefted the short sword and lashed out with it, more to convince his opponents that he was not hurt than to do them any damage.

The leader slashed out with his axe, shouting loudly as he did, his words shrill with rage. He rushed at Arkady, still keeping his axe in motion. As Arkady fell back, he struck out with his poignard, which glanced off the metal studding of Arkady's brigandine. He roared his outrage; his face, now close enough for Arkady to see his features, was distorted with ire. There were flecks of foam on his beard.

Near Arkady's left leg, the man on the ground reached for his axe. He was still clutching himself and moaning, but he had recovered enough to be able to fight again.

Arkady saw the movement, and he responded quickly, bringing the heel of his boot down on the man's wrist. He heard the snap and grind of broken bone and the miserable wail with a guarded confidence. He had been able to reduce his opponents to two, and if his left arm could hold out, he was fairly sure he could defeat them.

The man on his right shifted ground, looking for a way to get behind Arkady. He dragged his right leg, but not enough to make movement impossible. His axe swung ominously.

Sensing this maneuver more than seeing it, Arkady pivotted, slashing with his long sword. He felt the tip of it rake the limping man's mail, and saw the sparks where steel scraped steel, but then he lost his footing and stumbled backward.

With an enraged shout, the leader was on him, bringing his axe high for the dispatching cut.

Arkady thrust with his short sword, holding it low enough to get under the mail cuirass. With the other sword, he lashed out at the limping man, hoping to keep him back. The force of the leader on Arkady's short sword demanded all his strength and attention, for the bandit writhed like a gaffed fish as the point sank into his abdomen and drove upward under his ribs. Arkady felt blood on his hands and spatters of it on his face, and he dodged as the bandit leader's flailing arm brought his axe close.

The limping man shouted, and his leg went out from under him. He thrashed, trying to reach the new, wide cut Arkady had given him. His axe lay on the ground, and he made no move to grasp it.

Arkady rolled away from the body of the leader of the bandits. He felt weakness rush through him now that the urgency of battle had ended. Tears stood in his eyes and his left arm trembled so badly that he had to release his hold on the hilt of his short sword. He felt that he was about to be sick.

The limping man wrapped a length of cloth torn from his

sleeve around his leg, then struggled to his feet. He looked in silence at his fallen comrades, then stumbled off toward where the bandits had left their horses, gasping with every step he took.

Two of the others had recovered enough to shamble after the limping man, leaving their leader and the second man Arkady had wounded behind.

Arkady sat on the ground, his legs stretched out in front of him, his head lowered. He was panting and the cut in his arm ached abominably. He could not bring himself to turn his head and look at the bandit leader, though the dead man lay less than an arm's length away; instead Arkady peered through the darkness to the other remaining man, who lay unconscious on the ground. He knew that he should go to the fallen bandit and cut his Achilles tendons, crippling him and punishing him for his outlawry, but Arkady could not bring himself to create another beggar to sit by the side of the road with a bowl. Slowly he got to his feet and made his way back toward the faint glow of the dying campfire.

"Arkady-immai?" Surata asked tremulously as he approached, hearing his uneven steps.

"It's all right, Surata," he said in great fatigue. "They're . . . gone, most of them. The two that are left won't bother us." He sank down beside the campfire, seeking what little warmth it offered, his thoughts dazed. He cradled his wounded arm against his chest and fixed his eyes on a place in the middle distance. He could not tell how much he was bleeding.

Surata shifted the blankets and the shield away from her and sat still and alert, trying to locate Arkady by his movements and the sound of his breathing.

"Over here," he said after a brief silence. "I've got a cut on my arm and I'll probably have some bruises tomorrow." He had long since resigned himself to such hurts, for they were part of a soldier's life, but he was uncertain he had assessed all the damage that had been done to him, and he held his thoughts and worries within himself even though Surata could not understand them if he spoke of them. It was his arm that concerned him the most, and for that reason, he hesitated to probe the cut, for fear it would be worse than it felt.

Surata made her way on hands and knees to where he sat, and there she paused, not yet convinced that she could come nearer without hurting him in some way. "Arkady-immai?"

He raised his head. "What."

She wanted to ask him where he was wounded, but she had no words for it. She caught her lower lip between her teeth and wanted to shout with vexation. It was impossible to tell him that she had skills that would help. Finally she reached out and put her hand on his right arm. "Vaidatta," she said, hoping that he would sense her intention from the tone of her voice.

Firmly but without any roughness, he held her off. "It's nothing you can do anything about." He wished he had a few strips of cotton to bind the cut, but there was nothing he owned that would lend itself to making bandages. He told himself he was a fool for that oversight.

This time Surata's hands were more forceful, and she ran her hands over his arms and face expertly. "Dun'yatta," she said as she touched his helmet. Carefully she unfastened the chin-guard and lifted the thing from his head, smoothing his rough-cut hair back from his brow. Once she put the helmet aside, she renewed her examination of his face. She found a knot of a scar over the arch of his right eyebrow and deep lines around his eyes and mouth, but she realized that his features, while not fine, were attractive and well-cut.

"Ouch," he said as her fingers found a scrape on his cheekbone.

She drew back at once, murmuring a few apologies that he recognized by inflection rather than word. Her mind was still distracted as she reached out again, this time to his blood-spattered brigandine. She was deeply concerned until she realized that the blood was not his. "Shirad, immai," she said in her relief.

Arkady nodded, though he had no idea what she had said other than it was intended to reassure him. "The arm's the

35

worst, I think. They didn't hit me or cut me in the gut, that's what counts." That was a simplification but had enough truth in it to give him a little more hope. He winced as he tried to lift his left arm, and he felt the blood well around the edges of the wound. In spite of himself, he groaned.

Surata acted quickly, her hands moving knowledgeably over him until she found the cut. There was cloth and a bit of leather still embedded in his flesh, and it was bleeding sluggishly. She reached down to the hem of the robe she wore and strove to tear off a length of the fabric.

When Arkady realized what she was trying to do, he turned his thoughts to where he had left the cinquedea. "Under the saddle," he said aloud and leaned to the side, reaching across her with his right hand.

She protested at once, scolding him for such lack of caution. She grabbed him, trying to restrain him, but in the next moment, she felt the hilt of the little knife placed in her hand, and she nodded her approval. At once she set to work cutting two very long strips of cloth from the hem of her robe. The fabric was tough, polished cotton in the warp, silk in the woof, and it made a kind of scream when it was rent. When she had the two strips, she began the much more difficult task of cutting his sleeve away from the wound. She found the V-shaped blade awkward to handle, and for that reason, she took more time than she wanted to keep from injuring Arkady any further. At last she slit the sleeve from elbow to wrist and exposed the whole of his lower arm.

Arkady felt himself grow cold, and to his chagrin, his teeth began to chatter. He clamped his mouth shut, but the cold still seeped through his veins and bones. The sensation was not a new one—he had experienced it when he had been wounded before—but he disliked it intensely and irrationally, and he could hardly contain his anger as the inner chill spread.

As she worked to clean his cut, Surata wanted to find a way to comfort Arkady. She knew that in the morning, she would have to fetch water to wash the hurts he had sustained, but she doubted he would be able to make it to the stream to bring water for them, and she was afraid that if she attempted to get it, she would fall or spill anything she was able to get for him. She brought her special concentration to bear on his arm, and decided that as soon as the bandage was in place, she would have to wrap him in the blanket close to her so that he would not grow colder. Already his skin was clammy to her touch, and she knew that this would be dangerous if it was allowed to continue much longer. "Arkady-immai," she said, frustrated that she knew so few words he could comprehend.

"You're doing fine, Surata," he hissed, his wrath making his praise sound more like a condemnation.

She paid no heed to him but continued to bind his wound. When she was done, she finished her inspection of his arms and legs, and sighed when she realized that there seemed to be no other damage. She sat back on her heels and debated with herself briefly if she should bring the blanket to him, or take him to it, and decided on a compromise. "Vaidatta, Arkady-immai," she said, taking his weapons from him and giving them a cursory cleaning on the torn hem of her robe. That done, she reached over and took Arkady by the shoulders, pulling him gently toward where the blankets lay. She kept up a soft, steady flow of words, most of them the same sorts of things she might say to a frightened child. Steadily she coaxed him to stretch out, and when he had, she brought the blanket and began to wrap the both of them in it.

At first Arkady accepted this treatment, but as he became aware of what she was doing, he resisted. "No, Surata," he said, feeling her body pressing close to his. "This isn't right. It wouldn't work right now anyway. Surata . . . Surata, you've got to stop."

She paid no heed to him, knowing that the chill that held him was more dangerous than the cut in his arm. Calmly, she continued her work, and when she at last drew the blanket close around both of them and nestled her head against his neck, most of his protests were stilled.

"Surata," he said a bit later, "you don't understand what this could do to me." To his astonishment, he felt idiotic saying this to her. "You don't . . ."

She put her free hand to his mouth, wishing he would go to sleep.

"I have to tell you this," he said through her fingers. "And it doesn't matter that you don't understand what I'm saying. You have shown your worth to me, and I am in your debt. I won't disgrace myself by refusing to acknowledge all you've done for me. Without your warning, I would be seriously wounded or dead now, and the Holy Saints alone know what might have happened to you." He sighed, his strength going out of him more quickly than he wanted. "That's all." His head rolled back and he allowed himself to groan, now that he would not shame himself.

Surata brushed his hair back from his brow, letting her palm rest briefly on his forehead. She was not yet certain there would be fever, but she was content that he had got no colder. Before she started to drift toward sleep, she took hold of the cinquedea, in case the unconscious bandit should trouble them later in the night.

When morning came, both the bandit who had fallen by the fire and the body of the leader were gone. Surata propped herself on her elbow and listened to Arkady as he fumbled to start the fire again. "You did well," he said to her once again. Working with one hand, he felt incredibly clumsy. His head still ached and his arms and legs were stiff from hurt. "It will take me a little while to get this going," he explained.

"Arkady-immai," she reproached him, attempting to convince him to get back into his blanket. He resisted the tone of her voice and the gentle force of her arms.

"Leave off!" Arkady snapped, trying to shove her aside. But he knew that he was being foolishly stubborn. The night before, Surata had laid the fire and all that was needed was a spark from his flint and steel. When she urged him to lean back, he stopped fighting her. "All right, Surata. If you insist that I keep still, I guess I'll have to."

Surata wrapped the blanket around him and then set off to find more wood, walking with little steps and bending over to feel the ground in front of her. At first glance, it seemed a slow and inefficient method to find wood, blindness or no, but in far less time than Arkady would have thought possible, she had gathered up several dry branches and an assortment of kindling twigs and brought them back to their campfire. Then she set about laying the branches so they would burn well.

"You're good at that," Arkady admitted, doing his best to keep the grudging tone out of his voice. "I'm surprised at how well you manage."

She continued her work without any response. When she was done, she moved back and waited for him to spark the kindling.

Reluctantly, Arkady left the warmth of the blanket. He liked its comfort more than he wanted to, and yet he found fault with himself for enjoying it. "I'm turning soft already," he grumbled as he prepared to start the fire.

Surata came to his side and once again showed her skill in nursing a little red dot into a flame. As soon as there was enough kindling burning, she pointed in the general direction of the blanket, and for once Arkady obeyed her meekly.

When the fire was well-established, Arkady stumbled off into the trees to relieve himself, returning to find that Surata had somehow managed to find her way to the stream and bring enough water to make more gruel and to set out a little leaf tea, which Arkady regarded with suspicion. As he sat down on the blanket roll, his legs still treacherously shaky, he eyed the bowl of tea. "Where did you get that?" he demanded.

This time Surata did not respond quite as she had in the past. She pointed to Arkady. "Arkady-immai," she said, then pointed to the fire. "Chim?"

"Uh . . . fire," Arkady said.

"Uhfire?" she repeated.

"No, just fire, Fire." He took her hand in his and pointed to it. "Fire."

"Fire," she said. The next thing she touched was the bag of grain. "Chim?"

"Food," he said. "Grain. Food."

"Foodgrainfood," she echoed.

Chelsea Quinn Yarbro

"Food," he corrected her.

"Food," she agreed.

By the time they had finished their gruel, she had added five more words to her vocabulary and was smiling with pleasure.

Arkady watched her, surprised at how quickly she learned and how methodically she went about acquiring information. He could not help but smile at her, taking an unexpected pride in her abilities. There were so many others who were blind who would not have bothered to learn, but this foreign slavewoman was insisting that he tell her more words. She was moving her hand through the air, making it dive and tremble.

"Wind," he said, guessing at what she meant. He leaned over and blew on her fingers. "Wind."

"Wind," she agreed. "Fire, food, ground, rock, wood, sword, blanket, wind."

"Very good!" He laughed aloud. "You're doing very well, Surata."

"Chim?" she asked, and by now he knew the meaning of that word.

"Surata..." He tried to think of some way to convey what he meant. He reached over and patted her on the arm, very much as if she were a young soldier who had fought well. "Good."

Immediately she patted him on his arm. "Good."

"No," he sighed. "Never mind. I'll try to explain it later."

It was almost midday when they moved on, going slowly along the road, letting the horse choose its pace, making no effort to urge it. As they went, she learned more words.

"Tree. Horse. Hand. Foot. Head. Hair. Face. Arm. Fingers. Water. Boot. Saddle."

When they stopped to purchase dates and figs from a farmer, Surata learned her first abstract. She tugged at Arkady's arm and put her hand on her stomach. "Chim?" To make sure, she opened her mouth. "Food."

"Hungry," he said. "So am I." He chuckled as she repeated that along with her other words. "You're amazing, Surata. I couldn't do half as well, and I can see."

40

She caught the approval in his tone and smiled at him. Still smiling, she reached up, almost touching his eyes. "Chim?"

He swallowed hard before answering. "Eyes."

"Eyes." She hesitated, then pointed to her own. "Eyes?"

"Eyes." he agreed with difficulty.

She frowned shaking her head. "Dumet eyes." She passed her hand in front of her. "Eyes?"

"Eyes." he insisted. "Blind."

"Ah. Blind." This satisfied her, and she nodded, repeating the words to herself.

Arkady was grateful to see the farmer coming toward them with a jug of goat's milk and a few rounds of cheese. He finished the figs he held and reached into his wallet for one of the silver coins he had. "Good. Very good," he told the man and grinned at the farmer's blank smile.

The farmer had few teeth, and so he said very little, and what he said was in a sibilant whistle. He took the money Arkady offered, and pointed toward his well.

"Food?" Surata asked as she bit into a date. She was near the horse so that she could reach out and touch the sack of grain. "Food."

"Grain-food," Arkady explained, then touched the dates in her hand. "Fruit-food." He reached for the reins. "I have to water the horse."

There were two words she recognized, and she said them both. As Arkady started to lead his horse toward the well, she reached up and took hold of the unstrung bow hanging from the saddle and followed him toward the well.

"Bow. Arrow. Well. Bucket. Stone. Stirrup. Bridle. Rein. Sack. Cheese. Milk. Cup. Bowl. Sand. Bench. Sun. Shade. Grape. Vine."

They sat in the farmer's grape arbor out of the afternoon glare. The gentle drone of insects was the only sound they heard aside from their own voices and the munching of the gelding as he cropped weeds near the well.

Arkady stretched out his legs, wishing they were a little less stiff. It was so pleasant here, he thought, if only he were not so sore.

Apparently Surata noticed how he moved, for she suddenly put her cup of milk aside on the bench and reached out for him, her hands seeking out the bandage on his arm. Deftly she untied the cloth, paying no heed to his objections, then said, "Water."

Arkady sighed. "All right." He had to admit that it would feel better if some of the grit was washed out of it. He stood up and went back to the well, filling his empty cup with water and coming back to the arbor. "Here. Water."

She took the cup and sniffed at it. Then very carefully, she began to wash out the wound. "Arm. Water," she informed him.

"Yes," he said wearily. "Thanks." This last was half-sarcastic, but also grudgingly respectful. "You do that well."

"Well?" she repeated, surprised.

"No. Good." He winced as she deliberately set the cut to bleeding once more. "Don't do that."

"Water," she said patiently.

"Water, hell, that's blood." He took his free hand and touched her fingers near the cut. "Blood."

She sniffed her fingers. "Blood. Water blood," she said very calmly, and continued to wash. When she was through, she hacked off more of the hem of her robe—"Knife. Cloth." —to bandage the wound once more. "Water. Blood. Cloth," she declared, relinquishing her hold on him. "Arm."

"True enough," Arkady said to her, wondering what else she might take it into her head to do. He longed for a cup of wine but had discovered that it was not often found in this part of the world. Still, he thought lazily, trying to keep his mind off the throbbing in his arm, if the farmer here had this arbor, he might have wine. He was attempting to think of a way to find out when he felt Surata nudge him.

"Cheese?"

"Do you want some more?" he inquired.

"Cheese. Sack. Saddle." Her features were inquiring, and from the way she held her head, she was suggesting this to him.

"Good idea," he allowed and decided that it might also provide him a way to find out about wine.

"N'yeh, Arkady-immai," she said merrily, her manner growing more lighthearted. "Horse. Water. Food. Arkady-immai, Surata, water. Food. Cheese."

"Yes, I know," he assured her. "I'll talk to the farmer and see what I can arrange."

"Sack. Saddle," she added.

"Yes, I know," he answered a bit curtly, as much because he knew she was right as any other reason. "I'll take care of it."

"Fruit-food. Grain-food. Cheese," she called after him as he started toward the farmer's house.

"Fruit-food, grain-food, cheese. And wine," he whispered to himself. "For love of the Archangels, let there be wine."

He was pleasantly startled to find his prayers had been answered. The farmer produced several rounds of dry cheese; some hard, flat bread; a large jar of dates; and two skins of a rough red wine that was as welcome as any Arkady had ever tasted. As an afterthought, he also purchased a generous comb of honey and had it put in a tight wooden box. He paid two silver coins for the lot and thought himself very fortunate to have so much for so little.

"Tonight we will feast," he said to Surata when he came back to the arbor. "Cheese, bread, dates, honey, wine, it's all here. If I can get a rabbit for us, it will be fine."

"Cheese," she said, nodding happily. "Food."

In spite of the aches that plagued him, Arkady mounted his gelding in far better spirits than he would have thought possible. He reached down for Surata. "Give me your hand, Surata. I'll lift you up."

"Hand. Arm." She stretched toward him.

"Up you go," he said, pulling her up behind him.

"Up you go," she repeated.

"Up," he corrected her, then took her hand that had gone round his waist and lowered it. "Down." As he raised it, "Up," and lowered it again, "Down."

"Up," she said, bringing her hand back to his waist.

"Good," he said, starting his horse off toward the road once again.

Chapter 4

Not long before sunset, they found a goatherd; and after many gestures and two copper coins, he indicated in mime that there was a good place to rest for the night not far from the road. He led them part of the way and pointed out the spot.

"It looks fine," Arkady said, nodding emphatically, offering the goatherd a handful of dates in addition to the coins.

The goatherd smiled and bowed and babbled incomprehensibly, then went back to tending his flock, munching on the dates as he went.

"I'll gather wood for the fire," Arkady told Surata. "You wait for me."

She knew four of the words he said—wood, fire, you, me—and decided that she would be warm soon.

As Arkady unsaddled his gelding, he took his blanket and handed it to her. "You look chilly. Wrap up in this." He was getting more used to talking to her, and much of the frustration he had felt at the beginning was gone. Once he had set the saddle on the ground, he wrapped the blanket around her shoulders. "There."

"Blanket," she said, fingering it. "Fire."

"Warm," he corrected her. "Blanket warm."

"Warm," she said and stood beside the bay while Arkady hobbled him.

"I'll be back shortly," he said, and went off in search of wood, grateful that it was still light enough to make the task simple. He brought the wood back to Surata so that she could lay the fire and went to find a few more branches so that they could keep the fire built up at night. The air was already chilly, and he knew they would need to provide more heat than the blanket alone would give them.

"Fire?" Surata asked when Arkady returned.

"In a moment." He took flint and steel from his wallet, unwrapped them and struck a spark. As she blew on the kindling, he shook his head. "I don't know how you do that."

"Warm. Hands warm," she explained. Then, with the first blaze going, she turned to him. "Surata hungry. Grain-food and fruit-food and cheese."

"Sounds good to me," Arkady agreed.

"Good." She clapped her hands. "Fast. Arkady-immai make fast."

"Just as soon as I kill a rabbit or a bird." he promised her. "I'll get the grain out and you can start making gruel. Or we can toast bread if you'd like that better. I'll put some cheese on the bread and we can have it that way." He did not want to admit that he was getting very tired of gruel.

"Good food," she said. "Make good food, bread and cheese."

"All right," he said. "Shortly." He took his bow and strung it, choosing three arrows. He hoped that the next time they found a market town, there would be a fletcher who would sell him more arrows.

When he returned to the fire, the sun was down and Surata was contentedly eating a few dates. "Arkady-immai," she called out through the dates. "Here!"

"I'm coming," he answered. He had already gutted and skinned the rabbit he had shot, and it needed only the spit for cooking. "I've got food."

"Food here," she said, a bit puzzled.

"This is other food, meat-food." He came to the fire and found a long, thin stick that would serve for a spit. While the rabbit broiled, he cut cheese and put it on the hard bread, then set these on small rocks near the fire so that the cheese could melt.

"Good food," Surata declared as she had the first of the toasted bread-and-cheese. "More."

Laughing, Arkady gave her another but warned her, "Leave some room for the rabbit."

To his surprise, she shook her head. "Meat-food not good. Surata make cheese- and fruit-food."

Arkady looked at her. "Meat-food is fine, Surata. It's rabbit."

"Not good," she told him more firmly. "Arkady-immai make meat-food, good. Not good Surata make meat-food." She held out her hand for some more toasted cheese.

"Don't you eat meat?" he asked, recalling some of the monks he had met who had given up meat for the sake of their souls and to honor God's creatures.

"Not good meat-food," she said, taking another bite of the bread-and-cheese. "Here good, Arkady-immai."

Arkady shook his head slowly. "You can have more bread-and-cheese if that's what you want, but I'm going to have the meat, if it's all the same to you." He touched the spit and gave the rabbit another turn.

"Good Arkady-immai, not good Surata," she insisted and accepted more dates from him.

It puzzled Arkady to find her so determined, but he shrugged it off and helped himself to the rabbit, eating it off the point of his cinquedea. He wanted to ask her why she would not eat it, but she did not have enough words yet, either to explain or to understand his question. When he had eaten about half of the rabbit, he took one of the wineskins and drank some of the raw vintage. "Wine," he said to Surata, holding it out to her. "Try it."

"Wine?" She tasted it, made a face and handed it back. "Arkady-immai make wine, not Surata."

This was more surprising than her refusal to eat meat. "Try it again, Surata," he urged her, putting the wineskin in her free hand.

She pushed it away. "Not Surata."

He shrugged. "There's another skin, if you change your mind," he said and poured more of the wine down his throat. It eased his thirst and the ache in his body; he wanted to get drunk but could not bring himself to go that far. "I'll save the rest of this for later," he told Surata when he had half emptied the wineskin.

"Good," she declared, choosing the last of her dates to munch. "Arkady-immai . . . not hungry."

"No, not anymore," he said, taking a little more of the rabbit. The animal had been small, and he had to admit to himself that he was glad she did not want much—any—of it, though it still troubled him that she was not willing to eat meat. What would happen, he wondered, if that was all they had?

He put most of the food into sacks and slung them in the spindly trees. As he worked, he said to Surata, "I want to get the food out of reach. There may be wild animals who want our food as much as we do. This way, there's a pretty good chance they won't get it."

"Ah," she nodded.

"How much of that made sense to you?" Arkady wondered aloud.

"More," she answered, turning her face toward him, and once again giving him the eerie feeling that she could see him and was watching him.

"That's certain," he said quietly, adding more branches to the fire. "We'll have to sleep close tonight, Surata."

Again she nodded, and Arkady was more troubled than before. "Good ground."

He was puzzled by this announcement but did not argue with her. "Yes, I suppose it is." He got up and started to unroll his blanket. "It's dark now. I . . . " he faltered. "I'm sleepy, my arm hurts and I'm stiff from riding. You must be too."

"Dark," she said.

"Dark. Not sun. Night." He cleared his throat as he stared at her eyes.

"Night. Dark." She looked pleased.

"The blanket's almost ready," he went on in a determined way. "You can lie down when you like." He wished they had enough water to wash with, or a means to shave. His whole body felt grimy, and he was faintly embarrassed to be too near Surata. It was one thing to go without bathing or washing when surrounded by soldiers; but in church or with a woman of quality, then it was proper for a captain, even a disgraced captain, to present himself in a manner worthy of Court.

"Arkady-immai," she said as she finished licking her fingers. "Arkady-immai, blanket, down."

"Yes, it's down." he said, patting it, then reaching for her hand so that she could touch it.

"Not. Arkady-immai down." She shoved his shoulder, not roughly but with great determination. "Clothes down."

Arkady blinked. "What . . . ?"

She paid no attention to his question, but began to unwrap his arm. She touched the skin around the cut and sniffed at it. "Not good," she announced.

"I know that," he responded. He had known the wound would become infected. That was the way with wounds.

"Down down down," she insisted, pressing him back against the blanket and starting to unfasten his leather doublet.

"Surata, for the Saints in Heaven—" He tried to get her to stop, for he was now really distressed. It was bad enough that she knew he was hurt, but to discover the rest would shame him. He started to push her away, swearing to himself, when her hands touched his forehead.

"Arkady-immai," she said in a still voice. "Down."

Slowly he lay back with the languor of a dreamer. "Right," he murmured as his resistance faded and his body surrendered to the drag of fatigue. He was vaguely aware that he was not acting at all properly, but he did not care. The way her hands moved on his face and neck was more soothing than victory and wine. Even when she began to remove his clothes, he did little to stop her. There was too much—what? he asked himself: sweetness? pleasure? lassitude?—in him to stop her. Under her ministrations, he drifted, his mind roving back through his memories.

He had been so little that he could not see over the top of the table. He remembered peering at the rushes beneath, seeing the vermin there. At first they had fascinated him, but when he tried to get closer, a mouse had turned on him and sunk tiny teeth into his thumb. He had gone wailing to his mother who had bandaged the thumb but laughed at him. The humiliation of her derision still stung him, though she had been dead for seven years.

"Arkady-immai," Surata whispered as she pressed her palms to the place where his ribs joined, "do not hold back what is there. Release it to me."

There had been that big brute of a sorrel in his father's stable, and he had made a wager he could ride the horse, although most of the men avoided the beast. He had been able to stay on for a while, but he had been terrified the whole time, and when he was finally thrown, he had gone behind the stables to be sick.

He writhed at what these recollections did to him, afraid that he would be beneath reproach to anyone who learned such dreadful things about him.

"Arkady-immai," Surata urged him softly, "you must not be so distressed. There is no reason for it."

"Don't," he whimpered and was aghast at the sound of his own voice.

"No, no Arkady-immai, you have nothing to fear. I promise you, there is nothing to fear." Her hands were sure and so comforting that he did not force them away again. She continued to touch him, her hands strong and certain, never hard, never hurting, offering a kind of solace he had not known before.

A Turkish warrior, mouth open and foaming, eyes protruding, rushed toward him, scimitar up and ready to strike off his head. Arkady blocked the blow with his sword, but the sword had shattered. One of his soldiers, a boy of no more than fourteen who spent his evenings singing hymns, had got be-tween them and had been killed.

Arkady's eyes were wet and his hands could not stop shaking.

A woman with a brash sort of beauty strolled through the camp, offering to take on the soldiers for a price and a challenge. The Margrave Fadey had been horrified, afraid of pox and Turkish spies, and had ordered Arkady to drive her from the camp. She had taunted him in front of his men, and once outside the camp had tried to attack him with a knife. He had fought with her—the scar on his eyebrow was a token of that en-counter—and had left her unconscious. The next day she was found hanging, gutted, from the Turkish fortifications.

"Do not hide these things, Arkady-immai. I will not hate you or rebuke you or turn away from you, my vow on it."

He saw Mira's face the day she told him that she was preg-nant. He had listened to her in silence, then tried to make her believe that it did not matter to him, that he did not care, he would raise her child as his own if she would marry him. Her face had been tragic, for she had told him that the father had forbidden her to marry anyone, and would not or could not marry her himself. In vain Arkady had pleaded with her to change her mind, insisting that if the man treated her thus, he had no rights in the matter. Mira had heard him out, refused him then and later said he was not to visit her anymore. Three days after, they had found her body in the river, and the priest had excoriated her memory in church.

Surata's hands continued to work.

There was a boy in Sól who had been bitten by a mad dog and had taken the madness himself. Several other children had been terrified and had followed the miserable boy with stones. Arkady had been with them, but his thrill of overcoming his dread ended when he saw the boy lying on the ground, jerked and wracked by convulsions, bleeding from the stoning. The largest of his tormentors started to hurl a rock at the rabid child's head, but Arkady had tried to stop him, and a bitter, useless fight had ensued.

When he started to double over with shame and grief, Surata

gently stretched out upon him, holding him and warming him.

Arkady saw his father, still young and vigorous, riding off to do the bidding of his Margrave. He had made Arkady promise he would not waste his time, and had specifically warned him that his boy was not to spend more time playing the lira da braccio than practicing with his sword. He had patted Arkady on the shoulder, embraced him and had not come home for more than two years. And when he did return, he was a ruined, surly fellow, given to sudden outbursts of violence and long days of drunken recriminations.

His sister, so young and so pale, with strength that was easily sapped, every day growing weaker, sat in the door of the cooking house, weeping over a starved puppy.

The first time he had been wounded it was a pleasant spring day. He had fallen a little way out of the line of battle, an arrow in his thigh. He had lain, stunned, in the new grasses, with three tiny, blue-veined flowers, like stars, not far from his eyes. He had watched the flowers, and the life in the grass, and had wept for the beauty of it.

It was his turn to serve the priest, and he had come to the church to prepare for the Nativity celebration. In his zeal, he had decided to come early, to show that although he was only eight, he was devout. He had caught the priest with the wife of one of his father's officers, and for that he had been whipped and told he would never be permitted to serve in his parish church again.

"Oh, God, Saint Michael, what have I done?" he moaned, thrusting at Surata's shoulder to move her away. "I can't . . . I truly do not—"

Surata did not move. She appeared to use no might, but she kept him still, and when she spoke, her voice was low and untroubled. "You need not blame yourself, Arkady-immai. You have been alive, that is your only error. See that. Be awake to it."

"No. Please, no, no."

"Yes," she told him.

Deep snows had slowed the hunters, but they kept on, hunt-

ing boar. The Margrave was coming the day after tomorrow, and he and his retinue would expect a proper feast and reception. Arkady, the youngest member of the hunt, kept near his father, worried that he might attempt something dangerous, for he had been sipping wine since before dawn. Arkady knew his father was in an angry and capricious mood, reckless and impatient. He was concentrating so much on his father that he did not see the boar until it broke cover, already racing. Arkady's father had swung his spear around, but not quite quickly enough; he caught the animal, but the point entered the shoulder, not the chest, and by the time Arkady could cover the little distance between them, the hooves and tusks of the boar had done their work, and Arkady's father was cursing as he died.

The bishop had told him that ordinarily when a man is the last of his family, it was not expected that he should volunteer for battle, but this case was different. Arkady's father and his father's father, and his father before him had all been Marshalls for the local Margrave and were dedicated to preserving Poland and Holy Church. Now that the Turk, surely an instrument of the Devil himself, had come into Europe for conquest, Arkady should uphold the honor and tradition of the family, and fight against the invaders for the glory of God and the safety of the kingdom. For once, Polish and Ukrainian soldiers would fight together, not against one another, to banish the terrible threat to the peace of the world. Arkady had listened, and decided that there was nothing to keep him in Sól if the Margrave appointed another Marshall. On a whim, he had taken the commission offered him.

When Arkady was seven, his tutor, a frail man in late middle age, had fallen ill. Arkady had asked his father to permit the tutor to stay with them and recover his health, but his father had sent the man to the hospital run by the Benedictines, and the tutor had died there not long after. Arkady had mourned for the man, which had annoyed his father, and led to their first serious quarrel.

It was harvest time when his mother died, and they buried

her quickly, for the weather was very warm. Around the grave-
yard, the fields gave up their bounty; Arkady had not heard
the prayers for the dead, but the songs of the harvesters.

He had caught a thief: the man carried a tinker's satchel,
and in it were necklaces and bracelets and rings. Arkady had
fought with the man and bested him. The thief wanted Arkady
to kill him, for the penalty for theft was to have his hands
struck off. Arkady had refused, but a year later, seeing the thief
huddled in rags near the market square, he wondered if he had
been cruel where he intended to be kind.

Surata placed her hands over his closed eyes. "Arkady-
immai, tell me what you see. Let me see it with you."

The plain was vast, both fertile and rugged, and isolated.
In the distance, enormous mountains rose, blue and far-off.
Horses, wild but friendly, roamed the plain.

"How old were you? Show me how old you were, Arkady-
immai."

A child, scarcely more than a toddler, scrambled through
the fence and ran into the fields, waving his arms and shouting,
laughing at the birds that wheeled above him. In the distance
one of the horses lifted her head to regard the youngster.

In the church, the high altar had been draped in mourning
for Lent. Arkady had gone there every day to light candles,
thinking that the person being mourned must be an important
Margrave or the King to receive such distinction from the priest.
He hoped that his piety would be noted and reported to the
family of the deceased noble.

Arkady huddled on the riverbank, afraid to dive in as some
of the older boys had done. He did not swim well, and a child
had drowned in the river during the spring rains. He gnawed
his thumb, hugging his arms around his knees. His skin was
turning a mottled pink, and he wished he could bring himself
to go into the water and cool off. He finally pretended to see
a snake near him, which gave him the excuse he needed to run
away, and to send several of the other boys rushing for home
as well.

There were gypsies in the village, and they made a camp

not far from the Marshall's tower, where they kept a tawdry sort of carnival for more than a week. Arkady's father, who spent his days in drinking and self-pity, had warned everyone in the village to stay away, but of course, it was useless. Even Arkady had defied him, going to the gypsy camp at sundown to consult the heavy and moustached old woman who read fortunes. She had cast a knowing eye over Arkady and said that he would have a life filled with adventure and much honor. His destiny, said the woman, would take him into strange climes, and he would see things that were new to him. She cut herself off, hurrying her prediction for him, saying only that there were more foes that he knew of to battle. Her last remark came to him clearly—that there were more ways to see than with the eyes.

He came awake with a start and found Surata kneeling near his feet, busy massaging his calves and ankles. "What!"

"You are awake," she said, unperturbed as she kept at her task.

"I . . . I dreamed." He began to laugh and stopped when he heard the sound he made.

"You remembered," she corrected him, not taking her concentration from what she was doing.

"Perhaps," he said, feeling dazed. "It was so . . ." The words trailed off. "Say something to me."

"What would you like?" she asked.

"You're speaking well," he said, baffled and sarcastic at once.

"While I touch you, I can do this. If we are not touching, I have only the words you have taught me." She moved a bit and began to work on his feet.

He had to think about this, and finally asked, "Are you a witch?"

"No. You do not believe in witches, in any case," she said as serenely as ever.

"That what are you? How do you do this? What have you done to me?" This last question was the most frightening of all, and his voice rose as the words tumbled out of him.

"I am . . . an alchemist, you would call it. My family has followed that teaching and that life for many generations. It is the way of Bogar to do this. Bogar is my family, my . . . House. What I have done to you is minor. I have asked you for help, and you have given it to me." She turned her face toward him. "Arkady-immai, until you came upon me, I feared that my life was over and that there would never again be a chance to return to my home and undo the wrongs that have been done to us."

"What happens when you aren't touching me?" he demanded, still fearful of her and what she had done to him.

She released him and sat back on her heels. "Not good, Arkady-immai. Not many words. Not good talk."

"But you understand me?" he prompted her.

"Not good; some." She cocked her head to the side. "Hands, Arkady-immai?" As she asked this, she held out her own.

Reluctantly, he put his into hers. "All right, Surata, here."

"It is better, isn't it?" She smiled at him.

He sighed. "I hope so," he said after a moment. "But if you continue to do . . . this thing you do, I don't know how I will feel."

"There is only a little more, and then the worst will be behind you." She sensed his alarm at this and moved closer to him. "No, no, Arkady-immai, do not turn away from this. You will have some discomfort, and then it will be past you. If it were a boil, you would not hesitate to lance it, but because it is a memory, you enshrine it, though it infects your life." Again she stretched out along his body, not caring that he was naked. "It is not a great thing; you have only made it a great thing by denying it and hiding it."

"You know nothing about this," he said gruffly, twisting to break free of her.

"Arkady-immai, you bought me because you heard me cry to you. You may think of it any way you like, but that is the truth of it. You have returned my life to me. Let me do what I may to do the same for you." Her hand again came to rest where his ribs joined.

"Don't," he warned her, feeling the same strange sensation spread through him that had accompanied his memories.

"If you do not wish it, then I will not. But you *do* wish it, Arkady-immai."

"You *are* a witch," he muttered, turning his head away from her.

"You know I am not," she said. "I cannot force you, no matter what you fear. If you do not want to be free of this, nothing I do will take it away from you."

"From what?" he snapped.

"From whatever it is that you cling to and is so painful to you." She began to massage the center of his chest, from the base of his neck to his navel. "It is still there, whatever it is. I can feel it, like a cold current in all the warmth, like a death that strangles life. It has made you unworthy in your own eyes, and that is the saddest of all."

"I'm not unworthy," Arkady said curtly.

"No, you are not, but there is something within you that believes you are. Nothing exonerates you, or so you believe. You accepted your disgrace not only because there was no direct way to fight it, but because, deep in your heart of hearts, you were certain you deserved it. You are willing to be an exile because that part of yourself blames you, and welcomes your punishment." She pressed close to him.

"Those who have nothing of guilt are arrogant and uncaring," Arkady said defensively.

"Is that what you have been told: it is a lie." She touched his forehead. "Your eyes are pressed shut and your features are tightened. Your whole body is distorted. What brings you this pain, Arkady-champion?"

"Nothing!" he burst out. He shifted so that part of his back was to her. "It's nothing."

"Arkady-champion, it is something because you make it so." Again she put her hands on his face. "Though it is less than you believe it to be."

He laughed in despair. "How do you know?"

Seemingly without effort, she drew him around to her again. "Because it is always thus. It was with me, when I was brought to myself, four years ago." Her voice grew wry as she leaned her head against his chest. "I was filled with dread and the

57

certainty that it was not necessary for me to observe those disgusting parts of myself, for as an alchemist, I would put them behind me in any case. I tried to convince my master that there was no purpose in dredging in the midden"—she chuckled—"so you see how frightened I was."

"And?" he demanded in spite of himself when she did not go on.

"Oh, when I found out how I had deceived myself I was very irate, and it was some time before I could pardon myself and accept that I had permitted such things to happen to me."

The night around them had turned cold now, and the fire was burning down. The creatures of the dark had begun to emerge from their resting places. As if to signal the others, an owl hooted twice as it glided silently overhead.

"I've got to do something about the fire," Arkady told her, breaking away from her. He sat up, gooseflesh appearing all over him. Reluctantly he not deny that most of the aches that had made his day miserable had faded now and were nothing more than occasional twinges. Even the wound on his arm felt better, but he was not in the mood to see if there had been any improvement. He grabbed three branches and rather haphazardly placed them on the dying fire. "We'll be warmer in a little bit."

"Arkady-immai, down again?" She was not actually touching him, and most of her words deserted her.

"Not right now. I want to put on my tunic before I go to sleep." He started to get up, but her arm went around his waist.

"Not yet, Arkady-champion. Let me do this for you, so that the hurt will go away. Otherwise you will come to fear and mistrust me, and that would be . . . very hard for me."

"Because you're afraid of being a blind beggar?" He knew as he said it that he had struck home; it amazed him that he felt only contempt for himself rather than satisfaction.

"Or a blind whore," she said calmly. "As you fear begging or being a criminal." She continued to touch him. "Arkady-champion, I—"

"Don't call me that!" he shouted at her.

"What?" It was an effort to hold him now, but she did.

"Champion. It was bad enough using that other word, that 'immai' thing you attach to my name, but calling me champion..." He reached back for his blanket to wrap himself in it, away from her.

"But that is what it means, Arkady-champion. Immai is champion." There was no argument in her tone or her attitude, but she could feel his desire to lash out at her. "From the time you heard my call and answered it, you have been my champion, and I have said so."

"It's a stupid thing to say," he sulked, not succeeding in getting away from her.

She found an edge of the blanket and crawled under it, moving so that she lay against his back. "It may be foolish to you, but if you were not my champion, you would not have heard me call, for I called to my champion. That way, those enemies of my House who followed me would not sense my need or my intentions."

"It's all nonsense," he said gruffly.

"Then my blindness is nonsense, too," she responded in a still-low voice.

Arkady rebuked himself inwardly, although he could not bring himself to say so to her. Instead, after a little time of silence, he said, "This alchemy you do—do you change lead into gold?"

She shook her head, letting her dark hair brush against his back. "No. There are those who do, but it is a small matter."

"A *small* matter, to make gold from lead?" Arkady exclaimed, so incredulous that he forgot some of his resentment.

"Yes. That is only changing matter to matter. But to change, to transform yourself, that is an accomplishment. Those who practice this discipline strive to do that, not these minor... tricks." She did her best not to sound indignant, but she knew that some of her feelings could not be entirely disguised. "I do not mean to criticize you, Arkady-champion. I hope you will trust what I say. I do not intend to deceive you."

"How do I know that?" he challenged.

Surata let her breath out slowly, not quite sighing. "There are ways I could show you, and things I could show you, but it would take time, and you would have to study. Since there is no chance for that now, what can I do but ask that you test me. You need not tell me that you are testing, or when you are testing, simply do it and make your own decisions." Her voice trembled at the end of this, and for the first time some of her composure deserted her.

Arkady shifted enough to permit him to put one arm around her, holding her head close to his shoulder with his hand. "You've passed one test already. Two, if you count waking me last night." Without intending to, he bent his head and kissed her forehead, just above the blue mark.

"That is a start, I suppose," Surata said, snuggling closer to him.

"Right," Arkady whispered with a single twitch of laughter, thinking that she meant his attitude and not the kiss.

Chapter 5

"There are many skills we are taught," Surata told Arkady the next day as the rode toward the pass they had heard other travellers call Giants' Causeway. "Most of them are to strengthen us and show us the limits of what we do, but some are ... useful. There are ways to help a wound heal."

Arkady knew she was referring to his arm, for the infection he had feared had stopped for no reason, and now there was a red, puckering seam there, as if he had been cut three weeks ago, not three days. "And can you cure all things?"

"Of course not," she said wistfully. "I cannot cure age or mortal wounds or the sickness of rotting, or any other of the gods' maladies. I cannot cure blindness. I cannot make the dumb speak." She leaned her head on his back. She had grown used to the pace of the gelding, and it was no longer a constant struggle to keep her seat on the bay.

"Our priests said that the Son of God did those things," Arkady said, not to criticize her, but out of curiosity. "Do you think He did?"

"If he was an advanced Master, then perhaps he could. I've never known anyone who could, but there are always legends that say the Great Masters could do such wonders."

There were kites and other carrion birds hanging high in the air, dozing on the wind in ominous circles. "There might be trouble ahead," Arkady warned as he watched the birds.

"Why do you say that?" She had her hand inside his jerkin, resting on his skin, and their conversation was easy. "What do you see?"

"Birds," he answered tersely. So many boded ill, he thought.

"Ah," she responded with a wise nod. "I know of such birds, too. Outside of Samarkand, I saw them where a herd of goats had been slaughtered."

"Is that where we are going?" he wondered aloud. "To Samarkand?"

"We are going beyond Samarkand, into the mountains, near the city of Ajni. The Bundhi is beyond that." She sighed, this time with real distress. "You have no idea what power he has, and how ruthless he is in its use. He follows the Left Hand Path, and is rewarded for his destruction."

"And you follow the Right Hand Path?" Arkady said, still watching the kites. "You believe that you must oppose him?"

"He blinded me and killed half of my family." Her tone was matter-of-fact, but her breathing became deeper and more irregular.

"And you want revenge." He understood that need, that obligation.

"I want to restore order, balance." She paused. "And I want some recompense for the pain he caused my family and me."

"Revenge," Arkady said quietly. "I would want it, too."

"The Bundhi will do everything to stop our coming, once he knows that we are after him." She sounded distant. "He has a high redoubt, both here and . . . in another place. Here it is near the top of Gora Čimtarga, south of Ajni."

Arkady chuckled to hide his doubts. "These are the realms of Prester John, aren't they?"

"Prester John?" Surata repeated. "Who is this?"

"A king, or so I have heard. He is in the East and is the

most powerful monarch in the world. That is what is said, at any rate." He narrowed his eyes at the kites. "There are dead on the road, Surata."

She did not shudder, but her manner was remote. "There are always dead on the road, but most of the time we do not see them."

There was nothing that Arkady could think to say to this, and so he remained silent, watching the road ahead. "There's a party of merchants coming. A dozen asses and half that number of camels. I don't recognize their clothes, but they aren't dressed the way you are."

"What colors do they wear?" Surata asked with some interest.

"They're dusty," Arkady told her, squinting toward the little caravan in the distance. "But I'd say that they wear red-gold color and a very dark blue. They have turbans. I don't know if they are men of Islam or not." He had come to mistrust all the followers of Mohamet, and his battles with the Turks had given him a suspicious respect for them.

"Long knives in their belts?" Surata suggested. "Short beards, wide metal belts?"

"I can't see them that clearly yet. They're nearer than the kites, however." He took this as a good indication that whatever misfortune had brought the ominous birds, it had not been recent.

"They probably come from Kashgar. I know a few words of their language. Perhaps I can find out what the road ahead is like." She pressed herself more tightly to Arkady's back. "When I was made a slave, they sent me first to Tabriz and then to Trebizond. The Bundhi wanted to be sure that I was far away from Ajni and Gora Čimtarga, with or without eyes to guide me."

Arkady could sense an emotion in her that was not bitterness but had in it much deep-burning anguish, and he wished he had an easy way with words so that he could say the thing that would relieve her distress. Since he could not, he remarked, "We will want to stop for a while; the horse is tired."

"And you wish to have an opportunity to assess the merchants before we reach their party," Surata finished for him, apparently untroubled by his lack of response to her comments. "That is one of the reasons you are my champion—you are one who battles wisely."

"I don't like battling," he said curtly.

"Yes; that is why you do it well," she said in her tranquil way. "Find your place, Arkady-champion, and let us be done with this watching."

"Right." He began to watch the sides of the trail for a place where they might be able to wait. "I will be glad of tomorrow. By then, we should be out of the mountains and onto the plain."

"If that is what you think is wise, I will hope for the time," she said. It was pleasant to be silent with him, to turn her mind inward to the teachings she had mastered. She was young enough to be proud of her abilities, but wise enough not to be vain about what she knew. "Arkady-champion," she whispered, not caring if he heard her or not, "there is so much to do."

"What?" he asked. "What is there to do?"

"I will tell you soon," she promised. "But for the time being, watch the merchants. They are not all that they seem."

He was about to demand she explain herself but had sense enough to stop the challenge before he uttered it. "What merchant is?" This quip was meant to be amusing, but it did not succeed.

"There are those you may trust, but many that you may not," she said seriously. "It is a pity you don't have more arrows."

"True enough," he sighed and scanned the road ahead for cover. The mountains were rugged here, and the trees were sparse near the trail. It had been done on purpose, he knew, to make it more difficult for highwaymen to waylay travellers, but at the moment, he would have been pleased for the cover trees or brush would provide. "We'll have to get some distance from the road, I'm afraid."

"Do as you think best, Arkady-champion." She deliberately took her hand off his skin and held the cantel of the saddle. "There are more words now, but not . . . many."

"Not enough," he corrected her absently. He noticed a small track leading off the road not far ahead. "I think we have what we need."

"A tree? Many trees?" she asked clumsily now that she did not have direct contact with him.

"Not trees, but a road, probably a farmer's or a vintner's." He pulled the gelding toward the narrow, rutted path. "We can wait here until the merchants have gone by."

"Good," she said. "So many, you do not . . ."

"No, I don't," he agreed. "Even if only a few of them are fighters, their numbers are too great." He drew up in the cover of a large boulder. "This will do, I think. The merchants should be along in an hour or so. That will give us all a chance to rest." He patted the bay's neck.

"Horse has no . . . word . . . name," she said, commenting on something that had puzzled her for some time.

"No," Arkady said.

"What reason?" She was aware that he did not want to answer the question, which made her more curious about the circumstances.

He dismounted, pulling the reins over the bay's head before reaching up to help her. Finally he decided to tell her the reason. "You'd probably find out, anyway," he growled. "My first horse had a name, and my second. The first was killed. The second . . . the second went into the stewpot when my men had been three days without meat. Since then, I don't give my mounts names." He thought back, remembering Ruddy, his first horse, a big, raw-boned sorrel with a shambling trot and the smoothest canter. His second horse—he still winced when he thought of the liver-chestnut—was called Crusader and possessed enormous stamina as well as an uneven temper. There had been six horses since then, this bay gelding being the most recent.

"Good horses?" she inquired as she bent and twisted to work the stiffness out of her muscles.

"Most of them. One was too nervous, another was twelve years old and not up to fighting anymore, but they were good horses." He reached over and patted the gelding before loosening the girths. "This one is . . . reliable."

"What is that?" Surata asked.

Arkady reached for her hand and was surprised when she pulled away. "You were the one who started this," he protested.

"Not good to use it every time," she explained awkwardly. "Not always are hands touching. Not always . . . near."

"All right, all right," he said, reaching for his waterskin. "Have some of this while I fix a nosebag for the horse."

She took the waterskin and sipped at the brackish water. "More is needed," she said to him. "More new."

"But there isn't any nearby," he told her. "For the time being, you'll have to use that." He had taken a sack from the saddle and was putting grain into it. "As soon as I've got the horse taken care of, I'll get some fruit for us."

"Good fruit," she said.

"Yes." They were also getting low on food as well as money, and what they would do for more of either he was not certain, which troubled him. With just his brigandine, two swords, maul and bow, the most he could hope for was passage for him and Surata with a party of merchants going east. No lord or local Marshall would take him on with such equipment, even if he spoke the bastard version of Hungarian he had been told was the language of the area. For the first time he was convinced he had chosen foolishly when he had turned east, for the farther east they ventured, the more mute he would become. And there would be many, many leagues to cover before Surata reached her people again. He stared off into the distance, his thoughts bleak.

"Not good, Arkady-immai, to be . . . head down." She waved her hand to show that she had not found the right word and knew it. "You say."

"Cast down," he corrected her, motioning her to come closer, then cursing when he recalled she had to hear him speak. "Over here, Surata."

She obeyed at once, moving into the shadow of the boulder. "Good to be here?"

"Very good," he said. "The men are coming, and they out-

66

number us. With those kites in the sky, I don't know what we should expect, and so we'll wait here until they pass."

"Many . . . roads . . ." Her expression was exasperated, and she reached for his hand, smiling as they touched. "There are several trade routes once we leave these mountains, and there is no certainty that the kites have anything to do with the merchants you see on the road."

"And there's no certainty that they do not," he reminded her. "I don't want to have to settle that when they get here, do you?" He did not feel comfortable so close to her, for she was very attractive, and he did not want to add to his dishonor by using her badly. If she had been a campwoman, or a slattern in a village tavern, that would be different; but Surata, he knew in his bones and sinews, as he knew the weight of the sun's heat on him, was his true lady and deserved the best of him.

"Do not be troubled, Arkady-champion," she said quietly. "You could not disgrace me if you wished to. It is not in your nature."

He tried to scoff at her remark, but it so nearly caught his thoughts, he was not able to. "You're wrong there, Surata."

"I am not." She turned her head. "It is time to be quiet now, for the merchants will hear us soon."

"You blind hear better than those of us with sight," he said, hoping to still his lack of ease. "We had a blind priest for a while, and he heard everything."

"Not better," she said very softly. "We simply pay more attention to what we hear." Her hand dropped his, and she fell silent, her attention turned inward.

Arkady watched her closely, marvelled at her dark hair and smooth face. She was as beautiful as she was exotic to him, for all the dust that clung to her. He wanted to touch her again, to close the gap between them with his fingers, but he could not bring himself to do this. Then he heard the first, distant sound of the caravan coming toward them, and he went to his gelding, holding the bay's head so that he would not neigh to the other horses.

The sound of the caravan grew louder, and there were bursts of conversation over the shuffle and clop of hooves. One of the men was singing, the words repetitious and droning, the melody an eerie wail. The merchants moved slowly but steadily, almost without purpose; they spoke little, surrounded by the mountains and the dust they raised, which curled upward like an offering of incense.

In the shelter of the boulder, Arkady leaned toward Surata and whispered, "Listen, and if you understand what you hear, tell me."

"Yes," she promised. "I will understand." Then she settled back, her features composed, her body still and quiet.

Arkady watched her, both curious and apprehensive. He could not think of her without turmoil. He held the bay's bridle, prepared to pinch the nostrils closed at the horse's first sign of whinnying. He had done this many times before and did not need to concentrate on the task. Instead, he studied Surata. She was almost a decade younger than he, but she made him feel an untutored youth. It was more than her skills, he decided as he looked at her, at the way the shadow and sunlight crossed her face, revealing and obscuring at the same time. Her sightless eyes were closed, and had he not known better, he might have thought she was half-asleep.

The sun rose higher and the heat drummed down on the mountains. The caravan moved more slowly as the day advanced to noon and the way became steeper still.

Surata frowned and shifted her posture slightly, and her breathing deepened. Her chin tilted upward. Then another change came over her, one that made it seem her body was only a husk, abandoned, and that Surata herself was somewhere else.

Since the caravan was nearly abreast of their hiding place, Arkady dare not ask what troubled her, but it was evident that she was . . . different. He could not do more, for his horse was growing restive, and he had to devote more attention to the gelding. He strove to hold his bay's head while the horse's hooves slid and danced on the narrow track. Arkady could not risk speaking to the horse, or slapping him with the reins for fear it would alert the men of the caravan.

It took well over an hour for the strangers to pass, and once they were gone, Arkady insisted that they wait still longer before emerging from their concealment. "There could be stragglers, or they might have a rear scout."

"They don't," she said, slurring the words a little. She shook her head as if trying to come more truly awake.

"You can't be sure. I've seen impetuous men killed for leaving shelter too early." He reached down to help her to her feet.

"I can be sure." She held his hand without rising. "They have seen much trouble, and they are as frightened as they are tired. They have been moving since well before dawn, and they have not yet rested for a meal."

"Tell me," he said, fascinated by what she was saying even though he could not imagine how she had learned it. He could not doubt that she told him the truth.

"You're growing too dependent on this touching, Arkady-champion," she chided him gently. "There have been battles not far from here. The birds gave true warning. Many men were killed, and a village was burned. None of the merchants knew who had done it, for the villagers had been dead more than a day when the travellers came upon them. They were worried when they saw what had happened, because the village was a place where many travellers stopped. Now they will have to find another place, a safer place, to rest when they return."

"Why was this village so important, do you know?" Arkady asked, pulling her to her feet.

"It is . . . was a crossroad, or a fork in the road. Yes, I believe it was a fork in the road. That is where two roads meet and become one, isn't it?" Her hand trembled in his. "The killings were brutal, or so the merchants thought."

"Did you . . . ?" He could not ask the rest of his question, for his memories of battlefields were too stark.

She answered him anyway. "Yes, Arkady-champion. I saw it."

He could find nothing to say that would lessen her desolation; he did the only thing that came to mind. "Surata"—he put his arms around her to give her the warmth that had nothing to do with the heat of the day—"here."

Surata quivered but she did not weep. Slowly, very slowly, she relaxed against him, letting him support her until the worst of her wretchedness left her. "I'm . . . not sorry. This happens when I don't guard against it. I wasn't anticipating anything so . . ." She ended on a shaky laugh.

"It doesn't matter, Surata," Arkady said, taking unexpected pride in his ability to comfort her. He could remember all the despair he had felt after the dead were gathered at the end of a battle, and the black misery that had consumed him when they had to be left where they fell. For a woman like Surata to have such visions in her blindness gave Arkady a sensation close to sickness.

"Arkady-champion," she said, holding him in return, "do not fear for me. I'm not as fragile as you think me. And what I dreaded to find was not there."

He stared at her. "What was that? A sacked village was not as worrisome at this other?"

"For me," she said cautiously. "The Bundhi has those whom he . . . sends forth, to watch for him. There have been two before, but there might be more. He has used many. When he captured my family, he sent more than ten who carried staves." This time there was a silent terror about her that filled him with concern.

"Ten men with staves, what can they do against my swords and my maul?" He had seen soldiers who fought with long staves that he would not want to fight with anything less than a mace-and-chain, but refrained from saying so.

"If the staves are fed . . ." She stopped, forcing herself to a composure that was not as genuine as it appeared. "But you have your swords and your maul and your cinquedea. You are a good fighter." She turned her face toward him. "And you are my ally."

"A disgraced captain," he dismissed, unable to make light of his self-accusation.

The wind blew the last of the caravan's dust back to them.

"A sensible captain," she corrected him. "It is safe to leave now. They are all passed. Arkady-champion, watch carefully. The merchants have dropped something of value."

"Something of value? What use is it to us; we're not merchants." He was already busying himself with checking all their paraphernalia tied to the saddle. He had not wanted to release her hand, and he chided himself for letting her affect him so.

"Gold. Anyone can use gold." She went on awkwardly. "Arkady-immai, you are . . . not happy that there is not much money. Gold is good."

"Useful," he suggested. "Good or bad, it's useful." He took her arm. "Ready? Up you go."

She got onto the bay without fuss, holding the cantel, the hem of her robes hiked up to her knees, revealing the embroidered leather shoes with pointed toes that Arkady found fascinating. As he stared at her shoe, she said, "Arkady-immai, your head . . . what color?"

"My head?" He paused, his hand already on the saddle. "You mean my hair?"

"Yes; hair." She almost smiled. "I want to see you better."

"It's . . . uh . . . light brown, sort of like dry grass." He felt awkward answering the question, and wished, for reasons he could not comprehend, that she had not asked.

"And your eyes," she persisted.

"No special color," he said curtly, swinging onto the horse and narrowly missing her with his knee.

"What color?"

"It's not important," he snapped, kicking the gelding more forcefully than he had intended.

The bay jogged into a trot for a short distance but pulled back to a walk when they regained the main road.

"Tell me, Arkady-immai. It is good for me to know this," she said.

"Why?" he asked, perplexed and uneasy. His uncertainty was more with his own reluctance than her question. What was it about this that vexed him so? Was it only her blindness, or did it go further than that.

"There are reasons." She leaned forward so that her head rested against the back of his shoulder. "It doesn't bother me that you are not blind, Arkady-champion."

The acuity of her remark stung him. "I didn't mean—" He stopped. "Yes, I did. My eyes are greenish brown. My mother hoped they would be blue. My sister had blue eyes."

"Ah." It was a little time before she spoke again. "Watch with your greenish brown eyes, Arkady-champion. We are not far from where the thing was dropped."

He could not resist asking her, "How do you know that?"

She shrugged. "I know it. I saw it."

He had to be content with that, for she would say no more. As they rode, he watched the ground ahead of them and scanned the sides of the road. He had no notion what he might be searching for, but he could not refuse to look. He was not sure he knew what Surata meant when she said gold: a coin, a piece of jewelry, a small cast bar. Then he noticed a small leather sack, hardly larger than a pouch, half-covered with dust, and he reined in. "There's something," he said.

"Good." She sat still while he dismounted. There was a faint smile on her lips. The mark in the middle of her forehead appeared brighter than usual.

Arkady lifted the pouch, slapping the dust off it. He was surprised at its weight. "I don't know what's in it, but—" He broke off as he untied the thongs that held it. Inside the pouch, he saw the gleam of gold. "Coins," he said in an odd tone.

"Are there very many?" She did not seem the least startled by his announcement. "Are they all gold?"

"As far as I can tell," he said carefully. "There are quite a few of them," he admitted, bouncing the pouch a few times. He had never held so much money at one time in his life.

"Enough to take us to Samarkand?" she asked. "Will it buy us what we need?"

He swallowed hard. "I don't know what it costs to go to Samarkand, but I'd guess we could go to the court of the Great

Khan himself and return again on what's here." He told himself sternly that he would wait until they made camp at night to count their treasure. He tied the pouch shut and looped the thongs around his belt before he got back on his horse. As he tapped the bay with his heels, he tried to bring himself to ask Surata how she be so certain the gold would be there, but the words refused to come and they rode in silence across the Giants' Causeway.

Chapter 6

Eight days later they had left the mountains far behind and had come to the main caravan road running from Iaş to Tana and on to Sarai.

Still feeling giddy with wealth—the little sack contained a staggering sixty-three pieces of gold—Arkady suggested that they buy another horse or a mule for Surata to ride. "You won't be bounced around so much. You'll have a proper saddle. I'll see to it."

"What would be the point?" she asked, holding him closely. Her hands rested just above his belt. "You would have to lead the horse or the mule, and if there was trouble, I would be more of a burden to you on another beast than I am here."

"Not in a real fight," he said before he could stop himself.

"You do not know that, Arkady-champion. I have my own skills. And this way, we can speak easily. If I were on another horse, it would not be as pleasant, would it?"

"Well, you're getting better all the time." He had come to like having her near him, but he was concerned for the load his gelding carried as well as for his own desires. These he could not hide from himself, although he hoped she had not yet discerned the true nature of his feelings. He decided to try again. "Surata, if we are to cross the desert you say is ahead, then we must lighten the load my horse carries."

"Then buy a mule for the food and other provisions," she recommended.

"And if we lose the mule?" he asked. "It would be a risk."

Surata laughed outright. "Arkady-champion, breathing is a risk. Buy a mule or two, or a camel, if that is what you want. After Sarai, the way is difficult, and then you will be glad to have more than one animal, in case there are . . . problems." She lifted her hand to touch his face. "The scar over your brow isn't as serious as you think it is."

"Soldiers have scars," he said, attempting to turn her attention.

"Not like this one, for you did not get it in battle." Surata hesitated. "Do you want to travel with a caravan to Samarkand?"

He knew from her tone that she would not want this. "We'd be faster on our own, and you've said speed is important. There is more danger alone, but there is also speed. Also, if there are men hunting you for the Bundhi, it would be less easy for them if we are on our own." He looked into the distance, toward the eastern horizon. "We'll have to be careful if we encounter soldiers. I don't know how they would feel about a discharged captain like me."

"We will say that I engaged you to carry me back to my home. I will buy new robes so that they will think I am a fine lady." Again she laughed, this time lightly, teasing him.

"That's fine, *if* one of us can speak their language, and *if* they will listen." He shaded his eyes with his free hand. "I think there is a caravan ahead of us on the road. I see mules."

"How many?" The worry was back in her voice. "Can you count them?"

"Not accurately." He squinted with concentration. "Wait. They're . . ." He barked his laughter. "They're hogs and cattle. There must be a farmer nearby. He probably sells his beasts to travellers for food." Now he grinned. "Who knows what it will cost, but such farms usually have room for travellers to sleep for the night, if it's only a barn."

"It's shelter," she said warily. "And there will be a storm before morning. The smell of it is in the air."

He agreed with her. The sky had turned metallic early in the afternoon, a brazen sun hanging over the flat copper plain. Behind them, clouds gathered over the unseen mountains and the air was waiting. "We can find out how long it will take to reach Tana. The farmer should know."

"*If* he understands you," Surata reminded him, not quite seriously. "If the farmer is so near the caravan road, it will not be difficult to speak with him. He will have a way to do it." She sighed. "It will be good to sleep in a barn for a change."

"With the cattle and the mice," Arkady added.

"Cattle are not bad; even pigs are not bad. Mice are everywhere." She made a pleased little sound. "Go on, Arkady-champion. Find us this farmer."

"As you wish," he said, nodding instead of bowing. "You'd think," he added as he turned the bay onto the road, "that a man with sixty-three gold pieces could do better than sleep in a barn."

Surata did not sound amused. "Be careful with the money, Arkady-champion. Do not let it be known that you have so much, or our throats will be cut before the sun rises again."

"I'm not a fool, Surata," he responded. "I still have copper and silver. The farmer can have some of that." He patted the wallet tied to his belt. "We'll conceal the other."

"Excellent," she said with a hint of asperity. "Be sure you haggle the price. The farmer will be suspicious otherwise."

"I know." He was irked that she should question him as if he knew nothing of foraging and living in the field. He had been a soldier and knew how it was done. His jaw set as he urged the horse to a trot.

Their shadows reached far before them when they finally came upon the collection of huts, barns and pens where the farmer lived. The buildings were less than a league from the road, huddled together like enormous tortoises basking in the sun. Low stone fences marked the boundaries of the fields where grain and vegetables grew, and most distant from the buildings was a small vineyard.

"It will be soon now, Surata," Arkady told her as he tugged at the reins. "I can see men near the . . . I think they're barns. If we approach slowly, they should not be alarmed."

His prediction proved to be correct. As they drew near the huts, three old women, all wrapped in shapeless garments, came bustling out to meet them, waving, their smiles showing the gaps in the yellowish teeth. They indicated by mime that Arkady and Surata were welcome and that they could purchase food and a place to sleep and, for more coins, a bath.

"They have a bathhouse," Arkady told Surata, sighing at the thought of this luxury. All of his skin felt crusted and gritty, and he was sure she must feel the same.

"How much do they want for that?" Surata asked, her words eager.

"Two pieces of silver, apparently," he said as he watched the old women. "It troubles me that I see no men with them, just those coming in from the fields." He stared around the farmyard. "We must be careful tonight, I believe."

"If you think it's necessary," Surata said, not questioning his reservations. "Pay them the money for the bath, though. I feel as if all this dust is alive."

"It might be," Arkady told her, recalling all the times he had found lice in his hair. "It will be good to be clean, even for one night. We can wash our clothes, too."

Surata laid a warning hand on his arm. "Wet clothes can be a risk. The Bundhi likes to surprise his foes when they are naked."

Arkady nodded. "Very well. We will beat the clothes well before we bathe." He unfastened his wallet and handed down three silver and four copper coins to the old women and watched while they tasted them. When they beamed at him and motioned him to follow them, he dismounted. "I'll help you down once I find out where they're taking us," Arkady said softly.

"Good," Surata agreed. Her head was slightly cocked to the side, as if she were listening to more than his words. "There are many men here, Arkady."

"That's what I'm afraid of," he muttered as he led his horse through the gathering of buildings, following the three old women.

"We will be safe enough. The farmers will not harm us, but if other travellers come here, we must be on guard." She sagged against the cantel, revealing her fatigue for the first time that day. "It is good to rest."

"If we can rest, yes, it is." He stopped the horse as the three old women pointed to a building that was clearly a stable. Four large cart horses were stalled there, and half a dozen squat-bodied asses. The most wrinkled of the old women pointed to two empty stalls, side by side, and nodded her encouragement.

"We get a stall," Arkady told Surata. "It could be worse." He bowed his acceptance to the three women and nodded until he was afraid he might get dizzy.

One of the women pointed to the building next to the stable and indicated the three chimneys rising from it, then mimed scrubbing with outrageous swoops of her hands over her massive bosom.

"The bathhouse is next door," Arkady informed Surata.

The most wrinkled old woman indicated that a bell would be rung when the evening meal was ready, and Arkady relayed this to Surata as he went through the ritual of nodding once more.

Then they were left alone, and Arkady led the bay into the stable before helping Surata down.

"It smells of horses," she said.

"Small wonder." His hands lingered on her body, and he wanted to curse himself for giving her offense. His face grew red, as much from desire as from shame, and he stepped back from her.

Surata stood while Arkady led the bay into one of the stalls and began to unfasten the girth. "Arkady-immai," she said tentatively, "you will be with me in the bath?"

"Uh . . ." He wanted to say no, but he could not leave her

by herself in an unfamiliar place. "I suppose I'll have to," he told her at last as he tugged the saddle off the gelding's back. He lifted it onto the low wall separating the two stalls they had been allotted.

"Good." She folded her hands in front of her and lowered her head, the stillness that perturbed Arkady coming over her once more. She did not move again until he had finished with the bay and had come to her side. "Arkady-immai."

"I think the bathhouse is hot," he said. "Before it gets much later, let's get this over with." He took her hand and all but dragged her out of the stable. He walked quickly, his thoughts disordered.

The bathhouse was warm and dark, smelling of wet wood and the harsh soap made by the farmers. There was also a faint scent of sweat, sharp in the gloom.

Arkady found the benches near the wall and pulled Surata after him. "You undress here"—how could he stand to see her undressed?—"and then I'll take you to the sweat room."

"You will undress too?" she asked as she began to pull her robes off.

"I'll have to," he said reluctantly, staring at her in spite of his resolution not to. "Surata . . . I . . ."

She did not turn toward him. "I do not mind, Arkady-immai. There is no shame." She continued to take off her clothes. She made no attempt to be provocative or to affect a modesty she obviously did not feel.

With an oath, Arkady unfastened his belt and flung it onto the bench, then seized his brigandine and acton and worked them over his head. He looked at the acton and sniffed in disgust at the grime he saw on the padded cotton garment. If he were still in camp with the men of the Margrave Fadey, he would have given the acton to Hedeon with orders to clean it or burn it. He untied his breeches and, after a moment's hesitation, stepped out of them, reminding himself that Surata could not see him, so his nudity did not matter. He took the little sack of gold, slung the thongs around his wrist and cleared his throat. "The sweat room is that way," he said, pointing.

"I will go where you guide me," she said, her voice so even

and uninflected that it stung Arkady more than a reprimand would have.

Gingerly he took her arm, afraid that his touch would burn her skin. "This way," he growled.

The sweat room was smaller than he would have liked, and the close, steamy air enveloped them as soon as they were inside, wrapping them in its cocoon.

"You sit here," Arkady said brusquely, thrusting Surata down on the bench. "We must stay here a little time, then go into the next room and wash off. It's cooler in the next room."

Surata shook her head to loosen her hair. Now it fell over her shoulders and halfway down her back, shining black with the minute drops of moisture in the air. Arkady could not look away from her, so awed was he by her beauty. She stretched her legs out in front of her, flexing her toes. Then she rose, and to Arkady's amazement, placed one foot against her knee, pressed her palms together in front of her navel, and proceeded to stand in that position, humming to herself while the sweat ran off her body, leaving little trails down her bronze-gold flesh.

Arkady leaned back on the bench, glad it was rough wood, hard against his back. The scar on his arm where his wound had healed turned a raspberry color as the heat took him. His muscles protested this unfamiliar relaxation and he swore at them inwardly by every saint in the calendar. It relieved him to have something more on his mind than the presence of Surata. He decided that he stank, and that was good, too. He caught one of his hands in his thick, ill-cut hair, wrenching it through his fingers as if to uproot it. Sweat ran into his eyes and he blinked rapidly.

Surata took up the same position on her other foot.

He had intended to pay her no notice, but curiosity got the better of him. "What are you doing?" he asked when she had been still for some little time.

"It is . . . work." She faced his voice. "Your hand."

Very reluctantly, he took her hand in his, holding tightly because they were both so slippery.

"This is better. It is a part of my training, as prayer is a part of yours. It is for the body and the senses, so that they can work well, not in conflict with one another. There are other postures, but this one will help restore me for . . ." Her words trailed off.

"For?" he prompted when she did not go on.

"For later," she answered remotely. "There is so much we must do before we encounter the Bundhi."

"In the mountains beyond Samarkand," he said, turning on his side so that he could not see her.

"Yes," she replied vaguely, "that is one place."

"You mean he might be somewhere else?" Arkady asked, trying to sit up, to no avail.

"It is . . . possible," she answered after a brief silence. "You must learn to find it." Now she was standing on both feet, her arms extended above her head, crossed at the wrists, with the palms pressed against each other.

"What are you doing?" Arkady demanded, his attention distracted by her movements.

"This is . . . growing work," she said, not finding the correct word. "It is what I am trained to do."

"This is *alchemy?*" He wanted to laugh but managed to control the impulse.

"Most certainly," Surata said to him. "It is . . . knowing the letters in order to read." She lowered her arms. "Does it trouble you, Arkady-immai?"

"It puzzles me," was all he was willing to say.

"Soon I will explain it," she said, wiping the sweat from her body. "The bath is good."

"The bath is wonderful," he corrected her, then turned away as he heard the breathless sound of his voice. He was disgracing himself, and he knew it. He ought to leave the sweat room at once and ask her pardon later. His genitals felt heavier than the pouch of gold tied to his wrist.

"Arkady-immai, let me rub you," Surata offered.

Arkady yelped as her hand fell on his chest. "No . . . no," he stammered, trying to break away from her and ramming his elbow against the wall. Pain fizzed up his arm and he clutched at it, welcoming it for the diversion he provided.

"It will be better soon," Surata told him, her hands on his shoulders, pressing him back against the bench. "There is nothing to be afraid of."

"You don't know," he growled, twisting away from her.

"You mean this?" Surata's hand moved down his body and found his swollen flesh. "But Arkady-champion, this is good."

"Surata . . ." he protested, knowing it was too late and that he had disgraced himself.

"But this, Arkady-champion, this is the Four Petaled Center of the Subtle Body. It is the wellspring for what we will do." She moved her hand to the center of his chest. "You remembered so much, when we were lying side by side on the mountain, and the strength ran through you like a river, though you could not release all your fears."

"You do not know how I want to . . . use you," he said with disgust.

"As I wish to use you, I trust." Her voice dropped. "Arkady-immai, you have known nothing but urgency and longing. You do not know what it is to ride on the crest of the wave, and you must learn it if we are to find the Bundhi where he hides."

Thoroughly confused, Arkady lifted one hand to wipe the sweat off his face and gain a little time to try to make sense of what she said. "What does . . . using you have to do with finding the Bundhi?"

"He hides many places." She pressed her hands over his heart. "This is the Eight Petaled Center." Next, the base of his throat. "This Center has Sixteen Petals, and this"—her palm touched the center of his forehead—"Thirty-Two Petaled and the Center of the Moon."

"Surata, for God's sake—" He took one hand in his, wishing he could will her to stop.

"This center in the abdomen is also a Thirty-Two Petaled Center. And at the navel is Sixty-Four Petaled Center, the focus of the Sun and the seat of transformation." She smiled down at him. "Now you have begun."

"Begun *what?*" His throat felt unexpectedly tight. "Surata, a lady should not . . . it is proper that you should preserve your chastity." He repeated the words by rote, as his priest had said them to him when he was a child.

"Of all the qualities and virtues to treasure, chastity is the most senseless. Treasure wisdom or courage or kindness or integrity, but chastity—!" She shook herself with exasperation. "I prefer fidelity to chastity; I trust fidelity." Very deliberately she leaned down and kissed him, her mouth slightly open.

Arkady moaned as he locked his arms around her. How much he had wanted to do this! How he had longed to be near to her, to plunder her body with his own! His head ached with his need.

It was Surata who drew back first. "There," she whispered. "This is a first step."

He clung to her. "Don't deny me now, Surata."

She kissed his brow where the scar was. "I won't. But first we must be clean and fed, so that there will be enough time. It's a mistake to hurry the Opening of the Lotus."

He would not release her. "No. Now."

"So you may feel humiliation in lying with me?" Surata asked sadly. "So you can say to yourself that you and I are worthy of nothing but a hurried coupling? How can you think yourself of so little merit?"

"I . . . need." The shame he felt as he admitted this almost destroyed his desire.

"Arkady-champion, you're not a starving infant at the breast of his mother, you are a valiant man, with great courage and goodness of heart." She kissed him again, very softly. "You heard my call to you, because you called to me as well. Come." She stood up, holding out her hand to him.

"Now what?" He resented her for all she had done to him. It was bad enough that she knew of his desire, but that she would now refuse what she had seemed to offer was intolerable. "I can get up on my own." As he got to his feet, she gave him a companionable embrace. "Stop that."

She stepped back a little way. "Arkady-champion, listen to

me." She waited until he faced her. "I will refuse you nothing but your haste. I promise you that tonight you will have what you want, with the time to enjoy your desires."

He regarded her skeptically. "And there will be another reason to hold off then. I'll take you to fight the Bundhi without this, Surata. You don't have to . . . buy me." It was the cruelest thing he could think to say to her and he was rewarded when he saw her flinch.

"You may say that to me in the morning, Arkady-champion, if you believe then that I deserve it." She brought her chin up, but not in defiance. "Let's wash away all the dirt."

"Purify ourselves, is that it?" Even as he strove to hurt her, he wanted to give her comfort for his own harshness.

"Yes. So that you may be fulfilled." She hesitated. "Your desires are not . . . sullied, Arkady-champion. They are your strength." As she shook her head, she moved a little away from him. "We will wash."

He shrugged, annoyed that she was unable to see this. "Follow me." He did not to touch her again, not yet. "This way. There are two steps down." The door was heavy and he held it for her.

She stopped in the doorway, her milky eyes on his. "I am still your slave, Arkady-immai. You bought me."

"And the Devil alone knows why," he complained, pulling the door closed behind them. "Stay there. The tubs are just in front of you." With a sigh he put his hands on her shoulders and directed her toward one of the large barrels. "I'll help you step in."

"Let me wash you, since I am your slave," she said.

"Stop teasing me," he ordered her.

"I am not teasing." She sank into the water, smiling. "There is great force in water, if you have the skill to know it." As she took his hand, she added in her most practical tone, "Give me the soap and the brush, and I will tend to you as a slave should."

He was about to object but could find no reason to refuse. "Here's the soap, and here's the brush. See that you scrub hard."

"As you wish," she said, sniffing the soap suspiciously. "It is unfortunate that they do not use perfumes here."

By the time she was through with him, his body was rosy from the vigor of her ministrations, and his mood had lightened. He still viewed her with apprehension but was convinced her foreign teaching had confused her. He sat in the stable with her, eating a dinner of millet bread stuffed with spiced vegetables and a lentil stew. The three old women had provided a skin of wine and made it plain that if Arkady or Surata wanted pork, it would cost more.

"Do not eat it," Surata said to Arkady. "It is not good to eat pork now."

"There's money enough," he reminded her.

"I did not say this because of money." She wiped her fingers on the rough square of cloth the three old women had provided. "Arkady-immai," she said, smiling tentatively, "you are not to be afraid. You have no reason to fear me or anything about me."

"I'm not afraid," he said, taking another of the stuffed millet breads. "This is good."

She would not be distracted. "Arkady-immai, you are..." She reached over and put her hand on his arm, just above the scar, letting her fingers rest there. "You heard me call to you once; answer me again."

Though his skin was tanned and roughened by weather, he knew it darkened as he blushed. "I've got enough control now."

"But I don't *want* your denial. I want you." She said it gently. "Who knows when we will have so much time again, and it is necessary that we learn to... go to the other places where the Bundhi hides."

He brushed her hand away. "Don't start again, Surata."

"You no longer desire me?" Her question was calm, without a trace of accusation in it, but he reacted as if he had been rebuked and challenged.

"Listen, Surata, I won't add to my dishonor by making you a whore as well as a slave. I've lost too much as it is." He turned away from her and rolled far enough from her to be out of reach. The soft, new hay tickled his neck as he lay back. "I'm tired."

"Then I will rub your feet for you." She set two wooden bowls that had contained their food aside and found her way to him. "You would not mind that, would you?"

"Um," he grunted, letting her make of it what she would, smiling to himself as she began to pull off his leggings. He had to give her full credit for her talent for massage. The stiffness in his ankles and calves gave way under her capable hands. "That's wonderful," he said when she gave her attention to his knees.

"Good," she whispered, continuing her work.

Arkady was drifting into that luxurious half-sleep when he felt her pull his tunic off. He almost protested, then decided to let her continue. The sensations were too pleasant to stop them, and he would soon doze. It was too much bother to tell her to stop. His languor lulled him, the smell of horses and hay was friendly and familiar. When the first, soft drops of rain began to fall, its whisper on the roof was more soothing than a lullaby.

Precisely when it was that his contentment flickered into desire, Arkady did not know. One moment he was hovering on the edge of sleep; in the next, there was a stirring in his flesh that roused him only enough to remind him of his need. "Surata . . ."

"Hush, Arkady-champion." There was such serenity in her words that Arkady sighed deeply. She went on, kneading first his back, then his buttocks. When she was done, she rolled him from prone to supine. There she began with his face and neck, then moved down to his chest.

"It's raining harder," Arkady murmured.

"Yes," she replied, moving lower.

"Oh, God," he breathed, no longer wanting to object to how she touched him, or where. Her hands, the curve of her breast and waist and thigh were ineffably sweet, more gratifying than the swing of a perfectly balanced sword. When her lips opened to his, he forgot all his questions and doubts. He pulled her into his arms.

"Slowly, Arkady-champion," she whispered. "There is no hurry, Arkady-champion."

"Please," he moaned.

"It will be better this way, I promise you." She lay next to him from shoulder to toe. "The Lotus opens slowly."

"Now, Surata," he urged her.

"You will ride the wave with me," she said so softly that the gentle fall of the rain seemed louder.

He had never experienced such excitement before. There were sensations in his body that were new, thrilling and disturbing at once. As she pressed against him, even his breathing changed, growing slower and deeper. His senses were flooded with her nearness, and the only thing he felt was the magic of her flesh. Then she embraced his legs with her own and he rose into her.

Chapter 7

There was light around him, constantly shifting, more brilliant than stars and rainbows. Arkady stared in disbelief and awe at the splendor of it, gasping as the colors fluctuated and pulsed with every motion of his body. His body was without weight, suspended in the radiance as if he himself were a star. He longed for Surata to see what he saw, and heard her voice, so near that they might have been touching. "I see, Arkady, my champion."

As he watched, the colors became shapes, taking on the form of flowers and jewels, answering his whim. The most marvellous fragrances surrounded him, bringing him memories of everything pleasant he had known from his earliest youth. He wanted to laugh or to sing for the utter joy of it.

Like a butterfly, a cloud, a bird, he soared over the beauty, admiring it and feeling it stretch far beyond him. His arms stretched out to become enormous, brilliant wings, more glorious than any he had ever seen, even on the glass angels in the cathedral in Warsaw. He spiraled on vast rivers of light, high in the effulgent clouds, with flower petals falling all around him. His wings glistened.

Mountains rose up into the shining sky, magnificent as bishops in purple and white. They were as luminous as they were solid, alive with majesty. Arkady spiraled toward them, glorying in his freedom as much as he admired their great tenacity. How fine a part of the earth they were, how well they ornamented the world! He wished he had the means to tell Surata how it appeared to him, being free in the sky where he could romp with the sagacious mountains.

"I know this, Arkady, my champion. I am with you."

And to his amazement, she was, as close to him as his skin, or closer. He saw her face more clearly than he ever had, and saw who it was she was. He had never before noticed how black her hair was, or how young she must be. And her eyes! They were not the strange, frosted blankness he had known from the first, but a clear, deep, lustrous and glowing brown, warm and subtle. He stared into her eyes, aware that he had never seen anyone with eyes like hers.

"Surata," he said, without speaking, or if he spoke, it was in words and with a tongue he had not used before. "Surata."

Her answer was more stirring that any he had heard. It was like music, or the stillness before waking. He let those sounds go through him, kindling his soul.

Far below the mountains rolled the sea, vaster and more alive than water had ever been. Patterns of light played over its surface, shifting and changing with more variety than rainbows or the lights of the winter sky. Where the ocean met the mountains, spray and sand kissed.

How very far it was to the ocean, to the crags of the mountains! Arkady was caught up in fascination, thrilled and aghast at how far he had come. He turned to where he expected Surata to be, and could not see her. His vision was disoriented, for the mountains seemed to lose their shapes, growing fluid, melting, sinking toward the enormity of the sea. Around him, the light was obscured by roiling clouds, dark and sulphurous, threatening to lose him forever in the black clouds.

Abruptly he decided he must land, must not be at the mercy of the enveloping clouds. He was distantly aware that his body was changing, and that he had to protect it. Enormous, un-expected winds buffeted him through the darkness, battering at him, ready to dash him against one of the mountains that might be looming, unseen, with merciless rocks waiting for him. His arms—for they were no longer wings, but arms— flailed, and he plummeted

back into the hay, in the barn that smelled of horses.

Surata pressed her hand to his forehead. "You did this well, Arkady-champion. You surprised me." She smiled at him.

Arkady blinked, trying to regain a sense of where he was and what had happened. "There were mountains," he said slowly, shaking his head.

"Yes," she agreed as she pulled his blanket up over them both. "And the ocean and the air."

"But they were not the same," he said after a little silence.

"No," Surata said. She snuggled against him, one arm across his chest, her head on his shoulder. "Thank you, Arkady-champion, for all you have done."

Arkady blushed deeply as he remembered her body. Perhaps that, too, had been a part of his peculiar dream. It had been so real, while he thought he flew above mountains. If that had been his imagination, then she might have been, as well. Ten-tatively he spoke to her. "Surata, about . . ."

"You did well. It is possible, now." Her voice was relaxed and sleepy, and it was with a shock that Arkady realized they both were naked under the blanket.

"Ah . . ." He tried to draw away from her, but she would not release him.

"Arkady-champion, don't move away. It's cold, and after what we have done, it is lonely to lie away from you." She nuzzled his chest. "Most men who are not trained for this take much longer to have . . . separation. It is one thing to ride the wave, but it is not the same as transcending." She kissed his chest and shoulder.

"What are you saying?" he asked, already on the edge of sleep.

"Tomorrow I'll tell you, Arkady-champion. I promise you I'll tell you." She sighed, shifted her position so that it was more comfortable for them both, and slept.

Arkady wanted to wake her, to demand what it was she had told him, how it was that she knew what he had imagined. But the movement was too much, and his mind was already drifting. He was just able to mutter two half-remembered prayers before sleep claimed him.

In the morning, they bargained for more supplies and haggled over the price of an ass with a bridle and pack saddle, and then spent the better part of an hour haggling over sausages, cheese and grain. Arkady could sense that the three old women were enjoying themselves enormously. Their only expression of disappointment came when Arkady finally gave them three gold pieces and the last of his copper coins, then went to help one of the men bridle and saddle the ass before loading the pack saddle with their provisions.

"See if they will give us another blanket, as well," Surata suggested. "If there is more rain, we may need it."

Arkady nodded. He indicated his blanket and mimed that he wanted another. All three women laughed aloud and nudged one another, winking up at Surata while Arkady cursed them softly. Finally one silver coin bought two blankets and it was time to go. Arkady smiled and bowed from his saddle as he took the ass's lead from the farmhand who had helped him load the pack saddle. Behind him, Surata took a firmer hold of the cantel, and then they were out of the yard, going back down the track toward the wide swath of dust that was the merchants' road.

They had gone some distance in silence before Arkady said, "All right, you said last night you would explain."

"I will," she answered softly. "I'm sorry if I'll distress you." Her head rested against his shoulder and one arm went around his waist. "You will have to reserve your judgment until I'm through."

"Why's that?" He squinted ahead on the road but saw nothing but the dull earth cutting through the tall, rich grasses.

"Arkady-champion, you were not born to this as I was, and you have no idea what . . . happens. You did not take most of your youth to learn what I know."

"Most of my youth I spent learning to fight," he said roughly.

"And for that you are my champion," she said more confidently. "I know nothing of fighting and battle, and yet I must wage war on the Bundhi. Alone I am helpless, worse than a babe. But with you, I have strength, and there is much less danger."

"What does that have to do with last night?" He could hear the anger in his words, which startled him. "I . . ." he began, then could not finish.

Surata patted him. "Arkady-champion, the realm of this earth is not the only one."

"Heaven and Hell and Purgatory. Purgatory is a mountain," he said, repeating what he had been told as a child.

Behind them, the ass let out a loud, complaining bray which made the gelding bring his head up sharply. In the distance, another ass answered.

Arkady's heels urged the bay to move again. "Heaven is the Presence of God," he told her as his lessons came back to him. "It is where those who have been forgiven all sin may go. Purgatory is where the sins of the life are purged away without fault, where those of virtuous conduct but without the sacrament of baptism reside until they can come to Grace. Hell is for those whose sins condemn them to everlasting torment." He had sometimes joked with his soldiers about Hell, agreeing with them that those who have seen battle have little to fear from damnation.

"Karma will correct . . . errors. Until all karma is gone and all desire extinguished, we are bound to the Wheel." She thought a moment. "I have read of sin. I do not understand it. Surely karma provides . . . atonement." She tightened her hold on him, not enough to make him uncomfortable, but to give him a closer contact than they had had. "You do not need to have the Godhead forgive you, but to do in return what was done."

"You must have sin and atonement," Arkady said, shocked at the notion she proposed. "Without sin, there is no redemption."

"And must you be redeemed?" Surata asked quietly, her hands firm as she held him.

"Of course. Man is conceived in sin, and through God and His Son, we may be saved." He crossed himself.

"Do you think to ward off evil that way?" Surata wondered. "I know there are signs that are supposed to do that."

Arkady could not help but smile in his amazement. "You don't understand this at all, do you?" He had met pagans and heathen before, but no one like this young woman, who treated him as if he were the one without comprehension. "God sent His Son to die for mankind, so that we might be free from sin."

To Arkady's distress, Surata laughed out loud. "Oh, I know that one. My father knew a man from the West, who wore stinking black garments and had a tall hat on his head, who said . . . prayers all day for his redemption and salvation. My father tried to explain how misled he was, but the man from the West eventually said that my father was the servant of the Devil. You have such funny gods in the West, who do only one thing all the time. Think of Lord Śiva and Lord Kṛṣṇa. They are not at all like what your gods are. You have one goddess, don't you? Isn't that silly."

If Arkady could have managed it, he would have turned around in the saddle and slapped her for being so blasphemous. "You're outrageous. I should not even be in your company."

"You are truly offended," Surata realized and at once put a placating hand on his. "Arkady-champion, I did not mean to upset you, please believe that. But you see, with the studies I have done for so long, you sound like a little child, and not a grown man with courage and worth."

"You don't have to flatter me," he grumbled, trying to convince her that he would not be drawn into her heretical arguments. "I know that I am not a good Christian, but that does not mean I do not know what is right and wrong."

"And I am wrong," she said softly. "Your gods are very hard gods."

"Not gods, Surata; God. There is one God." He set his jaw and made a point of sitting straighter in the saddle.

"But what is the son, then? Isn't he a god? You said that he did a divine thing. Is he a god or a bodhisattva?"

"He is the Son of God, the Second of the Trinity," he insisted, wishing now he had paid more attention to the instruction of his priest at home. He felt out of his depth discussing such things with Surata.

"Then there is *not* just the one," she said reasonably. "That makes more sense."

"There are three in one," Arkady said with more determination.

"Father, Mother and Child," she said confidently. "That is very limited, but not unwise."

"No, Father, Son and Holy Spirit," he corrected her. "That is the Trinity."

Surata said nothing for a little way, then: "What of the Mother? How do you venerate the Female?"

"There is the Virgin Mary, the Mother of God." He cleared his throat. "Look, Surata, I didn't have that much of an education. I can't explain this very well. If you want to learn, then it would be best for us to go back and find you a priest who could make it all clear to you."

"You are doing very well, Arkady-champion," she said warmly. "You have some understanding, but you don't assume you know more than you do, which is very wise." She lapsed into silence once again. "The Mother of God is also a god?"

"Well, not exactly. She is the most exalted servant of God, for she brought the Son to earth." He remembered the way the priest had told his congregation that because of the Sin of Eve, no woman could ever aspire to the exaltation of the Trinity. Female Saints, he had reminded his listeners, were women who put their femaleness behind them for love of God.

"That is ridiculous!" Surata burst out. "What madness!"

Arkady pulled in the bay. "What is madness?"

"What you were remembering. That women must not be women or they are unholy. What would become of the world if this were true? There would be no love, no children, no transcendance." She shook her head, and Arkady could feel the movement through his brigandine. "I grow impatient with your priests, who are stupid and closed-hearted. No wonder you cannot trust what you achieved last night."

"And what *did* I achieve?" Arkady countered, his irritation becoming acute. "Men have . . . odd visions when they take a woman, especially when much time has gone by."

"Do you believe you took me?" Surata demanded. "I am your slave, but if I did not seek you, you would not touch me, no matter how your body yearned and throbbed for me." She took her arms from around him and deliberately clung to the cantel.

"Surata . . . Surata, I didn't mean that . . . I know it was something different, but . . ." Helplessly he got his horse and the ass moving more briskly. He had no way to tell her how his emotions and thoughts were troubling him.

By midafternoon, they caught up with a small party of merchants carrying salt and amber to Sarai, where they would trade them for precious metals and fine paper coming from China. Two of the merchants were Poles and were delighted to have Arkady join them.

"I don't hesitate to tell you, Captain, that out here, a man gets worried about thieves. It wasn't so long ago that the King of Poland ruled here, but now that the men of Islam are ravening like the Devil's lion all through Christian lands, we must be careful."

"We'll go part of the way with you, certainly," Arkady agreed at once without reference to Surata. "I gather you know the road well."

The oldest merchant, who was Georgian by the look of him, said in stilted Polish, "We have travelled this road for more than sixteen years. There have been many changes, but not even the Islamic heretics can change east to west, or deny their need for salt." He glanced once at Surata. "Your woman?"

"My slave. She cost me a good amount." Arkady read the lust in the old merchant's face. "I have no intention of parting with her."

"And you would not share her?" he asked. "Well, we can discuss that later, I suppose. Yevgen,"—one of the two out-riders swung around in his saddle at the old man's bellow— "this good soldier will go part of the way with us. He's a Pole!"

"A Pole," Yevgen shouted back. "Good enough."

At his back, Surata murmured to Arkady, "Be careful of these men. They expect . . . things of you."

"It will be fine, Surata," he told her softly. "You're being too cautious."

"Just because they are of the same country as you, and bow before the same altars does not mean that they are one with you in feeling and fellowship." She put her arms around his waist again. "I want to see them."

Arkady shook his head at this, struck by her plight once again. "There are seven men, all merchants, and two out-riders. You heard what they are selling."

"Yes, I heard. Take care of your pouch of gold while they are near." She rested her head against his shoulder and Arkady admitted to himself that he had missed that for the last hour.

"Tonight we can stop in a village that is another two hours along the road. They're Georgians, most of them, and they have good inns for travellers. The guard does not tax merchants too severely. You might have to pay a token for your slave, but if you don't plan to sell her, the sum should not be great." The oldest merchant chuckled. "If I had a slave like that, I wouldn't part with her until her hair turns gray. I've seen women like her in the East. I've gone as far as Khiva in the Timurid Emirate of Herat, when I was younger. There were many strange woman along the way, some as beautiful as the woman behind you, Pole."

"How fortunate for you," Arkady said, striving to keep the ire from his voice. "This is the first time I have travelled beyond the lands of Europe." He put his hand on the hilt of his longer sword where it hung from his saddle. "For as long as we journey with you, my sword is at your disposal."

"Captain Sól, that is an honorable oath," the Polish merchant who had spoken earlier declared. "What I would expect of a fellow countryman."

Arkady said nothing, though he could not help but think that these men would be less grateful for his presence if they knew how he came to be so far from his troops. He nodded his acknowledgment to the merchants and spurred toward the out-riders.

"Take the left point and I'll hold to the middle," Yevgen called out to Arkady, pointing to this position. "Do you have to keep that ass with you?"

"It has our provisions," Arkady shouted back, and was accompanied by a loud protest from the ass.

"Not very happy about it, is he?" Yevgen remarked, laughing at his own wit. "Keep a watch for men on horseback. There are parties of Islamites in this region. They want all the Russias as much as they want Europe."

Arkady made a half-hearted salute and took up his position on the left point. He had not been a scout for several years, but the habit remained and he fell into his watch easily.

"The merchants are afraid, Arkady-champion," Surata said some little time later. "They think they are being followed, and one of them is certain that you are with those who will prey on them."

"Surata . . ." He shook his head. It was foolish to challenge her. "How do you know this?"

"How do you know when there is an ambush ahead?" she inquired. "How do you know when your opponent is lying?"

He did not want to give this too much consideration. "You learn these things, in time," he dismissed the issue.

"And that is how I know," she said. "These merchants believe that you will be their hostage if they must bargain with thieves or . . . brigands." She paused, thinking about the word. "But a brigand is a soldier."

"Yes," Arkady acknowledged unhappily. "Cashiered soldiers often turn robber."

"Ah." She held him lightly. "You watch in your manner and I will watch in mine."

Arkady was content to accept this, still not quite prepared to question what she said to him. He kept his gelding to the same pace as Yevgen's heavy-barreled dun and the other out-rider's leggy chestnut mare. If he let his mind drift, he might almost convince himself that he was a young soldier again, on his first campaign, getting his first taste of boredom.

The afternoon faded into dusk and they had yet to reach the village. The other two out-riders had exchanged uneasy words, not wanting to remain on the road after dark. It was not very risky during the day, but once night fell, any travellers not safely camped ran an increased risk of robbery.

"How much further?" Arkady finally called to Yevgen.

"I don't know. I'll have to ask Old Milo. He's the one who knows the way." Yevgen rode heavily; both he and his horse were tired. "Hey! Tibor!" he shouted to the other out-rider, "See anything?"

Tibor yelled back, "Nothing but grass!"

Surata leaned closer to Arkady. "They will not find what they are looking for. They have passed the place. It is gone now. The last time the old man saw it was almost a year ago, and since then, disease has come to it and the whole place was burned to the ground. Everyone from the village fled if they were able, and died if they were not."

"How can you be certain?" Arkady asked, disturbed anew by her talents.

"I am certain. We passed the place a while ago, where the old and empty sheepfolds were." She sighed. "There will not be an inn for more than an hour. Do you think you should wait that long to camp?"

"You can't know this. You said yourself that you were brought to the West by another route." He resisted what she said more out of the fear that she was right than the concern that she might be wrong.

"I knew there was money on the road earlier. And what would it matter, since I am blind and have no means to see it, no matter which road it may be." She laughed slightly. "Trust me, Arkady-champion. It is hard for you to do this, but trust me."

He said nothing for a short while. "What do I say to the others? They will be suspicious of me, and I wouldn't blame them for it."

"Say that you are tired, or your horse is tired or the ass is tired, it doesn't matter. We must stop before it gets truly dark."

"And there is an inn ahead?" Arkady asked, not willing to question her too closely.

"Yes. It is off the road, but we can see it in the light. There are many merchants there, and several thieves. The landlord tolerates the thieves because they share their booty with him. Guard your pouch of gold closely, if we sleep there." She took a deep breath. "It is enervating, knowing so much."

Arkady grunted to show that he had heard, but would make no judgment either way. "An hour to the inn. All right. I'll suggest it to the others." He raised his arm to signal Yevgen. "How much further, do you know?"

Yevgen shrugged extravagantly. "I don't have a notion. Old Milo has said nothing."

"It's getting on. It will be dark soon." Arkady did not have to make this sound worrisome; for any traveller, being on the road after sundown was risky.

"I know. I'm concerned." He rode a little closer to Arkady. "The others want to push on, because they're afraid of being attacked in the night, or having their mounts stolen, but I don't know if it's worthwhile pushing on this way." Saying that, he glanced back over his shoulder toward the merchants. "They're strange men, so greedy and frightened. They will stand up to any man for two pieces of copper, but long shadows make them cringe."

Arkady nodded. "I've seen such before." He looked away and then back at Yevgen. "My slave says that there is an inn ahead, and we will reach it in an hour."

Yevgen raised his brows. "And how does she know this?"

"She has been on this road before," Arkady lied. "She said that the village Old Milo remembers has been burned. Those sheepfolds we saw—"

"I wondered about that," Yevgen said thoughtfully. "And your slave is certain she is right?"

"If she tells me she is, then I believe her," Arkady said, not entirely truthfully. "It is up to you, I think, to decide what's best for us to do."

Yevgen rubbed the stubble on his chin with his gloved hand. "So near an inn is a risk. There are desperate men who stay near the inns, hoping for merchants just such as these."

"True enough," Arkady agreed. "But there are three of us, and we should be able to fend off all but the most ruthless thieves." He did not relish another fight, but he knew he had to make it clear he would not refuse a battle.

"And the merchants will swoon if we find a boy with a skinning knife." He spat to show his disgust. "Very well. I will put it to Old Milo and see what he would prefer. They are paying me, after all. If I take their gold, I might as well do whatever they ask to earn it." He braced one hand on his hip as he turned his horse to ride back to the merchants.

"Why did you tell him that I came this way?" Surata asked when Yevgen was out of earshot.

"Because he would accept that more readily than if I told him you have ways of knowing things that are not Godly." He snapped this last at her, glaring with annoyance because she could not see his expression.

She reached up and touched his cheek. "Do not be angry with me, Arkady-champion. I do not know these things to shame you; I know them because I know them."

"But how?" Arkady pleaded, grabbing her hand with his own. "Tell me just that: how."

"I have *shown* you how," she said quietly. "You have left this world for that other world, and you know how different it is. Once you know how to travel in that way, you can learn many things." She paused, then said in a distant way, "There are men in this world who are far away, and so strange that we would find them more baffling than monsters. There are men who live in jungles so vast that no one has ever penetrated them, and there they wade in rivers that wind among trees, so that much of the forest is under water. There are fish there that are not fish, that swim amid the sunken trees. The river is more enormous than the sea, and where it meets the ocean, the water of the river drives away the salt."

Arkady shook his head. "That is your fancy, Surata. No such thing can be. It is like the mountains that melted . . ." His words straggled off.

"No; I have seen the river. It is not of that other world, but this one." She patted his arm and dropped her hand back to the cantel. "The cook at the inn is pregnant."

"What?" Arkady said, trying to swivel around far enough to see her.

"The cook at the inn is pregnant. I tell you that so you will be able to see for yourself that my vision is clear. Go to the kitchen and look for a young woman with yellow hair done up in a red cloth. You will know that what I said is true."

"All right. If we go to the inn, I give you my word, I will try to find this cook of yours." He was pleased to hear the sound of approaching hoofbeats. He saw Yevgen come up beside him. "What did they say?"

"They want to press on to the inn. They're frightened of the night and of bandits and of creatures of the Devil that are abroad when the sun is gone." He patted the hilt of his sword. "I say there are few Devils that can resist cold steel."

Arkady chuckled. "A good sword solves many arguments," he declared.

Yevgen nodded, then spurred away to inform Tibor of their plans.

Chapter 8

"She is pregnant," Arkady told Surata as they retired for the night. They had been alotted a private room that was only slightly larger than the wide cot it contained. One small window, now shuttered closed, gave a little ventilation to the close air, which smelled of old cooked onions, urine and sour wine.

"Yes," Surata said as she pulled off her clothes. "Be certain to put the bolt on the door. There is a rat-faced man who will come in, otherwise."

Arkady, holding the single candle they had been provided, watched her in fascination. He ought to blow the light out, he told himself with little conviction. When he looked at her, he sinned and sinned. It was not possible to remain unmoved by her, for to do that, he would have to be less than a man. He wanted to reach out and touch her hair, and could have done so with no effort, but he stood silently, unmoving, while she took off her clothes and folded them neatly. "Are you ready?"

"Aren't you?" she asked, turning toward his voice. "I have to unbraid my hair. Do you want to do it for me, or shall I?"

She had put her hand on his unerringly, as if she knew exactly where he was.

"I . . ." In order to say nothing more, he set the candle aside and began to scramble out of his garments, grateful that this inn had no bathhouse where they might wash themselves.

"Take all your clothes off, Arkady-immai," she suggested as she climbed into the bed. "It will be better if your clothes are off."

He stopped moving. "You're not going to . . ."

"No, not tonight. You are not ready for . . . all of it. I will explain as much as I can to you." She stretched thoroughly, like a cat, and unselfconsciously began to adjust their blankets.

"What kind of explanation can you give me?" It was a challenge now, and he meant to discourage her. His memories of the night before were as stinging as they were pleasant; he had no intention of inviting another such incident.

"Not much of one," she said with a diffidence that surprised him. "The best I can give."

Arkady followed her example and made an attempt to set his clothes aside neatly. He pinched out the candle, then crawled into the blankets and tried to find a position in which he could sleep without touching any part of Surata.

As he squirmed fruitlessly, Surata shifted her body so that it lay, so very naturally, in the crook of his. "Be still, Arkady-champion, and do not be troubled that we are close. No harm will come of it."

"You and I have different notions of harm," he growled but he resigned himself to her nearness. "I'm very tired."

"And am I. Transcending this plane is very exhausting, especially when you are not trained for it. Had I been with my family, I would have spent half the day in pleasant relaxation, reading, watching the birds and deer in my father's garden, and playing music. But that isn't possible now, and too much has changed." She fell silent.

"Surata?" Arkady ventured when a little time had gone by. He reached to pull her closer and discovered that she was crying, making no sound. "Surata."

"It's nothing," she protested in a muffled tone. "I thought I had stopped this." She wiped her eyes with her hands, then put one of her wet palms on the center of his chest. "You may feel what I feel, if you wish. It isn't difficult to learn how."

"Thanks; my imagination is vivid enough," he said, drawing back as much as the bed would allow.

"Arkady-champion," she wailed. "Don't do this. You can't want to be so . . ."

"Cruel? I'm a soldier, and I'm schooled in cruelty." He set his jaw, hoping that he had armed himself sufficiently to resist her tears. "You forget that sometimes."

"No," she said very unhappily. "Soldiers are often cruel, but you would not be my champion if you were. And if you were cruel, you would not have been able to transcend with me. Why do you persist in making yourself out to be the monster you are not? The Bundhi is cruel, and for him this is a virtue. He follows the Left Hand Path, and his manifestation of transcendence reveals this just as your transcendence showed that you were not cruel."

"You're talking nonsense; go to sleep, Surata," he ordered her, shutting his eyes as if that would keep him from hearing her.

"Arkady-champion, it's necessary that you learn to—"

"Go to sleep." He deliberately slurred his words, making himself sound more worn out than he was. Inwardly he doubted he had fooled her, but he trusted that she would not press him to talk more. He felt her hand on his cheek, and the curve of her thigh resting next to his, and told himself that was more than he could desire. He was grateful when he finally drifted into sleep and did not dream.

The inn was bustling before sunrise, and since the room where Arkady and Surata lay was near the kitchen, they were wakened by the clanging of pots and the sound of wood being chopped for the stove. One of the ostlers was shouting in the stableyard, and nearer, there was the clomp of wooden shoes on cobbles as one of the guests stumbled out to the privy.

"We will have to leave when the merchants leave," Arkady

muttered to Surata after she had kissed the corner of his mouth.

"If that's what you want," she said in a neutral way. "Tomorrow and the day after will be safe, but beyond that time, Yevgen will not be trustworthy." She had sat up in bed and was already gathering up one of the blankets, folding it first, and then rolling it so that it could be tied to the pack saddle on the mule.

"How can you do that?" Arkady marvelled at her in spite of his resolution to pay her little attention.

"You can dress in the dark, can't you? You've broken camp in the dead of night. This is no different." She presented him with the blanket and started on the second one.

Arkady dressed quickly, feeling his way in the little room. "They will have breakfast soon. Are you hungry?"

"No, but I will eat. We have far to go today, and we will have to move faster than anyone would like." She paused in rolling the second blanket. "Tell Yevgen that he should have a care to being followed. Today there is more to fear at our backs than what may be approaching from the east." Her face showed an intent curiousity, as if she heard something very faint in the distance.

"What is it?" Arkady asked.

"I don't know," she answered, making a sign for him to be quiet. "I fear that the Bundhi has sent his servants to look for me. They have assumed that I was taken away into the West where I could do nothing. If they discover that you are bringing me back, they will try to find ways to stop us."

"He'd have to send quite a few men to do that as long as we're with Old Milo and his crew," Arkady said, determined to make light of the matter.

"He would not send anything so simple as men, not now. He had men following me until I was sold to you, but now, now he must be more careful, in case I am able to detect his actions." She rose, tieing the blanket with a length of cord. "Here."

Arkady accepted the blanket but stared at her with a mixture of impatience and vexation. "Surata, even if what you say is true, don't let the others hear you speak this way. It wouldn't take much for them to decide that you are a witch, and I doubt they would permit you to remain with them."

"That doesn't worry me," she said as she began to dress, moving with great care as she adjusted her clothes.

"It should. Witches are burned by good Christians." He had wanted to frighten her into silence, but instead she rounded on him.

"I have said before that I am no witch. I am an advanced student of the Right Hand Path, and my skill is alchemy. Witches are not real, and you are a fool to believe in them. If those merchants think that they must burn me, you and I need only strike out on our own." She folded her arms stubbornly after she finished knotting her belt.

Arkady was not prepared for her outburst, and he lifted his hands, palms out, to pacify her. "Surata, please. I didn't mean to say anything to anger you. I only wanted you to be warned."

She could not see his gesture, but she heard his intent in his voice and was mollified. "Very well, Arkady-immai, but you are enough to enrage all the gods at once. And don't," she went on hastily, "tell me that there is only one god in the world. We've had enough contention for one day as it is." She bent and drew on her embroidered soft boots with the pointed toes. "I'm ready. Show me the way to the breakfast table and to the privy afterward."

"Right." Arkady was willing to suspend their disputes, perhaps more willing than Surata was. He took her by the arm and led her into the hallway, where he found Yevgen and Tibor emerging from an equally small room across the hall. "God be with you today."

"And with you," Yevgen said brusquely, turning away from Arkady to speak with Tibor again. "That is the best course."

"If you like," Tibor said, glancing nervously at Arkady and Surata. "But what..."

"It's not urgent," Yevgen muttered and stomped off toward the main taproom. "Be saddled and ready to go within an hour, Captain Sól," he ordered over his shoulder. "We won't wait for you if you're late."

"We'll be ready," Arkady answered. He was comfortable hearing his own language again, no matter how badly spoken, and he found himself seeking to prolong the conversation just to hear Polish. It was not the same with Surata, whose abilities made him wary of her.

"You may talk at breakfast," Surata said behind him. "Warn me where the steps are, Arkady-immai."

"Right," he said, following Yevgen down the hall. He could hear the heavy sound of Tibor's boots behind them, but he ignored their tread. He did not like to be caught between two armed men this way, friends or not, because such a position was dangerous. He was so preoccupied with the hazard he sensed that he almost forgot to mention the two steps to Surata. At the last instant, he put out his arm and warned her.

"Thank you, Arkady-immai," she told him softly, faltering in her movements and reaching out to brace herself.

"I forget you are blind, sometimes," he offered as an explanation, salving his conscience with the notion that he was not being entirely untruthful. It was not easy to remember her blindness because she was so strangely gifted in other ways.

"There are many kinds of blindness, Arkady-immai," she said, staying two steps behind him. "Mine is more obvious."

He made a noise to indicate he had heard her, but he gave his attention to the three long tables where many early-rising travellers waited for the pots and tureens to be carried in from the kitchen.

Old Milo waved Arkady to a place across the table from him. "You come in good time, Captain," he called out over the general hubble of conversation.

"Soldiers are used to rising with the sun," Arkady said, guiding Surata to a place on the bench beside him.

"They feed slaves in the kitchen," Old Milo reminded him.

"Not this slave," Arkady said. "She remains with me."

The old merchant laughed. "I suppose if I had such a slave, I would keep her by me, as well. I've been told—and when I was younger, had some hints myself—that the women of the East are very . . . capable." He waggled his thick eyebrows for emphasis.

"I've heard that," Arkady said in what he hoped was a bored tone. "I've also heard it about women of Africa, of Italy and of Russia. In fact, I have heard it of every nationality but my own and the Prussians. The farther away their homeland, the more fabulous the women." He braced his elbows on the table and reached for one of the hard, flat breads that had been carried to the table in baskets. "How far do you wish to go today?"

Old Milo shook his head. " I would like to get to the river crossing by tomorrow night, but who knows how it will be. They are saying that there is a windstorm coming, and if that is the case, we'll have to seek shelter while the blow is on. That will slow us down." He took one of the flat breads himself and murmured a brief prayer over it. "I noticed you did not offer thanks for your meal," he observed to Arkady after he had taken the first bite.

"I pray upon rising. It's a soldier's habit, good merchant. We do not always have the opportunity to offer thanks later on." He reached for another bread and handed it to Surata. "There will be more coming. Start with this."

"Thank you, Arkady-immai," she said, her attitude so subdued that it startled him.

"Are you well?" he blurted out.

"You are kind to ask, Arkady-immai. I am well." She started to eat, her face averted.

"Well, at least she shows proper respect," Old Milo said, cocking his head toward Surata. "Some slaves, when they have the pleasure of their master, think they have his mind also. It's wise not to give that impression. But that must be part of soldiering, too." He waved one of his merchants toward the table. "That's Jurgi for you, always late. Over here!"

The other merchant hurried to the table just as the kitchen door swung open and one of the potboys came out with a tray of boiled eggs.

"Make sure you eat two," Old Milo advised everyone in his party. "They will sustain you." With that, he fell to eating himself.

Within the hour, the entire group had assembled in the

innyard, ready to leave. The sun was not far above the horizon and it cast long, spiky shadows. The air had an ominous red tinge to it, and the animals all were restless.

"It must be the wind coming," Tibor said as he got onto his bucket-faced mare. "It always makes 'em crazy."

Arkady's bay was restless as well, and he sidled when Arkady tried to lift Surata to his back. He slapped the horse with the ends of his reins. "Stand!" he ordered and swung Surata upward as he spoke. Behind him, the ass brayed, his long ears turning and big teeth bared.

"We'll not make good time today," Old Milo declared and gave the sign for his company to mount up. "But the sooner we start, the better."

Yevgen mounted his dun and took his position at the head of the little train, gesturing Arkady and Tibor into their forward positions. "If you see anything, warn me."

It was all they could do to keep their beasts moving, and for the next two hours, most of the men were silent, giving their attention to horses and asses and donkeys.

"The wind will be here soon," Surata told Arkady as the sun approached mid-heaven. "There is still time to find shelter."

This time Arkady did not question her, for he had felt that change in the air and the scar over his eye had been aching for most of the morning. "I'll do what I can," he said and raised his hand to catch Yevgen's attention.

"Trouble?" the other shouted.

"The wind is rising. It might be best to make camp now, while we can." Arkady did his best to say this calmly, as he would have spoken to his own men, but he could see Yevgen bristle at the suggestion.

"I don't sense it," he replied. "You're too cautious, Sól."

"Rather that than capricious," Arkady snapped before he could stop himself. "We'll lose horses if we fight the wind."

That argument had an impact. Yevgen nodded grudgingly. "There is that," he said. "I've spotted some trees in the distance. We should be able to shelter there."

"Arkady-immai," Surata whispered, "there is danger."

Arkady nodded to show he had heard. "Very well. Should I warn the merchants?"

"I'll do it," Yevgen declared, turning his horse toward the men behind him.

"Do not go to the trees, Arkady-immai," Surata said as soon as Yevgen spurred away. "There are men waiting there already. They are eager for goods and slaves."

"Then Yevgen should—" Arkady began.

"Yevgen can deal with the men. He has done so before." She pressed closer to him. "If you let the ass run away, we may chase it."

"And lose it," he rejoined.

"Better an ass than a life, Arkady-champion," she said very softly.

He shook his head, but could not ignore her warning as he might have done before. His skin was prickly with apprehension, and he could not rid himself of the impression he was being watched. "Very well. In a little while, I will release the ass and we'll chase it."

Surata nodded. "It will go to the north and east, away from the road."

Arkady started to laugh at this, then stopped. "How can you be sure?"

"Because I will guide it," she said with a trace of mischief in her voice. "He will go precisely where I wish."

"But—" He could not bring himself to say anything more, especially since he feared her answer.

"Then we will follow him and the others will go to the trees on the south side of the road. We'll be safe, Arkady-immai, and we will be able to shelter from the storm."

"How can you be certain of that?" he asked curtly.

She sighed. "Arkady-immai, you have trusted me before and had no cause to regret it. Why do you hesitate now, when you yourself suspect the others?" Her hands pressed more tightly against him. "They go to a trap and you know it. Everything you ever learned as a soldier tells you that, and still, when I echo what your senses tell you, you question me as if you had no fear."

Arkady rode in silence a little while. "I do trust you, Surata, and that frightens me more than the swords of a few highwaymen or robbers."

For once, Surata said nothing. She clung to him, her head against his shoulder, her hands pressed to him where she had said the Sixty-Four Petaled Center was.

Yevgen rode over to Arkady, shaking his head as he came. "They want to make for the trees. Keep your eye out for a road. I don't want to have to cut across the fields unless we must. It always slows us down to do that."

Arkady almost added that it also left a trail to follow, but was able to hold his tongue this time. "I will. But Tibor is more likely to find it than I am, being on the south."

"True, but we should all watch, in case." He waved and started away, then glanced back. "The wind's starting to rise, did you notice?"

"I did," Arkady said.

As Yevgen hastened away, Surata said, "He is plotting death, Arkady-champion."

"But he speaks Polish!" Arkady protested, hating to think ill of the man when they were both so far from home.

"Even then," Surata said by way of consolation.

A little distance on, Tibor pulled in his chestnut mare and shouted, pointing ahead to a narrow pathway through the fields. "There! Yevgen, there it is!"

Yevgen signaled the men behind him to stop and rode ahead while the others waited.

"Let the ass run, Arkady-champion," Surata whispered. "Let him run now."

Reluctantly Arkady loosened the lead rein that was tied to the front of his saddle. He could feel the ass tugging on it as the length of braided leather pulled free. He forced himself to wait a bit before he noticed the ass. It was running to the north and east, as Surata promised it would.

"Sól!" Yevgen shouted. "Your pack ass!"

Arkady felt a great inward relief as he rose in his stirrups and swore. "I've got to catch him! He's got all my provisions!"

Yevgen shouted an objection, but Arkady had spurred his

bay into a tired lope after the fleeing ass. He was glad that the gelding was not too fresh, for it would have been an easy task then to catch the ass and bring him back. This way, it would be some little time before he stopped the runaway, providing himself with an excuse for not trying to return to the rest of the party. Arkady loved the feel of a running horse under him, and he rode now with exhilaration. This had been one of his greatest joys since he was a child, and to let the bay have his head delighted him, though he had sense enough not to let him run too far.

By the time they caught up with the ass—it was standing with sweat-daubed coat and heaving flanks—the merchants and their two out-riders were specks in the distance. Arkady leaned out of the saddle and caught the lead rein. "What do we do now, Surata? You said there would be shelter, and I'm damned if I see any."

Surata turned her head, for all the world as if she were looking over the landscape. "It is that way," she said, pointing off to her left. "Not far. Look for a stream and two tall rocks."

Although he was skeptical, Arkady did as she told him. "It had better be close," he said as they started off again at a walk. "The wind is growing stronger."

"Yes; we have time enough." She held him tightly. "It was fun, wasn't it, chasing the ass?"

"It was," he said with a smile. He leaned into the wind as he rode.

The first keening wail of the storm was sounding by the time he found the two upright rocks near the stream, and by that time he had almost given up hope of them. Arkady coughed as he tried to speak, for the wind had dried his throat. "The rocks are ahead."

"Then stop," Surata said confidently. "Take the blankets and make a shelter with the rocks and the saddles. Give me things to carry or hold for you. That will speed us." As he drew up the bay, she slid off the horse and stood, her arms lifted. "Give me your swords and maul for a start. I know how they should be cared for."

As he dismounted, Arkady did as she ordered him, no longer surprised at himself for following her orders. He blinked as the wind stung his eyes.

While Surata gathered small rocks to hold the blankets in place, Arkady secured both his bay and the ass in the lee of the rocks. He hauled the saddles off both animals and lugged them to where Surata waited for him. "They're safe enough, I think. I have tethers and hobbles on both of them. In wind like this, they won't want to go far."

"Good." She pointed out the little rocks and helped him with the unfolded blankets, giving him very little advice on what to do. "You have spent more time in tents that I have, Arkady-immai," she remarked when he expressed amazement at her reserve.

"I'm glad you're aware of that." He had to shout to be heard over the howl of the wind, and when, shortly after, he crawled under the protecting blankets, he said to her, "Not bad for makeshift."

"You've known worse," she said for him. "Now you can lie back, and I will rub your arms and legs for you, and while the wind blows, we can go elsewhere together."

He looked up sharply. "Surata, if you mean—"

"I mean only that we have the ability to wait out the storm in pleasant ways. Come, Arkady-immai, it isn't too cold and we are not in any real danger here. Why do you refuse something so pleasant and useful?" She was sitting with her legs crossed in a way that Arkady thought was impossible. Her hands were folded in her lap, first fingers and thumbs pressed together in two circles; she smiled at him. "Arkady-immai, where we go when we are venturing together, you can fight trolls and dragons. You are the warrior, Arkady-immai, and in that other place, I will be your weapon, whatever kind you want."

In spite of himself, he was intrigued. "It . . . isn't that, Surata. It's what you do."

"You mean that we unite our bodies? Why does this vex you?" She held up one of her hands. "You needn't tell me."

Arkady leaned back, saying rather dreamily under the wind's scream, "When I vowed to fight the Turks, I went to the church and did the Stations of the Cross. I said all the prayers, and promised God that I would be a worthy Christian soldier, so that He might favor us in battle. A woman like you . . . there's no way I can explain it. I've tried, and you don't understand. Every moment in the Stations, the Crowning with Thorns, the Driving of the Nails, I beseeched God to be the soldier He wanted me to be."

"And why do you fear you are not?" Surata asked, uncrossing her legs and crawling toward him. "Couldn't it be possible that your God sent me to you so that you could battle more than Turks? Think of it, Arkady-immai. You can conjure and defeat dragons." She touched him, seeking the place she had called the Center of the Heart. "Why not try, Arkady-champion? If your God disapproves, you will remain here to sense the storm. If your God does not mind, you will transcend to the other place and fight dragons." She took his face in her hands, tracing his features. "Arkady-champion, I know many things, but I never learned how to fight. Without you to aid me, I will be lost to the Bundhi. With you, there is a chance. If you are so anxious to serve the Right Hand Path, aid me."

He caught her hands in his. "Isn't there another way?"

She sighed. "No. You would need years of training and study, and even then, if we are to fight together, we would have to be together. That is where the strength of man and woman lies, Arkady-champion, in their unity, not in their separation."

One corner of the blanket flapped free, snapping in the wind. Arkady reached over to secure it again. "I should refuse," he said when he turned back to her. "I should not let you speak to me of any of this."

"But you are listening," she pointed out, her mouth turning up at the corners. "Arkady-champion, I am no different than you. I am far from my home and I am uncertain and lonely. But the Subtle Body is never away from its home, and there can be no loneliness when we are together." She ran one hand along the hem of his brigandine. "Arkady-champion."

The truth was, and he knew it, that he wanted her, and he welcomed her persuasions. He could convince himself that she was the one who desired their lovemaking, and that he had resisted until her presence overpowered him. He let her take his hand. "Dragons, you say?"

"Or anything else you can imagine. In that other place, everything is mutable. If you wish it to be, then it can be that way. And while I am with you, you are in no danger. You have . . . my word on that," she said, the last words a perfect imitation of him.

He laughed aloud. "Well, I admit I would like to fight a dragon." He remembered all the tales he had heard of Saint George of Armenia, who had been empowered by God Himself and the Archangel Michael with the strength to defeat the Devil in the form of a dragon. Was it the sin of vanity to want to emulate the great warrior-saint? He stared down at his large, blunt hands. Carefully he flexed his fingers and imagined his right hand closed around the hilt of a lance.

"Think, Arkady-champion," Surata said to him, "you will be able to do what you wish, and you will not fail." She had already unfastened her belt and opened her outer robe. "Arkady-champion, undress me."

"A true dragon?" he persisted even as he reached for her.

"As true as anything in that place. This is not the realm of dreams, but another place. Your battles there are as real as your battles here, Arkady-immai." She raised her arms so that he could take off her inner gown, shivering when she was naked.

"Oh, sweet Mother of God," he said to himself as he put her garments aside. "You are so beautiful."

"And you are beautiful, Arkady-champion," she replied, her hand on his. "Take off your clothes so that I can . . . see for myself."

He paused in unfastening his heavy belt. "Don't, Surata."

"But Arkady-champion, I *do* see you. When we are in the other place, I can see you with more than eyes, and what I see is beautiful." She took his belt from him and laid it aside. "Does that trouble you?"

"Of course not," he muttered, feeling his face suffuse with embarrassment. He could not make himself take off his brigandine and acton, or remove his boots and leggings.

Very gently, Surata took his left foot in her hands and began to draw off his boot. "You can remove the rest, Arkady-champion."

How he desired and dreaded her! He undressed without thinking, as if he were numb from fatigue and battle instead of stricken with lust. He did not try to stop her when she pulled off his other boot, or when she unfastened his leggings and codpiece. He folded his acton and brigandine as if his body belonged to someone else and what was happening had nothing to do with him.

But then she began to massage him again, triggering reactions that racked and delighted him. He was suddenly restless with his need of her; he reached out for her, all but dragging her across his body.

"Slowly, Arkady-champion," she told him. "You know that." Then she kissed him, her lips parted, her tongue just touching his.

He made a sound that was half moan, half sigh as he rolled on top of her, his whole body shivering for her as the blankets shivered in the wind. He felt her, supple and ardent, lift herself to him, and his head swam as if he were rapturously drunk

and the colors were all around him, vivid and intense as they shifted and changed, more beautiful than sunlight on the ocean.

"Arkady my champion," Surata said to him, "choose where you wish to be, and what you want to encounter."

He could not speak to her, so all-consuming was his vision and his passion. There was a current running through him, inexorable as the tide. Surata filled the lights, her face transformed with ecstasy. "You are the most beautiful woman in the world," he felt himself say, wondering if he had spoken at all.

"You want to battle dragons, Arkady my champion. Build a dragon from the light and make me your weapon." Her voice was all around him, tangible in the brightness, and it touched him in ways that her hands could not.

116

"I don't know how," he whispered and knew that his response was part of the light.

"Tell me what it is you wish, Arkady my champion, and it will be there. You thought of Saint ... George, who defeated a dragon. What was the creature? Tell me." She spoke in sounds more wonderful than music. *"Tell me, Arkady my champion."*

They glowed in the light. *"It was big, and clawed and scaled. It breathed fire, and it lived in a cave in the rocks, where it had piled up an enormous treasure, and where it brought the maidens it demanded in token ..."*

Around him the light coalesced into rocks, crags and canyons. Enormous, yawning darknesses punctuated these granite turrets, and in one of them, two chatoyant spots glowed. Arkady felt something in his hand and looked down to see a lance, so long and powerful that he was astonished he could control it more easily than his short sword. It fitted his hand and his arm so comfortably and lightly that he wondered how it could have the strength he knew it possessed.

"I am your weapon, Arkady my champion," Surata told him, her voice running up his arm. *"I will not let anything hurt or harm you."*

He was about to question her, when a shuddering roar burst from the distant cave.

Chapter 9

A dragon, twice the size of a horse, shambled into the brightness. Its scales flashed more than the sun off new snow, and when its spike-filled mouth gaped, ragged plumes of fire shone out. As he watched, Arkady marvelled at the beast and yearned for a horse to ride against such a monster, for surely, surely, he could not face it on foot with just his lance.

"Make it a good horse, Arkady my champion," Surata told him, her voice once more ringing in his flesh, moving up his arm like the strength of his muscles.

Arkady shook his head, trying to imagine all the attributes he could wish in a warhorse. And then he felt himself rise, his legs bowed out by the enormous red sorrel with flaxen mane and tail that formed out of nothing. The stallion lifted a polished black hoof, showing flaxen feathering. He was the most perfect warhorse Arkady had ever seen. Every line of his body showed strength and stamina, his head, properly bowed over his arched neck, showed how totally he devoted himself to the will of his master. His saddle and bridle were of tooled leather and studded with silver and brass. Arkady almost grinned as he couched his lance.

The dragon gave another roar, and smoke billowed out with the flames. It half rose on its hind legs and extended its talons toward Arkady, as if seeking to grasp him and rend him.

"He is your dragon, Arkady my champion," Surata said with the lance. "You have the right to defeat him."

"Then I will," Arkady promised, gathering up the reins in his left hand and preparing to spur his warhorse toward the monster.

The dragon bounded with uncanny lightness to a nearer crag, where its shadow loomed over Arkady and his stallion. It lashed its huge tail and breathed out streams of fire. The light glinted off the scales so that the dragon was almost as blinding as the rising sun.

Arkady's warhorse reared and pivoted on his hind legs, forehooves striking out toward the dragon. It whinnied out a challenge, unafraid of the hideous thing it confronted. Without effort, it sprang after the dragon as the enormous beast leaped to another promontory.

"Follow it, Arkady my champion. Do not let it escape you," Surata told him in the lance.

He did not need her urging, for the audacity of conflict had got hold of him, and he felt the terrible jubilation that he had known at the start of battle. It was good to ride after the raging dragon, to scorn the risk of its claws and teeth and fire! He almost laughed as the chase went on.

The dragon fled into a chasm, and Arkady hesitated only a moment, then spurred his horse, plunging down the rocky defile, lance poised for the fight to come.

At last the dragon could go no further, and it turned on Arkady, fire pouring out of its gaping mouth, its eyes glowing like coals in its massive head.

"Strike!" Surata called out to him.

An instant later, the great red warhorse charged the dragon, and Arkady, after one heartbeat of paralyzing terror, steadied himself for the fray.

The lance pierced the armored side of the beast, pressing deep into the monster's body, impaling its heart while the dragon writhed and howled, fire spurting from its mouth and nostrils.

Dizzy with victory, Arkady tugged the lance out of the dying monster, reining his warhorse back from the creature.

Gouts of vile-colored blood spattered from the dragon's wound, and where they touched, the earth sizzled. The dragon moaned and thrashed its head, growing steadily weaker.

The lance in Arkady's hand faded and became a long, shining sword. "Cut off the head, Arkady my champion."

Arkady dismounted and walked carefully toward the dragon, which seemed to grow larger with every step he took toward it. Once a few drops of its blood struck his unprotected hand, and at once the weal of a burn appeared. Arkady grew more cautious. Though the dragon was almost dead, it was still capable of wounding or killing him.

"I will not let that happen," Surata told him from the sword in his hand. Of its own volition, the sword rose high over his head as he came near the dragon and remained poised there until Arkady brought it down to sever the monster's neck.

At once the whole scene faded, leaving only the sword and the warhorse alone with Arkady in the many-colored darkness. "What now, Arkady my champion?"

"I..." He looked about in amazement, certain that the dragon was not far. "What...?"

"This place changes quickly," Surata reminded him. "What do you want to battle now? A Turk? Another dragon?"

A forest sprung up around them, filled with massive trees rising high above them, blocking all but a few shafts of preternaturally bright sunlight from the path where Arkady stood beside his warhorse. The air was still, not even the call of birds disturbed them, and the sough of wind through the branches was softer than prayers for the dying. The scent of green things and the bark of trees was heavy on the quiet, very nearly palpable.

The sword Arkady carried shifted in his hand, adjusting more perfectly to his grip. "What will you find here, Arkady my champion?"

"I don't know yet, but there must be something," he said, feeling a coldness seep through him. There was something about this place that made him more uneasy than all the rocks where the dragon lurked could. Yet he had grown up near forests, and trees had been his playground for much of his childhood.

"The root of your fear is in this place," Surata told him gently. "You have come here to settle things once and for all."

"But . . . I don't know what it is," Arkady said slowly, reaching back for his horse's reins so that he could lead the splendid animal along the narrow path.

"You will know it when you come upon it," Surata said.

Arkady did not respond. He gave his attention to the vastness of the forest and the strangeness of its silence. He went slowly, hearing the steady beat of his warhorse's hooves on the trail behind him.

After a while, Surata asked, "Why don't you ride?"

"I don't know," Arkady answered.

The shadows grew deeper, denser, and what light could reach them faded to an anemic shade of yellow. In the dimness now there were rustlings and sounds that might have been words whispered in angry snarls.

"Do you know it yet, Arkady my champion?"

"No," he said, shaking his head. "No."

"Then we must go on."

"You . . ." he began, feeling shame come over him again.

"I must go with you, Arkady my champion. We must go together or not at all." The sword thrummed in his hand. "You may have fear, but I do not. Your arm may falter, but I shall not."

Arkady managed a weak smile. "You don't know what you may have to face, Surata."

"It doesn't matter what it is," she said serenely.

"But . . ." He let his protest fade.

The forest was closing in on them, shutting out the light and narrowing the path so that leaves and fronds brushed against them with every step. The smell of the place was overpowering, rich and green; it might have been cloying if it were sweet.

The warhorse walked steadily, mincing his way on the path. Only once did he toss his head and snort in protest, and that was when an unknown and furry creature darted across the trail directly in his path.

Arkady stopped, holding the reins close to the bit while he peered into the foliage to see what the thing might have been. He saw the movement of low-lying branches and heard a curious sound, but nothing more. "I wish I could see better," Arkady said, then felt like a fool.

"Seeing is not important," Surata said. "You will find your way with or without your sight."

He wanted to ask her what she would do, but he was not able to make himself speak. He put his hands to his temples and drew in a deep breath, chiding himself for his growing unease. It would have been less worrisome if there had been birds calling in the trees, or the snorts and snuffles of badgers and wild pigs. He knew that boar were very dangerous, but he had faced them before and had survived. What bothered him here was that he did not know what he would have to face and what it would do when he faced it. Or what they would do, if there were more than one of them. His skin felt clammy at this thought and he could not shake it off, though he urged his horse to walk faster and he made himself stride along confidently, going toward the heart of the gloom. He tried to sing one of the marching songs he had bawled out with his soldiers, but his single voice, thin and shaky in the enormity of the forest, was more disheartening than the quiet had been. He lifted his jaw. "That's enough of that," he said, to his horse and himself.

Among the branches and leaves now there were vines— slim, dainty hanging things that dangled here and there like long tails of green rats. The sight of them made Arkady queasy, and he very nearly raised his sword to cut them down, but it seemed silly and useless.

"Why do the vines trouble you, Arkady my champion?" Surata asked the second time he hefted his sword a little way at the sight of the trailing vegetation.

"I don't know," he confessed. "But they are . . . wrong."

"Then you must be on guard against them," she said in a matter-of-fact way.

"They're just vines," he insisted, wishing he could be rid of his chill.

A wind ruffled through the trees, making the leaves and branches rattle against each other like fingers plucking at prison bars. Arkady looked up, his eyes narrowed as he tried to search out the danger he sensed surrounding them.

"What is it, Arkady my champion?"

He shook his head, unwilling to say again that he did not know. His hand ached where he held the sword.

"Arkady, Arkady, there is nothing you will have to do alone. While you are here, you are not alone. We are linked, Arkady my champion, in many, many ways."

He could say nothing in response, though he felt another surge of her presence in his body. His arm, his heart, the center of him was filled with her. He strode along with a touch more confidence as he let himself know her. "How do you do this?"

"When two are linked, transcendence can happen. The link must be total." This time it was Surata who hesitated. "That is why you are my champion and I am your weapon."

This was more than he could understand, and he shied away from it. With the excuse that he needed to watch the forest—which was steadily becoming more of a jungle than a forest—he searched the wide-leaved plants for some trace of life.

A thing that might have been a wyvern flapped away through the green twilight, calling in a harsh and plaintive voice to something that could not be heard answering.

"Is that what you fear, Arkady my champion?"

"No." He stared after the wyvern, wishing he had seen the thing more clearly. When he was a child, he had been told fabulous tales of the great, winged serpents that possessed all the wisdom of the ages and held everything but eternity and God in contempt.

"There is a clearing ahead, Arkady my champion."

Arkady wanted to feel relieved as she said this but could

not. "A clearing," he mused aloud. Why should a clearing bother him more than a narrow, unlit path did?

His red sorrel snorted, trying to toss his head free of Arkady's restraining hand on the rein. He moved more restlessly, lifting his feathered hooves higher off the ground with each step. White showed around his eye and the smell of his sweat was stronger.

"What bothers the horse?" Surata asked.

"Probably the same thing that bothers me," Arkady said, intending to make a jest of it, but realizing as he spoke that it was true.

"Then be on guard. That stallion is part of yourself, Arkady my champion, and he knows all that you know." The sword twitched, as if searching the clearing.

"There are more vines," Arkady said, trying not to be nervous at this announcement.

"Lianas. It is similar to the lands to the far south of my home, where the heat turns every leaf into an umbrella." There was a pause. "If you have not seen the jungle before, then this you have learned from me. It is part of the link."

"It's not my favorite part." He hoped that his casual lechery would improve his state of mind, but it did not. With every step he took, his thoughts became more disordered, and he had to resist the strong urge to turn and run from the place, to plunge through the green in mad and heedless flight.

"What is it?" Surata asked, her voice more commanding than it had felt before.

"I don't know!" he insisted, his breath coming faster. He crouched down, ready to fend off any attack.

Yet when it came, it surprised him, and he very nearly fell victim to it. He had been near the center of the clearing, testing the ground underfoot as if he expected it to open and swallow him up. He saw the vines, thick as his wrist around the clearing, but thought that where he was, he was beyond their reach. The first brush of one had seemed nothing more than the nudge of his warhorse's nose, and since the red sorrel had given an unhappy whicker, Arkady had not looked around.

In the next instant, he was wrapped around with vines

heavy as cables, and they were rapidly drawing him upward, tightening around him like a cage. If Surata had not been his sword, he would have dropped his weapon and been helpless. As it was, he had a brief and vivid recollection from the dimmest part of his childhood, when he had stared in horror at rotting corpses hanging outside the city's walls in cages only slightly larger than the carrion within. Arkady screamed even as the vines fell harmlessly away from him and he dropped slowly down onto the rolled saddle blanket that served him for a pillow. Around him, the wind still howled and the blankets flapped and he could hear the stamp of his gelding's hooves not far from their shelter.

Surata sighed with pleasure and regret. "One day, you will come to trust me, and we will manage better."

"Are you disappointed?" Arkady demanded, his body and mind still wrung with fulfillment and fear.

"Not with you, Arkady-champion." She lifted her head and took his lower lip between both of hers. Her kiss, deliberate and sensual, stirred his loins briefly. "You see? How could I be disappointed?"

"Then what?" He propped himself on his elbows and looked down into her face, sorry that here he could not see her eyes as he had that once in the other place.

"We have much to learn of one another, and there isn't much time to learn it." Her frown faded and became a smile. "It will be lovely to learn."

"You're shameless," he teased her, then heard the note of accusation in his voice.

"Certainly by your standards. Why should I feel shame for learning to love you, to link my earthly body and my Subtle Body to yours?" She clearly did not intend to argue with him; she kissed him once more, very lightly at the corner of his mouth.

"I'm sorry, Surata. I shouldn't have said that." He loved the feel of her body under his, and he thought fleetingly that he might want to try to join with her again, for the sheer pleasure of it.

Surata chuckled, and the movement in her flesh sent ripples

of desire through him. "Arkady-champion, first we both must rest. For it is as tiring to fight in the other place as it is to fight here. Later tonight, when you have slept and eaten, then if you wish it, we could begin again." She nudged him, and obediantly he moved aside but held her close so that he would not lose the joy of his contact with her.

"And you? Will you be tired tonight?" He let his lips linger at her ear as he asked.

"Undoubtedly," she said. "But perhaps not too tired. When the storm has passed, tell me what you wish." She had closed her eyes as she spoke and her voice faded quickly.

"Surata?" he said, nudging her shoulder gently.

"I regret, Arkady-champion, that I am . . . very tired." She had pillowed her head on her arm, but she braced herself on her elbow. "In that other place, it takes strength to act, just as it does here. To transcend is . . . an accomplishment, but not so difficult. To be as malleable as the other place and still yourself is . . . another matter. We both fought a dragon and the . . . other. Now it is good to rest, to restore ourselves."

Arkady nodded. "Yes." He often enjoyed sleep after love-making, but this had been so unlike anything he had ever done, there were many questions in his thoughts and they kept him from resting. "I hadn't realized that . . ."

"What?" she asked when he did not go on. "What is it, Arkady-champion?"

He leaned back, staring up at the roof of their makeshift tent. "The dead men in the cages," he said distantly. "I'd forgot them, until . . ."

Surata fended off her exhaustion. "No, Arkady-champion, you never forgot them; and for that, you made yourself one of them, a dead man hanging in an iron cage outside the city walls."

Arkady lifted his hand to cross himself, then hesitated. "Do you—"

"Why should it trouble me if you protect yourself?" Surata asked with a gentle half-smile.

126

"But you don't do this," he said, hastily moving his hand in the blessing.

"I do other things," she reminded him. "What about the men in the cages? Who were they?"

It was difficult for Arkady to speak; he had to clear his throat before he began. "They were traitors, ungrateful to the King and God. They had betrayed their trusts and..." He broke off, scowling as he tried to remember.

"But what did they *do?*" Surata prompted him. "For such disgrace, they must have done great wrong."

"I..."—he ground his teeth—"my father said that they had been paid by another nobleman, one in... I can't remember where, to reveal... to reveal what our King's wife brought as dowry." He turned to Surata in his astonishment. "Could it be that? Could it be such a little thing as that?"

"Is it a little thing?" Surata inquired. "How great a matter is a noblewoman's dowry?"

Arkady made a noise between a cough and a laugh. "They betrayed the King's trust. That made them traitors. They gained from their betrayal. My father told me that they were not worthy of the favor the King had shown them and had disgraced themselves forever." He snorted. "What would he think of me, I wonder."

"Oh, Arkady-champion, no." She leaned over and kissed him softly. "That's wrong of you, to think that because of your dispute with the Margrave, that you deserve to hang in a cage." She put her hand over his Center of Fears. "But that *is* what you think, isn't it? Every time you have done a thing that shamed you or brought you chastisement, you put yourself in one of those cages, didn't you?" She let her head rest over his heart where she could hear it beat. "Arkady?"

"But not champion?" he asked with false lightness.

"Always my champion," she reproved him kindly.

"A blind slave from a defeated family," he scoffed.

She did not move away from him, but her voice became sharper. "Stop that. I will not say you deserve to be in a cage no matter what accusations to make, so do not waste time with them." Her hands pressed under her chin, where his ribs joined. "I wish I were not so tired: we could rid you of the cages."

"Just like that," he jeered, snapping his fingers.

"No," Surata told him seriously, still listening to his heart. "But it need not be as impossible as you fear it could be." Her lips touched the place over his heart.

"Why bother?" He did not expect an answer and was about to shove her away from him when she answered him with an intensity that surprised him.

"Because the Bundhi will put you in such a cage, if he learns of it. In that other place, he will entrap you if you have such great fear in you. Understand that, Arkady-champion. The Bundhi will use all your fear to defeat you, as he will use mine to defeat me. There is fear enough in such a malefic man as he is, and battling with him will be hard in the best of circumstances. Fear like yours must be set aside. We cannot afford your fear."

Arkady heard her out without protest. "Right," he said when she finished. "You're right. If that's the risk, then . . ."

But Surata was not quite finished. "Every person has fear, Arkady-champion, but they are not being hunted by such a one as the Bundhi. Your fear, if we had to battle him now, would be . . . it would be the same as giving the Turks your swords and then riding against them with wooden sticks. He can take such things, and make them more binding than anything you imagine now. All the force of your fear and all his destructive intentions, wedded to bring you down."

"You make him sound like the Devil," Arkady said, not wanting to go on.

"The Left Hand Path is allied to destruction, to ruin, as the Right Hand Path seeks . . . transformation. We both wish a change, a revolution in the minds of men, but to what purpose and from what circumstances . . . there we cannot agree." Suddenly she raised her head, her eyes turned in the general direction of his own. "Arkady-champion, is it wrong to want growth and transformation? You are a soldier and you know death better than I do. Have I misunderstood?"

Arkady wrapped his arms around Surata, hearing doubt and despair in her words for the first time since they had met. "If you are wrong, then I am wrong with you." He kissed the top of her head. "Surata, there are so many dead men behind me that often I dare not look back. If anyone had told me that there was another way a year ago, I don't know how I might have answered him. But you, now, I tell you that I'm tired of battle and death and if I must choose, then I will ask for growth and life."

Surata drew a deep breath. "I am grateful, Arkady-champion. I cannot tell you how grateful."

He tried to find soothing words for her, and sometime between his first murmurs and sunset, he fell asleep, waking only when the braying of the ass grew loud and constant enough to disturb him.

"He's hungry, Arkady-champion," Surata said, stretching as she came to herself.

"And thirsty," Arkady said, reaching up to rub his eyes. "I don't blame him. So am I."

"You were very . . . active today," Surata remarked, her words still sleep-softened.

"You can call it that." He grinned suddenly.

She did not respond as he expected. "I've already told you that when we are in the other place, we are twice active. There is all we do here, that makes it possible for us to be there, and in addition, we are busy in the other place. In a sense, we work twice." She stretched. "It's going to be cold tonight, with that wind."

"We should push on, search for an inn," he said with a lack of interest that made her smile.

"It is more sensible to stay where we are; is it not, Arkady-immai?" She pulled the one blanket that was not sheltering them from the wind more closely around her. "When the storm has passed, then we will travel, but if we go now, with night near and the wind, what good is it to leave, when we would have to search out another place like this?"

Arkady had found his saddlebag and had pulled out his old

woollen tunic, but he paused before donning it. "How do you know what time of day it is?"

Surata cocked her head as if listening to a secret in the wind. "I know. I can't tell you how."

"The way you knew that the cook was pregnant or that Yevgen was up to something?" He saw her respond to his challenge.

"When we leave, we will go by the grove of trees and you will see what became of the others." She was somber now, unwilling to banter with him or make light of her knowledge. "I do not always like the things I know, Arkady-immai."

He drew on his tunic. "I accept that what you think happens is not always pleasant." Then he stopped. "My muscles are sore."

"You have been in a battle—in two of them. And you have shaped the other place to your vision. All these things take strength and . . . you are not skilled."

"But you are, and you can feel nothing," he suggested.

"I am very tired. My hands are sore and the river that flows through the Subtle Body is listless as a stream at the end of summer." She had reached out for him, leaning against his raised knees. "You are tired that way, as well."

"I've got to feed the animals. Do you want food?" He moved away from her, crawling toward the place where the blankets overlapped. One of the bags of food held this closed, and he lifted it with care, taking hold of the fabric as the wind caught it.

"When you've tended to the animals, yes." She gestured toward him, saying, "You want to do . . ."

Arkady let himself out of the tent, into the battering wind. He bent against it, his eyes squinted almost closed, his arms crossed over his chest. He made his way unevenly to the gelding and the ass, approaching them slowly, talking to them. In such weather, they would be wild and unpredictable. It took him some little time to calm them and bring them back nearer his shelter, and while he did these things, his thoughts drifted back to the dead men in metal cages.

When the nosebags were in place, and he had opened one of their three precious skins of water for the horse and the ass, Arkady stood, his back to the wind, his eyes fixed on the distant, ruddy glow of sunset.

By morning the wind had dropped enough that it was little more than friendly bluster, frisking with leaves and branches, teasing the hems of Surata's clothes and giving the day a vigor that was often missing so near sunup.

"We don't have to go to the grove if you don't want to," Arkady said to Surata as he lifted her behind his saddle. "I'll believe you."

"Perhaps I was wrong," she said, ducking as he swung onto the bay. "It would be better to see."

"See?" he teased, and in the same breath said, "That was uncalled-for. I'm sorry, Surata. I don't know why I say these things."

"You say them because you are afraid that I may be right, and that worries you, as it worries me." She slipped her arms around him. "Go to the grove, Arkady-champion. Then *both* of us can find out what happened."

He could not stop himself. "If anything."

"Yes." She was not offended. "It could be that nothing happened, and we'll have lost the company of men who know this route, which would be unfortunate, wouldn't it?"

"We can go faster alone," he said in a kind of compromise.

It did not take them long to reach the grove of trees, and even before they came within the shelter of the scraggly pines, marks on the ground told part of the story.

"Many men stopped here last night," Arkady informed Surata as they approached the trees.

"More than were in Old Milo's company?" she asked.

"Most of them on ponies, by the look of it," Arkady went on, holding the bay firmly as the gelding tossed his head nervously. Behind them, the ass gave a long, honking cry of distress.

"They are troubled," Surata said. "Go very slowly, Arkady-champion."

He did not need her warning to do this, but he took it to heart. "I'll dismount when we're in the trees."

"Keep your sword and that little knife handy," she recommended.

"The cinquedea?" It lay tucked horizontally in the back of his belt, where he always carried it.

"Yes. Keep it to hand." She was frowning as she spoke, her face intent.

Only one pitiful donkey was still alive, and it could only lift its head feebly and moan. The others—men and animals both—were dead.

"They were gutted," Arkady said with distaste. "Most were stripped. They hacked off Old Milo's head."

"And Yevgen?" Surata asked, holding tightly to the cantel.

"No. He's not here, nor is Tibor. They didn't do this alone, though. They were helped." He swallowed hard to keep from being sick at what he saw. The sight was bad enough, but the stench was appalling. Lengths of intestines like shiny ropes stretched over the ground leading to bodies lashed to trees. "Whoever did this wanted more than robbery."

"What more?" She shook her head several times. "It was more than fear, as well. They wanted to . . . put out everything."

"Like an extinguished candle," Arkady mused. It had been much worse than that, more deliberate and ruinous, but he wanted to spare Surata the useless pain of it.

"What makes you believe I do not know it?" Her question cut into his thoughts abruptly. "For one like me, there is no hiding, no deception." She leaned forward, bending over the high cantel, sucking in air as if she might drown. "There is something else here, something that hides and waits, like a shadow at midday that is darker for the light."

"If I had a shovel, I'd bury them," Arkady said, as much to himself as to the corpses. He went to the donkey and stared down at it, tears in his eyes. Then he drew his short sword and struck hard at the top if its neck, ending its suffering. While he wiped the blade on the hem of his acton, he caught sight of a bamboo staff leaning against one of the trees. Curious, he went and picked it up.

"What is it?" Surata demanded, her voice high with apprehension. "What have you found?"

"A walking stick," he said, glowering at it. It felt oddly warm in his hands, and a strange odor came from its surface.

"Describe it." Her order was cutting. "Now."

Puzzled, Arkady lifted the staff. "It's wood," he said as he examined it. "Smooth to the touch. Segmented."

Surata's head came up. "Let me feel it," she said, extending her hand toward him.

"If you wish." He held out the staff, expecting her to grasp it.

She shrieked. "Drop it! *Drop it!*"

Arkady had already released it and he stepped back as the bamboo staff clattered to the ground. "What?"

"The servants of the Bundhi!" Surata wailed. "They are searching for his enemies! They will know now. They will know!" Her sobs were deep and bitter.

"Surata!" Arkady cried, reaching up to her, wanting to offer her comfort without knowing why or how. "No, Surata. Don't cry." He was being foolish, he knew it. Whatever had distressed her needed more than a few words to relieve.

"He knows we are coming. He knows. He will be waiting for us, watching." She slid off the gelding into Arkady's arms. "We are not safe now. Nowhere are we safe!"

Chapter 10

Against Surata's advice, Arkady burned the bamboo staff along with the bodies of the merchants and their donkeys.

"They will know," she insisted in a low voice, as if she might be overheard.

"If the bodies are burned, the staff should be, as well. If I didn't, it might be thought strange." He spoke evenly, treating her like a young soldier before his first battle. "How could they know you would return? How can they know now?"

"The Bundhi will know," she said.

"Might not this be another . . . sorcerer? Surely the Bundhi is not the only follower of the Left Hand Path." He piled the last of the tack onto the fire. The acrid scent of burning leather mixed with the odor of charred cloth and flesh.

"The Bundhi has reason to watch, and to watch to the west. When he killed my father and my uncles, he swore that none of them would escape his wrath." She wrapped her arms across her chest. "There were servants of the Bundhi who followed me to the slave market. I knew there were others, but . . . I was hoping that there would be more time."

Arkady watched the flames, fascinated by the movement of the fire, the color of it, the way it changed constantly. "You can't let that stop you from thinking. That's not the way to win a battle, Surata. You can anticipate what you think your foe will probably do, and you then prepare to counteract the move."

"I think the Bundhi will send his agents to kill us." She said it harshly, her head coming up.

"Then we will have to be more careful and travel the rest of the way alone, as much as we can." He wrenched his eyes away from the fire. "What is the worst the Bundhi can do to you?"

"He can destroy me, as he destroyed my father," she said. "I don't mean just this body, but the Subtle Body as well, and the manifestation in the other place. All that could be gone, or worse." She shivered. "He'd prefer to subvert me, to make me his servant, but I won't let that happen."

"No, I don't think you will," Arkady said, coming closer to her and touching her shoulder with the tips of his fingers. "Don't be so frightened, Surata. That robs you of your strength. Anything that lessens your strength increases the strength of your enemy. Remember that."

"Your teachers would agree with mine on that," she said after a silence. Her attitude was chastened but not defeated. "When I think of what became of my father and my uncles, I..."

"Yes," Arkady said very gently. "I know how I feel about the loss of my father and my leaders. And I often disliked my father, yet it was a deep, abiding pain to lose him." He reached down and took her by her shoulders, pulling her to her feet. "You say you don't want revenge, but I think you do. And in your place, I would want it, too. If your vengeance restores order as well, that's an added benefit, but not the reason for doing it."

She nodded slowly. "I've been taught all my life that it is wrong to seek vengeance, because that is the way of the Left Hand Path."

Arkady kissed her forehead. "Worry about that when you have your victory," he told her. "Until then, you must fight against despair as much as the forces of your enemies."

"Whatever their form?" she asked. "He may send them as men, but he may not. They could come in the form of marauding animals or . . . or storms." She said this last very softly.

"Like yesterday's storm?" Arkady said for her. "You're assuming that the Bundhi has . . . God's power over the weather." He had intended to laugh at this, but the sound would not come. "Why do you think that, Surata?"

"The bamboo staff made me think it. All those who follow the Left Hand Path and have advanced in their studies carry such staves, and when there is work to be done, they . . . feed them." Her blind eyes gazed into the distance. "The staves . . . eat. They must be fed in order for the alchemists to do their work."

"Fed what?" Arkady asked.

"Meat," Surata answered. "You saw what had been done to Old Milo and the others. The Bundhi's servants would treat others the same way, so that the staves might have what . . . they wanted. You see, the center of the bamboo is rotten, and it is there that the power of the Bundhi and his servants lie, in what has been spoiled." She turned away from Arkady and from the fire. "You don't know what power the Bundhi can control. I have seen it. It was the last thing I saw with my eyes, the staves of his servants at their meals."

Although Arkady was almost certain that Surata exaggerated the might of her opponent, he did not want to question her now. He feared she might relapse into the strange apathy she had shown as he built the fire, and that he knew was a greater peril than any legend she believed about the Bundhi. He let her walk a little way by herself, and spoke only when she was about to blunder into a tree.

She gave a loud cry of rage and frustration. "How can I fight him now?"

"That is what you want *me* to do," Arkady reminded her, bowing to her as he said it.

Surata started to weep, more in anger than grief. "He has reduced me to this, and still he is not satisfied! He has taken everything from me—home, family, teaching, fortune, sight!—and yet he pursues me!"

"You must frighten him very much if he goes to such lengths," Arkady said, coming up to her and putting his arms around her from the back. "For a great sorcerer to bend all his attention to finding one blind girl . . . there must be more to that blind girl."

"I am one more thing to destroy," she said between sobs.

"A very special thing, or he would not take such trouble," Arkady pointed out, finding his observations troubling as he spoke them. He had meant to suggest that she had overestimated her importance, but now he began to wonder if her abilities might be greater than he already knew they were.

"It always enhances the power of the Left Hand Path when the number of those of the Right Hand Path are decreased," she said, trying to bring herself under control.

"But to make such an effort . . ." He touched her hair with one hand. "Surata, you'd better tell me all of it."

"All?" Her voice faded on the word.

"Yes." He said it softly, but it was still an order and they both knew it. "Listen, Surata; you are from a people and a place that are not like mine, but what you do is more than the strangeness of your people. Those who live in your country, no doubt, find you almost as strange as I do. Don't they?"

"Some of them," she admitted before she turned around to him.

"It's more than where you come from that makes you unlike me. It's more than a difference of religion and language. It goes much deeper than that." His hand on her hair pressed her head to his shoulder. "It's even more than the other place, isn't it?"

This time she did not answer him at once. "Yes."

"Am I guarding an angel, unaware, as the priest told us in the parable?" He expected no answer and got none. "Not now, and not here, but before sunset, you have to tell me the rest of it, Surata. I can't fight well for you unless I know what I'm defending."

She shuddered. "Arkady-champion, I—"

"Arkady," he corrected her. "We're not fighting now. I am Arkady Todor Sól, and you are Surata. I am not your champion and you are not my slave." He held her more tightly.

"Tonight I'll tell you," she said with difficulty.

"Good." He bent and kissed the tip of her nose. "Come. It's time we were on our way. If we can cross the big river ahead tomorrow, we will be making good time toward Sarai."

"And if you do not like what I tell you tonight, what then?" she asked tenuously. "What will become of us?"

"We will not know that until tonight," he reminded her as he released her. "Until then, I'm going to concentrate on going as many leagues as we can."

Surata nodded. "Very well," she said, taking his hand and permitting him to lead her back to the gelding and the ass.

The day passed quickly, and largely in silence. Twice they met traders on the road. One was a small party of Tartars carrying brasses. They were a jovial group, in no particular hurry, confident that they would have a good sale when they finally reached the country of Moldavia. The second band of travellers was smaller and less friendly. They carried bales of silk in two wagons and explained in a language that Surata barely understood that there had been fighting to the east.

"There is also fighting to the west," she warned them.

One of the merchants exclaimed, making loud protests to the sky, while the others conferred.

"They might turn north, to Poland and Lithuania, if they are looking to sell carpets and textiles," Arkady suggested, recalling how prized such items were.

"I'll try to tell them," Surata said and did her best to make this understood. She was met with a great outburst, and when there was a chance, she remarked to Arkady, "Two of them are very devout and afraid of the Christians. They think they will be made to suffer for their religion."

"And you, I suspect," Arkady said lightly, "are wording

their objections more kindly than they did. By the way they carried on, they did more than simply say they were apprehensive."

"They weren't very moderate," was as far as she would go, but her wry smile told him he had guessed right.

"Find out if there is still a way to cross the river," he requested before the merchants moved on.

Surata did as he asked, then said, "There is a village on this side that has a ferry. They charge to carry passengers and goods over, but according to the merchants the charges are not unreasonable, and for travellers like us, it would not be much."

Arkady tapped the leather sack containing their gold. "I doubt we have to concern ourselves with cost."

"Don't let it be known you have so much. We are not the only travellers on this road, and some of the others are more desperate than we are." She gestured toward the merchants, saying a few words and making respectful gestures toward them. "They do not like speaking to women, but since you do not know their tongue, they will condescend to address me. However, they have made it clear that they want only your comments and none of mine."

"Then tell them that is what you've done," he said with a shrug. "Why won't they listen to you?"

"Their religion is very strict about women," she said carefully. "It is considered dangerous to speak to women." This clearly annoyed her. "Among my people, we do not have such prejudices."

Arkady thought back to the afternoon before, lying in their tent of blankets, adventuring in the other place. He bit back a jest he was afraid would offend her but could not keep himself from saying, "Not all religions are like yours, Surata."

"Nor are they like yours," she responded, then lowered her head, saying, "I did not mean to say you are wrong, Arkady-champion. You have brought me a long way, and you have accepted much and asked little. It isn't good behavior on my part to speak to you this way."

Arkady wanted to talk to her, but could not say what was

on his mind while the merchants were still around them. "Tell them that we must be on our way and wish them good fortune, will you?"

"Of course." She spoke to the leader of the merchants using words that were spiky to Arkady's ears. Then she inclined her head as far as she could in the saddle and said to Arkady, "I've done as you asked, and they have told me to warn you once again of the fighting that we may encounter. I said that you are a soldier and prepared to do battle if you must. I hope that was what you'd want."

"What is this submissive attitude, Surata?" he teased as he nudged his bay and pulled at the lead rein of the ass. "It isn't like you."

"I am troubled," she said and would say little else until they stopped at sundown near a ruined stone building.

"This must have been a monastery," Arkady decided after he had looked around the rubble and discovered a broken Russian crucifix and two smashed censers. "It's been a while since any Brothers worshipped here." He pulled his gelding into the center of the broken stone walls. "So we can spend the night in a chapel."

"Is it safe?" Surata asked. "We can't be the only ones who have seen this place."

"Most of the Orthodox Christians believe that buildings of this sort are haunted by demons, and avoid them," Arkady observed. "If there are others, we will deal with them when and if they come upon us." He was kicking the rubble aside. "We can make a fire with the broken benches. There's plenty of wood. We can stay warm all night. You'd like that, wouldn't you?"

Surata did not answer him at once. "Do you think there might be a well? We're low on water."

"If there is one, it's probably poisoned. That's what the monks do when they're forced to leave a place." He reached to lift her down but hesitated. "Are you displeased with this place, Surata?"

"No," she said, sliding down into his arms. "I'm worried

that you will not like what I tell you tonight. It isn't the place that makes me nervous. Any place would make me uneasy this night."

He smoothed a few loose strands of hair back off her face. "I don't mean to make this an ordeal, Surata. If you cannot tell me, then I'll do my best to—"

"No. You have the right to know. In the other place I couldn't conceal it from you, if you were to look for it. I should not deceive you here, either." She pushed away from him. "But do not be too quick to assume terrible things of me." She tried to move away from Arkady but tripped on a broken stone and went down with a little whimper of dismay.

Arkady secured his horse and the ass, then went to her. She had managed to get to her feet, but her hands were cut and there was a scrape on her elbow that showed through the rent in her clothes. "You're hurt," Arkady said.

"Not badly," she responded. "I'd like to wash my hands."

There was not much water left, but both the horse and ass had drunk deeply at a stream not more than an hour before. "We can spare a little," Arkady told her, holding up her hands to study them in the fading light. "There's not much blood."

"Good," she said, pulling her hands away from him.

"After I get the pack and saddle off the animals, then . . ."

"That's fine," she said, making no attempt to be more forthcoming. "When you're ready, tell me." She turned her head slowly. "Where did they worship?"

"This was the chapel," Arkady said.

"What direction did they face? Where was their altar? They had an altar, I suppose?" She turned slowly, then pointed north. "Was it there?"

He took hold of her wrist and pulled it slightly toward him, so that she was in line with the walls of the ruin. "That way, Surata. There was an altar with a crucifix—God on the Cross—and icons of the saints and martyrs. That's the way I've seen most Orthodox churches. This chapel was probably no different. They could not take the crucifix, but doubtless the icons went with them." He released her.

"Where did they go?" She did not expect an answer and did not get one; Arkady began to set up their camp for the night, taking care to have his weapons where he could reach them.

By the time he had gotten a small fire kindled, it was dusk, and the broken walls appeared taller and more ominous than they had while the sun was up. He started a supper of cheese and a thick soup before he spoke to Surata again. "Are you hungry?"

There was no answer.

"Surata?" He looked around, expecting to find her still sitting on one of the tumbled stones, but there was no sign of her there, nor at any place the firelight reached. Arkady stood up. "Surata!"

Again his call was met with nothing but a few faint echos.

He turned back to the fire and pulled out the end of one of the burning lengths of wood, holding it up to serve as a torch.

The gelding brought his head around and whickered, his nosebag muffling the sound.

It was annoying to be unable to ask the bay what he had seen, if anything. Holding his torch high, Arkady began to search the ruins of the monastery, growing more concerned for Surata with every step he took. What could have happened to her, he asked himself as he went from the chapel toward the far side of the old courtyard. Had she gone away, feeling her way away from the monastery into the fields beyond? And why had she gone?

"*Su-ra-ta!*" he shouted, not entirely surprised at the anxiety he heard in his own voice. "Where are you?"

This time he heard a sound in answer. He was not sure it was her voice, and so he made sure he could reach his cinquedea before going toward the noise that had attracted his attention. For all his certainty that the deserted monastery would be empty, he could not believe it now. He went very cautiously, making as little sound as possible.

Surata was where the kitchen garden had once been, sitting in the shadow of the old bake-and-wash house, her face set in that strange and still way that made Arkady think that she was not actually there. Her hands were folded in her lap, and she was breathing so slowly that Arkady thought she might be deeply asleep.

"Surata?" He held the torch near as he dropped onto his knee beside her. "Surata?" He was tempted to shake her but could not bring himself to disturb her. "Surata."

At this third repetition of her name, a change came over her. Her composed features moved and her eyelids fluttered. She sighed, then drew in a deep breath. "Arkady?"

"I'm here, Surata." He wanted to know where she had been yet said nothing more.

"I think we'll be safe for tonight. I found no trace of the men of the Bundhi, or any others, for that matter. I was afraid that they might have left staves along the way, to watch for them." She reached out, almost striking his hand that held the torch. "There are only a few peasants nearby, and they do not venture out of doors once it is dark, no matter what may happen."

"That's usual," Arkady said, taking hold of her arm with his free hand. "Come on; I'll help you up."

She accepted his offer in silence and made no objection when he led her back toward the chapel. "I'm . . . hungry," she admitted to him as she caught the smell from his cookpot.

"So am I," Arkady said, making sure she did not stumble on the uneven footing. "They probably have flagstones under all the wreckage. Monks usually had stone flooring in their buildings. I've never seen a monastery that didn't have stone floors." He wanted to keep her from worrying and said whatever came into his mind as he found her the end of a bench to sit on and then set about serving both of them their food.

"Thank you, Arkady-immai."

He took his own bowl and sank down cross-legged beside her. "I was named for my great-grandfather. The Count of our district . . . his great-great grandfather, that is, hired my great-grandfather from one of the lords of Novgorod. That Arkady had the reputation of keeping order, and anyone who could keep order in Novgorod, they were certain could keep order in Sól. He must have done well, because we're still the Marshalls there. Or we were, until the Margrave Fadey..." He stared down at his bowl, trying to think what his great-grandfather would say to him if he knew how his namesake had disgraced the family.

"I was named for..." She put her hand on his neck. "The feeling, the riding the wave? The bliss of being together, that is *surata*. For those who are trained as I am, it is a very good name." She ate a few more bites. "Arkady-immai, what must you know?"

"Eventually, I must know all of it, if you want me to fight for you. Now, tell me as much as you are able." He put his spoon into his food but did not eat.

"I've said I'm an alchemist, and that is the truth. All my life, I've been trained in the way of transformations." She put her food aside. "That is what my father learned, and what his father before that, and so on back for nine generations. Men and women both have been trained, for the work cannot be done without both. Alchemy is the blending, and male and female are needed, and both must be skilled if the transformation is to take place."

"Like being in the other place?" Arkady asked.

Surata nodded. "That is one thing, a relatively simple thing. Being in the other place is not difficult, and there are many with no training at all who stumble upon it. But they do not know how to use it, or how to shape it, and so it's... not useless, but it is nothing more than an interesting event, without merit or lasting value."

"And you? What does this have to do with you?" Arkady had turned so that he could see her face in the firelight.

"There will always be darkness and light. Each depends on the other. The teachers from Cathay call it yin-yang, and those from the Land of Snows call in yab-yum. Night depends on day, and day on night. You have two faces for your Great God, haven't you—a face that is kind and one that is harsh?"

"God judges us all," Arkady said, crossing himself.

"Not that face," she said. "The other, the face called the Devil." She rested her elbows on her knees and dropped her chin into her hands.

"The Devil is the adversary of God!" Arkady burst out.

"Yes. And each depends on the other. We see the difference as dark and light, and you see it as evil and good, but the underlying principle is the same." She hesitated. "All my understanding comes from that teaching."

"It is not the teaching of my Church," Arkady declared.

"Let's not argue about it. I will do my best to follow what you say and not dispute with you." Out of habit, he reached for his bowl once more and ate the rest of his meal.

"Your Church distorts much," she began, then stopped. "I'll try not to say such things, if I can." This time she paused a little longer as she gathered her thoughts. "There are those who are born to families of the Great Teachers, the Bogar, who are especially skilled. It is our time on the Wheel to bring our experiences to the service of light. In another time, we have made great errors, and this is our way of . . . you would call it expiation."

"What could a woman like you have done that would—"

"Not as I am now," Surata interrupted him. "As I was in another life. Your Church does not teach this, does it?" She did not wait for him to explain but went on. "Here we know that each life is part of a greater chain of lives, and that the wrongs of one will be corrected in another."

"If that's so, then your Bundhi will be a very busy fellow later on," Arkady quipped.

"And so he will. But there are those who do not wish to remain on the Wheel, but to extinguish themselves utterly through great destruction, and the Bundhi is one such. He has chosen the way of the total darkness, and no longer accepts the balance of light and dark, but desires the triumph of darkness over all." Tears gathered in her clouded eyes. "And for this, he causes much suffering. He does not seek the balance that governs all things, but works to end the balance forever. If he succeeds, then all is ended."

145

"And you believe that you can change this?" He knew he could not keep his incredulity out of his voice. "You think that what you do, here or in the other place, can stop such things?"

"I believe that I must try to stop it. If I were one of the monks that lived here so long ago, and I had been asked to pray for the salvation of mankind, then no matter what I might think of my own worth, I would have to pray or I would not be a true monk." She stood up abruptly. "You would not be a soldier if you were unwilling to fight."

"Then I must not be a true soldier," he snapped.

"You were not willing to be destroyed. That isn't fighting, that's stupidity. A good soldier retreats sometimes, doesn't he?" She reached her hands up toward the darkness. "It is so huge, and it is vain, you think, for me or for anyone to believe what we do will change anything. But when you decided not to go into battle, your men lived instead of dying. You were willing to accept the wrath of your leader in exchange for their lives. What you did changed things. You made your decision because of your knowledge. I have to do the same thing. As you learned about weapons and war, I learned about the other place and the forces of balance. Arkady-immai, if you had an arrow in your arm, you would find your chirurgeon to take it out if you could, instead of asking a boot-boy, wouldn't you?"

"The boot-boy might do a better job, knowing the chirurgeon in the Margrave Fadey's company," Arkady said. "But yes, I would try to find someone with the knowledge needed in order to do a thing. I would not ask a shepherd to make me a bridge."

"Then understand that my skill has come from study and with it comes . . . obligation." She reached out toward him, seeking his hand with her own. "I will show you what it was like to learn and to study, and you will . . . sympathize with what I must do."

"All right." He set his bowl aside and looked for hers, noting that she had eaten almost nothing. "You said you were hungry."

"I am, but I can't eat," she said quietly. "You recall how you were able to go back in your memories, that time just after you bought me? Do you remember what that was like? And through that, I learned who you are?"

"I remember," he said awkwardly.

"Then I will tell you how, and you will learn the same of me, and you will think me less a stranger than you do now."

"You're hardly a stranger to me, Surata," he said, laughing a little, his voice turning warm.

"But I am. You know my body and a piece of my skill, but I am foreign to you. In some ways, I will always be, but it need not be as great a gulf as it is now."

"If you wish it," he said, feeling doubt as he studied her face. "I pray you will not . . . regret it."

"I won't," she promised. "Build up the fire, if you will, Arkady-champion, and then I will tell you how you are to do this. Don't be afraid."

"Me? Afraid?" Arkady boasted. "I'm a soldier, and I . . ." His voice changed. "And I am afraid. Any sensible soldier is afraid in battle."

"This isn't battle," Surata said. "How can you think that it could be when we have vanquished dragons and cages in the other place? You trusted me to be your weapon, but you cannot trust me to be myself."

This brought him up short, and he stopped in his search for more broken benches to feed the fire in order to look at her closely. "You . . . you're right. You've been my weapon and you have not faltered. Now I am failing you, and that is not honorable." The last words caught in his throat and he had to force them out.

"You're too severe," she said gently. "If this were simply another battle, you wouldn't hesitate or have doubts, you would decide if it was reasonable to fight and then you would do your best. But I am asking you to do something you have never done before, and to go where your skill and ability cannot help you. That requires more than just courage, it takes great trust."

"The man who fights at my back must trust me, and I must trust him," Arkady pointed out.

"In battle, certainly, but suppose you had to go back to the battlefield afterward, to account for the dead. What of the man who goes with you then?" She took an unsteady step toward him. "Arkady-immai, you are being prudent, not cowardly."

147

He put his arm around her waist to brace her. "Be careful," he warned her, but not entirely because of the risk of tripping. "Surata, I may not be as capable as you think I am."

"That isn't possible, Arkady-champion," she said. "Tend to the fire. It may be a long night."

"So it may," he said, having no idea what he meant by his remark. He cleared a space for her by the fire and spread one of the blankets for her to sit on while he set about stacking the broken lengths of wood that long ago had been benches for the monks. As he ventured to the limits of the firelight, he saw an owl perched on the broken wall, its face perpetually indignant. Arkady had always had a fondness for owls, and he stopped working long enough to admire this particular bird until it sailed away silently into the dark.

Surata had spread out the other two blankets and had made two rough pillows of their saddlebags. She patted the blankets as Arkady added more wood to the fire. "Put your clothes here," she said, indicating a place near her feet.

"We both need baths," he said as he undressed. "Does that trouble you?"

"It's inconvenient, but that's all," she said. "When we find another place with a bathhouse, or a pleasant river to wash in, we will do it." As she said this, she began to get out of her clothes. "I am sorry that I can't see how you look, Arkady-immai. My hands tell me you are very beautiful."

This casual comment amazed him. "What?"

"Wait," she advised. "Shortly you'll understand."

Chapter 11

Arkady took great care to follow Surata's instructions as exactly as possible. He rubbed her feet and legs the way she said it should be done and tried to keep his mind on what she felt instead of his own reactions. But as he moved from her knees to her thighs, it became more difficult to forget she was a woman whose body pleasured him as no other had.

"It's not wrong to think that," she murmured as his hands grew still. "But that is not all there is to think of. You must start at the Four Petaled Center."

Arkady's face went crimson. "Surata..."

"Think of the strength there, not just your enjoyment, and try to sense how it flows to the rest of the Subtle Body." Her words came slowly, almost as if she were dreaming.

"But..." He looked away.

"Arkady-champion, don't deny what you feel, but don't limit it, either. Go beyond what you have known. Learn what I know." She made a quick gesture with her hand. "Arkady-champion, there is so much more than you have let yourself know."

Swallowing hard, he began to rub her thighs once more, all the while doing his best to recall the prayers he had learned as a child that would protect him from sin. Most of the words were jumbled and he did not find the solace in them that he once had. He ached with desire. "I . . . I don't know if I can . . . do . . ."

"You are not doing badly, Arkady-champion," she whispered. "Move up, if you are troubled. Start with the Thirty-Two Petaled Center, but do not be put off by what you find there." She reached out and put the palm of her hand to his abdomen. "It is better while we are linked."

More than anything, he wanted to cover her with his body, to use her flesh to blot out the disturbing impressions that flitted through his mind. "I . . . Surata."

"You can sense a little," she said, softly but with great confidence. "Don't hold back from it," she said. "Arkady-champion, there is nothing to resist."

The palms of his hand felt . . . strange, as if the skin were buzzing. He found it too alien to be pleasant, but not so unfamiliar that he could not continue. Instead, he let his thoughts drift, as Surata had told him before he began. He thought of hills and the way horses moved when they trotted.

There were five naked children in the large, artificial lake, and they swam together, laughing and splashing. Most of them were no more than four, though there was one who was a trifle older than the others, and it appeared to be his job to watch the younger ones. He kept reminding them that the water was teaching them to stop struggling, and by that, overcome the trials of the world. The cool water was so unlike the heat of the sun that the younger children paid little attention to what the older one said, and let the cascades of water cool them and hold them up.

"You see?" Surata said softly.

There was an old man, and he sat in the Virasana Posture, his body showing perfect poise. He spoke to Surata, who knelt beside him. "When the mind is steady, and the transcendent state achieved, then the lie of time becomes apparent."

Surata repeated this to her self several times, trying with a seven-year-old's concentration to grasp what her teacher had said.

The walls were covered with pictures, showing every aspect and posture of union, and beneath, texts described the merit of each. Surata, in the Posture of the Cow Herder, studied all that she saw, and tried to ignore the ache in her knees. It was not long until sunset, when she would be permitted to cease her contemplations for the evening. The air smelled of lotus and burning amber incense. It had turned chilly, but Surata did not permit that to distract her from her learning. At ten, she had learned more than most of the other children, and she knew that she had been singled out for more rigorous studies. She wanted to be prepared for her next level of studies, where all she had been taught through instruction would be applied to her own exercises. That was more than a year away, but already she was eager. She said to herself, as she had been taught since she could remember, that it is not only what we do but how it is done that brings about self-realization, and from that, the way of transcendence.

Arkady felt his head, making sure that his beard was still there and his scar above his right eye. There had never been any sensation that was like the one he had experienced from—with?—Surata. He thought he was . . . her. He had known things, had assumed things that were entirely beyond him.

"There is more, Arkady-immai. Touch me again, and this time, choose the Center of Sixty-Four Petals," she said to him, as relaxed as he was tense.

"Surata . . . Surata, I don't know—"

Her hand closed on his. "Some of it is pleasant and some is not, but do not turn from it now, Arkady-champion. You are closer than before, aren't you?"

He was not certain he understood what she meant, but he said, "Yes, I suppose I am," and then he coughed once. "Surata, what was that place?"

"It was my home, Arkady-champion. I was a child there, as you were a child in Sól."

"It is . . . beautiful," he said, not used to the sights that were foreign and familiar at once.

"I have always thought so," she said, smiling more openly. "And it is *my* thoughts you are sharing."

"Is there more . . . you know the sorts of things I mean," he said, embarrassment coming on him in a rush. "Those pictures and the way you watched them . . ."

"There is more. That shouldn't surprise you. It is part of our teaching and our work," she said. "Arkady-champion, there is no shame in what we do. That is the shame of your priests, who have tried to pretend that the body has no bearing on their lives, and only the spirit is worthy of attention. But it is not just your spirit that rides to battle; your body goes with it, and it is the body that swings the sword and takes the blows. Does that deserve nothing but a bandage and burnt food?"

Arkady balanced back, buttocks resting on heels. "No, I suppose that is short shrift." He put his hands to her Heart Center. "Is this next?"

"It can be," she said, breathing deeply several times. "Do your best, Arkady-champion. There is only benefit in learning."

He thought of the captured Turks that the Margrave Fadey had ordered wrapped in the pages of a captured *Koran*, and then set afire, so that they and their heretical teaching should perish together. "I wonder if that's so," he said to the air.

"Learn of me, Arkady-champion, and decide for yourself." Her relaxation was almost complete as he once again put his hands on her, this time in the declivity between her breasts.

Smoke billowed up from the funeral pyre, and rose petals burned with the body of Surata's father. Many people, all of them with bronze skins and dark hair, stood around the pyre, most of them chanting or standing on one foot, in the Posture of the Stork in order to aid the transition of the soul from the confines of the earth to its new dwelling place. Surata tore her garments and wept, but her mourning was without guilt—to Arkady's astonishment—and her loss did not consume her. She threw incense and flowers into the fire, then pulled off all her clothes and threw them in, too.

"What of your mother?" Arkady asked, blinking against tears.

"She died long ago. Her body was discovered on the steps of the Temple of Ganesha. Her throat had been cut." She reported this with little emotion, which puzzled Arkady.

"Doesn't that . . . bother you?" he asked.

"Yes. It troubled me then, though I was only five years old. The Bundhi sent his men to my father and the others, saying that as long as new alchemists were trained for the Right Hand Path, he would kill those who could breed more, until they gave up their folly." She turned on her side. "I am the only female child who lived past the age of eleven, and that was only because I was carefully guarded and knew how to protect myself."

Arkady could say nothing at first. "I thought . . . you'll have to forgive me for this, Surata, but I thought from what you said, and what I've . . . glimpsed, that there was little . . . trouble in your childhood. I thought it was . . . study and pleasure."

"Much of it was," she said carefully. "But there was always the other. I never forgot that."

"Didn't you ever . . . think about leaving? It would have been safer." He wished he could take her into his arms to shield her as she had shielded him in the other place, but he was aware that she did not want that from him, not now. "Is there more?"

"Much more," she said quietly. "Do you want to see it, or do you want to . . . stop?"

"No. Not enough to . . ." He let his mind drift once again. He thought back to all the preparations for battle, and the constant trouble with supply. His hands trembled and he threw his head back as her memories displaced his.

The man was young, certainly less than thirty, and yet his hair was white and his features so haggard that he might have been closer to sixty. He staggered through the courtyard of Surata's home, his progress unimpeded by servants or relatives, for they all recognized Adri, Surata's youngest uncle, who had gone half a year ago to attempt to enlist the aid of other adepts in their struggles with the Bundhi. He fell to his knees by the fountain and tried to scoop out a handful of water, but he was shaking so badly that he could not do it. Everyone watching recognized the omen's intent and they withdrew as quickly as they could. One of the oldest servants went to summon Surata, who had been occupied with her studies in another wing of the house, or so they thought. She had seen Adri arrive from the window of her private chamber and had watched him with dread. She had been closer to Adri than any of the others and she knew he was lost to her forever.

The magician was known as Dandin, and as his name implied, he carried a staff. It was taller than he, and made of bamboo. He held it with great care as he entered the temple where Surata was preparing to be initiated. He made a courteous salutation, then came directly to the point. "I am an agent of the Bundhi, and he has given me orders to seek you out in order to warn you." "Why should you warn me?" Surata asked, though she knew that there could be no beneficial intent in the man or his master. "You are embarked on great foolishness, but you have a chance to refuse. Draw back before it is too late and spare yourself much suffering. What is the point in prolonging the way of the world when it leads to nothing but horror and ruin? It is time for the earth to be over and done, to return to the darkness forever." Surata heard him out. "Darkness and light are dependent one on the other, Dandin, and if your master is to achieve what he wishes, he will need light to balance him." "There is no balance, and you are deceiving yourself to try to create it, for it cannot be done." He held out the staff. "If you refuse, be warned that the time will come when this staff will feast on your entrails." "You have warned me, and you may tell your master that," she said with a calm that was as disturbing to her as it was to him. "The Wheel turns for all of us, and if it is my Path to be vanquished by your master, then it will happen. No one escapes karma." She reached for the mallet for a little gong by her side. "You are only compounding your error, Surata of the Bogar House." She rang the gong and said nothing more until Dandin had been escorted from her presence.

The two oldest adepts brought her news of the omens and

sat with her as she listened to them repeat what they had learned. "You may have power, but it is finite, and you will have to choose how you wish to apply it. There are many turns in your path, and where it will lead is up to you. The Bundhi will pursue you relentlessly until your power is gone or given over to him." Surata nodded slowly. "And the others?" "They say that this house will have no more women. You are the last of them. When you are gone, it will depend on the turning of the Wheel and the malice of the Bundhi if there will ever be another. As long as the Bundhi has power, ours will be reduced." Surata placed her hands to her head. "It does not all lie with me!" she protested. "No, but much of it does. You may do much with a champion, but to find him, you will have to call him from far off and seek him in faraway lands." Surata ran from the room, and would not see the two old adepts for more than four days.

"Then you expected to find me," Arkady said, straightening up.

"No," Surata responded. "I thought when the Bundhi blinded me that I was lost and that the little power I had left would do me no good since I was a slave far from my own land. I called out because to do anything else was more defeat than I could bear." She took his hand in both of hers. "Arkady-champion, when I felt you answer my call, I knew hope for the first time since my sight was taken."

"I gave you hope?" he asked, pleased and dubious at once.

"More than I had ever known, because my despair had been so great until then."

He laughed aloud. "My priest said that God is seen from the depths of the abyss, or something of that sort." He touched her face with the fingertips of his free hand. "Surata, don't give yourself any more pain."

"There are just a few more things, Arkady-champion," she said.

"You don't have to," he said more emphatically.

"Yes; I do." She directed her sightless eyes at his. "You need not be part of it, but I must do this for myself. I have stirred up so much that I have to go on. You can understand that, can't you?"

"Right," he said, feeling a kind of defeat as he said it. "I will do what I must. In the throat now?" He had already touched her neck, and started the gentle rubbing that brought his palms down on the place he could tell was a Center.

The Bundhi was not a monster—he was, in fact, slightly more than average height with a face that was remarkable only for its immobility and the flatness of his eyes. He paced through the rooms of the Temple of Śiva, apparently unaware of the bodies that lay scattered everywhere, all of them with their intestines pulled out of gaping wounds. He did not permit any of his servants to walk with him or to approach him while he completed his inspection. "And the young woman, have you got her?" he asked Vadin. "Yes, Great Lord," Vadin said from his prostrate position. "We have her. We have done nothing to her, as you ordered." His bamboo staff, lying by his side, seemed to shimmer and move as he spoke. "Bring her here to me. I want to see her for myself." He folded his arms, his larger staff in his hand still. "I do not wish to wait long for her." Vadin crawled backward out of the Bundhi's presence and returned almost at once with Mayon and two others leading Surata. "So much for one woman," Mayon said, and was struck hard with the Bundhi's staff for his words. "You are Surata," the Bundhi said to her, ignoring the others. "You do not need to ask that," she replied. "You know that as well as you know who all those you have killed were." Her head was high, but there was a sadness about her mouth and a tone to her voice that gave away her despair to her enemy. "You are going to be offered one more chance, Surata," the Bundhi informed her as he strolled nearer. "You may come to me as my servant, give your power—which I admit is considerable—over to me, and I will forget all that you have done to oppose me. I will honor your accomplishments by permitting you to aid me in my work. Think before you refuse," he warned her. "You will be allowed to touch my body when I need touching, and to be tool of my transcendence." He paced around Surata, his expression never changing. "Everything I have heard of you says that you have great dedication and abilities. Think of how well you could use that for me." *He paused, and the silence lengthened. There was a scorn in Surata's clear, dark eyes that was more scathing than words.* "Remember: whatever happens, you have brought it on yourself." "If you do not wish me to oppose you, you will have to kill me," *Surata said without fear.* "Kill you? So that you can return again to the body and perhaps battle me again?" *The Bundhi did nothing so human as laugh: he clicked his tongue as if coaxing a recalcitrant animal.* "I will deal with you more sensibly. If you are far away, in a place where no one knows you or your skills, or even your language, you will be in a stronger prison than stones and iron can make. I will sell you, slave that you are, to a distant land." "I will come back," *she vowed.* "Though it take this life, and every life to come, I will return." "It is regrettable that you are so stubborn. What is there left for you?" *he asked, waving his arm to indicate the desolation around him.* "Your citadel is gone, and you have no place to anchor another in the daily world, have you?" *Surata prepared herself for the blade in her stomach, or the terrible predation of a bamboo staff. She did not think he would spare her long agony before death, for he had not spared the others any pain or indignity. She thought he would destroy her, but she was mistaken. The pain in her head was worse than if her brain was boiling. She staggered, her hands pressed against her ears as the Bundhi continued to lean his bamboo staff against her forehead, its hungry mouth pressed between her eyes.* "You do not have to endure this, Surata. You have only your stubbornness to blame for this." *She felt that rats were in her skull, with millions of sharp teeth. Her vision swam, and then she could see nothing as the Bundhi laughed, a sound like falling pebbles.* "Take her far, far to the west and sell her to a slave merchant." *Surata, still reeling inwardly, turned too quickly and fell, landing against one of the bodies of her kinsmen.* "You did not think I would be merciful, did you, Surata? After you have denied me what I want from you? Death is much too easy *for you. Think of what you have lost, both here and in that other place. Think of what is to come, of the long days and years in darkness and isolation without a citadel in this daily world to return to, and no means of reaching that other place. Mayon, see that she is sold and that she does not return." His footsteps and the tap of his staff receded in her darkness.*

This time Arkady did not stop himself. He drew her close against him, his arms holding her securely as he wept for her. "Surata, I . . . you didn't have to relive that. I don't want to cause you more torment."

"There is one more thing, Arkady-champion," she insisted. Her voice was tired, and he could see dark circles under her blighted eyes. "Just one more, and then we will rest, if that's what you want. Is there enough wood on the fire?"

Such an ordinary request threw him. He glanced over his shoulder, trying to make sense of what he saw. "It needs a little more wood," he said at last, when he had puzzled it out. "I'll tend to it." He eased her back as if she were a wounded comrade, then built up the fire. He was slightly dazed from all he had witnessed, and his thoughts were disordered. What more could she reveal to him? There had been so much already that he could hardly make sense of any of it. To have more could only add to his bafflement.

"The center of the forehead, Arkady-champion," she instructed when he touched her again. "This is the last, I promise you."

He could not agree or protest. He stared down into her face, which was less than an arm's length from his own, and marvelled at the serenity he saw there. "If it is painful, you need not do it," he said once more. "Surata, you don't have to hurt yourself anymore."

"But I'm not hurt, Arkady-champion. I have only remembered, and a memory may sting, but it cannot hurt me." She attempted a reassuring smile, which only served to make him more apprehensive. "This will make it . . . clearer."

He could think of no argument to use against that, and so, with hands that shook a bit, he touched her forehead, in the Center of the Moon.

In the doubt and the darkness, which had been filled with movement and travel, there was suddenly something else, a presence that responded to her, that shone like a torch in her mind. Surata reached out for that light, using everything she had learned as a child to call the presence to her. She heard a voice in a language she did not know—Arkady nearly broke his contact with her when he recognized, with some difficulty, Polish, and his own voice, saying, "Be quiet, you. How much?"—*address the slaver, and that voice began to give the presence form. A man, a foreigner, young, but not too young. She sensed that the warning of long ago was accurate, and that she had found what had been promised for her, not where she expected him, and not at all what she had thought he might be, but now she knew beyond any doubt that he was everything she needed. She went with him willingly and turned her attention to finding out about him.*

Arkady was fascinated and repelled to perceive himself through Surata's eyes. He knew he was not as courageous as she assumed he was, and he resented her ill-concealed disgust with his religion. He discovered her understanding of his language, almost laughing at some of her early mistakes. Slowly he caught bits of himself, first his voice, his sex, his origin, then his general size and build. Then, even more slowly, details of his appearance—the scar over his eye, the shape of his hands, the color of his hair and eyes—and last, her desire for him. "Surata . . ."

"Hush," she whispered.

They were in the bathhouse, and her longing for him was so intense that she thought the air was thickened with it. He was so reticent, so sure that she could not want him, and that his own desire was unacceptable. Her flesh tingled when she was near him, and when she touched him, she felt she had been wounded, so tender was her skin where it met his. She could not bear to believe that he might be able to defend her without any greater intimacy than they had known already. It would not be possible to fight the Bundhi with such limitations. And even if it had been, she admitted to herself, her yearning for him was almost unbearable. She refused to have less than all

159

his passion and decided that it was time to try to convince him that he had nothing to dread in her. All through the meal they ate in the stall, she strove to contain her erotic eagerness, so that it would be at full force when they lay together. It took all her discipline to calm him once again, and to focus her ardor on waking him from the numbing stupor of shame that had possessed him. All the men she had known before had been lifetime students of the pleasures and uses of the body, and now she had before her a man no more experienced than a little child.

"Surata," Arkady said, his mouth dry.

Apparently she did not hear him, but one hand moved, keeping his hands on her forehead. "There is nothing . . . to be afraid of." Her voice was so soft that Arkady was not entirely sure she spoke at all.

"Surata, I don't think I . . ."

When at last they came together, she opened every center of the Subtle Body to him, seeking transcendence as well as the gratification of her desires. The links, which were more than simply the meeting of bodies, began to be forged as the currents of the Subtle Body moved from one to the other as their souls reveled in astral pleasures.

Without intending to, he fell on her, seeking her with body and soul. His hands still on her forehead, he went into her. How strange it was, and how wonderful, to feel his body through hers, to know what she knew, to sense his own body with her hands, to press close to her and have the experience of his weight.

He braced himself. "I didn't know I'm so heavy," he murmured in apology.

She turned her head and kissed him, her tongue touching his. A gentle push and they were both comfortable, much closer and more intensely united

in the shifting light and the endless variety of the other place.

"What can we do?" Arkady asked.

"Anything we like," Surata answered. "But now we cannot forget that the Bundhi knows we are here, and that we are

capable of seeking him out." She was a long, broad-bladed *glavus, larger and more formidable than any that had been forged, with a glint on her steel that was deadly in its promise.*

"And you a sword?" He touched the blade with an affection that bordered on reverence.

"It is what you need and trust. Here there are dangers that no sword could fend off, but that doesn't matter. Whatever comes to you, I will resist it. You might falter, through fear or through shame, but I never will." The metal hummed, and in his hand the hilt grew warmer. "No one could pick me up and turn me against you. No foe could hide me far enough away that I would not find you and return to you. It could not be possible."

Arkady said nothing, knowing now without doubt that there was no reason or need to speak. He lifted the sword and watched the light glint along its steel. "You are the other side of me," he said to the weapon.

"And you of me, Arkady my champion," came the answer.

"Well, what will it be this time? More dragons?" He chuckled as the light around them began to take on a rocky look, more friendly than what he had conjured the time before.

"You're learning to like dragons," Surata said. "You would enjoy another such battle, wouldn't you?"

"Of course," he admitted, feeling pleased that she knew so much of his inner thoughts. That in itself was surprising, for he had always resisted permitting others to know him too closely. Soldiers were cautious of close friendships, for so many of them ended in battle. Yet the bond, he thought, the bond was there.

"Be certain, Arkady my champion, that you choose wisely, for we may be watched, and what you bring forth may not be entirely in your control." The concern was genuine, and he accepted her words without hesitation.

"What could he do?"

"Almost anything. He could take your monster and make it his own. He could change where you are so that the battle would be on water instead of land. You must recall that here the distances are not what they are in the daily world." She shifted in his hand. "If you want a battle, then let me suggest *that this time you choose something that flies. Your dragon had wings but did not use them."*

"Very well," he said, considering what she said. "I think that you're probably right. I've never fought anything in the air. No matter what the Turks think, they cannot fly through the air, though they fight as if they could."

"What do you want it to be?" she asked.

He hesitated, then said, "A gryphon. They guard treasures. I have seen them in heraldry and once in a tapestry. That would mean that I can conjure it up, wouldn't it?"

"That, or anything you can imagine," she said. "It's easier if you are familiar with the form and nature of the thing." She shifted again, growing a bit longer and developing heavier quillons to compensate for the added weight of the blade. "This might be tough to fight without a shield."

"Can you do that?" He had not considered this before.

"As long as what I am touches you, I can be anything you need to fight with or to protect you: any weapon, shield, armor or other guard to keep you from harm." She shimmered and he felt himself clad in fine scale armor. "This will make it more difficult for your gryphon to hurt you."

They were now standing on a ridge above a vast copse of trees. The ground underfoot was rocky, and behind them rose huge mountains; they were in a place that showed them beauty without demanding all of their strength to sustain themselves.

"Where is your gryphon?" Surata asked, her voice caressing him through the armor.

"I . . . I don't know yet. They were supposed to guard treasures," he said, trying to think where such a beast might hide. "They were part eagle and part lion. It might wait on the crags, but it could just as easily have a cave in the woods. You never know about such things. They are not the same as game in the forest, living always in the manner of their kind."

"Then decide, Arkady my champion, and begin your battle," she urged him. "The longer you debate, the more easily the Bundhi can search you out and do damage to you."

"And you?" he asked, not needing the answer. "Very well. It is in a tower on"—he turned and pointed—"that mountain, *and once I have my destrier again, we can start out to hunt it,"* he said.

The red sorrel came up behind him and nudged Arkady's arm in friendly greeting, and pranced forward so that Arkady could mount him easily.

"I wish my bay were this cooperative," Arkady said as he got into the saddle, noticing that while he mounted, his armor felt much lighter, and did not impede his movements.

At the most gentle of kicks, the red sorrel started off at a smooth, effortless and untiring canter, a gait that was a pleasure for the rider and that covered ground at a speed that Arkady knew was flatly impossible for any horse he had ever ridden. The stallion snorted, as if disdaining to be compared to any horse from the daily world. Arkady laughed out loud for the utter pleasure of his adventure.

A shadow passed over him, a shadow of tremendously wide wings and a long body ending in a tail not of a bird but a lion.

Arkady drew in and looked up.

There overhead the gryphon hovered, watching him with its keen eyes, dropping lower for a better look.

"It's a beauty!" Arkady shouted, raising his sword and grinning.

It was enormous, the gryphon. Its head and wings and front talons were like the eagle on the royal arms of Poland. The lion's hindquarters were tawny and massive, the fur as plush as velvet. Lazily, it came lower, letting out a loud cry in recognition or challenge.

"Watch it!" Surata warned. "Things that fly are often full of tricks."

"You're worried," Arkady said, giving his words a light, teasing rebuke. "There's no reason to worry."

"I hope you're right," she said, lifting in his hand.

"It's almost a pity to fight something so splendid," he said, watching the gryphon with a little regret. "If it doesn't attack, I'll let it go free."

"Whether it attacks or not should be up to you," Surata said, with a faint emphasis on 'should.'

"Then eventually, I suppose it must. But I don't have to

163

kill it, do I?" He was entranced by the mythical animal. It was so incredible and glorious. Arkady studied the size of its wings and the curve of its beak and decided that it was larger than any animal he had ever seen before, and that included the rhinoceros that had been displayed in Hungary that he had seen when he was younger and going to visit one of his mother's relatives. "See how well he flies, in spite of how large he is?"

"He's a fine beast," Surata agreed.

Arkady lowered his sword and sat still, watching the gryphon. He wanted to sing to it, or declaim great poetry. "Gryphon!" he shouted, waving his left hand, showing it was empty.

Majestically the gryphon descended and came to rest not very far from Arkady. It sat like a cat, talons together, wings folded back along its body, the lion's tail tucked neatly around his glistening front claws. It regarded Arkady without fear, its large eye turned slightly toward him in order to watch what he would do.

Arkady dismounted and walked slowly toward the gryphon, taking care to keep his sword sheathed. Since the gryphon was considerably larger than his horse, Arkady stopped a little distance from the animal and bowed to show his respect. "You are the most awe-inspiring creature I have ever seen..." he said to the gryphon, adding in an undervoice to his sword, "can he hear me? Can he answer?"

"That's up to you," Surata said with amusement. "He's your gryphon. Do you want him to answer?"

The gryphon had a voice that was harsh, like an eagle's voice, but not unkind. "You do me great honor," it said, its huge head dipping courteously.

"You are...most generous to talk with me like this." It was a foolish thing to say, but it was true enough. Arkady wished now that he had conjured up a gift for the gryphon. "What can I give him?" he whispered to Surata.

"Whatever you wish to give him," she replied, a smile in her voice.

A golden chain with a dazzling badge of the Knightly Order of Saint Michael appeared in Arkady's hands. He was pleased *that the chain seemed long enough to go around the gryphon's neck. "This isn't much in tribute. You should have more than this," he apologized to the gryphon.*

"It is a great honor," the gryphon said and once again lowered its head so that Arkady could approach it and place the chain around its neck. It nodded twice in acknowledgment of the act, then spread its huge wings in a leisurely fashion and without the least effort, rose into the air.

As the wind from its ascent buffeted at him, Arkady shaded his eyes to watch the gryphon. A peace and satisfaction that he had never felt before came over him, a sense of humility that was almost more consuming than pride.

"You did that well," Surata said. "Not all battles are fought with weapons, are they?"

"No," he said, still watching the owl that had returned to the broken wall of the ancient monastery.

Chapter 12

If Surata had shown the slightest trace of shame or embarrassment, Arkady could not have endured it. He regarded her warily as she curled up beside him and pulled the blankets over them. "Do you want to say anything to me?" he asked.

"I *have* said it to you, better than I can in words," she said gently, touching his cheek.

"After that, no avowals of love?" He wanted to sound worldly but even he knew he was being petulant.

"You had that long before we were born." She smiled with such exquisite tenderness that he was almost unable to look at her.

"Surata . . . what"—he slipped his arms around her, holding her in the curve of his body—"what if I'm not what you think I am?" It was so hard to ask her, for he was staggered by what he had discovered. "You see me . . ."

"I see you as you are, Arkady-champion. I could not see you any other way." She sounded very tired.

He could not argue with her, but he had to warn her. "I

might not be that . . . admirable." He moved her hair aside and kissed the back of her neck as if to make up to her for saying such things.

Sighing, she turned her head, resisting the lure of sleep. "It isn't a question of what I see, but of what is there. I don't know what you see of me, but it is . . . more than I can know, most of the time. Your limits are not as stringent as you think they are. Doubtless the same is true for me."

"Your gifts . . ."

". . . Yes? They are not the same as yours, but that is why there is so much we can do, and do together." She kissed the air near his cheek. "We have a very long way to go. Tana, then Sarai, and on to Khiva and Samarkand." She was quiet, then said in a very small voice, "If you are willing to go. I shouldn't have assumed that you—"

Arkady put one hand on her shoulder and very, very gently shook her. "Why would I not? Fine sort of champion I'd be, if I refused."

"You *are* a fine champion," she said, trying not to yawn.

"And you are the finest guardian any champion ever had." He held her until he knew she slept, and only then did he relax enough to doze.

The next day they ferried over the river Dnepr, pausing on the far side for the rest of the day and the night.

"We will have to buy more supplies in Tana," Arkady decided as they sat together that night. "Another ass or a mule. I don't know how much longer the gelding can keep up this pace if we don't lighten his load."

"Do you intend I should not—"

"You ride with me; that's certain. But if we're going as far as you say we are, we will need another ass and more supplies. And a change of clothes, at least. I don't want to see this acton again once I buy another." He patted the garment and shook his head at the scuffed brigandine. "All our clothes are worn, and if there is hard country ahead, we must plan for it."

"You know what's best to do," she said. "I can't advise you. You're the soldier. And you're not blind."

"Ssh." He took her hands in his. "Don't, Surata."

She took her lower lip between her teeth. "I didn't mean that as you think I did. It's not you. I am . . . bitter with myself."

"Surata, you're my guard, my weapon against an enemy I can't begin to recognize. If you . . . if you lose heart, what will I be able to do on my own? Nothing."

She could not dispute this. "There is not much chance. You admit that." Tears welled in her eyes, and she tried to pull her hands away from him, but he would not release them.

"You've made me your champion, and for that, if no other reason, I must try, with you or without you. You know I am worse than helpless against the Bundhi if I must face him alone." He looked at her, measuring the emotion he read in her face. "Oh, Surata, with you, there is a chance that I will reclaim my honor—"

"You never lost your honor," she corrected him.

"You may not think so, but when I am in despair, I fear that the Margrave Fadey was right to cashier me as he did. You know what it is to have such fears; you have them now, when you anticipate meeting the Bundhi again."

"He is searching for us. I know the feel of him and his men, and I know." She broke his hold on her hands but only to pull him closer. "If they were to do anything to you, I—"

"I know," he cut in. "That's my one worry, as well, that something might harm you."

She gave an unsteady laugh. "Well, what are we to do, then? You're determined to save me from myself, and I want to do the same for you."

"Would abandoning your . . . quest save you or me from the Bundhi?" He asked it calmly, the same way he would have asked one of his lieutenants what the strength and disposition of an enemy force was during a campaign.

"No," she said, her manner growing somber. "Sooner or later, he would have to seek me . . . us out, and then . . . there would be no choice."

"So if we have any advantage at all, it is in making that decision for him, taking the battle to him rather than waiting for him to come to us." He looked around the room the landlord had given them. "From everything you've said, doors and bars and walls are not enough to keep him out."

"He can strike out at us from the other place." She was thoughtfully silent. "Since you sensed you with me, you have changed, Arkady-champion. You speak of us as . . . as . . ."

"As a unit?" he suggested. "You've made the same change." He moved away from her so that he could take stock of what was in their saddlebags, which he had dropped in the corner. "I don't know what happened then, but . . . we *are* different than we were."

"Yes," she said, seeming a bit distracted. "Do you think we should ask the landlord where to buy another ass, or should we go to the center of Tana and see what's offered there?"

Arkady took his most bracing tone. "Better to ask the landlord. We're too foreign, and that would be an invitation to scoundrels to try to foist poor animals and supplies on us."

"You'd know the difference," she pointed out.

"But there would be delays while we established that, and we might bring attention to us that would not be wise." He patted their pouch of gold. "The landlord can aid us if we provide the proper incentive, and he might be less willing to boast of it if he has something to lose for his trouble." He pulled his tunic out of the largest of the saddlebags. "I think that when we have the new animal and a good pack saddle for it, that we should find new clothes, with no lice, that are not so—"

"—So obvious," she finished for him. "That would be wise. The agents of the Bundhi are looking for foreigners, not ordinary travellers. What they see in the other place cannot be disguised, but here, at least, we can confuse them for a time."

"Perhaps we should buy the clothing in Tana, where it will not be so much noticed," Arkady mused. "The less that can be traced the better. Don't you think?"

"I'd agree," she said, and though it was apparent that her attitude was still troubled, she was no longer expecting defeat.

"Then tomorrow, livestock and then on to Tana." He gave

her a quick hug. "Don't forget that I am helpless in this fight without you, Surata."

"I won't," she vowed.

The next day, Arkady bargained and haggled with two different traders and in the end, gave up the ass and two gold coins for two strengthy mules and their tack. It took the better part of the afternoon to purchase the rest of the supplies and another hour to find bags and sacking to carry it all, but by the time he came back to the inn, he was satisfied.

"First thing in the morning, off we go to Tana. There are no merchants leaving from here, but there may be some on the road," he said, determined to be cheerful. "The mules are satisfactory—they're a bit larger than the ass, and clever. I think mules are born clever." He lugged the rest of his purchases into their room and described them in detail to Surata.

"I wish there was more I could do," she said when he was through. "If I had been bought as a slave, not as you bought me, but as others are bought, what would have happened to me, once the buyer got tired of the novelty?" She shook her head. "That was what the Bundhi intended should happen."

"Are you always so gloomy when you've been cooped up all day?" Arkady asked. "Because if you are, then I'll be sure we keep moving once we leave here. Since you're the only person I can talk to, I'd like it better if you were not so downcast." He flipped the end of her braid. "Tomorrow, Surata, tomorrow we start our hunt."

She smiled, but there was no real delight in her face. "Tonight, Arkady-immai, do you want to take the chance to . . . spy on the Bundhi, in the other place?"

"Yes," he said with conviction. "Do you think that . . ."

"What?" she asked when he did not go on.

"That we could be exposing ourselves too much by searching for him?" He paused, then added, "Mind you, I want to go to the other place. I think both of us would find it . . . refreshing. It would make us feel less alone." He reached out and touched her face very lightly. "I . . . miss you, Surata."

This time her smile was more genuine. "And I miss you, Arkady-champion. You're right."

It was late when the inn at last fell silent, and Surata wakened Arkady from his half-sleep. She did it with kisses, most of them so soft that they could hardly be felt. Her lips grazed the scar over his right eyebrow, then brushed his eyelids.

"Keep doing that," Arkady whispered.

"I am your slave, Arkady-champion," she replied, her mouth becoming more emphatic.

"God, how long did it take you to learn how to do this?" he asked as his body quivered with pleasure and anticipation.

"Years and years and years," she murmured, her tongue tracing out the Centers of the Subtle Body.

A little later, he gasped. "They were worth it."

"I think so," she said, sliding onto him.

Arkady brought his head up in alarm. "This isn't right to—"

"Hush." She kissed him, pressing him back beneath her.

The protests faded from his thoughts as he reached up to fondle her breasts. He had done so many things his priest would disapprove of, one more could make no possible difference, especially one so sweet as this. He felt the current between them, a tingling in his chest, his lips, his spine, his groin, and sensed a similar awakening in her. He tossed his head

and lifted his gold-and-iron mace before mounting his red sorrel stallion.

This time, the other place was more sinister than it had seemed before. The colors that swam and faded were more acidic in their tinges, and Arkady had to quell the finger of dread that pressed on his throat.

"Take care," the mace warned him. "Your fear is nectar to the Bundhi and he will be drawn to it as you are drawn to good food."

Once in the saddle, Arkady took the time to be certain that he had all the equipment he needed, and was distressed that he could find no shield.

In the next moment he was clad in the same light scale armor that had appeared before. "If you need a shield, you will have it. For the time being, the armor and the mace will be sufficient," Surata told him.

"Where is the Bundhi, do you know?" Arkady asked, turning as much as his saddle would permit. He saw nothing but fluctuating light and shifting shapes that made no sense. "How am I to go through this, where there is no . . . footing?"

"You don't need footing. Just go," Surata said through the armor. "The horse is the same as the lights. So are we."

"What are we looking for?" he asked, growing annoyed at the uncertainty of it all.

"The Bundhi maintains a bastion in this other place, where he can retreat from his enemies in the daily world. It does not change much, since he uses it for shelter. It is a fortress on a high crag, a fortress made of bamboo." The last repulsed her and the scale armor clicked and rang with her feeling.

"Bamboo—like the staves?" It was a guess, but a sensible one and he knew when he asked it that he was probably right.

"It is made of those staves. They have the same habits here that they do in the daily world, and . . . they are very dangerous. They can sense the presence of . . . food." She became quiet.

"What do I do?" He still felt at a loss and she did not appear to know how to aid him.

"Set your horse in motion. You are looking for the Bundhi and agents of the Bundhi. That is all you need to think of. The rest will come."

It seemed ridiculous to go about a hunt in this way, but Arkady did as his armor told him and tried to picture the Bundhi as he had seen him through Surata's eyes and memories. He was startled to see his red sorrel raise on his hind legs and then start off through the constantly changing shapes.

"Remember, the Bundhi is also looking for you," the mace warned.

"I won't forget it," Arkady promised, wondering if he would recognize the presence of the Bundhi when and if he came across it. What was this sorcerer that he would employ so many disguises?

"It is part of the destruction he desires," Surata explained as the mace. "Nothing is accurate, and that leads to doubts and to illusions."

"But this is an illusion, isn't it?" He moved his arm to indicate all of the insubstantial forms around them.

"No, this is the nature of the other place. When it appears to be a solid thing, that is the illusion," she said.

"My horse? My dragon? My gryphon?" He found it difficult to speak.

"Oh, they are real, in the way of this place. They are real because they come from you. A stone that contains a jewel is only a stone until the jeweler touches it. And when it is a jewel, it is still a stone." The mace swung in his hand. "Arkady my champion, you must not resist the duality of what we are. That will only rob you of your strength."

Ahead—at least, Arkady thought, in the distance in front of him—there was something that appeared to be a stretch of desolate land. The patterns of light grew more cohesive and took on the appearance of rocks and scrub. The whole world appeared empty. "What is this?" he asked, disliking everything he saw.

"It is where we are going. We are seeking out the Bundhi where he has his stronghold. Across that waste, there are mountains, as barren as the moon, and they are where the Bundhi has made his redoubt."

The red sorrel shook his head, snorting and stamping his feet. He had slowed his pace, and now he resisted going further into the parched landscape that had developed around them.

"He's edgy," Arkady said, patting the red sorrel's neck to give him some reassurance. "There must be something he's aware of that bothers him."

"This place would bother anyone or anything," Surata said, her voice not entirely calm. "This is very dangerous now."

"Why?" Arkady asked.

"Because this is the Bundhi's land, and everything here is part of him. Nothing comes here that he does not know of it." The mace twitched. "Arkady my champion, be very cautious, for anything might turn against you."

"There's nothing here," he pointed out, rising in the stirrups and shading his eyes against the glare of the sun. "There are mountains, but they are a long way off. If the Bundhi is in his stronghold, he cannot know we are here."

"This is part of his stronghold. This place, all of it, is part of his redoubt. Everything originates with him. Don't be fooled by what you see here." The scale armor grew heavier to add to his protection.

Arkady shook his head. "You're worried over nothing. Even if it is as you say, the Bundhi cannot be aware all the time of what transpires here." He gave the shaft of his mace a pat.

"He has agents for that," she snapped. "Go very carefully. Your horse can stay above the ground, not that that would help for long."

"Stay above the ground?" he repeated, laughing in spite of himself. "He can do whatever you wish him to do. But if you want him to act unlike a horse, you will have to concentrate all your attention on that, and not on what is around you." This came from the armor, which rang softly with her voice.

"But—" Before he could go on, he saw the ground ahead of him shimmer and shift. Out of the flat and empty plain, something rose up, a massive cliff of loose rocks that tumbled toward him as the ground gaped open. A rock struck his arm, and at once a shield took the place of the mace. His helmet became a helm; greaves covered his lower legs.

"Get away!" Surata shouted to him, her voice almost lost in the rattle of the avalanche that poured down on them.

"How!" Arkady yelled, tugging on the blankets that covered them. His upper arm ached where a bruise was already forming. Surata lay atop him as if shielding him with her own body.

"Arkady-champion!" she cried, her hands moving over him as if searching for damage. There was nothing amorous about her now.

"I'm . . . all right, Surata," he said as he tried to take stock of himself. "My arm, that's all."

"What's happened to it?" she demanded, her urgent, gentle fingers trying to discern the injury.

"A bruise. How can I be bruised here, if I was struck there?"

He felt mildly disoriented, as if he were slightly drunk, or had not slept enough.

"Injury is injury," she said brusquely. "Come, we must leave here. Now. Before his agents can follow where we have gone."

"It's . . . the middle of the night!" Arkady protested as he watched her get to her feet and feel for her clothes. "For God and the Angels, Surata, what are we to do at this hour?" He felt so sleepy, and the thought of moving was wholly unwelcome.

"They will be here. They will know where we have gone. We must not let them find us, or we will never get to the mountain stronghold in this daily world, let alone in the other place." She had already pulled on her embroidered boots with the upturned toes and was now slipping into her underdress.

"Surata," he complained.

"Arkady-immai, you must hurry. We haven't got much time. Get up, for the love of . . . your soul," she pleaded, pausing to stare in his general direction. "You've seen what the Bundhi can do in the other place. He can do many things in this daily world through his agents and his abilities. *Please!*"

Reluctantly Arkady got out of bed and reached for his acton. It was in a wadded heap where he had left it, and it took him a moment or two to sort the garment out. "Where are we to go at this hour, Surata?"

"Away from here, that's all that matters," she insisted. Her outer robe was in place and she was knotting her belt. "Hurry, hurry."

He sighed to let her know he was not pleased, but he pulled his acton on over his head and tried to locate his leggings.

"I'll tend to the blankets. Get up." She shoved him aside and set about folding and rolling the bedding. "Where are the cords to tie them?"

Arkady, who was now half-dressed, reached for the two cords and held them out for her. "Is it really so urgent?" he asked, no longer mocking her for her dread was as real as the darkness around them.

"Yes. He was more prepared than I thought he would be.

175

I assumed that he no longer concerned himself with me, but..."
She broke off as she finished tieing the blankets. "They're
ready. How much longer will you need?"

"Not long," Arkady said, recalling all the times he had had
to arm himself for battle in far less time than this. "Can you
carry three of the bags? If you can, we won't have to make
more than one trip to the stableyard."

"Yes. Yes, I can. We must not come back once we leave,
for that would tell him everything: where we are and that we
have fled." She clapped her hands in impatience. "Listen!"

"What?" he asked as he fastened his belt and picked up his
helmet.

"That sound," she said.

"Mice," he told her after listening briefly. "Or rats. Most
inns have mice. You said so yourself." He chuckled and was
worried when she grew even more agitated.

Surata reached down and gathered up the blankets, slinging
the two rolls over her shoulder by the cords and then fumbling
to carry more. "Where is the door. Quick!"

"They're just mice, Surata," he said. He reached for the
two leather bags and hefted them to his shoulder. "It's not as
if they can do—"

"Don't you understand?" she demanded, rounding on him.
"They can be instruments of the Bundhi. They can be after us
now, and if they are, it is too late already!"

From the next room, someone banged on the walls and gave
an incoherent and angry outburst.

Surata swung around toward the wall and thumped it as
hard as she could with the largest sack she could. The thump
was a resounding one and made the man in the next room more
outraged than ever.

"What the Devil...?" Arkady demanded.

"If he becomes active, the mice may go to him instead.
Since he is not the one they search for, he will not be harmed,
and by then we will be away from here. Get the bags and
move!" She felt her way to the door and pulled it open. "Arkady-
immai!"

"Right." He could hear the mice more clearly, along with

the outbursts of the man in the next room, who had started to drum on the wall between their chambers with something very solid. Arkady hesitated just long enough to make sure he had their gold and the flint and steel for lighting fires, and then he left the room, pulling the door closed behind him.

Surata stood at the head of the stairs, waiting for him. "You must lead me down. I can't manage them on my own, not with everything I'm carrying."

He reached for her arm and half guided, half dragged her down the stairs. Behind them, the man in the next room let out a loud and indignant yell, and as Arkady and Surata reached the bottom of the stairs, another one of the guests was shouting, and there were more sounds of mice, scampering and skittering through the inn.

There was a stout bolt across the door of the inn; Arkady dragged it from its housing and flung the door wide open. Pulling Surata after him, he kicked the door closed and sprinted for the stables. His arm braced Surata, and when she might have stumbled, he held her up and kept her moving.

In the stable, he forced her to stand to the side, all their gear at her feet, while he saddled and bridled his bay and the two mules. It did not take long to load the pack saddles, and to bring his two scabbards with their swords to a position of easy access on his gelding's saddle. "Almost ready," he called to Surata.

There was an outburst from the back of the stable and a sleepy voice shouted at them.

"What's he saying?" Arkady asked as he led the bay out of his stall to where the two mules waited, their long ears twitching at this unusual behavior.

"I don't know," Surata replied, not amused by the question. "He probably wonders what's going on."

"Natural enough. Come here." He held out his hand to her. "Get up." He had lifted her onto the horse enough times that he could do it easily, and this time was no exception. He did not wait to be certain she was well seated, but swung into the saddle, trusting her to duck out of the way of his leg.

An old man carrying a lighted candle appeared at the far

end of the stable, a pitchfork in his hand. He shouted indignantly at Arkady and Surata and stumbled forward as if to stop them.

"Hang on!" Arkady shouted and kicked his gelding sharply, jolting himself, Surata, the bay and the two mules into action.

The little party was almost halfway across the innyard when the bay brought his head up, snorting and neighing in distress. His hooves struck sparks from the cobbles and he pulled at the reins, attempting to bolt. Behind him, the mules brayed at the ends of their lead lines.

"What is going on?" Arkady demanded of the sky as he struggled with the animals. However late it was, he doubted that this was reason enough for the strange reaction of his horse and the mules. He used all his skill to bring the gelding back under control and finally was able to do it.

Surata, who had clung to Arkady without speaking, released her hold on him a little. "Do you know why they did that?" she asked him when the gelding had ceased to toss his head.

"I don't know," Arkady answered, becoming as worried as he was puzzled. "He doesn't do that."

"The mules too," she said, turning toward the sweating beasts. "They are mad with fear."

Arkady once again started his gelding across the innyard, but this time was much more deliberate in his actions. He rode as far forward as the saddle would allow, half standing in the stirrups, his eyes scanning the building and the ground. "Steady," he ordered the bay as they inched toward the gate. "Keep going, fellow."

The gelding made a quiet, uneasy whinny and began once again to sweat. He panted as if he had been running for an hour.

"It is the Bundhi," Surata said to herself, with conviction and misery. "He has found us after all."

"You can't be certain of that," Arkady told her without letting his attention be diverted from the ground ahead.

"He has found this inn. I know that," she replied. "You heard the mice. You know that they were not . . . natural."

"I heard mice, but that . . ." He halted his gelding and stared down at the ground.

The cobbles appeared to heave and slide in the dim moonlight. It was a little time before Arkady realized that what he was seeing was not stones at all, but a huge tide of mice sweeping toward the door of the inn. They made almost no sounds and they ran with grim purpose that was not like what Arkady had seen mice do before.

"You'd better hurry," Surata said. "There must be a back way."

Arkady knew he did not need to tell her what he saw. "They are going to the inn."

"We still have a chance," she said with a little hope in her voice. "Find the back way."

Arkady wheeled his bay—which was plainly relieved to be sent in another direction—and started back toward the stable.

The old man with the pitchfork was blocking the way, his candle flickering in the wind. He bellowed some sort of order or insult at Arkady and shook the pitchfork at him.

"Behind the bakehouse," Arkady said as he caught sight of a break in the high fence that surrounded the innyard. "We can get out there."

Surata said nothing but held on with determination as Arkady kicked his gelding to a fast trot. For once the mules were willing to move, and they both broke into a jagged, rocking canter as Arkady got them away from the inn and its visitation of mice.

Chapter 13

At Tana there was a constant confusion, with merchants from all quarters of the world—Greeks and Byzantines from the fallen empire; Arabs, Turks and Persians; a few Egyptians; traders from Moskva and Kiev and Kazan—gathered there on the edge of the Sea of Azov, for the purpose of selling and exchanging wares.

In an outburst of pleasure at the variety around them, Arkady bought three changes of clothes for each of them, rationalizing this extravagance as a good precaution. "The Egyptian cotton will do well on the long trek from Sarai to Samarkand, where it is hot and the sand is mixed with salt. This"—he lifted his second ensemble—"is Byzantine and should do me very well when we are riding. It looks prosperous without appearing rich, and the armor is good. I think that the mail is old-fashioned, but it is versatile and it doesn't need a squire to help me into it. This for you"—the garment was also old-fashioned, of patterned silk from Antioch—"will do you well when we are in cities or other places where a great many people gather. No one will approach or insult you in garments like this. I'll show you how to wear them, so that you can dress for yourself."

Surata could not help laughing. "What else have you got?"

"The last I bought from a merchant from Smolensk. He has brothers who are priests there, and they are anxious for him to purchase goods for them. I have a priest's habit, and a nun's. They will help us while we travel." He wished she could see these last two, very dark, woollen garments with belts and crucifixes with the two straight bars at the top, and an angled one further down. "I'll show you how to handle the things so that you can convince others that you know the rites of the Christians." He knew that he was fairly ignorant of the Orthodox ceremonies, but he was determined to continue in this plan. "While we're by ourselves, we can decide when it will be best to wear the clerical garments."

"The further east we go, the fewer Christians we'll find," she pointed out, not entirely convinced that this ruse would work. "Think of what could happen among followers of Islam. They are already battling with Christians. Might it not be dangerous to appear as members of Christian clergy where Islam rules?" She did not expect an answer, but Arkady gave her one nonetheless.

"You're right, for some of the places we must go. But there are others where it would be to our advantage to be *any* sort of clergy, so that we may excuse ourselves from battle or from joining with other company that might be more dangerous than these robes are."

She shrugged. "Well, later today, you can explain the significance of the dress to me. That should be the first step in any case."

"You're not convinced it will work, are you?" He respected her enough that this question was quite serious.

"No, I'm not. It's too chancy, but if you think we'd be safer, you are the one who has fought most of your life, and you know far more than I about avoiding conflict. That is why you are my—"

"—Champion; yes, I know," he countered with impatience.

"For the time being, I also have travellers' cloaks for both of us. I trust you won't object to wearing them?"

"No, not at all. I've wanted a cloak for... some time. I thought..." She broke off, her face very still. "We must be careful tonight, Arkady-immai. There is danger waiting for us. The Bundhi is searching for us, and it would be simple enough for him to..." Her hands came up to her face, covering her blind eyes. "I *hate* this darkness! *I hate it!* To be able to see only in the other place, where no one needs eyes... It's impossible!"

Arkady, distressed at her outburst, came quickly to her side and took her in his arms. "Surata, no. Don't let yourself give way to despair. For my sake, if not for yours." He kissed her hair, then her forehead. "With determination, we can prevail, but if you abandon our fight before it has even begun, what will we do then?" He felt how fiercely her sobs tore through her, and that caused him more anguish. "Surata, please."

She did not respond at once, but when she did, she had brought herself back under firm control. "I didn't expect this would happen. You will have to pardon me for carrying on in this way."

"Everyone has times on a long campaign when it presses them. You're no different than a green soldier. But Surata, this is just the beginning of the fight. Until now, there was no campaign. You will have to watch yourself, or you will be exhausted long before we reach the Bundhi or Samarkand." He held her less tightly and took a more comradely attitude.

"And if the Bundhi reaches us first? The mice were little more than an entertainment, a warning that our presence was known, and our intent understood. The Bundhi has done nothing difficult yet, that I am aware of. That frightens me, as well," she went on in a hesitant way. "I know that the Bundhi is capable of ... much more than ... a sea of mice. He had great power. It could be demonstrated in weather or enemies or animals or ... anything. I know that I should be able to recognize him and his agents, but what if I don't? What if I fail to ... see? It's possible, Arkady-champion."

"That shouldn't bother you," he said, hoping to cheer her up. He realized that her new worries were well-founded, and he could not deny that she had good reason for her concern.

"Don't dismiss me so easily," she told him with some spirit. "I don't want to be killed, or worse. It could happen, more easily than I want to think it could. If you won't listen to me, and help me to take precautions, then we might as well turn around now, and go back to the West, where I will be your slave for as long as you find me . . . desirable. After that, it will not matter." She pushed away from him.

"For the love of Saint Michael!" he exclaimed. "What's come over you? For almost three weeks, you can say nothing but how urgent it is that we get to Samarkand and that place beyond it, so that we can engage the Bundhi in combat. Now that we're on our way, you're talking as if we had already been defeated. What's the matter with you?"

Her hands knotted together and she remained stubbornly silent for a little time. "Arkady-immai, I don't want to see you hurt or harmed. I have been raised to this battle, but you're not born to it as I am, and . . . you're from another people, another country, another faith. You have no reason to risk so much."

"Yes, I do. I'm your champion, remember? You've been telling me that since before you could speak my name. If that's the case, then your battle must be my battle as well. Right?" He was secretly deeply touched that she had so much concern for him. With the suggestion of a chuckle, he reached for the cloak he had bought for her. "Here. You might as well try this on. I think it's long enough, but I couldn't be sure when I bought it."

She grasped the sand-colored garment. "Arkady-immai . . ."

"It's cut very full, so that you can roll up in it at night if you need to," he went on, as if he had not heard her.

"Arkady-immai, let me speak," she said very quietly.

"All right." He stood facing her, looking into her face, wishing that he could see her thoughts in her eyes instead of the blankness that was there.

183

She began slowly, chosing her words very carefully. "You have shown me much ... consideration since you bought me. Sometimes more consideration than I wanted or needed, but that's of small matter now. You have accepted our joining and our venturing to the other place, and so far you have not complained. But soon it will be more hazardous. That avalanche was just the beginning, to be sure we were aware that the Bundhi knew of our presence. It was not ... when I realized that you had been bruised by the falling rocks, I was very troubled."

"Any soldier knows that he can be hurt in battle. A bruise is nothing. I've had worse than that during training, let alone in battle." He swung his arm. "It's fine now, Surata. Nothing lasting, just a bruise. You're overly worried on my behalf."

"No, I'm not," she said, frowning. "You haven't seen what can become of those who oppose—"

"Stop that," Arkady interrupted her. "You're frightening yourself. If you must be frightened, let the Bundhi do it himself; you're doing his work for him."

Surata laughed unhappily. "You're right, Arkady-immai. I know you're right. But ... I've been thinking about what happened to my father and uncles, and it *does* frighten me."

"Then think of something else," he advised. "Why am I telling you this? You're the one who should be saying this to me. You're the one with the understanding of what thought and all those other things can do. Have you forgot everything you ever learned?"

She brought her head up. "Are you accusing me of ..." She could not find the right word.

"I'm not calling you a coward, if that's what you're worried about," he said, taking a milder tone with her. "But you are not being sensible about this. You're succumbing to all the things you know are not right, and you're excusing yourself because of your memories. All of us have memories, Surata. We must deal with them as best we can."

This time she was much chastened. "I ... ask your pardon, Arkady-immai," she whispered.

"There's nothing to pardon. You're spooked, that's all. It happens to all of us, one time or another." He changed tone with her again. "The cloak?"

"Oh, yes," she said, lifting the wadded fabric in her hands. "It goes around the shoulders, doesn't it?"

"And ties at the neck and over the heart. There are two long ribbons you use . . ." He reached out and took them, wishing he could demonstrate the tieing for her.

"I'll do it," she said gently, not a trace of rebuke in her voice. "You just wait a bit, won't you, while I work it out. When we travel, I will have to fend for myself. I should start now."

Arkady nodded, then said, "Yes, I suppose you're right."

Surata struggled with the unfamiliar garment; it was difficult to adjust the voluminous folds so that the cloak was properly balanced on her shoulders. "It is very warm," she said, approving of the cloak. "At night I'll be glad of it, but during the day, it might be too much." She untied the ribbons in the front. "I had these wrong, didn't I?"

"You did," he said, looking down at the scuffed toes of his boots.

"If I make that mistake again, you must correct me," she told him as she pulled the cloak off. "I won't improve if you don't correct me."

He remembered the many times his teacher had made him repeat exercises with his weapons for exactly the same reason. "All right, I'll tell you." His promise did not come easily, and he wondered if it was because he knew how bitterly she hated her blindness.

"Arkady-immai," Surata said, breaking into his thoughts, "you let yourself worry about the wrong things. If you are afraid to mention my blindness, then I will become ashamed of it. If I had lost a hand in battle, you would not think twice of it. You would help me when I needed your help and you would encourage me to excel where I could. Wouldn't you?"

"Possibly," he hedged. He wanted to take her in his arms and soothe her, vowing that she would never have to suffer for her blindness, giving her his word that he would be her eyes and her hands for as long as he lived. None of these sentiments reached his lips, and his hands stayed at his sides.

Surata smiled wistfully, the corners of her mouth not quite turning up properly. "I wish..."

"Yes?" Absurdly, he hoped that she would be the first to speak, to offer assurances and oaths to him.

She shook her head. "Never mind. Let me inspect these other garments you've brought. And tell me which you want me to wear when we leave tomorrow."

Arkady swallowed his disappointment. "Well, here the religious robes would be best. By the time we reach Sarai, there may be other clothes we ought to buy."

"And the gold? You have been free with it, Arkady-immai." She was not critical, but curious.

"There is no reason to worry about poverty yet. We are not in danger of running out of money for quite some time." He patted the pouch that hung from his belt. "Soldiers know how to haggle. And how to forage, if it comes to that."

"Beyond Sarai, it may. There may be a trade route through the desert there, but it is a bleak land, from all I have been told of it."

"Bleak," he said. "A stretch of desert and salt marshes by the old sea."

"There are tigers that follow the caravans, feeding on stragglers." She paused, giving him time to consider this. "They might follow us, since there are only two of us, and the mules would be a good meal for a tiger."

"And the Bundhi?" Arkady asked.

"Yes, he might use them. He likes them, respects them. They are so good at killing."

"I have heard that," he said in a neutral voice while he thought back to the tales he had heard of the enormous striped cats that would fix you with their hard stares and sap your will before they attacked. Legend was that if you threw a glass ball in front of them, they would become fascinated by the reflection they saw and mistake it for their young, and would abandon the hunt. Arkady did not want to put that theory to the test.

Surata reached toward him. "Arkady-immai, I would not fear for you if you meant nothing to me."

"I know." He took her hand in his and bent to kiss it.

By that night, the worst of their fears were forgotten, and they enjoyed a lavish meal before going up to bed. In the dark they lay side by side, hardly touching under their blankets.

"Surata?" Arkady ventured after they had laughed about the pompous way an old Greek merchant had ordered the porters around in the taproom.

"Yes?"

"Could we . . . would you take us to the other place tonight?" It was wrong to ask it, and he knew he was succumbing to worse sin than before. It was one thing to respond to her when she made the advances, but it was another to be the one initiating their intimacy. He could no longer pretend that he did not seek her love.

"If you wish," she said, a warmth in her voice. "It's also possible simply to be lovers, if you would prefer that."

"No," he said, too quickly, though he was curious to discover what it would be like to lie with her without being transported to the other place. But that would be admitting more than he could bear. "If we can be in such danger, it might be best to scout the activities of the Bundhi."

She turned so that her body met his. "It might be more dangerous than wise, Arkady-champion."

"Not knowing anything would be more dangerous," he said stubbornly. Now that he had gone so far as to ask, he was determined to proceed, no matter how great the risk.

"Perhaps," she said doubtfully. She was still a short while, then said, "I am glad you have asked me, Arkady-champion. I was afraid that you would never want to ask, and that in time you would distrust all that we do together because you never sought it."

She was so close to being accurate that he could not answer her for a moment. "I . . . I am not used to your ways, Surata."

"And there are times that they cause you chagrin," she added for him. "I know that what I do is contrary to what your priests told you. I know that you are disturbed by it, and that does

187

not surprise me, though it . . . saddens me." She kissed his cheek, her tongue brushing the stubble there. "You will have quite a beard soon."

"With no shears to trim it," he said, more pleased with her comment than he could express.

"Buy them, if you wish," she said, grinning toward him.

"I will. With our other supplies." He whistled a bit, suddenly nervous as an untried boy; the tune was a marching song his men had sung before battle. The words rang in his head:

"Saint Michael and Saint Barbara
How bright their banners glow!
For glorious Saint Raffael
We arm against our foe.
The mighty hosts of heaven see,
And promise us the victory!"

"What is that song?" Surata asked.

Arkady stopped whistling and his memories faded. "A soldier's song." It was strange to feel so bashful with a woman he knew so well.

She hesitated. "Do you miss being a soldier, Arkady-immai? No. You don't need to answer," she went on before he could speak. "You miss it very much, don't you?"

"Yes," he admitted.

"And this battle, the one you have taken on with me, does it mean anything to you?" She made no condition with her voice, no implication that he could give her any answer she would not accept.

"I don't know," he said slowly. "I have never fought this way, and there are times it doesn't seem . . . real." He made an apologetic gesture she could not see but was able to sense.

"It is real, Arkady-immai. The other place is real, what we do there is real, and what happens there is real. You saw some of my memories, and you know that the Bundhi will not let you or me or anyone else set against him live. In the other place on in this daily world, he has power and he will not hesitate to use it."

"But..." Arkady did not finish.

Surata went to his side and put her arms around him. "Arkady-champion, you are more able than I am to triumph. You know what it is to fight, and how to fight, which I do not. Tonight, we can... scout? Is that the word?"

"That's the word," Arkady said, bending to kiss her forehead, just where the caste mark was.

Again they waited until the rest of the inn fell silent before she approached him. The room they shared was on the second floor and had three large windows that were shuttered at night against the hordes of demons that were feared as much as the more immediate unpleasantness of insects. Their bed was covered with coarse muslin sheets and two blankets, but it was far too hot for either Arkady or Surata to use them.

"Later, we will want them," Surata whispered as she rolled them toward the foot of the bed.

"But it's so hot," he protested, kicking at the weight of them.

"The night will grow cooler, and after being in the other place, you will be tired. Those who are tired often feel cold." She patted the blankets, then crawled back up the covers to him.

"This Bundhi—where do we look for him this time? In his redoubt, or some other place?" He could not stop himself from chuckling.

"You are amused?" Surata demanded.

"A little. I'm used to scouting in other ways." He still wondered about what she had told him, but he had learned to withhold his doubts.

"Why does this make you laugh?" She was rubbing his chest lightly, her hands describing brisk, interlocking circles on his skin that made him shiver. "Am I tickling you?"

"That's not it." He reached up and stopped her so that he could speak without distraction. "You're more than I thought you were when I... bought you. I don't know what I assumed then, but you're much more."

She smiled, her teeth bright in the shadow of her face. "I know that of you as well, Arkady-champion. You're more than

I thought you were. You are almost what I hoped you were."
Leaning down, she kissed his lower lip, nibbling it gently.

"The Bundhi is a fool to hunt you," Arkady said roughly
as he felt the deep stirrings of desire.

"On the contrary—if he is to have his victory, he is wise."
She resumed the feather-light massage, matching this with a
rain of fast, tiny kisses over his face.

"Surata . . ." He could not stop the long, luxurious shudder
that moved through him, exciting him almost unendurably. He
was so consumed with her that he nearly forgot to breathe.
Then with a low, ecstatic cry, he pulled her to him, rolled onto
and into her

*and the light blossomed around him, engulfing him
in its luminosity. For a moment, he felt he was falling, and
then his hand closed on the sturdy support of a pike shaft; he
found his footing in tall grasses.*

*"This time you must take great care, Arkady my champion,"
Surata warned him from the length of the pike. "The Bundhi
knows this other place far better than you do and can shape it
as he wishes. You are his enemy and he will seek to bring you
down."*

*Arkady looked around him as he might have done at the
edge of a battlefield, looking for the places of advantage and
disadvantage. "You are more his enemy than I am," he said
to her without thinking.*

*"Yes," she responded mournfully. "Because of me, you have
the Bundhi for your enemy."*

*"No matter, Surata. Anyone seeking to harm you will have
to answer first to me."*

*Some of her dejection lifted. "And yet I am the one who is
your weapon." The pike moved in his hand. "You were bruised
in this other place once, and the bruise was with you in the
daily world. Remember that when you fight, your wounds will
be as real to you in the daily world as they are here. And here,
they can be used against you."*

*He did not entirely understand what she meant, but he did
not question her. "I'll do what I can, Surata." Carefully he*

looked over the vast, grassy plain that seemed to stretch farther than any expanse he had ever seen. "We seem alone."

"Seem," she mused. "That's correct. What is there but sky and grass, you wonder, and you are lulled into thinking that you are not watched. But the ground is alive with insects and little animals. You saw what the Bundhi could do with mice in the daily world. He could make far worse than mice here."

"I'll be on guard," Arkady promised and slapped at a mosquito that lit on his arm.

"What was that?" Surata demanded.

"Nothing. A mosquito." He shrugged. "I probably have fleas here, too, just as I do in the daily world."

"How foolish!" Surata burst out, sounding frightened and angry. "I never thought of . . ."

"Surata, don't—"

She did not let him go on. The pike he held became a long maul with a massive head. "Something will have to be done. We must get camphor and Arabian gum, and see that our clothes are redolent with them. We must bathe much more often."

"Surata, what are you going on about?" He did not want to tease her for being too worried, but he also did not want to encourage her in this latest outburst.

"Fleas! Mosquitos! Ticks! They sap the blood, and if the Bundhi has that, he can work magic with it, use it to feed his staves, drain us of more than blood." The maul lifted of its own accord and swung slowly around his head. "If anything— anything at all—bites you, tell me at once. While I am a weapon, there is nothing that can be had from me. Remember, here you shed something more precious than your blood if you are bitten."

Arkady frowned, grasping some of her concern. "But a mosquito, Surata—"

"There are no mosquitos in this other place unless they are conjured, as this grass is conjured, as your weapons are conjured. The Bundhi can come against us in many forms. Why not a mosquito, when you barely notice it?" She sounded impatient but no longer as dread-filled as she had at first.

"Right," he said, accepting her order reluctantly. "But if I have to worry about every gnat and louse, I won't be much use as a scout." His tone was calm enough, but he was not pleased with her. "If the Bundhi's to be found, then—"

"You had best pay attention to gnats and lice and lizards and ants and all the rest of them. Moles in the earth and birds over it, they can all be formed by the Bundhi." The maul twitched ominously. The smell of cedar and camphor spread around him. "These pests are not . . . real as they are in the daily world, but this will serve to aid us. The Bundhi must withdraw the pests or reveal himself in them."

"If you insist," Arkady muttered. "And what am I to do, other than count everything that moves in the grass?" This was not soldier's work and it shamed him to have to do it.

"You are to wait. If there are creatures in the grass, then we must know what they are. If there are things in the sky, watch them. The Bundhi's army comes in many forms, and in this other place, they are more mutable than ever." Now the scent of pyrethrum and wormwood was added to the camphor and cedar.

"Won't all this perfume attract the Bundhi?" he challenged her.

"No more than the stuff taken by the thing that was not a mosquito will," came the somber answer. "Take great care."

Arkady nodded, feeling more apprehensive than he wanted to admit to her. He looked down at his arm where the mosquito had bitten him and saw a mark like the kiss of a leech.

There was a rustling in the grass, and a stoat peered out at him, its narrow snout twisting at the various aromas that filled the air. It was larger than any other stoat Arkady had ever seen, close to the size of a fox. Its eyes were oddly blank.

"What is it?" Surata asked sharply as the maul swung around once more.

"A stoat," Arkady answered in a strange voice. "Over there." He pointed to where he had seen the animal, but it was gone. Not far away from where the stoat had been, three badgers hunkered together, watching him suspiciously.

"And now?" Surata inquired, her maul-self swinging faster so that Arkady felt the strain in his arm from holding it.

"Badgers."

"How many?"

"Three. No, four." He noticed that the animals were moving nearer, not close enough for him to do much about them, but keeping their presence apparent. "And some foxes too."

"It will be bear next," she predicted. "Be careful of the bear, for they might rush you."

"Not wolves?" Arkady asked with forced gaiety. "In Poland, we pay more attention to wolves than bear."

"The Bundhi would send dholes, if he sent coursers." The maul settled, angled in front of him where it could be used swiftly and lethally.

"What happens to the Bundhi if one of these creatures are killed?" Arkady inquired lightly enough, but he was beginning to want to strike back at the elusive sorcerer.

"It depends on what the . . . things are. If they are extensions of the Bundhi himself, their hurt will be his hurt. I do not think," she went on, darkly thoughtful, "that the Bundhi is foolish enough to take such needless risks when he has so many agents to do his bidding."

Five bear, their maws gaping, had ambled up behind the badgers. They stood, heads lowered between their shoulders, snuffling the odors that enveloped Arkady and his maul.

"You were right about the bear," Arkady said softly.

Off to his left, a huge, sinuous shape crept nearer. "What else?" Surata demanded urgently.

Arkady stared at the animal, which held his attention with its beauty as much as its menace. "It's a tiger, I think."

"Yes, a tiger. I should have anticipated that," Surata said with self-condemnation.

The colors and shapes blurred, as if a clumsy artist had smudged a drawing, and then solidified once again.

"What was that?" Arkady said nervously.

Surata did not answer at once. "Insects. Are there insects?"

Arkady had been so intent on the creatures that gathered around them that he had neglected to pay attention to his skin—if he had such a thing as skin in this other place—and what was on it. As she asked, he became aware that his legs and arms were itching, as if he had been set upon by the most voracious lice. He gave a frustrated shout and tried to slap at the places that were the most irritated.

"No!" Surata ordered, swinging upward and lengthening into a halberd, with a long spike and a wicked hook on one side and a hatchet blade on the other. She moved in his hands even while he was trying to scratch, and the swing of the weapon whistled as it sliced toward the advancing animals.

"Watch, Surata!" Arkady shouted as he caught the first, swift rush of the tiger toward them.

The point of the halberd thickened into the striking head of a battle hammer, descending on the rushing cat with deadly force.

The tiger disappeared; in its place, a vulture flapped into the sky.

Arkady, pulled by the weight of his weapon, took a hasty step forward, crying out in dismay as he began to fall.

Chapter 14

Where the grassland had been, there gaped an abyss deeper than anything Arkady had ever seen. In his attempt to keep from falling, he let go of the halberd. "Surata!" he shouted, trying to reach her, to catch her before he, too, dropped

off the side of the bed. The blankets were wrapped around his ankles, and he was still panting and flushed. "God and Saint Michael!"

Surata extricated herself from the tangle of the sheets and reached out for his hand. "Arkady-immai. Are you . . . ?"

His fingers closed on hers. "I am well, Surata," he said in a shaken voice.

"Your legs . . . arms?" There was greater concern in her question. She tried to touch him.

"Insect bites," he admitted shakily. "They sting," he added when he scratched at them.

"Don't. You'll give more blood, and it is like a scent for dogs to follow. If you can, avoid touching them. The Bundhi already has some part of you. Don't let him have blood as well, or we will never be able to escape detection." She held on to his hands tightly.

Arkady felt a tingle where the bites had been, and then a mild numbness took away the irritation. "What . . . did you do?"

"It will last for most of a day," she said, letting go of him and starting to gather up the bedding. "By nightfall, we must be far away from here. The Bundhi will send his minions tonight, and it would not be good for us if they found us. Can you find a vendor of salt before we leave?"

"Salt?" he repeated, puzzled by the request.

"We are going into a hot and arid place. And salt can be used for other things." She had most of the blankets gathered up and was trying to straighten out the sheets. She paused in her work to sniff the muslin. "I like the smell of you, and the smell of us together."

Arkady knew he was blushing; women did not say such things to men. If they mentioned smell at all, it was to compare him to a goat.

Surata was apparently unaware of his discomfort. "There are baths in this place. We must go there before we leave and make sure we clean ourselves with the salt as well as water."

"Salt?" He thought of the bites on his arms and legs and he shuddered. "Not salt, Surata."

"It will not hurt, Arkady-immai," she promised him. "I will make sure of that." By now she had most of the bedding gathered together, their own blankets folded and ready to be packed. "It's almost dawn. We can get up."

"How do you know that?" Arkady asked, not truly doubting that she knew, but unable to figure out how she came to the knowledge.

"Sounds," she said after a little hesitation. "Rhythms. There are scents in the air, in anticipation."

Arkady unbarred one of the windows and looked out. Overhead the sky was slate, but far in the east, there was a silvery tinge. The air was rustling. He stood still, thinking of the many times he had waited for the dawn, knowing that battle would come with it. Twice he had risen late in the night for a camisado attack with his men, but for the most part, dawn had been the signal to prepare to fight.

"Do you still miss your soldiering?" Surata spoke softly, barely above a whisper.

"Sometimes. Perhaps not as much as I thought I would." He closed the window again. "Come here. I'm going to put you in the nun's habit."

"After we have a bath," she told him. "Until then, our other clothes will do. And when we bathe, we can leave them behind to be burned or sold, as the bathhouse owner chooses." She folded her arms, her unseeing eyes staring. "We must move quickly, Arkady-immai. Does that bother you?"

"Only that I don't know what I'm fleeing, or why." He touched one of their packs with his toe. "It won't take long. Shall I tell the ostler to ready our steeds?"

This brought a faint smile to her mouth. "Yes. And I will take care of everything here. How clumsy to have to tend to all this material, when, in the other place, you have only to conjure a thing and it is so."

Arkady laughed obediently and hurried out of the room. He rubbed the places on his arms where the bites were as he hastened to the stable, all the time marvelling that Surata had been able to take away the sting and itch of the bites.

The sun was not far over the roofs of Tana when Arkady and Surata entered the bathhouse. This time the rooms for men were separated from the rooms for women, and they could not be together as they washed. Arkady followed Surata's instructions carefully, cleansing himself three times, once with the rough soap provided by the bath slaves, once with salt and once with clear, cold water. He did not touch his old garments again but donned the priest's robes, taking care to conceal his pouch of gold in the long folds of the black garments.

Before the sun was halfway up the morning sky, Arkady and Surata were outside of Tana, going north and east toward Sarai, the city of the Golden Horde. For the sake of the illusion that they were in religious Orders, Arkady had insisted that

Surata ride one of the mules while he led on his bay gelding. He discovered he missed having her behind him, arms around his waist. That startled him, and he resolved to find the means to resume their old method of travel before too many days had passed.

For three days their journey was uneventful; from time to time they passed other travellers—sometimes large and prosperous caravans, more often smaller bands of merchants, or the occasional solitary wanderer—going toward Sarai, or come from there toward Tana. Although it was not yet the height of summer, the way was hot and dry, with silky dust rising at every step their animals took.

At Surata's insistence they spent their nights in unexpected places: a barn, a deserted hermit's cell, under the branches of a fallow orchard. When Arkady balked at the last, Surata faced him very directly.

"The Bundhi knows that we are coming to him. He knows where we were, and he played with us for a while." She let him think about this. "But the closer we get, the more he will need to stop us. Do you think that he would let us sleep if he knew where we are?"

"If he's as strong as you say, he will be looking for us," Arkady reminded her, a note of doubt in his words.

"Yes, and he will be looking for us in the expected places, which is where we must not be. If one of us has to spend the night in wakefulness, I'd rather it be the Bundhi, not us."

Arkady nodded, smiling a little. "I have heard of fighters, far in the north, who have a way of distressing those who invade their land: whenever the company of invaders camp by a river—and there are many rivers in their land—all night long they send wooden boats downriver past the camp of their enemy. In some of the boats, there is one archer, while others are empty. Yet the enemy cannot take the risk of ignoring one single boat, empty or not, and they pass the night with very little sleep. A few nights of this and the invader no longer wishes to fight, only to sleep in peace."

"You see, you do understand." Surata smiled at him.

"Right," he admitted as he began to plot out their campsite.

For the next week, they went quickly, setting out shortly after dawn and finding shelter at sunset. They pressed for a fast pace during the day, pushing their animals as far as their strength would permit.

"In Sarai, we'll have to get remounts," Arkady said as he examined his gelding. "This old fellow's beginning to feel the press." He patted the bay and set about cleaning his hooves.

"Will you keep him?" Surata asked.

"Probably, but I'd like to have a second horse, just in case." He braced himself to lift the bay's off-hind foot. "We'll need to find a farrier as well—he needs new shoes, and his hooves have to be trimmed. Same thing with the mules." He wielded the hoof pick expertly. "Hard earth hurts their feet, Surata. They'd rather run on grass."

"So would I," Surata said, unwrapping their bedding. They were in the lee of an ancient wooden wall that still showed the marks of charring. "The tinker who told us about this place," she went on in a different tone. "He said it was haunted, didn't he?"

"I think that's what he said. I don't understand much Georgian." He was avoiding her question and they both knew it.

"Did he say—" she began more forcefully.

"Yes," he admitted. "There was something here, a place for unwelcome persons, and it burned down." He indicated the remaining portion of the wall. "There's sign of fire."

"What sort of unwelcome persons?" Surata asked.

"I . . . I'm not sure. I think they might have been mad, or suffering from degenerating disease. I told you I don't know the Georgian tongue well." He had finished with the bay's hooves, so he hobbled the gelding and went to work on the larger mule. "Remind me to keep an eye on these shoes. They're not holding up very well."

"If you wish." She continued with her labors. "Might they have been lepers?"

"It's possible. Why?" He disliked discussing such matters, for the plight of the mad and diseased inevitably left him with a great desolation of spirit.

"There are lepers I have seen who had learned many things

from their afflictions. Some of them acquired power." The blankets were in place and she felt her way toward him. "I'm worried, Arkady-immai."

"I know," he said gently.

"It's been ten days, and nothing has happened." She reached out for him.

"Could it be that we've fooled the Bundhi?"

"By now, he knows we are not staying with other travellers, and therefore he will have changed his manner of searching. He could find a thousand ways to watch us and never reveal himself to us or anyone else." She leaned against him. "I am afraid that we're not as safe as we've hoped."

He sensed how much this confession cost her. "Surata, we can search for him, too," he reminded her. Since they left Tana, they had slept chastely, as much from fatigue as from the unspoken agreement to avoid greater risks by more exploration of the other place.

She gave a long, shaking sigh. "If there is no change after tonight, I fear you're right."

"Fear?" he repeated, stung that she should speak of their joining in such a way.

"Not for loving you," she qualified at once. "I fear that in loving you, I may bring you to harm." She reached up and touched his face. "In Sarai you must buy shears. Your beard is getting like a bramble."

"Lend me your comb and I will do what I can for now," he offered, not letting go of her.

She would not be drawn into banter with him. "When you cut your beard or pare your nails, burn what you cut away."

"I will," he said, not wanting to dispute anything with her now that she had come to him. "The Bundhi puts hounds to shame."

"Yes," she said, frowning to herself. "Is there any honey left, or did we have the last of it yesterday?"

They had gotten a piece of a honeycomb two days before, savoring its sweetness as a special treat. "There's a little left. Some cheese and some dried fruit as well. And a bit of hard bread." He grinned. "If anyone comes near, Surata," he said, hoping to reassure her, "they will think we're ghosts. They will leave us to ourselves in a place with the reputation this has."

Finally her mood lightened. "Yes; I hadn't thought of that." Impulsively she hugged him. "Even the Bundhi would think that this burned place is haunted and would ignore whatever he sensed here. He wouldn't think that we'd take such a risk, if he searched for us here."

"And is there a risk? Is this place haunted?" It was a question he had wanted to ask but did not want to hear answered.

Surata laughed. "Ghosts can't hurt you, Arkady-champion. They are . . . echos. You might hear them, but it would mean little."

This lighthearted explanation did not make Arkady feel more secure. "You mean there *are* ghosts here?" he demanded.

"Oh, yes, of course. They are very miserable ghosts. There is no harm in ghosts, only harm in your fear of them." She moved away from him. "I'm tired, Arkady-champion. My bones ache. I don't understand how you can ride for so long and feel nothing."

"I haven't said I feel nothing," he reminded her. "When you've asked me before, I've said I'm used to it, which I am. I'm a soldier. Long rides and sore bones are part of a soldier's life." He led her back to where she had spread their blankets. "I'll light a fire and then we can have supper."

"I'll take care of the fire," she said, a hint of reproof coloring this.

"Fine," he said, too quickly. "Good." That made it worse.

Surata did not respond, but her silence was louder than words. She made her way through the tall grass, finding bits of wood, some burned, some not, which she gathered and brought near the blankets. She pulled up the grass where she intended to put the wood and then began to place the wood and small dry branches so that they would burn most efficiently. Her back was stiff as she worked, and although it was dusk, Arkady could see that she was upset.

"Surata." He hobbled the second mule and came to her side, kneeling next to her. "Surata, I didn't mean to criticize you. I didn't mean that you weren't able to make a fire. God in Heaven, it's hard enough to remember that you're blind, with all that you can do. If I say things . . . without thinking, well, I hope you can forgive me. I don't mean anything unkind, or . . . or . . ."

She reached over and found his hand. "Arkady-immai, try to understand: my blindness shames me."

"Yes, I know that," he said. "I wish I knew a way to convince you that you have no reason to feel that way."

Her smile was slight and sad. "And I wish I could convince *you* that you have no reason to be shamed by what you and I do when we are joined. You have no reason to be shamed, but you are."

Arkady nodded slowly. "Right."

She lifted his hand and kissed it. "If the ghosts do not bother you, we can go spying tonight, if you are not too tired."

He patted her hand, holding it between both of his. "If I fall asleep, then I'm too tired. If I don't, then I'm not."

This time Surata was able to laugh more openly. "Let's wait, then. Once we've eaten, we'll decide."

"At least we don't have to stay awake until everyone else in the inn is asleep." He got to his feet, releasing her hand reluctantly. "There's work to do."

She made a sign of agreement, then said, "The ghosts will help, Arkady-immai, whether you believe they are there or not. They'll confuse the Bundhi, and we need that. But don't be alarmed by them. Truly, they can't hurt you."

Arkady indicated that he had heard, then did his best to put the whole thing out of his mind. All that he considered was that once again they would be lovers, and that no matter how sinful and damnable their actions, they would be joined in delicious frenzy before the night was gone.

"I think they were mad," Surata said some time later as they rolled into their blankets.

"Who?" Arkady asked, not paying too much attention.

"The ghosts. They feel as if they were. It's more than the

terrible way they died, it's a feel of . . . madness." She slid close to him.

"Surata, don't joke about such things," he warned her, more worried than he cared to admit. "If . . . if there are ghosts here, then they are sent to bedevil us, and it would take a priest to exorcise them." He crossed himself, just in case.

"I'm not joking, Arkady-champion," she said, her lips against his shoulder. "It is a good thing for us that they are there and that they are what they are." With the tip of her tongue she found her way along his collarbone and up his neck, over his beard to his mouth. "I have wanted this."

"Oh, yes," he groaned as he wrapped her in his arms, holding her as if he could absorb her through his skin. There was a distant echo of condemnation in his thoughts, the voice of a priest far away thundering about the evils of the flesh, but Arkady shut the priest away, delving into the mystery that was Surata, exploring her with his body and his senses.

Surata licked his Sixty-Four Petaled Center, murmuring, "You are not as afraid as you once were, Arkady-champion."

It was an effort to speak, so he gave a laugh low in his throat instead. He shivered as she kissed him, then reached for her, impatient for her. His desire—more intense than any lust he had felt—coursed through him, relentless as a river in flood. He wanted to touch, to taste, to *know* her as if they lived in the same body.

"This is good," Surata whispered as his hands slipped between her legs. Her back arched as he moved over her, and she opened to him as he went deeply into her, sighing her name

so that the echos of "Surata" made the colors around him change, becoming more luminous and brilliant from his love.

"We will have to take care," his chain mail reminded him. "The Bundhi has been waiting for us to try something. It must be that he anticipates some action from us."

"Then we must be more prepared," Arkady observed quietly.

Surata did not speak for a moment. "Do you want to try to reach his redoubt again?"

"Not if I have to go through more chasms," Arkady an-

swered, faintly amused. "It might be entertaining for a sorcerer, but for a soldier, it is simply hard work."

His chain mail jingled in a feeling that was part sympathy, part laughter. "Arkady my champion, you are proud of your ability to endure these things. You would be disappointed if you were given a clear path and an easy assault."

He did not reply to that accusation at once, but finally he smiled. "True."

"And the redoubt? What do you want to do?" Surata persisted. "We can go there directly, we can approach it many different ways, but how you wish to go is up to you."

"If the Bundhi can sense when we approach, then there must be some way that he would not notice, or would not anticipate," Arkady said, thinking aloud.

"But what, Arkady my champion?" she asked patiently.

He thought a bit longer, then chuckled. "It's too bad we can't fly. A man in such a fortress is watching the ground, not the sky. And small wonder," he added in a more critical tone.

"Why can't we fly?" Surata said. "Do you think it isn't possible?"

"I haven't got wings," he reminded her, holding his arms to the side.

"But I can become wings for you. I can be any weapon you need, and if that means wings, so be it." The chain mail slithered and slid over him, gathering at his back and clumping there. It chimed softly, then changed, stretching out, expanding, until two huge expanses of silver feathers framed him and towered over him. "It will take this much to lift you, if you wish to remain as you are."

He was caught up in the wonder of this transformation and so took a little time before he said, "I wish I could do the things that you can do. To be able to alter so much..."

"It takes many years of study, Arkady my champion. As much as I would wish it, I cannot learn to be a fighter in a week or a year. To have your skill, I would have had to begin as a child, as you did." Her voice in the wings was breathless, softer than the clarion chain mail.

"I suppose you have the . . . ." He shrugged and felt the wings ride on his shoulders with the movement. "How far is it to this redoubt?"

"How far is anything in this other place?" she asked. "It is where it is. We will fly there and find it as quickly as we can. The more closely joined we are, the faster we will go."

She had never before made reference to the duality of their existence when they were in this other place, and it took him aback to hear her mention it now. "Surata, what we are doing . . . ."

"We are united, Arkady my champion. Our Subtle Bodies are linked as our flesh is linked. We are still in the daily world, and our fulfillment in each other is the riding of the wave that brings us here." The huge wings expanded and cupped the air, beating slowly at first and then faster. "As long as we are united, then this, the Divine Child of the Jiva, can be freed in this other place. The way we are here is the offspring of how we are in the daily world. If we should end our lovemaking, or if there should be discord between us in our joined bodies, then we could not be able to function in this other place. That is why the Bundhi wishes to disrupt us and cause . . . frictions between us that will interrupt our joining." They were into the air now, soaring through a sky that was as many-hued as a rainbow.

The wings were silent, beating steadily, carrying him with a sureness that heartened him. Below them there were shapes in the bright patterns that might be land, but it was impossible to tell with any certainty, for this other place was so malleable that nothing here was immutable.

"There's something up ahead," Arkady said after a passage of time—whether it was long or short, he had no way of knowing. "Do you think it's the redoubt?"

"It may be," Surata whispered in the rush of the wings.

"It looks like the fortress we saw before," he said, not quite as certain as he had been.

"Yes, but that means little here." The wings spread, holding him in a slow, steady turn over the steep-rising mountains below. "This may be a sham, a false image established to turn our attention away from the real stronghold."

"Then how can we ever know if we are actually battling the Bundhi and are not simply wasting our strength on illusions?" he asked, feeling the cold touch of despair within him.

"We will know," she said grimly. *"Do not give way, Arkady my champion, or . . ."*

("Surata," he breathed, her hair moist against his brow. "I don't think . . . God, I can't hold back . . ." Her mouth was warm and open under his.

("Slowly," she murmured when she could speak at all. "Go very slowly, Arkady-champion. Slowly." She moved so that he could penetrate her more fully and moaned with the pleasure of him.)

"Surata!" He felt dizzy, disoriented in the shifting lights.

The wings flapped listlessly, then opened, holding him in a steady coasting while he strove to regain his equilibrium once more. He was giddy with fear and exhilaration, and was not certain which was greater. The mountains beneath them wavered, shrank and rose again, as the space around them turned blue and clear at last.

"Hold on, Arkady my champion," Surata called in the beating of his wings. *"Hold on."*

He could not answer but did not have to. He all but willed himself to ascend, rushing higher than he would have dared to go before.

Far below them, the redoubt of bamboo staves loomed over the crags. It was livid as a bruise and filled with menace.

"What do you think? Is it the Bundhi?" Arkady asked as they swung over the peaks.

"It may be," she said again. *"I hope it is."*

"Why hope?" he said.

"Because it would mean he does not know we have come so close once more. If the Bundhi knew we were near, he would seek to show us illusions and other distortions. This may be just that, and a very persuasive one, but I doubt it." She carried them in a long arc that brought them directly over the redoubt. *"It does not look as if it is an illusion, unless the Bundhi is aware that he must attend to his citadel from above as well as below."*

"You don't believe it, do you?" he asked. "You're afraid that he does know we're here and is seeking to divert us from our goal." He could feel her lack of conviction in the movement of his wings, but how it could be, he had no idea.

"Yes," she said finally, and they dropped a little in the air. *"Yes, I am afraid that the Bundhi has anticipated us and has already made up this ruse to . . ."*

When she did not finish, Arkady said for her, *"To keep us from his real stronghold. That is what worries you the most, isn't it?"*

"It is." The wings beat steadily, but there was no more from her but the force of their flying.

"And if this is the redoubt, what then?" he asked her when they had circled the fortress for the third time.

"Then we must find a way to destroy it, and to end the protection it gives the Bundhi, both here in this other place and in the daily world." She sounded hopelessly determined and it touched his heart to hear her.

"Surata, don't. You have courage and dedication and—"

"You had those things and you were cast out of your own ranks for them," she reminded him.

"Listen to yourself," he said when he could think of no reasonable argument. *"You warned me that the Bundhi could sap your strength with doubt, and you are the one who is questioning everything here. I have no way of knowing what is and is not right in this other place; you do. If you can't be certain of what is here, how can I?"* He was not angry, and there was nothing in his voice but his concern. *"Surata?"*

She did not answer him, but his wings carried him more quickly, and that gave him hope.

(He felt his release start to build, from the base of his spine to his throat; his body strained against its demand.)

The redoubt shuddered, the bamboo staves quivering as if they could sense the two far overhead. A soundless wail drifted up to them, as eerie and frightening as the cry of wolves in a winter's night.

"They sense us," Surata cautioned.

"This is the Bundhi's redoubt, then?" Arkady asked, feeling terribly vulnerable.

"Yes. And they will be hunting us if—" She had no chance to complete her warning; he trembled in the embrace of the wings.

"Su

rata," he cried as his body succumbed to its need, and she pressed tightly to him, shaking and laughing with him as the air around them snapped and quivered with the turmoil of the disturbed, unhappy ghosts.

Chapter 15

For the next three days, they went even faster, driving their animals and themselves to the limits of their strengths. Only when the larger mule went lame did they stop their flight, knowing that to do anything else was folly.

"We could abandon the mule," Arkady suggested without enthusiasm.

"And half our supplies," Surata added. "It wouldn't matter. The Bundhi's agents would find it, and they would know too much."

"It takes more than the threat of a spy to frighten me." His bravado fooled neither of them. "Besides, with your insistence on baths every other day, and making me darken my hair and beard, who would know me?"

"The Bundhi follows other trails," she sighed. "Arkady-immai, I know you want to cheer me; I wish I could be cheered."

Arkady patted the rump of the lame mule. "All right: I admit I'm worried. But I won't be dispirited. That's doing the Bundhi's work for him." He put his hand on her shoulder.

"We're not far from a village, it won't take us long to walk there, and they must have a farrier and a smithy. I can get another shoe for the mule and see if he can go on."

"Better buy another mule," she said. "I know it is more than the shoe. It is the hoof." Her eyes were fixed in the middle distance, as clouded as fine opals.

Arkady did not dispute this. "And if we can't find another mule, what then?"

"An ass, a horse, it doesn't matter. So long as we can travel."

"What about staying there for the night? It will be late afternoon by the time we get to the village. You need rest, Surata. One of the reasons you're downhearted is that you're exhausted."

There were tears gathering in her eyes now, very shiny. "I realize that. But it frightens me."

"Oh, Surata." He put his arm around her shoulder. "Listen to me, girl. I'm a soldier, I have better sense than you."

She tried to laugh, sobbed instead, as she rested her head against his neck. "Much better sense."

"No trooper fights well tired. It's worse than hunger and wounds, because it slows you down, it distorts your judgment and makes you hesitate when you should act. With a foe like this Bundhi, if you hesitate, you're damned. One good night's sleep will make all the difference."

"Sleep?" she asked, with the hint of provocation in her tone.

"Sleep," he repeated emphatically. "I need it too."

She patted his back. "You've convinced me."

"Good." He kissed the top of her head and stepped away from her. "I'm going to put you on my horse and I'll lead all of you. We'll make better time that way."

Though he had not said it, she added for him, "It would be faster, wouldn't it, if you don't have to wait for me to shuffle after you."

"Stop that," he ordered her. "I'll take almost anything from you, Surata, but not self-pity."

This brought her chin up. "I was not being self-pitying, just saying what is obvious."

"I won't argue about it," he said firmly as he took the reins of his gelding and led the bay nearer to her. "Get ready to mount."

"Arkady-immai . . ." She was uncertain now, and once she said his name, she faltered.

"What is it? We don't have time to waste." He could sense something in the air, the same sort of tension that he had felt before he learned of the ambush, the same he had felt on the eve of losing a battle. "There's thunder in the air," he said aloud, to explain his feelings to himself.

"It's not that," Surata said, her face averted. "Help me up."

Silently he tossed her into the saddle, then went for the two mules. The irregular clop of the animals' hooves was all that passed between them for most of the walk to the village.

Surprisingly, no barking dogs hearalded their approach. The whole collection of rush-thatched huts was unnaturally still. No livestock bleated or grunted or lowed, no birds shrilled.

"What is it?" Surata asked as Arkady slowed them to a walk.

"I don't know," he answered. "It's as if . . . no one's here."

"How close are we?" Surata said, her head cocked to the side.

"Close enough. Someone should have noticed us by now." He could see the door of a shed swinging lazily on the summer breeze.

Cautiously they entered the village, only to find it deserted. The squat houses stood untenanted, the barns and pens were empty. Nothing, not a chicken, not a rat, moved in the stillness.

"This is the Bundhi's doing," Surata said from her seat on the bay, for Arkady had refused to permit her to dismount.

"Surata . . ." He could not continue; he had no other explanation to offer for what they had found, and it perplexed him to see no reason for the place to be empty.

"An emergency would not take all the animals," Surata said, anticipating Arkady's protests. "There would be signs that the people had left in a hurry, but not that they had never been here."

"Maybe there was a battle nearby and they decided to take all that they had. It's happened before." He did not believe this, but he wanted to.

"Then why are there wagons in the barn? You said you found three of them." She did not want to ask him this and both of them knew it. "There is food in the houses, and fuel in the sheds, you said so yourself. The water is not brackish in the pails you found, so they cannot have been gone long. The smell of pigs and sheep still lingers." She shifted in the saddle, patting the bay when he gave an uneasy rumble in his throat.

Arkady felt the same distress that his gelding did, but he would not allow himself to surrender to it. "I'm going to make a thorough search. I haven't examined everything."

"And what do you think there is to find—skeletons?" She stopped herself. "Forgive me, Arkady-immai. I am not being sensible, am I?"

"I don't blame you," he responded. "Do you want to come down? It may take me some time to look everywhere." He held his arms up to her.

"Even if something happened, I could not see where to go, and this poor creature would not know what to do with me," she said, resigned to their uncertainty. "Let me down, by all means." She felt for his hands and came out of the saddle. "Find me a place where you will be able to reach me quickly, if you must."

"By the well," Arkady said at once. "That's central. There's three houses close to it, and a cattle barn." He led her and their three animals to the well. "Don't let them drink. You can give them their nosebags, if you want."

"Better not," she said as she almost stumbled beside him. "If we must leave quickly, it wouldn't be—"

"You're right," he interrupted. "Well, watch them for me."

"Of course," she said, taking a seat on the wooden bench beside the well where he had led her. "I'll try to find out . . . anything I can while you search."

It was almost sunset when he came out of the bathhouse,

pale and shaken, to tell her that there was a body. "It's a man," he went on. "Dead. Young. No more than a day dead."

"What is it?" she asked sharply, hearing the strain in his voice.

"He . . . he's pretty horrible."

"Plague?" she ventured.

"I don't think so," he replied carefully. "I've never seen a death like this before." He was shaken, and he sat down beside her abruptly. "He's . . . very white."

"Oh?" She wanted to know more but knew better than to press him. "Why does that bother you?"

"There are other marks . . . " He shut his eyes and swallowed hard. "I . . . I found him in the bathhouse. He was . . . just lying there peacefully. He was as calm as an old, old Saint dying in the odor of sanctity." Automatically he crossed himself, aware that his hand shook as he did it. "But there were marks."

"What marks?" Surata demanded, her patience almost gone.

"You remember the mosquito bite I had in the other place? The one that looked as if a leech had been at me? They were like that only . . . much larger. Much, much larger. As big as the palm of my hand, and . . . deep. They had . . . sunk into him." He had not been speaking loudly, and by the time he had finished, he was barely whispering.

"The Bundhi. I said it was the Bundhi," Surata said, her hands knotted together in her lap. "He took them all. Every one of them. He's taken them and made them . . . his."

"A whole village, dogs and all?" Arkady asked in disbelief. "How could he do a thing like that?"

"I've said he's powerful. He yearns for destruction, and each destruction adds to his power." Suddenly she reached out for him, holding on to him as if he were keeping her from drowning. "If the whole world disappeared, he would be content and pleased."

Before he found the young man's corpse, Arkady might have doubted her; now he nodded dumbly. He pressed her head to his shoulder, his hand stroking her hair to soothe himself more than her. He could not get the picture of that pallid body out of his mind, nor the red, red circular impression that covered most of his skin.

"He wants us to know he did this. That's why you found that body, just the one." She shuddered. "The staves took him. They fed on him."

"The bamboo?" he said numbly. "The bamboo did that?"

She put her arms around his waist, moving closer still. "I didn't know he had advanced so far. It's been little more than a year, and he has gained all that strength."

Arkady had no answer for her. He did not want to think of facing an enemy capable of making a whole village cease to exist. They sat together as the sky grew darker.

It was twilight when they left the village. "He will know where we're going now, I think," Surata said listlessly as she got onto their sound mule. Arkady held the animal's head for her, steadying her so she could mount.

"We'll get another in Sarai. We'll get three mules." He tried not to think about what they had found, but he did not succeed entirely. "We can't go very far tonight, but at least we can get away from here. That's something."

"For what little it is worth," she added for him. "There will be other agents. He is amusing himself with us. That's clear. If he thought we might actually be able to fight him, we'd be one with those villagers, wherever they are."

"Maybe they're with the ghosts in the burned madhouse." He had intended this to be funny, but it came out badly and he looked away from her. "I'll get mounted."

"We could turn around, Arkady-immai," she said in a small voice. "We could go back."

"To where?" he asked as he mounted his bay. "Where would you be safe?"

"I don't know. There might be somewhere." There was only a forlorn hope in this, no confidence at all.

He turned in the saddle to face her. "And if you could find this place, could you rest there, Surata?"

She did not answer him at once. "I would try."

"Well, I wouldn't. I've been dishonored once. I will not be

dishonored again, not even for you." He jabbed his heels into the bay and swayed as the horse lurched into a canter. The mule snorted and brayed as it was dragged after them.

"Arkady-immai!" she shouted, clinging to the saddle desperately. "Arkady-immai!"

He slowed his horse and the mule at once. Behind them he could hear the abandoned lame mule bray to the others as it tried to follow after them, limping painfully.

Surata had steadied herself and turned her head back toward the other mule. "I hate to leave him in this place."

"So do I. But he will slow us down and ... Surata, his hoof is split. There's nothing I can do for him but put my last arrow into his skull."

"No. Not that." She held up her hands in protest. "Let him do the best he can. Don't kill him."

"I won't," he promised her. "But he might suffer and die, no matter what we do for him."

"We all suffer and die," she said, some of her tranquility returning. "Arkady-immai, there is nothing to fear in death. We will come to life again."

She had told him similar things before, and he always shied away from such heresy. "We will come to life in God," he said curtly in order to end her comments.

She said nothing for a long moment. "I do not want to turn away from the Bundhi. If he attempts too much, there will be nothing to return to. If I die, then there will be karma that will bring me ... whatever I deserve."

Arkady shrugged. "Whichever of us is right, *I* won't turn away from the Bundhi."

"You can do nothing against him without me," she reminded him with a wry smile.

"And you can do nothing without me," he said, his smile echoing hers. He wondered if she knew it somehow.

"If that is the way it must be," she said, then added hesitantly, "Arkady-immai, I do not want you to die because of me."

"And I don't want you to die because of me. You see,

Surata? We're in perfect agreement." He started his gelding moving again, but this time at a walk. "A little way and then we'll find a place to sleep. Tomorrow or the next day, we should reach Sarai, and then we can choose the supplies we'll need."

"And there is still enough gold?" she asked.

"Enough. Not as much as we might like to have, but yes, certainly enough. I will even have money for arrows."

"This time, get more then ten," she suggested. "The ones you bought in Tana did not last long."

"They never do. Even if I recover them, they are often no longer true." He remembered the archers he had fought with years ago, all of whom had complained that an arrow once fired could not be counted on to fly straight.

She rode quietly, letting him choose the pace and their direction while she strove to regain her inner peace.

A little while later, as he drew them up beside a wide, shallow stream, he said to her, "I know you better than I have ever known anyone in my life; I see you more clearly than I've seen anyone; I love you more than I've loved anyone: yet you're an enigma to me." He was not upset and he said this placidly enough, but he knew as he spoke that words alone were inadequate, and that saddened him. "Surata . . ."

"I know," she said as he hesitated. "I'm hungry, Arkady-immai, and I'm frightened. Can we sit together and talk about, oh, the games we played when we were children, or what we ate at great feasts? I don't think I can speak of other things yet."

"Right," he said, relieved. As he dismounted, he heard the distant sound of the lame mule trying to catch up with them.

The next night they slept within sight of Sarai, and by noon the day after they were in the shadow of its walls. Here, east of the Don, west of the Vulga, the Kazakh city served as a crossroad for Asian merchants bound northward to Moskva and Novgorod and westward to Tana, Venice and Constantinople. A century before it had been ripe with prosperity, but since the men of Islam had taken up the sword against Christians, Sarai had suffered as trade and traffic diminished.

Arkady regarded the battlements with a critical eye. "There hasn't been any real fighting here for a little while. The walls are in good repair and there's only a token Guard on watch."

"Is that good?" Surata asked.

"Well, we're not arriving between skirmishes; that's something," he remarked. "By the look of it, they aren't expecting any attack or enemy soldiers to come soon."

"What enemy?" Surata asked.

"Islamites, Cossacks, Russians, who knows? There are Tartars on this side of the Don." He looked along the battlements again. "They haven't got very new equipment up there."

"Perhaps they have it elsewhere."

"I doubt it," Arkady said as he caught sight of an inn outside of the walls. "There's a place we can stay and we won't have to answer too many questions."

"Why would we have to answer questions?" she wanted to know.

"Because we're foreigners and we aren't merchants. That makes us suspect. I carry arms and I have the look of a soldier. That makes it worse." He interrupted himself to signal a young merchant in Lithuanian clothes. "Hey! You there!" He knew very little of the Lithuanian language, but enough to get a meal and good directions.

"You talking to me?" the young merchant cried, astonished to hear his own tongue in this remote place.

"I am," Arkady said as pleasantly as he could. "I need a little . . . advice." He hoped he had the word right.

"At your service. I'm Lauris Trakiv." He bowed to Arkady, ignoring Surata completely.

"Arkady Sól," he responded at once. "From Sól."

"Where's that?" Lauris asked, cordial and curious.

"Poland. Not far from Sandomierz." He saw the Lithuanian's smile broaden.

"I know some Polish," he said in that language. "Not much, but enough to get by. My grandmother's a Pole."

"My uncle married a Lithuanian," Arkady answered at once and was certain that he had the interest of the younger man. "You're a long way from home, Trakiv."

"Lauris," the young merchant said warmly. "We're practically cousins." He cocked his head. "You looking for a place to stay the night, get a meal, have a bath?"

"Yes," Arkady said baldly. "I hoped that you might be able to guide me. That inn by the wall, there"—he pointed to the one that he had noticed earlier—"what of that place?"

"Not bad. Russians own it. They take in all kinds of Christians. No questions asked. But there's another place, around the corner of the wall. Greeks own it, and it's more pleasant. More costly too."

Both of them laughed and Arkady said, "That's a Greek for you."

"The food's good, they have a bathhouse, they take in everyone but Islamites, and that's because the Islamites start arguments and brawls, or so they say." He gave a jovial wave of his hand. "I don't mind an occasional good grapple, but those fellows, they carry knives, and they like to use them." He cleared his throat. "Wine's good too."

"Excellent. Show me where I can find this Greek paradise," Arkady chuckled. "And then, if you are willing, I'd like to know where there's a good horse dealer, and a good fletcher."

Lauris wagged his head from side to side. "In a hurry, are you, soldier?"

"Yes," Arkady said with no apology for his brusqueness.

It was obvious that Lauris would have asked more but could think of no pretext to do so. He made a gesture showing that he would be willing to accommodate them.

"Arkady-immai, who is this man?" Surata asked softly as they followed him through the bustle that swarmed around the walls of Sarai.

"He is a Lithuanian; he comes from a country that is next to mine. He's probably a rogue, but he can help us, I think." Arkady smiled, then said, "I don't mind rogues. A great many of them have been soldiers at one time or another. This one is a merchant. I'll find out how he comes to be here a little later."

"Where is he taking us?" she persisted.

"To an inn run by Greeks. They probably pay him something

to provide them customers, but that doesn't trouble me." He had to admit, if only to himself, that he was grateful to find someone as familiar as this Lithuanian in this remote and foreign city. It made him feel less a stranger himself.

"And then what?"

"We'll see. We'll get more supplies, more pack animals, and try to find out what lies ahead. It's unfortunate that it's summer. The journey will be hotter than the inner circle of hell, but for all I can tell, the winter is worse." He peered through the crowd, keeping an eye on Lauris.

"He's not taking us to a robbers' den, is he?" Surata asked.

"I don't think so," he answered. "We don't look prosperous enough."

They threaded their way around the tower in the wall, hurrying to keep up with Lauris. They passed merchants on donkeys and mules and horses and camels. Some were swathed and turbaned, some were in layers of rough silk, some were golden-skinned, some were bronze. There were large groups of children, and beggars who held out their hands and bowls for the occasional coins that might be dropped for them.

"Here! Here!" Lauris called out in excitement. He stood in the gateway of a large inn, waving them forward. "This is the Greeks' place. You see, a Pole like you will like it."

Arkady had to say that it was a pleasant surprise. "I owe you for bringing us to this place." He held out two silver coins. "Take them."

"Thank you for that, soldier," Lauris said, whisking the coins into one of the capacious pockets of his long woollen cote. "The owner is named Eudoxius. When the Turks came to Constantinople, his family came here, or so he claims."

"It looks pleasant enough," Arkady decided aloud as he rode into the innyard. "There is a bathhouse, Surata, and the stable is good-sized."

Lauris came up beside him. "Where are you bound, soldier?"

"Samarkand," Arkady answered, knowing it was true enough, though not the end of their journey.

"Ho!" Lauris exclaimed. "You've a way to go. And in summer too. You'd better buy some of those Tartar robes if you don't want to be baked before you get there." He stood by the bay's head while Arkady dismounted. "No wonder you want more pack animals. Are you taking the woman with you, or are you going to sell her here?"

Arkady's expression hardened. "She goes with me," he said tightly.

Lauris brought his palms up and shook his head. "No offense, soldier. I didn't mean anything. If you wanted to sell her, I know someone who'd take it on, but—"

"She's not for sale," Arkady told Lauris in a soft, steely tone.

"Sure. Fine." He backed away and covered this retreat by indicating the entrance to the public room of the inn. "If you go in there, Eudoxius will be happy to provide you a room and whatever else you want."

"You're being very good to us," Surata said suddenly, making both men turn to her.

Lauris colored to the roots of his fair hair. "I didn't think you knew enough..."

"My owner has taught me to speak his language," Surata went on. "He would not go to that trouble if he intended to sell me, would he?"

"Of course not," Lauris said, babbling now. "You have to understand, in a place like this, there's always an active slave market, and a man with...well, it...I..." He ducked into the door and called for a servant.

"He works for a slaver," Arkady said softly to Surata. "Be careful of him."

"I will," she vowed. "With men like this about, the Bundhi need not bother with risking his agents."

"I'll keep my cinquedea with me all the time." He patted the back of his belt where the little knife was concealed. "If he tries to take you, he'll find this blade through his hand."

Eudoxius came bustling out of his inn, bowing obsequiously to Arkady. "A Pole!" he said with a heavy accent. "Very rare."

Arkady gave him a gold coin. "I and my slave will need food and a bath. Our mounts should be watered and fed. We will want a room for the night and food in the morning."

"Just one night? The kyrios knows that in Sarai it is difficult for a stranger to buy supplies and that such transactions always take time." He spoke in Greek and Lauris translated for him.

"Then I'd better start now." He had intended to leave Surata to rest at the inn, but he no longer thought she would be safe. "My slave and I will bathe now, and when it is cooler in the afternoon we will go to see what we can purchase without a long wait." He smiled at both men and went to help Surata dismount, whispering to her as he let her down, "Be clumsy. Clumsy slaves are not as attractive."

"Shall I stumble as well?" she offered.

"If you like." He took her by the arm and started across the innyard to the door, biting his cheeks to keep from smiling when she managed to trip twice.

"Blind and clumsy as well," Lauris said, shaking his head. "She must be very good in other ways."

"She was part of my battle prize," Arkady lied. "You know what commanders can be like when it comes to awarding battle prizes—they keep the gold for themselves and parcel out the rest as they see fit."

"You must not have been a favorite with your commander," Lauris sniggered as he pointed toward the public room. "There may be Islamites all around us, but here a man can find a cup of wine if he wants one." He straddled a bench between two tables. "Join me in a cup, soldier. Wash the dust out of your throat."

Arkady knew that it would be insulting to refuse. "One cup *would* please me. Let's have it while Eudoxius gets the bath-house ready." He sat Surata at the table across from Lauris, pretending he had not noticed the look exchanged by Lauris and the Greek landlord.

Eudoxius bent at the waist and through Lauris told Arkady that he would hasten to the bathhouse just as soon as he had brought their wine.

"The wine's from Hungary," Lauris explained. "They bring it twice a year, four big barrels of it on bandy-legged mules." He slapped the table with the flat of his hand. "It's good to hear Polish again. I go for most of the year without seeing a proper Christian. These Russians are hardly worthy of the name, the way they carry on."

"I confess that I was growing very lonesome for a few familiar words," Arkady said, looking up as Eudoxius approached with a tray with two large earthenware cups.

"There you are!" Lauris shouted at Eudoxius as if the landlord were in the next room. "In good time. Wine for the soldier first, then for me. That's the right way." He was speaking Polish for Arkady's benefit, but Eudoxius knew what was expected and served Arkady first. He bowed to both men, then hurried away, calling to someone at the rear of the building.

"Well, to Poland and Lithuania, then," Lauris toasted heartily, lifting his cup high.

Arkady reached for his cup, but before he could grab it, Surata turned toward him and upset the cup as she steadied herself with her arm. "Surata!" Arkady burst out.

"Master . . . do not . . . Master, I am sorry," she uttered faintly, cringing as if waiting for a blow from his hand. "I did not mean to . . . Master, don't . . ."

Wine spread over the table and ran into Arkady's lap. He glared at her. "Slave, you will try your luck too far one day."

"Master." She bowed her head and blocked her face with a raised arm.

Lauris let out a long whistle. "You sure you want to keep a creature like that? What's she good for, beyond the obvious?"

Arkady did not trust himself to answer. He stood up. "Come, slave. We'll get out to that bathhouse at once. You'd better find a reason for what you did." Saying this, he seized Surata by the elbow and dragged her to her feet. "Now, slave."

Surata quivered and winced. "I will do what you ask, Master."

"Yes, you will," he bullied, tugging her after him as they went the direction that Eudoxius had gone. "And when we come back from the bathhouse, you'll make your apology to Lauris for spilling the wine."

"Yes, Master," she said, her chin quivering as if she might burst into tears at one more harsh word.

Arkady stormed through the kitchen, still railing at Surata, and continued to upbraid her as they went across the rear of the innyard toward the bathhouse. Only when they were inside and Eudoxius had been given four copper coins and told to go away did Arkady's demeanor change. "All right," he said in his normal voice, "what was it? Poison?"

"Yes. There was a smell of almonds in the wine." She shivered and this time it was no performance. "They wanted to be rid of you. Who knows—the rulers of the city might pay a price for a dead Christian, especially if he is a soldier."

Arkady took her in his arms. "Surata, Surata." He had no words to tell her of his gratitude.

"There is danger here," she said with no particular emotion.

"We're used to danger. Aren't we?" He bent and kissed her forehead. "We'll have to be very careful."

She almost laughed. "To think that a greedy slaver and an innkeeper might do the Bundhi's work for him."

"Very amusing," he said sarcastically. "Come on; we'd better bathe now that we're here."

Chapter 16

By the following evening, Arkady had found another horse and three mules as well as tack for all of them. He had paid more than he wanted, but there were still a good many gold coins left in the little leather sack, and he counted himself lucky that he had been asked no more difficult questions by the city Guard than where he had come from in Poland and who had commanded his fighting troops in Hungary. He had had some trouble in finding a fletcher and even more in persuading the man that it was acceptable to sell arrows to a foreigner. Finally one of the Guard officers had been summoned and gave the fletcher permission to sell Arkady two dozen arrows, for which the fletcher charged more than twice his usual fee.

"But," as Arkady told Surata that evening as they ate a salad of cold cooked grain, shelled nuts and shelled peas with sliced lemons, "it could have been much worse. It's because I'm only passing through and have no one with me but a blind female slave. I gave the Guard my word that we would be gone by day after tomorrow at the latest, and that we would not return for at least six months."

"They have strange ways, these Guards," she said thoughtfully. "As if six months would make a difference if you were determined to do the city harm."

Arkady shrugged. "Well, they required it, and I gave them my word as a soldier."

"Did they respect it?" She turned her head, raising an admitory finger toward him. "Did they?"

Puzzled, Arkady watched her as she listened, and after a brief pause, he answered her question with all the appearance of calmness. "They seemed to. A soldier's word should be binding—faithful unto death are often the terms, after all."

"But if you . . ." She stopped, concentrating on something that Arkady could not sense. "If you had already given your word elsewhere to be faithful unto death?"

"But that is not the way it's done," Arkady said reasonably, leaning toward her as he spoke. "What is it?" he whispered to her.

She shook her head, but continued to give her attention to whatever it was. "Have more of the food, Master. You must not neglect your body in this way, for on the road ahead, there may not be much to eat."

Arkady helped himself to more of the salad. "Speaking of food, I have been to the marketplace, and tomorrow morning before we leave, I will take you there so we may gather up everything we need for the next leg of the journey to Samarkand." He said this a bit more loudly, in case they were being overheard.

"Good." She signaled him to continue.

"That will get us and the animals through a month of travel at the least, and that is all we need to the next market town, no matter how slowly we travel. They say it should take sixteen to eighteen days to reach the northern shore of the Caspian Sea."

"Then supplies for a month would be more than enough." She turned her hand so that her fingers pointed toward the door leading to the kitchen. "You are very wise, Master."

"I'm glad you realize that," Arkady told her, staring at the doorway. "Oh." He feigned surprise. "Lauris. I didn't know you were there."

The Lithuanian came slowly into the public room where Arkady and Surata were having their meal. "I've just come back from visiting with . . . my uncle."

"The one you told me about while we were buying arrows?" Arkady asked with an expression of mild curiosity. "He's a merchant, you said, didn't you?"

"Yes. He has no sons and has been teaching me his trade." Lauris coughed diplomatically. "When I told him about you, he said he was eager to meet you. He misses our homeland."

"It's a pity that I'm leaving tomorrow. I would have liked to meet him myself." Arkady indicated the remains of their meal. "We were going to retire shortly. The ride ahead is a rigorous one, from what I've been told."

Lauris looked distressed. "But Arkady, night has just fallen. You needn't go to bed quite yet. There is still time for you to come with me to my uncle's house. It would give him great pleasure to entertain you for an hour or so."

"That's kind," Arkady said. "Another time I would be delighted, but . . . no, it wouldn't be prudent. The Guard was not suspicious of me today, but if I were to visit another foreigner, then it might be another matter. I don't want to repay your hospitality and the offer of your uncle by bringing you such misfortune."

"But . . ." Lauris glared at him. "He won't like this."

"I am shocked to know that I have caused him displeasure," Arkady responded.

"He was anxious to tell you," Lauris said with renewed intensity, "of the troubles his men have had crossing the lands of the Khan of Astrakhan."

"But we have already come through the Crimea without mishap," Arkady said, thinking that the problems they had encountered had little to do with the Khan. "The Cossacks here have left us alone. Why would it not be the same in Astrakhan?"

"There is fighting," Lauris insisted. "And you have a woman with you."

"What Islamite cares for that?" Arkady chuckled. "From what I have been told they prefer the backside of a boy any day. More fool they."

Lauris took a step closer. "Soldiers' words," he spat.

"I'm a soldier," Arkady agreed, unruffled. "Tell your uncle that I'm grateful for his invitation but that it would not be sensible to join him this night. A successful merchant like your uncle will certainly understand that I mean him no offense, but that I have tasks I must accomplish. The Guard expects me to leave, and leave I will." He tossed two more coins to Lauris, one silver, one brass. "Take these with my . . . appreciation, Trakiv. You have been very generous with a stranger." Rising, he tapped Surata on the shoulder. "Come, slave. It is almost time to sleep."

"Yes, Master," she murmured obediently.

"What will I tell my uncle?" Lauris called out as they left the public room for their chambers.

"Be sure you brace the door," Surata said softly as they ascended the stairs.

"I'll do more than that. I wish I had a crossbow." He guided her into the room, and while she gathered their things together, he rigged a deadfall over the door.

"Did you get the clothes you wanted?" she asked as Arkady began to undress.

"Yes. Lauris thought I was buying a tent—which I did— but I found desert robes for both of us, and a good shirt of chain mail. Even if Lauris wants to find us, he will be looking for the wrong thing."

"There are the mules and the horses," Surata reminded him.

"He hasn't seen them. He knows my bay and that's all." He set out the clothes he intended to wear the next day. "It's odd," he said as he pulled off his boots. "When I was a captain, I owned two horses, a mule, my weapons, tack and two kinds of armor. Now that I am disgraced and fleeing for my life, I have mules and horses and new armor and six sets of clothes, more tack than ever before, my weapons, gold and a slave."

"The Wheel turns for all of us," she said as she slipped under the sheet. "We won't need the blankets. It's too hot for them, anyway."

"Will the heat be worse, do you think?" he asked as he sat down beside her.

"Yes. It can't be helped. After we cross the Volga, it will be worse."

"I've bought two bags of salt and a box of salt fish. Will that be enough?" He had fought in heat before, but nothing like the relentless, enervating swelter that had begun at Tana.

"I hope so. Salt and water, for us and the horses and mules." She sighed. "In my homeland, the days are often very hot, but we lived in the mountains, and at night it would grow cool. Here the whole world is an oven."

He laid his hand on her arm. "I stink like a goat, Surata."

"I do not mind the smell. What troubles me is the landlord and Lauris." She stared at the ceiling. "Would you mind leaving at midnight? There will still be moonlight."

"Why?" he asked, knowing that she was worried.

"I think that Lauris may go to the Guard and denounce you. And if he does, they will be here before dawn to take you away. They . . . at the best, they would make a slave of you." Her breath caught in her throat.

"And the worst? Kill me?" He did not need to hear her answer. "And you?"

"A brothel if I'm lucky," she said, revulsion in her voice.

"But . . . Surata, you would be a treasure to a brothel owner." He was puzzled by her; after all she had done to his body, why would a brothel offend her.

She turned on her side, speaking softly and fiercely. "Do you think that after we have had all this together, that I would ever want less? When you and I have ridden the crest of the wave, and wakened the Subtle Body, do you truly believe I could endure having that gift made tawdry and trivial by men wanting only to spend themselves in female flesh? Do you?"

Arkady caught her hands in his and held them, silent. Finally he said, "Surata, you shame me."

"Still?" she whispered, a wail in her voice.

He shook his head. "Not that way. You shame me because . . . I thought . . . never mind what I thought. I do not deserve your fealty."

"But you do," she said. "You would not have it otherwise."

He nodded, humbled and strangely shaken. "We'll leave at midnight. I'll wake you."

She kissed his cheek just above his beard. "It won't be necessary. Sleep, Arkady-champion."

He started to protest, then accepted her order, sinking back on the pillows and sighing, certain he would never be able to rest. And then he felt her hand on his shoulder and her voice saying that it was nearing midnight.

"Lauris left the inn a little while ago. I heard him talking to Eudoxius."

"Is the landlord still up?" Arkady asked, trying to pull himself out of the last hold of his dreams.

"No. He went to his chamber as soon as Lauris left. I heard the bolt put in place." She threw back the sheet. "Where are our clothes, the ones that Lauris did not see?"

"I have them set out," Arkady said, getting up and rubbing his chest and arms to bring himself completely awake.

"You will have to dress me," she reminded him. "I know nothing of these garments."

"I don't know them too well, either," Arkady said as he lifted the fine-spun wool and studied the thing in the dim, dim light. "I think that is what you put on first. Over the head." It took him longer than he had anticipated, but he was able to dress her and himself without too much fuss. After a brief inner debate, he pulled on his mail shirt over his robes and buckled on his wide leather belt with the scabbard hanging from it. He tucked the cinquedea into the back of it and slid his long sword into the scabbard. "The helmet's with our tack."

"The stable, then." She found her way to his side. "We seem to leave inns at peculiar hours."

"And in strange company," Arkady said. "At least this time there are no mice."

"There may be Guards if we don't hurry."

Arkady nodded. "Quickly, Surata. You carry two of the bags and I'll take the other two. The saddles are all packed. All we have to do is put them on the mules and horses. If you can do their bridles, I'll handle the saddles."

"I'll do them," she said, holding on to his arm as they descended the stairs.

They were mounted and about to leave when there was a sound in the innyard. Arkady swore.

"What is it? Guards?" Surata asked. She was astride a small Russian mare, and she turned awkwardly in the saddle, trying to hear over the sound of saddle squeaks and the hooves of the horses and mules.

"Probably," came Arkady's grim answer. He had put on his helmet, more from habit than any real sense of danger, and now he was glad he had taken the precaution. He gathered all the lead-reins in one hand and drew his sword with the other. The gelding could be guided by the pressure of his knees and would not falter in the face of armed men. Since he knew nothing of the other animals, he had a moment of apprehension, then he clapped his heels to the gelding's flanks and rushed out of the stable into the innyard, Surata and the mules clattering after him.

Five Guards were at the door of the inn, all on foot. Two of them had the elaborate helmets that identified them as officers, the other three were heavily armed.

"Fiends!" Arkady yelled at them as he rode down on them, his sword swinging up.

The Guards turned as one man. At first they were too amazed to do more than stare; by the time they had recovered enough to draw their weapons, Arkady had already struck one of the officers a glancing blow on his helmet and was pulling his bay onto his hind legs over two of the other men.

Arkady rammed his bay into one of the men, knocking him over as the gelding thudded his forehooves onto the packed earth. The nearest Guard had drawn his sword and was swinging it back to cut the horse's legs out from under him. Arkady hit the man across the side of the head with the flat of his sword.

"Arkady-immai! Hurry! More will be here soon!" Surata shouted to him.

"Right!" Arkady swung the sword again, this time cutting the nearest officer in the shoulder before forcing the bay to move on. The other animals lurched after him, following the pull on their lead-reins.

"Go east!" Surata yelled, hanging on to her saddle with both hands. "Otherwise you will find more Guards."

"Damn that Lithuanian slaver!" Arkady bellowed as he did what she told him. Arkady set their pace at a trot, knowing that they would go farther at that pace than at a gallop.

When they had finally slowed to a plodding walk, Arkady shortened the lead-rein of the Russian mare so that he and Surata would be close enough to talk comfortably.

"They were acting on the suggestion of Lauris. You realize that, Arkady-immai."

"He's a slaver. That's obvious. But why did they want me?" He could understand Trakiv's desire to get Surata, but he was perplexed about what the slaver would want with him.

"You're a good fighter. That's of value. You're foreign, and that means there would be few questions asked. Perhaps it's because you're Christian, and Lauris needs to keep in the favor of the city leaders by giving them an occasional Christian slave. Who knows, Arkady-immai."

"When we reach Itil, we may be able to learn something," he said, though he had little hope of it.

"I don't know the language there, and neither do you," she pointed out, smiling a little. The moon was almost down, casting long, faint shadows over the arid land, giving her face a sheen as if she had been dusted with silver. "Arkady-immai, what color is my horse? And my clothes?"

Arkady hesitated a moment. "Your horse is a brown-gray color, with a dark mane and tail. The French would say it was mouse-colored. It's darker than dun and the coat never has much shine to it. Your clothes are almost white, except for the veil, which is light blue."

"And your clothes, what color are they?" She seemed content to let him talk.

"My clothes are the same color. My armor is mail and the links are polished. Some of them are steel and some are brass. The brass ones run down the center of the front and back, around the armholes and the lower border, and along the shoulders. My helmet needs polishing. My belt is about the same color as my horse—a brown that is almost black." In the moonlight, few of these colors could be seen at all: the whole world was white, black and blue-gray.

"Do you think there really is fighting ahead?" She sounded unconcerned.

"I don't know. It's always possible. If these Islamites are anything like the Turks, they fight for the pleasure and glory of it and care nothing for their own lives." He paused. "And the Bundhi? What of him?"

"He has not forgot us," she said with quiet determination.

"Do you think . . . Surata, would he try to lead us into danger?"

"If he could. He would find it amusing." She shook her head twice. "His agents are good at deception, and without my eyes to aid me, I cannot always tell . . . I dread that one of them will find you, and I will not know of it. You would be in danger and helpless. I've dreamed of that, Arkady-immai, and in my dreams, I hate myself because of—"

"Stop it," Arkady ordered her. "When I've led men into battle, Surata, I have never allowed them to say that we might not win. You say that the Bundhi is a formidable foe, and I believe you. But you are a formidable foe as well, or the Bundhi would not be bothered by you, or attempt to stop your return. Remember that when you are tempted to tell me that our chances are slim."

For an answer, Surata smiled.

They continued on through the night, stopping shortly after sunrise for food and water and to rest their animals. They resumed their trek as soon as Arkady was certain the horses and mules could take it, and kept on through most of the day, halting only at the hours of greatest heat. They made camp shortly before sundown, and Arkady pitched their tent with great ceremony, saddened because Surata could not see it. They retired shortly after their evening meal and slept deeply until dawn.

The next day went more slowly, for the steady heat taxed the animals more than it drained the strength of their riders. Arkady warned Surata that they would have to rest earlier in order to give the mules a chance to regain their strength. "One of them is breathing too hard. I don't like it."

"Should he have more salt?" Surata asked.

"If we find a well tonight, yes, but otherwise we might not have enough water to go around." He was more concerned about their water than he liked for her to know, but she was not deceived.

"Arkady-immai, there will be wells. And there are still the two casks you loaded on the third mule." She made a curious gesture. "You may not want to open them so early, but you take no risks by doing it."

Arkady did not answer her.

That night there was a well, and the night after that. Surata helped him refill all the skins they carried and said, "Tomorrow will be dry, and most of the day after. Is the salt holding, or must we purchase more in Itil?"

"We'll get more whether we need it or not." He checked the mules to be sure their feet were all right, and he took great care with the pick around the shoes. He did not want another animal going lame on him.

In the tent, Arkady and Surata lay back together, lightly embracing, their eyes half-closed. Arkady felt the beginning of desire stir deep within him, and he smiled lazily.

"You would like this, Arkady-champion?" Surata asked, her hand moving over the Centers, touching each one in a different and stimulating way.

"Yes, I would like this," he said softly. "*All* of this." He let his hand drift over her breasts, cupping, fondling, gentle and forceful at once. "I love your skin," he said, brushing the backs of his fingers over her ribs and down to her hip.

"It is better when I have bathed and been rubbed with sweet

oil," she said but without any particular regret. "One day, you will learn this, I hope."

There it was, the faint but constant reminder of why they were together. Arkady did not argue with her, for it was apparent to him that this could serve no purpose but to keep them from their enjoyment of one another. "I hope so too." He kissed her mouth the way she had taught him to—slowly, lightly, the tips of their tongues touching. He could not imagine ever again being content with the grapplings he had known with women before.

Surata did not hurry her caresses; she took time to explore, to bring every part of Arkady's body to the highest pitch of sensitivity. Her hands, her body, her lips all played a part, and Arkady fell into that languid frenzy that made the rest of the world seem distant and unreal. She moved over him, reaching over his head to pull one of the packs nearer. "Use this for a pillow," she whispered, helping him rise so that he was half sitting. "Now."

Too elated to question this, Arkady leaned against the pack and watched with bemused delight as Surata settled in his lap, taking him into her with a long, ecstatic sigh and

the soft chimes of distant music that was part of the shifting lights.

Arkady felt no armor on his body and there was nothing in his hands. He was clothed, he saw, in white shining cloth, so soft that he decided it must be silk. There were designs worked in gold on the cloth. He shimmered more brightly than the shapes around him and when he walked, the distant music grew louder, more beautiful. He looked around him. "Surata?"

"Here," answered his silken garments.

"You've changed from armor." He chuckled, making the lights around him reel and dance. "Why?"

"Just as there are more ways to fight than with swords, so there are more ways to shield than with armor," she answered.

"If this is a shield, it's very pleasant," he told her, sliding his hands over the marvelous fabric. "Although I can't imagine this would stop any sword I've ever seen."

"It would depend on the sword, Arkady my champion, and on the silk. I could be nothing more than a mist hovering around you, and there is still no weapon that could penetrate it."

He had heard that note in her voice before, under the loving, an implacability that he wished he had had in all his soldiers. "Right." He walked on a little further, although he did not sense anything solid under his feet nor have an idea where he was going.

"Make what you want here, Arkady my champion. If the Bundhi wants to plague us, then he will have to come to us, this time." Surata pressed her silken self close to him, as if a breeze were blowing his clothes against him. "For once, this is for us."

Arkady grinned, taking great satisfaction in her announcement. "How good, to have this all to ourselves."

"Perhaps, when this is finished, it will be possible for us to have this for ourselves often." She did not sound very confident, but there was no lack of courage in her. "Then there would be no reason for caution or doubt, and there would be so much more pleasure in doing this."

"Are you still being cautious?" he asked, hearing what sounded like the susurrus of a river not far away.

"Yes. If I were not, I would be here as myself, and we could do here what we do in the daily world." The silk caressed him. "It would be like nothing you have known, Arkady my champion."

"Everything about you is like nothing I have ever known, Surata," he said to her with a deep affection that pleased and surprised him. "Surata?"

"I am listening to the river. Did you want a river?"

He shrugged. "I must have. After spending the day in the hot sun, a river, and grass, would be so nice. We could swim, and then lie on the bank until we were dry."

"We can be wet and dry in an instant in this other place," she reminded him and added more softly, "It would be very welcome, wouldn't it?"

The sound of the river was louder, more luring in the melody *of its current which blended with the haunting sound of chimes that remained with them. "And perhaps we can conjure up a feast, with all the foods that are rich and rare to give us luxury and delight." He was beginning to give his imagination free rein.*

"What foods do you want, Arkady my champion?"

"Oh . . ." He thought about it a moment. "Pomegranates, for a start. I've never tasted them, but I saw some once. And then . . . honey wine. I have had that, twice, at weddings. And fresh buttercakes, with raisins." He thought a little more. "Capons soaked in wine and oranges. I've never tasted it, but the Margrave Fadey served it to his noble officers once, and I still remember how it smelled."

Surata hummed, making the silk quiver on his skin.

"And spiced barley, with green onions. My mother used to make that, with lots of pepper when we had it." He looked ahead and saw a grassy riverbank forming out of the shifting colors, as beautiful as any he had ever seen as a boy. "Ah!" he cried out for sheer satisfaction.

"Is that what you wanted, Arkady my champion? The riverbanks of my home are not like that." Surata had very little apprehension in her voice, but enough for him to realize she was not certain it was quite right.

"They weren't like this at my home, either, but I wish they had been. Look at it. And the river!" They had come to the place where they could look into the water, and Arkady stood not far from the little bank of sand and pebbles that framed the river, smiling down into the clear, rushing water. "It's so beautiful." He reached for the hem of the silken tunic to pull it over his head, then stopped as Surata tweaked his arms.

"Arkady my champion, don't take this off. It won't matter that I get wet. The clothes will not be hurt and you will feel all of the river that you wish to feel. Let me stay with you, Arkady my champion." There was sweetness in her tone, and the cloth rested softly on his arms.

Arkady chuckled deep in his chest, a low, sensual sound. "If we can stay close, it's fine with me."

"We are close," Surata said.

("So close," Arkady murmured to the rise of her breasts.)

He shouted, running over the spring-smelling grass to the bank of the river where the little pebbles rolled underfoot. He felt the first splash of the river as his left foot hit the water, and he made a half-dive into the ripples, gasping a breath of air just before he hit. The water was cool but not cold. It closed over his head as he started swimming, then lapped around his chest as he came up once again. Arkady tossed his head, shaking the water from his hair, a joyous grin stretching his mouth. He let his feet drift down and was pleased that they touched bottom at a depth that allowed him to stand with his head and neck out of the water. There were rounded stones under his feet, and the light pressure of the current to remind him of the strength of the river. He wondered, briefly, if the water would harm Surata, and he called out her name, not knowing what he would hear.

"There is nothing that will bother me, Arkady my champion," she said, sensing his concern. *"Silk does not breathe air, and this water is like the other things in this other place."*

"But if the bruises I get are lasting in the daily world, can't I drown here, or you?"

"If you truly drown, then it would be in both worlds, yes," she said. *"But do not let that ruin your pleasure. It would not be easy for you to drown in this river."*

"But not impossible," he qualified.

"No, not impossible." There was a pause, and the touch of the silk seemed to warm him in the cool embrace of the river. *"But I am here, Arkady my champion, and I would not permit you to drown or come to hurt, I promise you."*

Arkady began to swim again, going slowly across the river, floating every now and then with the current. He turned and looked up at the fleecy clouds in a sky so blue that he thought he might be able to rise and swim in it as well.

"If that is what you wish, Arkady my champion," Surata said.

Arkady shook his head. "No. It sounds like too much work

for both of us." He let the current carry him a little way once again. "This is like being a boy once more. All those days when I was terrified of the water, this is what I really wanted to do. When I finally learned to swim, it was too late to take off an afternoon and spend my time on a riverbank. My father was dead and I..."

"Then this must please you very much," Surata said.

"More than I can tell you, Surata. I wish I had some way to explain it to you." He noticed that the current was a little faster, and he sighed. "I suppose it's time to dry off."

"Unless you'd rather not," she told him.

"I don't like swimming in fast water—I never did. It's too much like battle." He struck out toward the bank, taking long, powerful strokes with his arms. The exertion was as pleasurable as the floating had been. He glanced at the shore, calculating where he would land, and his eyes widened in terror.

Chapter 17

There were scorpions on the riverbank, thousands upon thousands of them, all with their tails lifted for the deadly sting. Their carapaces shone in the fading sunlight, and Arkady was certain he could hear the clicking of their legs on the pebbles.

Arkady yelped in distress and felt the silk he wore tighten on his body, not binding, but guarding.

"What is it?" Surata asked, distressed at this change in attitude he revealed.

"It must be the Bundhi," he said, trying to turn away from the bank, but being swept further downstream by the current.

"Scorpions!" she exclaimed in recognition. "He has found us."

"Did you think he wouldn't?" Arkady asked bitterly.

"I hoped he would not; you know that," she answered, beginning to alter the silk to something more buoyant and substantial.

The current was increasing, and there was the distinct sound of rapids ahead. Arkady turned in the river and started to swim against the weight of the river.

"Arkady my champion, don't. You'll only exhaust yourself, and that is more dangerous than any rocks can be. If we must go through rapids, then let it be while you have strength left to fight them." She was more like woven reeds now, encasing him in a suit like armor that held him up and provided some cushion against impact.

The current grew more ferocious, and Arkady was swept downstream at an increasing speed. He felt his legs slap against a hidden rock and tried to gauge how badly hurt he might have been if it weren't for the woven armor. He was spun once as the water eddied and swirled, and he looked toward the shore in the hope that it might be safe to swim toward it. The scorpions were there, and with them other creatures that Arkady had never seen and could not name.

"They are made by the Bundhi." Surata said breathlessly. "They are only found in this other place; they are not of the daily world."

Then the river had them again and they were carried toward the rapids.

Arkady gathered himself into a tighter form, hoping this would make injury less likely. He felt helpless to resist the river. In the next instant, he had slapped against a rock, crying out

and holding Surata fiercely, his fingers sunk into her shoulders as he gasped for air.

"Arkady-champion," Surata panted, her head pressed against his shoulder. "I did not think that would happen. Truly."

"I believe you," Arkady said after a moment. His arms ached from fighting the river, and he was dazed from the suddeness of his return to the daily world. He shook his head, feeling the excitement fade from his flesh. "Does that happen every time I spend myself?"

Surata smiled slightly. "For those who are advanced in their studies, no, because they can sustain their desire after spending themselves. For most men, Arkady-champion, it is as it is for you."

"And for you?" he asked, touching her face with the tips of his fingers. Her blind eyes were on his, and he had the uncanny feeling that she was *looking* at him.

"It is different with women, Arkady-champion. It is not our part to give but to receive, and because of that, we are . . . capable of longer unity."

"What do you mean, you don't give? You have given me . . . everything." He leaned forward to kiss her. "Surata, no one has given me more than you have, ever."

"With my body I receive," she said patiently. "The female is made to give love and receive the flesh, as a man is made to give flesh and receive love." She tossed her head. "You wish to argue now?"

"Yes," he said emphatically. "Surata, I love you. Don't you understand that yet?"

"Ah, but which comes first? Did you know of this love when you bought me? When you allowed me to touch you the first time, was that for love, or the need of your body?" She kissed the lobe of his ear, his jaw, the curve of his collarbone.

"It was . . ." He stopped. "I don't know *what* it was, Surata."

"But you see, I loved you from the very first, because you heard my call and answered it." She moved off his lap. "Arkady-immai, I am tired. Do you mind if I sleep?"

He shook his head. "I'm tired too." He felt around them for their blankets, shoved the pack away and in a little while was lost in his dreams.

In the morning he saw the bruises on her arms and hips and legs. "What happened? What . . . who did that to you?" He feared that he might have hurt her without knowing it, and the very idea sickened him.

"In the river, the rocks did it," she said matter-of-factly. "It doesn't matter that I was not in this body, I still was present and this—"

"Do you mean that any time you are . . ." He coughed and

started again. "When you are my protection, it hurts you?" He made no effort to conceal his indignation.

"Not always, Arkady-immai. But when there are blows, the blows are real, whether they are in the daily world or the other place and . . . Are they very bad?" She moved a little stiffly.

"You look as if someone has beat you." Arkady could hear the anger in his voice, and the force of his emotion surprised him.

"Well, someone has," she said, still in a very reasonable tone. "I do not mind, Arkady-immai. Truly, I do not."

"*I* do," he shouted. "I won't have you hurt for me, Surata."

She set aside the blankets she was rolling to put in their pack. "Arkady-immai, that is not for you to choose, it is for me. You are my champion, and I am your protection. You may choose to fight or not, but you cannot stop me from defending you, for that is *my* choice."

Arkady had almost finished tightening the girths on three of the pack saddles. "And if I don't fight, what then?"

"Then I must face the Bundhi as best I can," she said with no particular emotion.

"I can't let you do that!" His voice was so loud that the nearest mule laid back his ears and made a distressed sound.

"That is not for you to say, Arkady-immai." She went back to the blankets. "We should be away soon. Unless you would rather not go on."

"If I don't, I suppose you will try to get to Samarkand and to Ajni by yourself? You're my slave; I can take you away with me if I want to." He folded his arms to keep himself from going to her and embracing her.

"You can do that. But you would no longer be my champion," she told him very calmly.

"Right." He turned back to the girths, tightening them so forcefully that one of the mules tried to kick him. Suddenly Arkady came to her. "It's just that I can't bear to see you hurt, Surata."

"I know," she said to him as she handed him the filled pack. He took it silently and went on with breaking camp.

At the mouth of the Volga, the river split into many little rivers divided by marshy islands. It was on one of these islands at the edge of the Caspian Sea that Itil stood, its spires and domes rising over the water like enormous marsh grasses.

"They're Islamites here," Arkady said to Surata as he paid the bargeman whose boat had carried them to the gates of the city. "We'll have to be careful. There have been other religions here, or there must have been, but no longer."

"Very well," she said serenely. "Pull the veil over my face, Arkady-immai. I know that they do not wish to look on me."

This time it took more than four days to find a caravan going to Khiva, and it cost Arkady four gold pieces to be allowed to join it. He complained to Surata that since he could not speak the language of the men of the caravan, he would have to rely on pantomime and signs. "I can't draw well, or that might be a way to tell them what I need to know."

"When we reach Khiva, then I can help you. I know some of that language; not much, but enough." She paused. "They will not like to speak with a woman; Islamites don't."

"We'll manage somehow," Arkady said bracingly. "We will have to eat apart from the others; they've insisted on that, and it might be best if . . . if you and I don't—"

"Go to the other place," she said for him. "Yes, I've thought of that. There is too much of a risk."

"Do you think . . ." He made a gesture which she could not see. "The Bundhi has agents, you tell me. Would these be his men?"

"Islamites? No, they would not. To them, the Bundhi is an evil sorcerer and an Infidel. They would never deal with him." She fussed with her veil. "This is foolish, veiling a blind woman."

"Surata, it would take little for them to abandon us, and it would not be easy for us to reach Khiva without them." Arkady put a consoling hand on her arm. "It is only for the length of the journey, and then it will be different."

She nodded once. "We must do what is easiest." Her expression was not clear to him, and he waited for her to say more.

When she did not, he dropped his hand and went to find the caravan leader to make his final arrangements.

They were required to stay at the back of the caravan, behind two old and vile-tempered she-camels that stank and spat if Arkady let his gelding get too close to them. In the heat of the day, the dust raised by the caravan forced Arkady and Surata to ride in a perpetual gritty cloud; in the evening, they sat together in isolation while the men of the caravan ate, prayed and joked.

By the time they crossed the Ural River and entered the city of Gurjev, Arkady was so vexed that he was tempted to leave the caravan and wait for another.

"It would mean a long wait," Surata reminded him. "This is the height of summer and few caravans venture across the desert at this time of year. The longer we stay here, or anywhere, the greater are our chances of being found by the Bundhi."

"He must be as reluctant to go across the desert as anyone else," Arkady said in disgust. His eyes ached and he was furious.

"He need not cross himself. His agents are eager to have his good opinion and will undertake . . . anything he wishes." She caught her lower lip between her teeth. "I am sorry, Arkady-immai, that we must do this."

Until she said that, he agreed with her, but now that she had apologized, he felt his attitude change. "Well, if this discomfort makes it easier to reach the Bundhi, then it is good strategy for us to do it."

They were in their tent outside the walls of Gurjev—since they were foreigners and Infidels, they were not permitted to sleep inside the city. It was a still, baking night, one that stifled the very air. Since sunset, they had been alone; the men of the caravan had been accorded a welcome Arkady and Surata were denied.

"Suppose they simply leave without us?" Arkady suggested some little time later. He had tried without success to fall asleep, and now lay staring up at the peak of the tent, feeling the rivulets of sweat run off his body and soak into the blanket beneath him.

"Do you think they would?" Surata was drowsy but still awake.

"They might. What could we do to them? Where could we complain? Who would listen to us? Who would understand?" He sighed and turned over, willing himself, unsuccessfully, to rest.

Surata had no answer for him, and said nothing.

Two days later they once more took up their position at the rear of the caravan and set out across the desolate lands east of the Caspian Sea. Four days out from Gurjev, they encountered a west-bound caravan from Kabul, and the two groups camped together for three days, the traders exchanging information and gossip while Arkady and Surata waited in their tent, forbidden to let themselves be seen by the Kabuli merchants.

Among the Kabuli was a strange, wizened man, gnarled by disease into a skinny gnome. He was regarded by all the merchants with a reverence that bordered on fear. He took an immediate dislike to Arkady and Surata, castigating them in a frenzy of incomprehensible words. The caravan leader who had accepted Arkady's gold began to make the sign to ward off evil every time he came near anything belonging to the foreigners. There was no doubt that the misshapen mystic had influenced the caravan leader.

"I don't like it," Arkady grumbled at the end of the third day. "That magician, or whatever he is, he's up to no good."

"I wish I could leave this tent," Surata said. "I might be able to understand him."

"No. The leader made it plain that you're to stay out of sight. So am I." He could not pace in the limited area of the tent, but he moved restlessly, glaring at the wedge of sunlight that slanted in at them.

"Describe him to me again," Surata requested.

"Little, bent, knobby, old." He ticked these features off on his fingers. "Falls into trances, harangues the others, eats only cooked grain. I don't know, Surata. I can't understand most of what they're saying, and even if I did, they wouldn't let me near him long enough to find out much." He snorted. "Fools!"

"Yes, but they know the way." She rubbed her face. "Do we have our packs ready?"

This question was so unexpected that he turned and stared at her. "What? Why do you want to know that?"

"Because I'm worried," she admitted and would say nothing more.

By nightfall a slow, persistent wind had come up, and with it, a pervasive sense of unease. The camels became more obstreperous than ever, the mules balked at their feed, and Arkady's gelding tried to nip him when Arkady brought him a leather pail filled with water.

"They sense something," Surata told Arkady when he complained of the way the animals were acting. "I don't know what it is, but they can tell there is trouble coming."

Arkady knew better than to discount this. How many times had he felt the same disquiet before a battle? He strove to remain composed, but his inner anxiety grew as the night deepened and he heard the animals grunting and stamping.

"It's that damned holy man of theirs. He's making everyone upset and the animals feel it." Arkady slammed his fist into his open palm. "By tomorrow, they'll all be as mad as he is."

Surata shook her head. "That might be part of it, Arkady-immai, but it isn't all of it." She had been sitting quietly, in one of her ritualistic postures. "He's . . . summoning."

Arkady stared at her, the back of his neck prickling. "Summoning what?"

"I don't know. I'm not sure what it is." She gave an impatient clicking of her tongue. "He is . . . masked to me. I have tried to reach him, to learn what he is doing, but . . ." Helplessly she opened her hands. "Arkady-immai, I can discover nothing."

"Well," he said wryly, "then we're both confused." He sat beside her, his legs crossed. "I wish they'd all go to bed.

They're still eating and talking. They might be up half the night." He faltered, then went on. "I don't want to sleep while they're in the state they are. If I have to fight them off, I want to be awake enough to know what I'm doing."

"I don't know if that's the problem," she said somberly. "I think it is something . . . different."

"Worse?" he asked.

"I don't know." In her frustration, she struck out in the direction of his voice, but succeeded only in hitting the heel of his boot. With a cry she pulled her hand back.

"Surata, I . . ." He tried to comfort her, but she wrenched away from him.

"No. I've failed you."

"What are you talking about?" he demanded, a trace of unbelieving laughter tinging his question. "How have you failed me?"

"I can tell you nothing, yet we're in danger. You are aware of it, and so am I, but I have no skill to find out what it is. Fine protection!" This time she brought her hands down hard on her own knees.

Arkady was reaching to stop her when a shattering roar filled the night. "Christ in heaven!" he burst out, crossing himself at the sound.

The animals echoed this dire sound with whinnies and screams.

Surata sat very still. "A tiger."

"By Saint Michael," Arkady whispered. "Near?"

They could hear the men of the two caravans shout and lament. There was a flurry of activity as they hastily armed themselves and prepared to fend off the huge cat.

A second roar sounded, nearer than the first.

"It's closer," Arkady whispered.

"No," Surata corrected him. "There are two of them."

He did not doubt her now; she had that stillness that was part of her certainty. "They're hunting?"

"Yes. Camels and mules and horses. They're afraid of the fire, but their hunger may be greater than their fear." She raised her head. "Can we build up our cooking fire?"

"There isn't much to burn," he warned her.

"Still," she said, her brows drawing together.

"The merchants won't like it." He said it in a rush, and harshly. "They . . ."

When he did not go on, Surata folded her hands, and her expression changed to that vacant look that Arkady knew he should not disturb no matter how much it puzzled him. He moved closer to her, waiting for her to come back to herself. He listened to the sounds of the mules and horses, their increasing agitation and fear. One of the mules let out a high squealing bray that started the others doing the same. The noise was almost worse than the tigers' roars had been, and Arkady held his hands over his ears, hating himself for doing nothing.

There was another roar, and the sound of snapping cord as one of the mules broke free of its tether, racing away in panic.

"God," Arkady muttered, waiting for what he knew he would hear.

It came quickly. the galloping was interrupted by a few irregular hoofbeats, and then there was a shriek and growl and the sound of the mule falling, kicking and grunting, and then there was another roar.

"The tigers are sent. So is the holy man," Surata told Arkady in a remote way. "They have been sent. They are . . . following us." She lowered her head.

"And?" Arkady said, knowing there was more. "The Bundhi wants to stop us?"

"Yes. He wants us to die." She leaned toward him. "I think I've held the horses and the other mules for the time being, but I can't do it for long. If the tigers stalk us, they'll flee."

"If the tigers stalk us, I want them to flee," Arkady said. "I hope they chase our stock all over the desert. I hope they glut themselves and die of it." His vehemence was so intense that he hardly noticed his fingernails digging into his palms.

"First we should be sure we can go on," she said. "The holy man will try to stop us now. I wonder, does he carry a staff?" She did not expect an answer but Arkady responded.

"I didn't see one, but to walk so far, and twisted as he is, he must have one." There was a softer tone in his voice now, one that revealed his fatalism. "I ought to have thought of that before now."

"It doesn't matter. If it had not been him, it would have been another." With a sob of frustration, she reached for his hand. "Arkady-champion, it's as much my error as yours. I'm going distracted sitting in this tent, like a piece of meat in an oven. I've lost track of what I must do, and it's caused me to . . . make mistakes."

There were sounds from the merchants' camp, a steady shouting like a chant. Above it all, the high, wailing voice of the holy man screamed in demented fury.

"They're as frightened as we are," Surata said.

"They're angry as well." He brought her hands to his lips and kissed them. "I think . . . we'd better be ready to get away from here."

Surata's hands tightened. "We can't."

"We can't stay with these merchants either. Not tonight, but perhaps tomorrow night or the night after, they will decide that there has been too much wrong, and they will know it's our fault. I don't want them to be able to find us when they make up their minds. I've seen what Turks do to their enemies. I don't want to learn that these men are cut from the same cloth." He pushed the images that had formed in his thoughts to a far corner where he would not have to look at them too closely, but one refused to be banished: a sergeant, massive and dependable as a workhorse, strapped to an X-shaped cross, held in place with long strips of his own skin.

"What should we do?" Surata asked.

"Give the tigers time to feed, then make sure we have all our goods ready. Tomorrow when we start again—they have said we must resume our journey tomorrow—we will follow as always, but we will fall behind, so that by nightfall, we'll be on our own." He cleared his throat. "That ability you have, the thing you do when you . . . go look at things. Can you use it to guide us to Khiva?"

She considered his question. "I don't know. I've never tried to do it, but . . . I suppose it's possible. We know the direction we have to go, and some of the route is marked. If I take care, I think . . ." She sighed, shaking her head. "Arkady-immai, I will do the best I can."

"Fine," he said with enthusiasm. "That gives us a chance. If we continue southeast, we must come upon *something* eventually." That sounded dreadful to him, and he knew it was terrible to her. "Surata, don't be troubled. I'm saying these things wrong."

"No," she said with resignation. "You are saying them truly. I don't mind that you do. I would rather not fool myself or you. There is a good chance we will go astray, and then . . . the Bundhi need not trouble himself to send agents after us. The sun and thirst will be enough."

He could not contradict her. "In the morning, be prepared, Surata."

"I will." She turned away from him, listening to the shouts and chanting from the merchants, and the nervous sounds of the animals while the tigers dragged their prey off to feed.

Halfway through the next day, the caravan was so far ahead of Surata and Arkady that it appeared to be nothing more than a cloud of dust, like a distant storm, or the funnels that towered up out of the desert, swaying and coasting with the wind.

"Do you think they know we've gone?" Surata asked as they watered their animals.

"Probably. They will have stopped for food and water by now, and that should let them know that we're missing." He took his hoofpick and went to work on his gelding's feet. "This hot, hard earth is bad for them."

"After Samarkand, we will soon be in the mountains." She patted her mare's nose. "At Ajni we turn south. There is a canyon that will lead us toward Gora Čimtarga. The Zeravšan and the Jagnob are the rivers we will follow."

"Tell me when we get there," he recommended. "For the moment, all I wish to do is reach Khiva."

"And Samarkand," she added.

They deliberately went slowly that day and the next, putting as much distance between themselves and the caravan as they could without actually stopping.

"Do you think the tigers will be back?" Arkady asked as they made camp the second night.

"Yes," she answered. "They have been trailing us since they killed the mule. They have the scent of us and the Bundhi to keep them constant on their hunt."

Arkady still found it difficult to believe that the Bundhi could control such beasts as tigers and he said so. "Even the Pope cannot command animals, and he speaks for Christ on earth."

"And did your Christ have power over beasts?" Surata asked while she gathered dried camel dung to burn in their fire.

"I . . ." He had never actually thought about it. "Well, he cast demons out of a woman so that they entered swine."

"And what did the animals do? Did your Christ rid them of the demons as well?"

"No," he replied after he had thought about it. "At least, the priests don't say that He did." He looked at the pile she was gathering. "I should have remembered that all we had to do was follow the camels. That will guide us where we wish to go."

"Not all camels are bound for Khiva," she pointed out. "Some are bound for Bukhara and some for Rai. Doubtless some are wild and are going where wild camels go."

"Right," Arkady said, not quite comfortably. "It was just an idea."

"It was cheering," Surata said, continuing in a lighter tone, "Arkady-immai, we have already come a great distance, more than I would have thought possible, and faster than I assumed I could go. For that alone, I am grateful to you."

"I don't want your gratitude," he said kindly. "I have not done this for gratitude."

"Then why have you?" She was searching the folds of her clothes for the flint and steel to start the fire.

"Does it matter?" He had asked this facetiously but stopped

himself. "It *does* matter. It would be a simple thing to say that I was captivated by you—and I was—but that's not why I did this. At first I was running from my own disgrace, and saying that I was aiding you, or embarking on an adventure made it less like flight. Then . . ."—his thoughts turned inward—"I found that I wanted to do this. Expiation? Exoneration? I don't know. I do it for myself." He saw the trouble she was having with the fire and came to her side, handing her flint and steel. "Here. Use mine."

She took it from him. "Thank you, Arkady-immai." She patiently struck several sparks before she was able to get a little flame, and all that time she did not respond to him.

"Well?" he said when she had got the dried dung burning.

"Your flint and steel," she said, giving them back to him.

"You have nothing to say?" He could not imagine that she would refuse to talk to him after what he had said to her.

"Arkady-immai, do you want me to make light of what you've told me? Do you want me to say the easy thing or the true thing?" She remained silent while he thought this over.

"The true thing, Surata." He turned away from her and took the tether-stakes from one of the packs.

"That will take a little time," she said, adding more dung to the growing flames.

Arkady set the tethers and unsaddled the animals, then tended to their hooves once more. By the time he was through, Surata had grain and fruit cooking. "I'm hungry," he said as he unpacked their tent. "You?"

"Yes." There was something in her expression or the tone of her voice that caught his attention.

"What is it, Surata?" He looked out over the dry land, the occasional bits of brush and withered grasses. The shadows in the fading day were long and deep like fresh scars.

"The tigers are near." She sighed. "Tonight or tomorrow night, they will be after the mules again."

Arkady knew better than to doubt her. "When do you think they'll get close?"

"I don't know. There's a dry wash to the south, and we

could move over there for the night. There's more fuel for fires," she said.

"I don't like to fight in a trap," Arkady said, thinking back to the battle he had refused that brought about his disgrace.

"Nor do I," she said, "but for different reasons. I want to know what is coming after me, and in that wash, I might not be able to find out."

"Then we stay here and hope that we can keep the tigers away." He came and patted her shoulder. "I'm glad you warned me, Surata. It's easier to have a defense if there's a warning."

"I'll stay awake tonight. If there is reason, I'll wake you," she said.

"You are as tired as I am," he reminded her.

"But I can sleep in the saddle tomorrow. You can tie me on. You must stay awake while we travel." She hesitated. "If we lose another mule, we'll have to leave some of our supplies behind, won't we? The others can't carry it all."

"If we lose another mule, then we'll talk about it," Arkady said, and went to work putting up their tent.

Chapter 18

Two nights later the tigers moved in, killing Surata's mare and raking the flank of the smallest mule, leaving deep, bleeding furrows.

Arkady had stumbled out of the tent, his bow strung and the arrow notched. He let four shafts fly after the tigers and struck nothing.

"What about the mule?" Surata asked when Arkady came back into the tent.

"She's not going to be able to carry anything. I'm not sure she can walk. In the morning, we'll see."

"At least we can ride together, the way we used to," she said a little while later. "That's something."

"I've missed it," he admitted.

"Yes. I have too." She thought a moment. "The tigers won't be back tonight. Do you want to ride the wave?"

He had missed the solace and elation of her body. "I have wanted to very much."

"Do you still?" She was fussing with the blankets, trying to smooth out the rough parts where the ground protruded.

254

"Of course." He had thrown on his outer robe when he had left the tent to try to kill the tigers, but he was naked beneath it. He untied the belt and tossed it away, letting the robe hang open. "You are better than wine and the intoxicating smoke of the Turks."

She rose on her knees, arms around his hips, her cheek resting on the top of his thigh. "Arkady-champion."

His skin tingled as her lips touched his flesh, feather-soft kisses on his hip and abdomen, then moving down, to his rising manhood. She roused him still more, her mouth and hands finding new ways to excite him, until he was afraid that he would topple over on her. He breathed her name.

Surata left off her tantalizing ministrations and reached up for him. "Come. We can be together, Arkady-champion." There was a low, almost drugged sound to her voice as she pulled him down to her.

"God and Saint Michael, Surata," he cried softly as he opened her legs. In the next instant, her ankles were joined behind him and he plunged into her, his head flung back, his mouth open for the wonder of

the luminescent colors that surged around him, filling this other place as far as he could see. This time he was as naked here as he was in the daily world, but a glow, silver-blue and glinting, surrounded him.

"*Surata?*" *he said tentatively.*

"*Arkady my champion?*" *the glow responded, the voice a sensation almost like tickling.*

"*What now?*" *he asked as he looked around.*

"*We are trying to find the Bundhi. But we don't want him to find us. Last time he was able to, but perhaps this time he will not.*" *The glow pulsated, revealing an emotion between ire and mischief.*

"*Why?*" *Arkady wanted to know, thinking that she had gone beyond anything sensible when she said that.*

"*Because there are ways to deceive him. To begin with, you may not believe it, but to anyone else but yourself and me, you are invisible. That is what this aura does for you. I have*

255

given you another kind of protection." The silver-blue light shifted, turning the brilliant colors pale with its radiance.

"And what good is that?" Arkady asked, trying to determine what was happening to him this time. *"There isn't any land."*

"We haven't made any, and we won't. This time we will see what the Bundhi has done instead of letting him see what we are doing." She laughed a little, glimmering around him.

"Will it work?" He was feeling disoriented because there was nothing solid or recognizable emerging from the shifting lights. He felt the current between him and Surata more powerfully than before and tried to think why it would be so.

"I hope it will," she answered. *"For now, we must . . . drift in this other place, looking for signs of the Bundhi."*

"But . . ." he objected, trying to find a way to express why this troubled him.

"Arkady my champion, you will know him if we find him. You will feel a stench on your soul, for the Bundhi is a charnel house. You will sense the reek of him." There was quiet passion in her description. *"You have seen what he can do. Now we will watch him do it."*

"And if he's waiting for us, as he has before?" He could feel a movement that was like wind, and he assumed that they were starting their search.

"That's a risk. It's always been a risk. But I think he assumes we're too worried about our animals and the tigers to venture into this other place tonight. He has always believed that those who follow the Right Hand Path are too cautious and too reluctant to act. This time we will not hesitate, and we will not give him a target to aim for."

Arkady considered this, and though it made him uneasy, he could not argue with it. *"You're basing most of your strategy on what you assume your opponent will do,"* he pointed out to her.

"What else can I do? What else have you done?" The brightness was different now, the areas of light larger and less iridescent. There was a quality about them of vast distances.

"I don't know." He could not say that he felt too vulnerable

as he was, that he feared her protection would not be adequate if they were pursued in any way.

"Do not fear, Arkady my champion. You are as safe now as if you were girded in steel." There was that note in her voice again, that determined implacability that he respected utterly.

"Right," he said, squinting into the expanses of brightness. Before he had been reminded of the wings of butterflies; now he thought of the light through stained glass.

"The Bundhi is trying to stop us and to deceive us. We must not let him do that," she reiterated. "I must do everything I can, you know that, Arkady my champion. If I do less, I would not be worthy of you."

Arkady sighed. "Surata, don't let that trouble you. It means nothing to me." He knew he had said it badly, but the smooth, facile compliments would not come to his lips.

"But it does to me," she responded. "You see, there is nothing that—" She broke off suddenly and Arkady had the sensation of coming to an abrupt halt.

"What is it?"

"We're not alone here," she said.

"The Bundhi?" He had no inkling that their surroundings had changed in any way.

"I don't know." She became very still, and he with her. "I think it is . . . someone else."

Then something was changing in the lights—the brightness became music as well as light, a deep, sensual, exalted melody that came from the throats of hundreds of singers and from instruments that had never been heard before.

"It's . . . wonderful," Arkady whispered, the word wholly inadequate to describe the music. "What . . . where does it come from?"

"From a musician," she answered very softly.

"But what is it?" It was so unlike any music he had known, and so total in its harmony that he listened to it in growing awe.

"It is what the musician envisions his music to be. In the daily world, it will be an echo of this. It happens sometimes.

There is a vision of the art, known only to the artist and those of us fortunate enough to stumble upon the vision here. I have seen statues here that the gods must envy for their sublime beauty." She was barely speaking; her voice seemed to come through his skin rather than his ears.

The music continued, growing more rapturous and vast. Then it faded, not quickly or distractedly, but from within the music itself, until it was two crystalline, pure, high notes suspended together like stars.

("Surata, Surata," he murmured, finding music in her name.)

Then they were in silence again, and sliding through the brightness toward an area of enormous blackness.

"Does that trouble you?" Surata asked as Arkady grew tense at the sight of it.

"It . . ." He had recollections of what the priests had said about limbo and thought that this must be what they meant.

"It is like the night sky, Arkady my champion, huge but clear, clear as water." She shimmered, carrying him a little way into the blackness. "You see? . . . clear and deep. This is not like what you fear, something muffling and enclosed. In this other place, the darkness is open and free."

Arkady tried to be calm, but he grew steadily more apprehensive. "Does a comet feel like this?" he asked her, trying to make a joke of it and failing.

"Who knows what happens in the heart of a comet?" she replied. "In this other place, there are no comets. You and I are free to do as we wish."

This did not reassure Arkady, who still anticipated falling with every breath. "I . . . I don't know if I can keep this up, Surata. It's too . . . difficult."

The silver-blue glow around him grew brighter, larger, so that he seemed to float in an enormous bubble or a translucent pearl. "There. You see, you are quite safe now. You are not hampered by the daily world here, and you are taken care of differently."

Arkady almost smiled. "The best of both worlds? To have you this way and the way . . . we get here."

Surata did not answer this, but within the bubble, Arkady

grew warmer, almost cozy. They continued into the darkness, going in contented silence.

Arkady watched the darkness from the center of the silver-blue sphere, awed at the scope of what he saw. "Who would have thought that there were such expanses beyond us?" he said to ward off the isolation and panic that wriggled like an eel in his chest.

"Not beyond us, Arkady my champion: within us. This other place is reached from inner transcendence." She swung them through a long, slow arc. "Everything is within you."

Arkady nearly burst out with wild laughter, but he was able to control himself enough merely to say, "How can this be within me?"

"Where else would it be?" she asked kindly. "If it were not, it could be reached other ways, but being within, we must be . . . within one another." Once more she was quiet. "The Bundhi," she warned quietly.

"What? Where?" Alarm caught his attention once more.

"Not far. He is . . . busy. He has released the tigers for the night and now he is going to return to his redoubt, the one in this other place, not where he is in the daily world."

"And where is he in the daily world?" Arkady inquired, wishing he could find a way to sense what she sensed.

"A city, with domes, in blue and gold. There are cobbled streets and high walls, and pointed arches. There are tigers with the sun on their backs walking amid flowers." She hesitated. "A garden, do you think?"

"With tigers the way you describe?"

"The walls are the color of the dry hills, and the gates are surmounted with blue domes." She kept them hanging in the darkness, poised to react swiftly if they had to.

"Another deception," Arkady suggested. "He's created a place other than his redoubt to confuse us or has disguised his redoubt to make you think that it is another place. You've told me he can do this."

"That's true," she said dubiously. "This does not have that feel to it." The brightness of her sphere dimmed. "We must go carefully, so that he does not see us."

"You said that we're invisible."

"And so we are, but as he leaves a presence behind him, so do we, and he has the skill to track us, whether we're visible or invisible." She sailed them away from the thing she had perceived, expanding the darkness between them and the Bundhi.

"But he is alone, isn't he?" Arkady asked.

"He . . . has agents with him, two of them. They know me. They are the ones who followed me when I was sent into slavery." There was real fear in her voice now. *"They will recognize me, never mind what precautions I take. They are like hunting dogs, who can follow a scent anywhere but through running water. We leave a scent in this other place as surely as if we were crossing a field with hounds behind us."*

"Then," Arkady said lightly, *"we must find some running water."* He chuckled, hoping that she would not be so frightened.

"Yes," she said eagerly. *"But if we create it, then it will be the same as leaving yet another scent for them to follow. They leave us so little . . ."* Her voice trailed off. *"Arkady my champion, what would be better: creating water or making a false scent for them to follow?"*

"Can you do that—make a false scent?" He was intrigued by the idea as much as he was uncertain of the outcome of such action. *"What would you do?"*

"I think I can create another bubble like this one, but empty, and send it far out into the void. They might think it was you and me, because of what we have done already." She glowed a little brighter. *"If not, they will find us in the daily world soon enough, and we will have to be ready for them. The Bundhi does not want me to return, and he warned me that he would do everything that he can to stop me."*

"But why? Surely you aren't so great a threat to him now." Arkady reached out to her with his mind. *"He could have killed you many times before now."*

"But you know he does not desire my death. He wants my power to use, not my death." Her strength thrummed through

him. "He wishes to have what I have given you, and refuses to share it, not with me, or with anyone. You heard what he said when he blinded me. He has not changed his mind."

Arkady thought this over. "A false scent, then. Another bubble might confuse them, that's something. They are not seeking to strand us here, are they?" He wanted her to be amused, but neither of them thought it was a joke. "They might not be aware we're here, if they think that . . ."

She did not respond at once. "When they serve the Bundhi and he transcends through the ministrations of his slaves, they will know we are here and that we have been here. And they will search for us, Arkady my champion."

"You're certain." He did not have to make this a question; he knew from the scent and the feel of her that she was.

"Yes." She trembled, and the light of the bubble glistened like frost on a winter morning.

"Then it would be best to return before they know we've been here. We've learned a little something, and that's to our advantage, Surata. If we can get away without the Bundhi and his agents knowing we've been here, spying on them, so much the better. They've found us out every time before. This time it can be different." He felt her shrink in close around him, and the vertigo he had experienced when they had first entered that limitless darkness returned.

("Arkady-champion, you . . ." She took a long shuddering breath, then gave two small cries, the sound of birds at dawn.

(He pulled in his breath sharply through his teeth. "Holy Saint Michael!")

"Come away, Arkady my champion."

Already the darkness was fading, and the glow that surrounded him expanded rapidly, pulsating, then burst into many brilliant colors, glorious sparks rising

as the last light from the fire outside the tent made their skins glisten.

"Did we get away?" Arkady whispered to the lobe of her ear, kissing her softly.

"I think so," she answered when she could speak. "They

were not in that other place when we left it. They didn't discover where we were."

"Then they won't be able to follow us back here, not from that other place, will they?" He traced the line of her cheek with his fingers, wishing he had the means to tell her how precious she was to him.

"Probably not. There are other agents, but we know about them, don't we?" She caught his hand in hers and kissed it, holding the palm against her lips.

"The tigers and the rest of it?" He saw her nod. "It means that we need only worry about being eaten or dying of thirst," he jested, his smile genuine, marred only because she could not see it.

"Which are minor matters," she appended, going along with his lightly taunting mood. "To say nothing of collapsing from exhaustion."

"Are you exhausted?" His sympathy was mixed with contented pride.

"Perfectly." Her legs slid over his hips and along his thighs. "It is better to sleep this close to you, Arkady-champion, than anything else in the world."

Hearing this, he was consumed by a tenderness that was almost painful in its intimacy. "I will not lose you, Surata."

She held him fiercely. "No. Never lose me, Arkady-champion."

They clung together through the night, unwilling to be parted even in sleep.

In the morning, Arkady decided to abandon the injured mule; the animal was clearly suffering and Arkady had no means to tend to the deep gouges the tiger had plowed in her hide. He looked at her pack saddle and tried to make up his mind what could best be left behind. He did not want to discard any of their food or water, but one of the bags contained their religious garments, and these, he knew, were expendable now that they were outside of Christian lands. He tossed the pack aside and divided the others between their other mules. While the extra weight would slow them down, Arkady was also aware that with Surata riding the bay with him, they would not travel quickly in any case. All that he had to do in the end was to make up his mind if it would be kinder to kill the injured mule. He walked to her side, making low, reassuring sounds as he bent to examine her flank. The wounds were puffy, with blood and watery fluid seeping from them whenever she moved. Arkady noticed that her breathing was labored, and she held her head low, long ears drooping. "Bad for you, old girl." He patted her rump and nodded to himself as she shied, grunting. Regretfully he reached out and patted her cheek before going back for his maul.

Surata touched his arm. "It is wrong to kill her, Arkady-champion."

"What else can I do? She's in pain now, and the scratches are very bad. This afternoon or tomorrow at the latest, the wounds will be infected. She will die slowly, in thirst and in pain. This way it is over quickly and she will not have to suffer." He lifted the maul. "I don't like killing animals, Surata, but I don't like seeing them suffer needlessly, either."

"It is not the way I have been taught," she said stiffly but let go of him. "You are the one who understands these things as a soldier. If you must do it, you must."

He kissed her cheek. "If she could understand, she could make the choice herself, and I would abide by it—I have with my men more times than I want to remember—but she cannot, and because I brought her to this, I must do what I think is best. I'm responsible for her being here in the first place."

"It is karma, Arkady-immai."

"It's also my obligation to that animal." He felt a bone-deep sadness as he went back to the mule. "I'm sorry, girl," he told her just before he swung the maul, striking her with full force between the ears. The mule went down with only the sound of her fall.

Surata was quiet for most of that day and the next, and Arkady was unable to break into her reverie. The heat dazed him, his eyes ached in his skull and the only thing that gave him any relief was the steady pressure of Surata's arms around him.

Four nights after he killed the mule, the tigers returned and claimed another.

"We'll have to leave most of the extra clothes behind," Arkady said when he had taken stock of what they had to carry. "There's too much weight otherwise."

"That's all right," Surata said, sighing a little. "You choose what we should keep. You know better than I what will be the best use to us." Her face was drawn and thinner than when they had started from Itil. She had deep smudges under her milky eyes, and her skin was chapped in many places. Arkady felt a pang as he looked at her, wishing that he could deliver her from this dangerous predicament.

"You're troubled, Arkady-immai," she said, turning herself toward him.

"The mule . . . we really couldn't afford to lose it," he hedged.

"It's more than that," she said. "You're worried about the tigers still, and there is something more."

He did not dare to say what had been gnawing at his thoughts for three days: what if they missed Khiva? They had no guides to take them to the city, and they had met no one coming toward them since they left the caravan. Arkady had been using the sun and the stars to point the way, but he knew only too well that it would not take much of an error for them to miss either city—Khiva or Samarkand—completely.

"Tomorrow we will make good time," Surata said, trying to encourage him.

"We won't, but it's good of you to say we will." He made a surreptitious check of their water supply and was not comforted by what he found. They would have enough water for another ten days and then they or the horse and mules would have to go without. Idly, he thought that it was possible for the tigers to take another mule in that time, and that would give them a day or two more water. He laughed unpleasantly.

"You're angry, Arkady-immai," she said.

"Not at you." He reached over and put his hands on her

arm. "I'm angry because we're in a hazardous situation. Risks always make me angry "

"Water?" she guessed.

"In part." He cleared his throat. "Would you mind if we rationed the water? We might find a well soon, but we can't depend upon it, and I wouldn't like to . . ." He made a resigned gesture.

"If you think it is wise to ration the water, then do so. I can manage with less." The weariness in her face softened. "You have done what is best for us since you bought me. You will do the best now."

"Thanks," he said, rubbing his eyes. "Those damned tigers will wear us down. They're staying on our trail."

"You know why that is," she said. "The Bundhi does not like to have to wonder where we are."

"You're certain they're sent by him?" Arkady believed her most of the time now that he had been with her for so long, but he could not rid himself entirely of doubt. "Couldn't they be just a pair of tigers?"

She shook her head. "Tigers hunt in their own areas, and these follow us. They take no prey but our animals. If you were to put a goat out with the mules, they would still take the mules or our horse if they could get him."

He made no argument; he was aware that they were under scrutiny. There had been many times in the past when he had felt that odd sensation, a prickling of his skin, and never more strongly than now. "Right," he said to her, hoping to find a way to divert the tigers before they killed the rest of their animals.

They pressed on for more than a week and lost another mule to the tigers. The low salt flats gave way to hard scrub land with dust-colored grasses and occasional thorn bushes. They saw no one. Finally, sitting by a dying fire, Arkady voiced the fear that had been plaguing him for more than three days.

"Surata, it's possible that we're lost." He thought of their waterskins, now almost empty, and their diminished food. "We might have passed Khiva and . . . not known it. There should have been some sign by now that we were still on a caravan route, but... there's been nothing."

"What should we do, Arkady-immai?" She sounded calm enough, but he could see that her hands shook.

"Go on, I guess. There is supposed to be a riverhead somewhere and once we find it, we can follow it southward."

"Will it take us to Samarkand?" she asked, dipping her fingers into the meager serving of peas and millet. It was all they had left to eat in their supplies, and Arkady dared not leave her to hunt for fear of what the tigers might do. He could tell from the way his gelding fretted that the enormous cats were not far off.

"No, but we should cross a caravan route eventually, and then we will be able to find where we're going." It was a remote hope, and he took refuge in petulance. "And if you'd use your powers to see where we are, you could get us away from here."

Surata set her food aside. "Arkady-immai, when I am tired I can see no farther with my skills than you can with your eyes. Beyond those limits, how can I or anyone tell where a place is? Once we are beyond the confines of the earth, we can be anyplace we wish to be in an instant. How far do we have to go to be there? How do you measure such a distance? And how can I guide you here with what we might learn there? It's useless, Arkady-immai. It's no aid to us to search where there are no landmarks and no roads to..."

He sighed. "I know. I know. I want a miracle, Surata. There are times I hope that you can give me one, but..." He did not know how to go on.

She had no comfort for him. She rested her head on his shoulder, then carefully scooped out the last of her food, licking it off her fingers with care. "We will have to find a well, won't we? And soon."

"Yes," he admitted. "For the animals as well as ourselves. Since I can't see anything hopeful, I don't suppose you..."

"I will do what I can," she promised him, her face wan.

They found no water the next day—neither dared to speak

of it—nor the next. The skins they carried became flaccid and empty, and the parching sun did not spare them. Their lips cracked and bled, their skin chapped, breaking at elbows and knuckles. Their heads throbbed from heat and sun, and when they moved, there were roaring tides in their heads that frightened them as much as the inexorable, festering sun.

And when Surata insisted that there was a spring nearby, a cool place in the hard, rocky ground, Arkady was sure that she was suffering from the sun and thirst, that she had conjured up a vision of what she wanted for them both to make their ends a little more bearable. He did not have the heart to challenge her.

"We'll try it," he said through his crusted mouth, knowing they had nothing better to do. "Where is it?" As he asked, the bay tossed his head, snorting and trying to bounce on his forefeet, though he tottered like a newborn foal with the effort.

"He smells the water," Surata told Arkady.

"I hope so," Arkady responded and let his horse have his head. He wobbled in the saddle as the gelding stumbled into what once would have been a brisk trot. "How far?"

"Not very," she said, her voice cracking. "We can go a little further without food if we have water."

"Right." He tried to make out what lay in the distance, but his vision was blurred, and when he blinked, it made him feel dizzy.

The bay snorted again, moving more actively. Then he whinnied and started to run, going toward a place in the rocks where the shadows fell deep and cool.

Arkady blundered out of the saddle and stepped into the darkness. His foot slipped on the moss growing around the spring. He dropped to his knees, catching himself on his hands, then brought them to his face, seeing how wet they were, and how chilled. "Surata!" he shouted. *"Surata!"* He lurched to his feet once again. "There's water!"

"Yes," she called to him. "I can smell, as your horse does."

Leaning down, Arkady sunk his hands into the spring and brought up a handful of water. He drank it greedily through his palm, begrudging every drop that trickled through his fingers. After four such frantic gulpings, he knew he should stop, or he would get sick. Reluctantly he came out into the light again. "I'll help you down, and get the pail for the horse," he said, reaching up to Surata and taking her around the waist.

"He is half-crazed, poor beast," Surata remarked as she was led into the cave.

"Drink, Surata, but not too much at first." Now that he had had some water, he became light-headed. He giggled as he filled the pail, and he was whistling when he gave the pail to his gelding, finding it amusing to listen to the horse blow through his nostrils as he drank. He looked up at the sky, and it no longer seemed to be made of heated brass. He pulled off his knotted cotton headgear and flung it away from him, then sunk his hands in his unkempt hair.

The bay brought his head up, snorting. He stamped twice, as if trying to dig more water out of the ground.

A little of Arkady's euphoria faded and he came back to his horse. "Not yet, old fellow," he said, patting the dusty neck. "Wait awhile and I'll see you get some more." He bent down and picked up the leather pail. "Surata? Are you all right?"

"Yes, Arkady-immai." She sounded stronger. "It is pleasant to be out of the sun."

"Good." He found the hobbles on the saddle and knelt down to fasten them on his gelding. He had made up his mind that no matter how much sunlight was left to them, they would remain here for the night, and he wanted to make sure the gelding did not wander off. On impulse, he took his sword and scabbard, belting them on as he went back into the cave.

"The water is sweet," Surata said to him as he came to her side.

"Don't drink too quickly or too much," Arkady warned her again. "If you do, you may become ill."

"Yes, I am aware of this," she said, reaching out and dangling her hands in the water. "This is very nice."

He copied her hesitantly, wondering if it would make his thirst more acute. "It's . . . restful," he said a bit later.

She did not speak at once, and when she did, her tone was thoughtful. "Arkady-immai, doesn't it seem odd to you that this spring should be here and there be no signs that men come to it? Animals must—I can catch their scents a little—but there is nothing to say that men know of this place, not so much as a bucket or a pitcher."

Although this bothered him as well, he said, "We're in a remote part of the world, Surata. Perhaps the men who know of this place aren't here often."

She shook her head slowly. "No, Arkady-immai, that is not the reason. The reason is that we are far from any roads, aren't we?" She did not sound frightened, but still, it was hard for him to answer her. "Arkady-immai?"

"Right," he muttered. Then he turned to her. "Yes, Surata, yes. We're lost."

Chapter 19

They did not so much sleep that night as collapse. Both lay in an exhausted stupor that held them even when foxes and wide-eared, flat-headed sand cats came to drink in the night. Once a golden civet sprayed its penetrating scent at an unknown threat, and that odor hardly disturbed Arkady and Surata, though she sneezed.

When they woke, it was slowly and groggily, moving as if they feared their bones would not support them.

"I'm hungry," Arkady said when he had blinked and stretched and tried to remember where he was.

"So am I," Surata said. "But the horse needs food more than we do. He will not carry us much longer unless he has food and a rest. He is as tired as we are."

"I know," Arkady grumbled. "He can eat grass and leaves if he must. I'll try to cut him something when I get up. Can you tell if there are any trees or shrubs that he can eat?" His mouth was dry, but that no longer weighed on him as it had the day before. He remained still, hoping that he would be able to keep down the little moisture he had taken.

She started to speak, but began coughing from the effort.

He reached out to her, touching her hair. "Are you all right now?"

"I'm tired." She stretched. "I don't think I have been this tired in all my life, not when I was going with the slave caravan, not when I fought with my family against the Bundhi. My bones long for sleep."

"I'm sorry, Surata." His sympathy was deep and genuine. "I'm truly sorry."

"But why? I am the one who should say that to you, since I am responsible for us being here at all." To her chagrin, she started to weep. "I . . . it's the fatigue, Arkady-champion, it means nothing. I can see why you do not trust me at other times when I nearly brought us to death by getting us lost."

He understood her better than she knew. "Surata, after I take care of the horse, I'm going to find us something to eat, even if it's only grasshoppers. We can't keep on this way. One of the reasons we're lost is that we're too tired and too hungry and too worn out to be able to think clearly. And in this condition, we haven't a prayer of getting to that other place for help." Or for relief, or for love, he added to himself.

"I wish I could help!" She brought her hands to her eyes. "I *detest* this blindness!"

"I know," he said, confining her hands in his own. "I know, Surata."

She turned on him, as if she willed herself to see him. "Why do you bear with me? I have led you into this . . . desolation. I have cost you more than gold and livestock. I have failed you, and—"

He sat up. "You know why. I've told you before. Surata, you hate your blindness more than I do. That's natural. It saddens me that you're blind. But I'm damned if I'll pity you for it, or let you pity yourself." He pulled her up. "I know how you feel. You've told me before."

This outburst quieted her, and she composed herself. "You're right to rebuke me."

"For all the Saints in Heaven . . . !" He unwrapped himself

from the blankets. "I *didn't* rebuke you." He glared at her in exasperation. "Or if I did, it wasn't meant to—"

"It was meant kindly," she interrupted him. "I realize that."

"But?" He smiled down at her.

She shrugged. "It still irritates me."

"Not surprising." Arkady just managed to suppress a yawn, then looked about for his horse.

The bay was near a few low-lying bushes, stripping the few leaves off the branches. His ribs showed and his dark coat was almost without luster. But he was eating, and Arkady knew that in time he could grow sleek and glossy once more.

"Doing better?" Arkady asked as he came up to the gelding. He patted the horse's shoulder. "You've done more than I should have asked of you, fellow." He looked for the shears in one of the packs and started away, still weak and unsteady, for the hillside, where he set himself to cutting the clumps of grass and other low vegetation he found. It took him longer than he thought possible, but when he came back, he had an armload of fodder for the horse. "I'll get you more water in a bit," he said to the bay, then looked around for Surata.

She was not where he had left her: the blankets were neatly rolled and stacked together, but she was nowhere in sight.

Arkady knew a moment of consuming panic, then steadied himself. "Surata!" he shouted.

There was no answer at first, and then he heard her call his name. She was in the cave of the spring. "Come here, Arkady-immai."

He found her seated by the water, her legs drawn up and crossed in the manner she had, soles upward in the bend of her knees. She had regained some of her serenity. "I have been wondering why the tigers did not come here. It would have been an easy thing, a natural thing for them to attack and drink as well."

Arkady had been able to keep the tigers from his thoughts, but her reminder brought back all his apprehension. "Do you have any reason?"

"Yes, I think I do. This spring has a guardian." Her smile widened.

"What do you mean, a guardian?"

"You know," she said impatiently. "There are forces that are partly of the other place and partly of the daily world. They are often very ancient things. This guardian is one such."

"You mean it's haunted?" He crossed himself quickly, remembering everything he had been told as a child about malevolent ghosts and evil spirits.

"Not haunted," she corrected him. "This is a . . . being that watches this place. Perhaps other men think it is holy or haunted, and that is why they do not come here. The animals know better, and visit it regularly." She rocked a little.

"Then the tigers might—"

"The tigers are agents of the Bundhi. They cannot come here. The guardian does not permit that." Her voice was light and happy. "We can remain here another day or so and be safe. The Bundhi will not be able to find us, in the daily world or in the other place: the guardian has power in both and will stop him."

Arkady could think of nothing to say to her. While he knew she did not doubt what she was telling him, he could not accept it without dread. He muttered a prayer under his breath and looked around the darkness uneasily. "What makes you think this is so?"

"Because I can . . . touch it. Not as you and I touch, but there are other ways. This guardian is strong and does not want this spring to be contaminated with such as the Bundhi. The spring is restorative."

Was it because they had been in the sun and heat and emptiness for so long that Surata imagined this? Arkady asked himself. Why did she want to convince him that they had stumbled upon anything more miraculous than water? "Surata, there's no reason . . ."

When he did not go on, she turned toward him. "The guardian cannot harm us, Arkady-immai. It will not harm foxes, either, or the other animals. It will be kind to your horse."

He thought her words were madness but he said nothing. "I've got feed for the horse. I ought to find something we can eat, Surata. The water is wonderful and without it we would be dead, but we must have food."

"There is a fig tree up the hill and behind an outcropping of stones. It was planted long ago to give food to the guardian." She waved him away. "Find that tree, Arkady-immai. Then we will eat."

He supposed, as he left the cave, that he would have to do her the service of looking. It would be difficult to tell her that he found nothing. He went with growing regret, for it pained him to consider how their ordeal had changed her. As he made the climb up the hill, he did his best to think of ways he could ease the distress that had so clearly taken hold of Surata. "Guardians," he said to the air. "Guardian beings taking care of springs!" He was able to scoff now, where she could not hear him and he would not have to see her anguish.

Near the brow of the hill there was an outcropping of rocks, and this surprised him more than he liked to admit. He stood looking at it, deciding at last that in an area like this, she would know there had to be occasional outcroppings of rocks. There was nothing significant in finding it, he insisted to himself.

Behind the rocks stood an old fig tree, the ground beneath it sticky with fallen figs. Flies and other insects droned among them. Arkady stood staring at it for some time, then went cautiously toward it, expecting to find it gone. But the smell was real, and the leaves rustled in the wind, and when he pulled one of the remaining figs off its stem, it was believable enough. Shaken, Arkady peeled back the skin and bit into the rich, sweet fruit.

He came back to the cave with the leather pail full of figs. On the way, he had given three to his horse and watched the gelding extend his neck and half-close his eyes with pleasure. As he entered the cave, he called out to Surata, adding, "They were there," rather sheepishly.

"The guardian said the tree was—" she began, only to have him cut her off.

"I doubted you. I thought that . . ." He could not go on.

"You thought that I had gone mad. But you see, I had not. The guardian is real and has told me things we must know. Now I tell these things to you, so that you can get food for us and keep us safe."

"It's too bad we had to leave the tent behind. In a place like this, it would be pleasant to have it to climb into." He sat beside her and held out a fig. "Here. There's more." While he watched her eat, he had another fig himself. "We shouldn't eat too much. It's like the water, it could make us sick."

"Three figs will not destroy us," she said lightly. "Oh, this is so good."

By nightfall, Arkady had been guided to more food by Surata, who insisted that her information came from the guardian of the spring. He accepted this unwillingly but could think of no other explanation for her remarkable knowledge. It was against everything he had been taught, and he said this to her as they pulled their blankets up to their necks that night.

"But you've said that you believe in devas, winged spirits—"

"Angels," he supplied.

"Yes, that guard you. And you said that there are miraculous shrines that your holy men protect. How is this any different?" She stretched one last time before securing her blanket.

"It ... it is." he was as puzzled by his answer as she was. "This isn't a Saint or the Virgin, or ... I don't know what it is."

Surata touched him gently. "Arkady-champion, that is why you don't want to believe it is there—because you don't know what it is, and that troubles you. You cannot trust it, as you do not always trust what I tell you that you cannot verify for yourself. If calling this ... guardian a saint or an angel will make you less apprehensive, then call it one of those things."

"And how do you know that it isn't a demon or ... anything like that?" He was being stubborn, and he acknowledged it to himself, though not to her.

"If it were malignant, those tigers would be here, and we would not. The guardian is neither of the Right nor the Left Hand Path. The guardian keeps to its own way and will not permit those that are not peaceable to come here. The tigers are not peaceable, and for that reason, they cannot find this place. If the guardian did not have this power, the Bundhi would know where we are, and he would have taken some action against us by now, because we are weak, and we're . . . in no condition to reach the other place, let alone battle him or anyone once we reached there." She paused, then pointed out, "We have food, don't we? And water? Then stop asking so many questions and be glad that we stumbled onto this spring."

There was nothing he wanted to do more, but the uncertainties nagged at him. "If neither the Right nor the Left Hand Path is welcome here, why have we found this place?"

"Because we are peaceable. If we carried on our fight here, the guardian would not permit us to remain." She sighed. "It is sad that the guardian will not take sides, for we need an anchor in the daily world before we can establish a sanctuary in that other place. But the guardian will not do this, not for us or for anyone."

"But can we stay here?" Arkady dreaded the thought of going on before they had regained some portion of their strength.

"We will be permitted to do that, and the guardian will protect us as long as we do not bring our battle here. We may travel in that other place and the guardian will not interfere, but we are not to bring our fight to his spring."

"Right," he said wearily, closing his eyes.

They spent one more day and night there by the cave and its spring. In that time, some of their energy was restored, and their bodies no longer ached from privation. The gelding grew restless and his coat glistened in the sunlight. Arkady combed and braided his mane, having nothing better to do. He was delaying the hour of leaving, and he admitted it, if only to himself.

"We'll have to travel soon, Arkady-immai." Surata told him later that day. "The guardian will not permit us to remain once we are strong enough to fend for ourselves."

"We are a long way from any merchants' route," Arkady said pensively. "You said that you can see no farther than I can, and all that is around us here is empty, dry land. We don't know where we are, so it will be difficult to find where we are going."

"There is a way," she said with more enthusiasm than she had shown before. "We can return to the traders' road."

"Possibly," he said. "We can't be very far from the Oxus, and if we take care, we can reach it, then—"

"But Arkady-immai," she cut in, "you may be limited and I may share your limitation, but the guardian is not like us. The guardian knows where the spring is and sees distances not as we would in that other place, but as we do in the daily world. Through the guardian, I *do* know where we are, for the guardian has shown me, with his wider vision."

"Surata . . . you don't need to say these things. I am content to go. We'll find our way." He looked down at her, admiring her and yet exasperated with her for persisting in her story of the guardian. He was willing to believe that she had somehow found the well for them and wanted to press on to Samarkand, but her invention of a guardian spirit that would let them rest but was doggedly neutral as a cloistered monk was more than he would accept.

"Arkady-immai, we are to the east of Khiva. We passed the city while we were in the grip of hunger and thirst. There is a river—the Amu is what the guardian calls it—not more than a day ahead of us. We must continue east and then bear slightly to the south. Samarkand is at the base of the mountains. The caravan route is more to the south than we are, and passes through Bukhara before reaching Samarkand. The guardian tells me that we can take three or four days off our travel by going directly to Samarkand. It will also give the Bundhi fewer opportunities to spy on us. Undoubtedly he has sent agents to both places."

Arkady stared down at his large, blunt hands, looking at the scars on his knuckles. He listened to Surata as he flexed his fingers, wanting to trust what she told him but unwilling to do so. "Surata," he said when she had finished, "you've got too pardon me if I am suspicious of what you . . . Look, Surata, I know you're convinced that you've found something that

277

helps you, but I . . ." He thought a moment, then tried again. "I'm not convinced that there really is a guardian, or that it can tell you anything, but I'm willing to give it a try, for your sake. After all, the fig tree was there."

"You want me to know that you're not accepting the guardian, is that it?" she asked him when he was through.

"That's more or less it," he confirmed. "The river may be there and it may not. You want us to find something, don't you? So do I."

"And you're trying to prepare me for disappointment," she added with great candor. "That is dear of you, Arkady-immai, but it isn't necessary. The river is there, and the way to Samarkand is clear. We will pass two empty cities and a tower filled with bones, and those will be signs to us that we are in the right."

Arkady thought carefully as he listened to her. He wanted to trust what she was telling him, and all her past skills argued that he could, but this was different. What they did now would determine if they would live long enough to confront the Bundhi, or sleep in a bed instead of a roll of blankets. He patted her hand. "Surata, if we don't reach that river, what then?"

"We will," she said tranquilly.

They reached the river late in the afternoon of the following day. Arkady drew up his gelding and stared as if he were seeing a mirage. Surata, riding behind him, tightened her arms.

"What is it, Arkady-champion?"

In a voice he thought must belong to a stranger, he said, "It's the river."

Surata gave him a playful jab in the ribs. "There, you see?"

Three nights after that, after they had eaten and night enveloped them, when their campfire had burned down to a glowing molehill, Surata said softly, "I have missed our union, Arkady-immai."

"So have I," he said, then amended this. ". . . When I wasn't so frightened or so weak that all I could think about was the danger we were in."

"There is always danger," she said in an abstracted way.

"To breathe is dangerous. To wake in the morning is dangerous. There is no reason to spend all your days thinking of the danger."

"I'm a soldier, Surata," he reminded her. "I've lived this long by recognizing danger in time." He took one of the blanket rolls and braced it behind him, so that he could rest his elbows on it and look up at the stars. "You watch after us in that other place; it's my responsibility to look after us here."

"That's true, I suppose." She felt around her for his hand, and when she did not find it, she stretched out her arms until she touched him. "Still, it would be pleasant to be in that other place. It would be pleasant to awaken the Subtle Body."

"Is that the only reason you do it, to reach the Subtle Body and get access to that other place?" The question bothered him, had been nagging at him since Sarai, but he had not had the courage to speak of it.

Her face turned to the sound of his voice. "No. That is not the only reason."

The relief that came over him was far greater than he had expected. He did not realize he had been holding his breath, but now he let it out explosively and made a grab for her, pulling her down across his chest and laughing joyously. "Thank God for that," he said before he kissed her. As she began to rouse him, he knew he would never grow weary of her, never regret being with her, never doubt that buying her was the wisest thing he had ever done. He met her kisses with his own and tentatively explored the places on her body where she said that the Centers lay.

She got him out of his clothes and was soon naked herself. "Arkady-champion," she crooned as her tongue circled the center of his chest.

He took her face in his hands. "No, Surata. This time let me try, for you."

She made a sound that was not quite a laugh. "You know nothing," she protested happily.

"Then teach me, Surata," he murmured as his lips grazed hers. "Teach me."

"I have studied a lifetime," she breathed, her head flung back as he circled her breast with his hand.

"Good." There was a hint of a sensation in his fingers, like an inner tingling. "It will take me a long time to learn." Was it possible that she had been telling him the truth, he marvelled as he ran his hand down the Centers. Was there really a force that was triggered by this contact?

"The lips first, Arkady-champion," she whispered unevenly. "Then the throat, then the heart." She stopped as her whole body trembled with the movement of his mouth on her salty, sweet flesh.

It was the most exquisite delight to waken her passion. There was no part of her—not a toe, not an eyebrow, not a Center of her Subtle Body—that he could touch without bringing sighs of pleasure to her lips. He knew he was clumsy, that he had learned only the few things she had shown him, yet he had no doubt that her rapture was genuine. How much better it would become when he had been instructed in all the nuances and exercises she already knew. His own body thrummed with excitement and expectation.

"Do not wait . . . too long, Arkady-champion," she urged him a short time later. "It will be over too . . . soon." The last word was hardly more than a flutter in her throat. Her hands moved over his body ardently.

He could not speak, so consumed was he with apolaustic need. As he drew her close, onto him, around him

they soared through vast expanses of many-hued light, around vistas and spires of light, along avenues and under seas of light. He no longer felt separate from her; his unity with her was as intense—more intense—in this other place than in the daily world. He thought it possible that they might fuse, be one being, made of the same light as the spaces around them.

"Arkady my champion," she said with the sound in his mind, "it can be possible."

He could sense a little of the knowledge she had in her as part of his own memories, but so remote and hazy that he could not discern any specific part of it. Wavering images, phrases, events flickered at the edge of his thoughts, but they escaped quick as fish when he tried to hold them. "You . . ." *He had no way to express his frustration to her.*

Surata understood. "It will come in time, Arkady my champion. It will be clear to you."

"Does this happen to you about me?" *He did not actually speak aloud, but his words were distinct and separate from her words, and that reassured him.*

"Not as much," *she confessed.* "I know your confusion; I have experienced it, when I was younger."

"Then you have done this with others?" *His jealousy was foolish and unnecessary but he felt it as keenly as a knife in the back.*

"This? No. Not this." *She soothed him, rocking him gently as if he were her child and not her lover.* "There are other means, but this is what I was being trained for, this unity."

He was mollified by her confession. "We are united, aren't we? Completely?"

She hesitated. "Not completely. There would not be you and I, there would be the Divine Child, which would be both of us in a new being. It would be yin and yang at once, male and female, light and dark. Then we would be one." *She felt his hesitancy and faint revulsion.* "There is nothing wrong in such a being. It is the greatest achievement of any Adept, any alchemist. It is the end of alienation."

"The end of being myself," *he objected, fear cold within him.* "Would I ever be myself again, after that?"

"You would be all yourself, Arkady my champion. You would be all the things that you truly are, in the daily world. Here we would be the Divine Child, if you wished it." *Her voice ached with longing for it, and he could feel it distantly.* "When one has learned to transcend, to ride the crest of the wave, that is just the beginning, not the end of it. A student soon learns to transcend alone, roaming this other place and shaping it according to whim or desire. That is not what you and I do, and we do not do what the Divine Child can do."

"So that's what you were after," Arkady grumbled with resentment growing in him. "We're an excuse to . . . advance your studies."

Her chuckle was heartrending in its sadness. "Arkady my champion, you must know better than that by now. If that were all I wished of you—"

Her pain was a hurt within him, and he cringed at it and what he had done. "I didn't mean that, Surata. Not the way it sounded."

"You did mean it," she corrected him softly, "but that isn't important. The fear that you have is important."

Arkady was almost overcome with shame. He had intended to hurt her, and he had, but he had not anticipated her compassion, and her care. They hovered together, their shifting environment less brilliant than it had been an instant ago. "I . . ." he began contritely. "Surata, what can I—"

"You need say nothing, Arkady my champion. I know what you feel, as you know my emotions." Her voice was serene, accepting. "Your turmoil is needless, believe me."

He tried to let her gentleness replace his hostility and was abashed to find he could not. "I don't . . ."

"It will take time, Arkady my champion. Do not be troubled that you are not ready to learn so much. Most of the world cannot bear to know the smallest part of what you've already done." Her tone was calm without being dispassionate, encouraging him while she excused his reluctance.

"I'll try," he promised. "Each time, I'll try."

She was about to say more, but there was an abrupt change in their surroundings: darkness like banked flames erupted in front of them, and a sound worse than thunder and the firing of many cannon shot the air. Lurid shadows fell over them, and the air echoed with screams.

"What . . . ?" Arkady demanded, suddenly wishing that he was armed and mounted with a full troop of cavalry behind him.

"The Bundhi. He has found us." She turned them around, away from the ghosts of battle and death that loomed before

*them, and pointed to the rising walls of the bamboo redoubt.
"Don't let that touch you, Arkady my champion; it is dangerous in this other place as well as in the daily world."*

With an unconcealed shudder, Arkady remembered the body he had found in the deserted village, and he could not deny his repugnance. "I won't touch it."

"The bamboo is alive. It feeds." She was on the verge of panic as the redoubt walls rose higher behind them.

"Surata!" His tone was sharp, deliberately jarring.

"They're seeking us." Everything about her urged flight.

"Steady," he ordered as if he were leading his men against overwhelming forces. "We can manage it, with a little good sense."

"We can leave this other place," she suggested.

"And then the Bundhi would send his tigers after us while we are still naked, lazy from fulfillment? No thank you. I'd rather throw him off the scent." He pondered the problem. "Surata, does he know what . . . we're doing? Now, in the daily world?"

"Yes," she answered.

"Does he . . . have the means to follow us because of that?"

"How do you mean?" Her apprehension was controlled now, but the redoubt was increasing in size at a steady and alarming rate.

"I mean that being together could be something he can use. He might be able to know that we are together here, and will use that as a link to where we are in the daily world." He waited impatiently for her to answer him. He had been sliding away through the air, but the redoubt did not become a distant place as he had hoped it would.

"He could," she said carefully, her words ringing their warning in his skull.

"But . . ." Arkady began, feeling his way, "what if we were to make him think we were in another place, would he believe that? Would it be possible to make it appear that we're in a barn or . . . any building, or ruins? Could he be made to assume that we were there and not where we are?"

She strove to match his composure. "I really don't know. It was never suggested that we could lie about such things. Still, it . . . might work."

"Is there anything else that we can do instead that you know of?" He was not challenging her; he wanted nothing more than to learn she had a trusted and successful way to avoid the Bundhi and the voracious bamboo staves that made up his redoubt and the strength of his agents and himself in the daily world. "Did your father or your uncles tell you that they . . . ?"

"Nothing," she admitted sadly. "Before, the Bundhi always knew where we were, in any case. Our redoubt was an old one, one that had been established generations upon generations ago. It was part of our power, as his redoubt—this one and the one in the daily world—are part of his. There was never any need or inclination to dissemble." She trembled as the bamboo expanded, appearing now to be the size of the pillars of temples and throbbing with vile appetite.

"Do they know we're here?" He dreaded what her answer might be.

"They know. But they are as blind as I am and have no way to locate us beyond the sense they have of . . . prey." If it were possible, she seemed to become more completely part of him.

"What do they want to do? Feed on us here and in the daily world at the same time?" It was a guess, but one that made a curious sort of strategic sense to him.

"The Bundhi would like that, but he would want to be able to find us in both places himself." She gave a little shriek that came through his mouth. "Arkady my champion, look! There are more staves."

The redoubt had more than trebled in size since they had first seen it, and now it appeared to be enclosing them in vast, ascending walls.

"Where is the Bundhi?" Arkady demanded, wondering if he dared to attack the sorcerer directly.

"There! All around us! Don't you understand that he is the redoubt. This is not only where he comes in this other place,

it is his manifestation." She shook as if consumed with fever. *"Arkady my champion, we must leave and be sure that . . . your trick diverts him and his agents."*

"Right," he said harshly.

("Arkady-champion, are there any rats in the hay? I don't want to ruin this with rats." The words came out in a rush and she rolled them so that neither of them could see the last embers of their fire.

("There are usually rats in stables. But cats live here as well. They'll keep the rats away." He blinked, trying to concentrate on what sort of stable they were in. "Don't light the lanthorn, Surata. The dark is better.")

Together Arkady and Surata put on a burst of speed, then, as they moved beyond range of the staves, Surata whispered urgently, "Quickly; think of a place or other grand place—the biggest and most beautiful building you've ever seen."

Confused, Arkady did his best to remember the castles and cathedrals of his youth, and came up with an immense building that was a fortress version of Saint Stanislas as he recalled it from his childhood. It was so vast, with tall, buttressed arches and windows of stained glass letting in light of so many colors that the air of the place seemed tangible with it. Statues of Saints and the Virgin and Our Lord were everywhere, all in the scale a seven-year-old boy would perceive.

"Did you like this place?" Surata asked as the structure soared around them.

"I don't know. It awed me too much to like it." He was amazed at what she had done, and he hesitated only a moment before he said so. *"How can you do this?"*

"It is what we learn, when we are trained for this life. This was strange for me; I have never been to such places. Is all your stone so dark and your ceilings so high? They did not appear so in your other memories."

"You're . . . tired," he blurted with surprise.

"This takes strength," she said by way of explanation. *"It will not protect us for long, but long enough, I hope, to confuse the Bundhi while he tries to determine where the stable is."*

She changed her tone. "You saved us this time, Arkady my champion. I was useless when I should have been fighting with you. I am abashed."

"You were afraid." He did not accuse her, but it was apparent he would not allow her to protest his judgment. "You needed me at first because I can fight. I've shown you now that you made a good choice."

"I knew that from the first," she said, not willing to accept his implied excuse for herself. "I did what I have been taught I must not do, and for that we were nearly consumed. I was not worthy of your defense or your trust."

He was aware of how great her disgust with her actions was; it was as keen a sense in him as his own feelings. "Surata, look at me. Look. You have no reason to do this. You have to accept that even the most seasoned soldier will sometimes freeze, for no reason at all, in the face of the enemy. Others will weep like frightened babies at the sound of cannon-fire, though it has never troubled them before. You know the strength of the Bundhi, and you know it far better than I. It was too hard for you to think about it, for a little while."

She was not consoled by his kindness. "I should have acted. I knew the consequences, for both of us, and still—"

"Stop that. If you spend our time berating yourself, we won't be ready to meet the Bundhi's next attack. There's one sure to come." He wanted to take her by the shoulders and give her a quick shake, but it was impossible, with her a part of him.

"If the Bundhi comes again, we have this, and it will give us some protection." She paused. "We ought to do more with that stable, but I'm worried that if we give away too much, it will become apparent that it is our imagination and not a real place."

"We haven't given much willingly—this can be no exception, or the Bundhi might grow suspicious. It would be the sensible thing to do, under the circumstances. You've said that he has very little trust in anything." His cool attitude at last had the effect he had hoped it would.

"Yes; all right." She shivered with disquiet. "I don't know these places, Arkady my champion. This building is . . . strange and forbidding to me. What do you do in a place like this?"

"Worship God," Arkady answered, aware that she did not and would never have the same sense of comfort he did. To her the stone room was stark, the towering statues cold and un-responsive, inhuman in their holiness. He studied the sur-roundings with his shared knowledge of her and could not believe any longer in the succor of the cathedral-fortress he had brought forth out of his memories.

"Arkady my champion, what is wrong?"

"Nothing."

"What is it?" she insisted.

Before he could answer her, a bamboo staff the size of a tree trunk fell through one of the stained-glass windows, scattering bright shards of the Martyrdom of Saint Boniface of Querfurt over the stone floor.

Chapter 20

Arkady shouted, feeling Surata's alarm as well as his own. The stones shook with the impact of the bamboo, and he realized his hands were burning where he had accidentally touched the surface of the tremendous staff.

"We can't stay here," Surata said, spurred to action. "And it is not yet time to go back. We are not ready to go back. We can still do a few things to protect ourselves, and we must try."

"But the Bundhi," Arkady protested as he watched the stones melt like ice at the end of winter. The staff lay across them, filling the air with a charnel-house stench. "The Bundhi will try to find us here in this other place as well as in the daily world."

"He has found us already," Surata said. "And that is not a good thing for us. You have seen men surrounded, haven't you, and cut off?"

"Yes. It's rare that anyone gets free of such a trap."

She could feel his bitterness but chose to ignore it. "Then think of what you would do then and we will do it now."

Arkady laughed, and with his laughter, the walls of the cathedral-fortress broke and dissolved. The bamboo staff hovered not far from them, undulating slightly. "And what now? We're still exposed."

"But not enclosed," she pointed out. "In this other place, it is difficult to build walls that last forever." Her strength was returning, making him feel stronger and more capable than he had since they fled the expanding walls of the redoubt. "We can go through this other place with great speed. It will lengthen the time we are gone from the daily world, but it will divert the attention of the Bundhi."

"Where did you get an idea like that?" he asked her, surprised at her acumen.

"From you, Arkady my champion," she said with a trace of amusement. "It is your mind that tells me these things."

He knew what she meant, as he knew her thoughts, but he could think of no way to acknowledge this, and so he said, "It's a good idea, and we'd best act on it quickly, before the Bundhi finds another way to capture us."

At that, he felt himself made lighter, lighter, until he was nothing more than thistledown floating in the vastness, Surata with him, and lighter than he. There was no voice left to either of them, but Surata said softly in the long fibers that radiated out from the center of him, "You are learning, Arkady my champion. Until now, you've been anchored in your own shape. This is great progress and it pleases me that you have done it."

He wanted to respond, but found no way, and in his confusion, he almost forced her to return him to his proper body. "What is this?" he finally was able to inquire, although he had no notion of how he had managed it.

"It is a start toward your growth, Arkady my champion," said her voice without sound. "With this, we have a chance."

He tried to deal with her praise, but found his impressions so jumbled that he could not fasten on any idea for very long. His consternation increased. "What good is this?"

"We will be able to meet the Bundhi with some of his abilities for ourselves." She hesitated. "Aren't you aware that the redoubt of the Bundhi here is the Bundhi, in another form? What the bamboo eats in this place nourishes the Bundhi. What the bamboo eats in the daily world nourishes the bamboo." She grew more somber, and the thistledown no longer wafted on unfelt breezes.

Arkady thought of what she had told him—that in this other place, the Bundhi and his redoubt were one in the same—and it worried him. It was one thing to storm a fortress; he had done it enough times in the past to know how it was done. But this was another matter entirely. He had never had such a battle to fight, and he did not know what he ought to do. No matter how he puzzled over the matter, he thought of nothing. He let her carry them wherever she liked, and experienced something that might be speed, or simply distance.

"Arkady my champion," she said some little while later, "we have come far, and if the Bundhi wishes to find us, he will have quite a search on his hands. That gives us time to make a safe place to use later on."

"How do you make a safe place here, where everything changes?" He could not hide from her the disgust he felt, nor the futility that had taken hold of him.

She did not upbraid him for his melancholy but said, "There are things that can be made here that will last as long as your will lasts. That is the nature of this other place. You will have to join with me to make such a place for us. If we could unite to the point that we became the Divine Child, then we would have no need for the protection of a fortress or other barrier, but you are not so advanced that it is possible for the Divine Child to manifest yet." Her tone changed. "You have heard of a castle, I perceive, that is in an island in a low salt lake. That would provide protection. It is a thing that the Bundhi does not know, and because he does not know it, he will not be looking for it. Your . . . cathedral"—the word was strange to her and she pronounced it clumsily—"was too much like a temple, and for that reason, the Bundhi sought us out. But a place that you think of, that stone fortress in a salt marsh, that should stop him for a little while."

"Why would it stop him, when the other didn't?" Arkady asked, confused and irritated.

"I have explained that. The Bundhi will not look for it at first, and that is the advantage we need." Her tone was becoming more enthusiastic. "You must understand, Arkady my champion, that we need a haven, one where we will be able to resist the Bundhi for the time he pursues us."

Arkady shook himself in confusion, and the thistledown quivered in the emptiness. "Right. I will try to remember everything I know about that castle. It's old, and it's held off more attacks than most. The marsh around it is filled with sinking sand, so that any approaching without knowing where to step will be sucked under the water." He put all his effort into recalling the vast salt marsh. The place was desolate but secure.

"Very good, Arkady my champion. For a man untrained to this study, you are apt." She was more encouraged, which communicated itself to him. "Let us establish this place, and then we may come to it when we need it."

In the void, there was shimmering light, the color of the sea and the color of stone, green and gray, with a somber shine that looked like the glint of sunlight on polished armor. Arkady felt an inner pride as the fortress took shape before him.

"Is this right, Arkady my champion?" Surata asked, her voice more thready than it had been.

"Yes, it's right," he said with satisfaction. "There is a causeway to approach it, and a drawbridge, so that the castle can be completely isolated." As he described it, the thing came into being. "Beautiful, Surata."

". . . grateful," she breathed, her strength almost gone.

"What is it?" he asked her, feeling how exhausted she had become.

"It takes . . . strength to . . . keep such a place . . . real." Her sigh was fluttery, so soft that there might not be any breath at all behind it.

"Surata!" Arkady demanded, afraid of the sound of her.

"I am both here with you and there in that castle," she forced herself to say. "It is . . . what I know to do."

"Almighty God!" he protested. "You're hurting yourself." He felt it as keenly as he felt his own tenuous existence in the thistledown.

"Not badly, Arkady my champion. Here we can defend . . ." Her failing accents gripped him in fear. *"No, Surata—"*

"It is protection," she insisted, so feebly.

"Enough of this. I won't have you risking yourself to make a place for me to hide." He attempted to change his form, or to be able to reach her in her efforts. *"Surata!"*

"It is . . . good, Arkady . . . my champion."

"Not if it hurts you, it's not," he countered, feeling her fading in his thoughts. "Stop, Surata."

("Surata! Surata!" He took her by the shoulders, then held her tight against him.

("Arkady-champion," she murmured, sounding a long way off.)

"Arkady my champion, the castle is for you." She was struggling to be stronger. *"Together we can be there."*

"Not this way, not losing you!" He wanted to be more than thistledown, more substantial than anything in this other place. *"Damn everything!"* He shook with the violence of his feelings and the spiky ends of the thistledown quavered for the inadequacy of their form.

"The castle," she pleaded. "Go there."

He could not bear to listen to her, to know how much she had sacrificed of her own power to make him safe. He felt himself drift forward, over the shine of the salt marshes toward the castle and the safety of its massive walls. He strove to resist this, certain that Surata was so enervated that she would not be able to continue the transformation for long.

"Arkady my champion, this is for you," she repeated, almost begging him now.

He made one last effort, infusing the delicate, fragile spines with his determination and his

shattering fulfillment and release. He lay beside her, holding her, warming her, urging her back to him. "Surata, don't ever do that again," he whispered to her as he stroked her. "Never endanger yourself that way for me again." He could not tell if she was responding, and he missed the profound link he had had with her only moments—if the time of that other place and the daily world were the same—before. He cradled her, rocking her gently, saying things to her that he could not remember as soon as he spoke them. His hands stung where he had been burned, and he forced himself to examine the weals on her hands as well. The sight of the burns shocked him, for though he had seen daily world echoes of injuries received in that other place, this was different, as if it were tainted with the malice he had felt in the presence of the bamboo redoubt.

Shortly before dawn, when the sky was slate and rose, she turned in his embrace, and her breathing changed, no longer shallow and slow, but the steady, deep rhythm of sleep. Her eyelids fluttered and then were closed, the lines at the corners of her eyes smoothed now, and at rest.

"What happened?" he demanded of her when she called out to him in the morning.

"The Bundhi very nearly had us. He is strong, with his redoubt in that other place anchored to Gora Čimtarga in the daily world." She hid her hands as if unwilling for him to see the burns she had received. "Everything the Bundhi touches is contaminated by him."

"But our castle in the salt marsh..." he protested, not knowing what else to say to her.

"It is a haven of sorts, but... ephemeral. It is not anchored to anything in the daily world, and that makes it much more vulnerable. If the Bundhi wishes to raze it, he could do it." She sighed. "We worked so hard. But..."

"But what?" Arkady asked. "What is it, Surata?"

"Without an anchor, we cannot stand. I wanted to ask the guardian of the spring, but it wasn't possible. With a place like that protected spring, the castle would have been able to stand against the Bundhi whether or not we were present to defend it, but since it wasn't anchored, there was..." Her hands fluttered in distress.

"You speak as if it were no longer there," Arkady said, unable to rid himself of the foreboding that crept over him. "After all you gave to that castle, it couldn't simply . . . fade, could it? It was so . . . real." He could still see it in his mind, and its indomitability was apparent even to him.

"It was real," she said softly. "But it might not be now. I hope I'm wrong. I'm afraid to look for it, or to search." Her eyes met his without the light of recognition. "If I had nothing else to do but give my concentration to it, then I could serve as the anchor, and for a time we would have it. There are too many things we must do in order to live. The castle . . . I hope it will still be there when we return to that other place, but Arkady-champion, I—"

Arkady held her face in his hands. "Surata, you are more to me than any castle in this world or any other." He recalled his village priest describing Paradise as the palace of God, a great, magnificent castle of gold and jewels that floated above the clouds. He kissed her forehead. "What castle is worth you?"

In the next days, she recovered slowly. She was content to ride with him and let him care for her. She had few objections to anything he did, and only once betrayed her feelings, and that was when they came to the first empty city.

"It's very old." Arkady said, holding the bay near the ruined gates. "No one has lived here for generations upon generations."

"What manner of people were they?" Surata asked.

"I don't know. I've never seen anything like this place before and there isn't much left to see of it. I don't know what they were like, Surata." He stared at the gates, the wood almost entirely rotted away so that the ancient hinges hung in the opening like broken teeth. The massive walls of wind-polished stone were rounded and smoothed, so that if there had ever been crenellations along them, they could no longer be seen. "I think they must have been pagans."

"I am a pagan," she reminded him, reaching down to pat his shoulder.

"Not that kind of pagan," Arkady said grandly and vaguely.

"There's a piece of decoration here," he went on. "There's a woman with many breasts and a . . . crown, I guess that is what it is, or a wreath. She has something on her head. There are horses at her dugs, feeding like children." He was both curious and revolted.

"They say there was an ancient people who lived in this area who made gods of their horses," Surata said.

"This might be their city." He recalled that she had said the guardian predicted they would come to two empty cities and a tower of bones before they reached Samarkand. "This is one empty city," he admitted grudgingly. "If there's another one, that should indicate something."

"There are many strange things in these wastes. My uncles said that there were once statues of cats as large as several tall men, and they looked out over a broken courtyard. The emptiness claimed them long ago."

"Do we go in, or go on?" Arkady asked. "It's a little after midday. We can cover much more ground before sundown."

Surata shivered. "The Bundhi may be looking in these remote and empty places, thinking that we would hide in them. Let's go on, and camp in the open."

There had been no tigers for the last four nights, and Arkady was beginning to hope he had outrun them. "What agents would the Bundhi send to a place like this?"

"Anything," she answered very quietly. "Men. Tigers. Scorpions." At this last, she shuddered.

"I wouldn't like to find a nest of scorpions in that place," Arkady said, pulling the reins and turning his gelding away from the ruin. "We'll go on, then."

"Good." Her relief was genuine, and she did not excuse her desire to be away from the arid, desolate place.

Four days later, they came to the second city. This one was older than the first, hardly more than mounds of rubble with scrub grass and thorn bushes growing out of the drast.

"What is it like?" Surata asked as Arkady dismounted, prepared to lead his horse through the declivities that might once have been streets.

"It's like . . . nothing. It's just . . . heaps." He tried to imagine what the place had been like, but it was not possible. There was not enough left to give him any feel of the place. He stared around him. "We might get rain tonight or tomorrow," he said inconsequentially as his gaze went from the wreckage around him to the horizon and sky beyond.

"It will not be tonight," she said confidently. "Tomorrow before mid-morning, there will be rain, but not near us, I think. We will have to avoid low places—washes and riverbeds—if we do not want to get trapped in the floods."

Arkady laughed. "Floods? Out here?"

"Oh, yes, most certainly," Surata said in her most serious manner. "This country has floods. They come suddenly and are gone as quickly, but you can drown in them, just the same." She turned her face toward the south. "Are there mountains yet? Can you see them?"

"Perhaps," Arkady answered, squinting against the dry wind that frisked over the parched grasses. He wanted very much to see the mountains, to tell Surata that they were looming there at the edge of the world.

"Then you *don't* see them," she sighed. "They will be there soon. Tomorrow or the next day, you will see them, to the south. They are very tall mountains."

"I'll look for them," he assured her. "You'll know when I see them. I promise you that."

"Thank you, Arkady-immai," she said, relaxing, her hands wrapped around the tall cantel of the saddle. "You do not believe that the mountains are there, do you?"

"Of course I do," he lied valiantly.

"Arkady-immai," she rebuked him gently. "I know from the tone of your voice that you do not expect to find the mountains—not tomorrow, not the day after, or ever. You will be satisfied if we find an inhabited city, and it need not be Samarkand." She was able to laugh a bit. "Will it trouble you very much when we come to Samarkand?"

"I want to find the place," he said carefully. "We're down to nothing on supplies, and we can eke out a few more days without real strain, but after that, a marketplace would be much appreciated." He paused. "We've been lucky in that respect—the foraging has been good, and there has been feed enough for the horse. There is still enough water to last us a little while longer." He kicked at a loose stone and watched it bounce away through the weed-covered rubble. "I'll say this for that other place: you don't have to worry about food and water and all the rest of it."

"Just bamboo staves that leave burns on your hands," she said.

"How . . . ?" He turned back toward her, rubbing his hands together guiltily. He had convinced himself that he had concealed his injuries successfully. "You didn't mention it before." There was a sulky cast to his expression and that embarrassed him more than her knowledge of his hurt.

"I have the same burns. We were together when the staff came through the window. The burns will heal, Arkady-immai. But it troubles me that you were not willing to tell me about them." She held one of her hands out toward him. "See? Does this look like the burns you have?"

He glanced at her hand, recognizing the shiny, stretched-looking skin across the heel of her palm. "Yes," he said. "It looks the same."

"We shared the hurt, Arkady-immai. There is nothing wrong in that, is there?" She waited for him to answer her, and when he remained stubbornly silent, she added, "If we are to battle the Bundhi, Arkady-immai, we will take the same blows and feel the same pain. It is best to know that now, while you can get used to it."

He wanted to argue with her, to insist that there was no possible way for them to have such close unity that they would have the same wounds. The half-healed scar on her hand matched the one on his, and he could not dispute it. "Look, Surata, what you say might be true, but you could be making too much of this."

"If you want to believe that, it is your right," she said in a soft voice. "I don't wish to wrangle about it." Her chin lifted and her manner became aloof.

Arkady led them through the tumbled wreckage, watching

for animals and reptiles. He was very much afraid of snakes; he listened for the slither in the dry grass most intently.

"There are scorpions here, and lizards, Arkady-immai. They are in the hidden places, waiting. If you do not disturb them, they will not harm you." She listened to the sound of the bay's hooves, then said, "You do not like me to say these things."

"There's nothing wrong with it," Arkady snapped, perplexed by his resentment.

"You fear that I will intrude, that I am intruding, as we are intruding in this old fallen city." She was confident of herself but saddened by what she perceived. "Arkady-immai, you have nothing to be ashamed of, not in your dealings with me."

"It's not that I'm ashamed," he argued, glaring at an overgrown hillock. He knew that she was distressed, but he could not stop the words. "Talk about something else if you must talk, Surata."

She was silent and said nothing until they were beyond the tumbled humps that had once been the city walls. "We will see the mountains soon. And then Samarkand."

"Right," he replied, and kept his eyes on the clouded horizon.

"The wind has shifted, Arkady-champion. There will be rain soon, I think."

"Then we'd better find a roof for the night."

The rain struck late in the afternoon, and by the time they found shelter in a grove of scrub, they were drenched and miserable.

"I don't know if I can get a fire going in this," he mumbled as he brought the bay to a halt. "The ground's wet, and if there's any kindling to be found, it won't take a spark." He had known other such nights, on campaign, and the memory of huddling in dripping tents, clothing damp and stinking of sweat and wool made him grind his teeth.

"It won't trouble me," Surata said, sniffing once. "It is a shame we had to leave the tent behind."

"It's a shame that the tigers got the mules. It's a shame that the caravan became unsafe. It's a shame that—" He made himself stop. "Don't pay any attention, Surata. I'm disgusted with myself for not thinking ahead. I should have found us shelter before the storm broke."

"I have no objections, Arkady-champion."

The saddle groaned and squeaked as Arkady dismounted, and his boots squished as he walked. There was a finger of water down his back. He shook his head and water flew off his hair. "I'll have to dry my weapons somehow. I don't want them to rust. If we find the Bundhi, I'll need them."

"Yes, you will," she agreed. "Are there boughs enough to bind them together, to make a shelter for us?"

"Probably," he said, thinking that he could use a hatchet now. Cutting boughs would be bad for his swords. "There's some thongs we can use to tie them."

"That's a start. If you will help me down, I will help you all I can, Arkady-champion."

"Thanks," he said curtly. He reached up to her and brought her down, noticing that the water in her clothes made her much heavier than usual.

"There must be a place where the trees are thick enough to block most of the water. If we go there, that will be a good place to make our shelter."

Because that was exactly what he had been planning to do, he had an irrational desire to suggest something else, but he suppressed it. "Sounds like a good idea," he said in the flattest tone possible.

Three hours later they huddled together under a makeshift lean-to, eating cold, dry fruit and shivering under their sodden blanket.

"Does the horse have enough food?" Surata asked Arkady, her teeth chattering.

"For tonight and some for tomorrow. We have some gold left, and when we find a village, we can buy food and new provisions." He had been worried about the bay but hated to admit this to Surata, since without the big gelding, they would be on foot and almost helpless.

"Samarkand is not far," Surata promised him.

Arkady bit back a challenge to her calm assertion. "I hope so," he forced himself to say.

She leaned back, trying to sleep. "My bones hurt," she said, not so much in complaint as in surprise.

"That's not surprising in weather like this," he told her, cuddling close to her, grateful for the warmth she provided.

"Tomorrow it will rain, as well. The day after it will be clear."

"You can't be certain of that," Arkady protested but knew inwardly that she was telling the truth.

"Perhaps we should carry this shelter with us, so that to-morrow night, we will not be entirely without protection." She did not wait to hear his comment but yawned and turned on her side.

Arkady dozed through the night, never fully asleep, and in the morning, he was dull and irritable. He saddled up and packed their belongings with little more than a few forbidding grunts, and as they resumed their way through the rain, he began to feel a certain grim satisfaction that they had come so far, endured so much, to end up this way.

Surata endured his surliness, willing to let him sulk. She suggested once that they might make camp early, to give the horse some relief and let themselves get warm.

"What good is that?" Arkady muttered. "We won't be dry and it would mean using up our supplies faster than we have to."

"It would give us all a chance to rest," she ventured, making every effort not to be daunted by his mood.

"And then what?" He sighed heavily. "I don't know where we are, and neither do you. If we stop, we might as well wrap up in shrouds and be done with it."

"That's not necessary," she said, a faint irritation in her voice. "We are still going the right way."

"With nothing to guide us?" he sneered.

"I am here, and I know that we are going in the way that we have been sent." She sounded stubborn now.

"More from that guardian, I suppose." He wanted to shout

at her, to force her into denying that she had known anything of what was ahead of them, that she was trying only to keep them from losing hope back there in the wastes.

"Yes, in part. You think we are lost because you cannot see the stars or the sun." She was upset now, and she did not guard her tongue as she usually did. "Well, I cannot see the stars or the sun in any case, and I know that we are going to the east and a bit to the south. You may be lost without the stars, but—"

"Surata, don't," he said to her, embarrassed by his own callousness as well as wearying of their animosity. "I hope you're right, but you don't have to claim this to cheer me."

"I am *not* trying to cheer you!" She grabbed his soaked brigandine in her hands and jerked at it. "I am telling you that I know this is the right way. If you cannot trust me so far, what has everything we have endured, in this daily world and in that other place, been for?"

Arkady shook his head. "I believe that you are convinced you're right," he said carefully, shocked at the depth of her feeling.

"Then what harm is there in trusting me? You have no better alternative to offer." She released her hold on his clothes. "I do not mean to . . . impose on you. I want only to . . . bring us to a safe place."

"I realize that," he said, more kindly than before. "And you're right, I have no better plan than you have. I suppose we might as well go where you think best as let the horse follow his nose."

"Thank you," she said, mollified by his change in attitude. "So far, the horse's nose has been pointed in the right direction."

Arkady did not think he could laugh, but he smiled a little and hoped it would be clear to her. "No harm in that."

They rode on in silence through the weeping, fading day.

That night they came upon more ruins, not as old as the ones they had passed through most recently, but more ancient than the first empty city they had encountered.

"What place is this?" Arkady asked as they came to an avenue of broken pillars.

"I don't know," Surata admitted when he had described it to her. "The guardian mentioned only two empty cities." There was a flickering of doubt in her words.

"Well, perhaps he forgot to mention this one." He peered through the mizzle, trying to find a place where they would be out of the wet for the night.

"I..." She could not go on and said very little when he brought his bay to a halt in a vast, broken doorway.

"We will be dry here," he said as he dismounted. "The ground is damp, but we can put the branches underneath us, and that will help a little."

She permitted him to decide what they were to do; she remained silent and withdrawn, caught up in her fear that they once again were lost.

As they had the last of their food that night, Arkady put his hand on her shoulder. "It's all right, Surata," he said awkwardly. "We'll do what we can, come morning. It could be that the Bundhi is too much for us."

"You mean, that he has forced us to lose our way? That is good-hearted of you, Arkady-immai. But I have been riding with you, not the Bundhi. If we are lost again, it is because I have not..." There was a sudden tightness in her throat.

"You aren't to blame." He kissed her forehead. "Go on: get some sleep. We'll both feel better in the morning."

She nodded miserably. "I did not think it was my karma to do this. If I had known, I would not have brought you into it."

"Just as well you didn't know, then," he said affectionately. "I don't like to think what would have become of me without you. And if this is the end of it, then praise God and amen." He crossed himself before pulling her into the circle of his arms.

"Arkady-champion," she protested softly.

"Shush," he whispered.

Chapter 21

There were rag-tail clouds in the morning sky, and the shadow of mountains in the south. Arkady stretched, hearing his joints crack from stiffness and the damp. His attention was held by the sight of the mountains and the nearer structure that he had not bothered to explore the previous evening. He walked toward the enormous conical structure, noting its age and the utter quiet of it.

At one time the tower had been fronted in marble, but most of that was gone now, leaving rough bricks exposed, which made climbing the thing relatively easy. As he clawed his way toward the top, Arkady felt the stiff leather of his boots, and he hoped he might find some wax to rub into them to restore their suppleness.

"Arkady-immai!" Surata's call from below, not urgent but not entirely at ease.

"Here! Up here!" he shouted back to her. He was almost at the top of the structure now, and he felt a cold certainty at what he would discover within it.

"Up where?" she inquired. "Where are you?"

"There is a . . . a tower," he answered, a bit uncertain of how much more he should say. He clung to the bricks, breathing hard from the exertion of the climb and the sudden rush of apprehension that came over him.

"And?" she persisted.

He did not answer at once; he went the rest of the way up the hive-shaped building until he reached the open top. He balanced there, staring down into the interior in excitement. "There are . . . bones." The last word was hard to say, and he felt a moment of vertigo as he stared down at the bleached skeletons that littered the inside of the tower.

Surata clapped her hands. "We are not lost, after all!"

"I suppose not," Arkady said, more to himself than to her. He looked into the distance, shading his eyes. He was not sure what to expect, yet he discovered he was holding his breath as he stared east, toward the foot of the mountains. At first he saw nothing more than the blue and tawny yellow of the peaks rising out of the plain. Then he noticed the shapes against the foothills, and slowly he picked out the walls and towers of a city. "Samarkand," he breathed, certain that was what he saw.

"What is it, Arkady-immai?" Surata shouted. "What do you see?"

"Walls and towers. A long way off." To his astonishment, his voice cracked as he told her, and he felt his eyes fill with tears that were so unexpected that they baffled him.

"Ah!" she yelled. "Tell me!"

Very slowly and carefully, he answered her. "The walls are as yellow as the sands and rocks, and the domes are blue."

This time she said nothing, but her laughter was eloquent.

As Arkady climbed back down the tower, he searched his mind for explanations and could find none but the one Surata had given him. He whispered a prayer, but to whom and for what he did not know.

They entered Samarkand shortly before midafternoon three days later and heard the men at the gates call their city The Most Splendid Face of the Earth.

"Do you know the language, then?" Arkady asked Surata when she had translated this for him.

"A little. Enough." She hesitated. "I will tell you what to say, and you must speak for us. The Islamites do not like to deal with women."

Arkady shrugged. "The Islamites are heretics and fools," he said automatically, repeating what he had been told for so long. They were making their way down a narrow street paved with hexagonal stones.

"Do not let them know you think so, or it will go hard with both of us," she warned him.

Ahead he saw a feathery ornamentation of blue-and-gold mosaic tiles covering a square, closed building surmounted by a blue dome. The structure was surrounded by trees and borders of sweet-smelling herbs.

"Is it beautiful?" Surata asked him softly.

"Yes. After the plains, it is paradise." He did not like to admit how much the city awed him. They passed the closed building and continued on, nearing another stone box topped with a fluted dome. "What are these places?" he wondered aloud.

"I will tell you what to say to find out," Surata offered, and painstakingly repeated the syllables to him, insisting that he do his best to imitate her accent.

At the first opportunity, Arkady stopped one of the turbaned inhabitants and repeated the sounds Surata had taught him. His inquiry was met with a flurry of words and abrupt gestures that made Arkady nervous to hear. "What did he say?" he asked Surata.

"He says that they are tombs for noble families," she told him. "Say this to him next," she instructed, giving him some more incomprehensible things to parrot.

This time the outburst was different, more voluble and definitely more cordial. At the end of it, the man made the Islamic bow of respect and passed on.

"What was that? What did I say to him?" Arkady demanded of her as soon as their helper was out of range.

"You asked him where the market was, and who had built so beautiful a city. He told you that it was the design of Timur and of the great Ulug-Beg, and that there are many market-places in Samarkand. The greatest is at the Registan, amid gardens, or so he claims." She smiled. "He loves this place."

"It *is* beautiful," Arkady said. They continued along the narrow, crowded street in the direction that the friendly man had indicated they should go. On their way, they passed several more of the ornate mausoleums, and on the front of one, Arkady saw the image of a pacing lion with the sun—a face smiling amid golden rays—perched on the lion's back. This sight stirred some recollection, but he could not grasp it and, after a short time, dismissed it. He was too caught up in the glory of this magnificent city. Even the towers that marked the Islamite mosques could not detract from his admiration.

The streets grew more crowded, and among the throng were merchants in strange Eastern garments, leading Bactrian camels and asses laden with goods for trade. Arkady threaded his way toward the square his informant had indicated, trying hard not to dawdle and stare at the city around him.

"We're being followed," Surata warned him softly when he paused to let a band of scrawny children run ahead of them. "There are three men who are coming after us as if coming after . . . prey."

Arkady felt a twinge of worry but said to her, "Surata, we've been out in the wastes by ourselves for a long time. We have seen almost no one. In such a place as this, it would be an easy thing to assume that all those around us are trying to follow us." He patted the flank of his gelding as if this simple gesture would make them all relax.

"They are following us," she insisted. "They are the Bundhi's men, and they have been sent to find us for him." Her hands were white-knuckled with emotion, and she set her jaw. "It is a trap, Arkady-immai."

"It's only the main square of Samarkand," he corrected her, then tried to soften his blow. "Even if the Bundhi has sent men to watch for us, what can they do here? They might want to denounce us, but for what?" He patted the gelding as the noise around them grew louder. "We've been so isolated, Surata, that so many people are . . . troubling. It isn't just you, it's the horse and me as well. The city is unfamiliar, and that makes it worse."

"That isn't what I sense, Arkady-immai, it is the presence of the staves."

Arkady shook his head and shouldered past a tinworker and his donkey. "We are almost to the square, and once we arrive, we can purchase food and grain and water, for us and for the horse. You're tired and you've let your fear get hold of you," he admonished her, trying to be pleasant in his manner.

"You are certain?" she challenged him. "Why not look behind you for two men in tan silken robes? One is carrying a tall bamboo staff. You know what that bamboo is."

"Surata," he said with a greater show of patience, "you're being . . . impulsive." He had nearly said arbitrary, but he was determined to make full allowances for their arduous journey and their fatigue. To satisfy her, he turned around, and saw a mass of men, none of them looking like the agents of the Bundhi. "There are merchants all around us, but I see no one with a bamboo staff. If you still think we're being followed after we've had a meal and the gelding's been stabled, then there might be reason to be on guard, and I promise you I'll take every precaution."

"This *isn't* hunger and exhaustion talking, Arkady-immai; it is certainty. I know the Bundhi, what he is, and I can scent him, though we were in a jungle of animals and men. Believe me, I beg of you. I know that you have reason to doubt when I . . . when I lost us as I did. This is different."

Arkady did not know what to say to her, and he was inclined to admit his doubts. "We're coming to the marketplace. They say it is part of a garden."

She looked defeated. "That is delightful," she said tonelessly.

"There are men everywhere."

"I can hear them," she conceded.

"We're almost there," he said, wanting to cheer her.

"And the Bundhi's men are almost upon us. But do not let that deter you. The horse does need grain and we're both hungry. We ought to take care to eat enough, for the Bundhi might not want to feed us, once he has us."

The narrow street opened onto a large sandy square, flanked on two sides by large buildings, one of which was the famous Madrasah of Ulug-Beg. The central massive gate was flanked by two tall towers, and the whole was ornamented with white, gold and blue mosaic tiles. At right angles to it, an ancient mosque of crumbling stone rose in majestic decay. There were fountains, the largest of which provided water for camels, horses and asses. The air was alive with the cry and chatter of the merchants who brought their goods to this enormous marketplace.

"What place is this?" Surata asked nervously.

"The market square," Arkady said in relief. "I'm going to get water for the horse and then we can see about food."

"And perhaps take the time to find out if we are being watched," she suggested.

"We're foreigners, Surata. Undoubtedly someone will be watching us." He said this easily enough, but as he spoke he realized that there would be few places in the city that were better suited to watching them. Here no one would think another stranger unusual, and any odd behavior would be ignored. In a place where so many merchants from so far away gathered, a few more foreigners would mean nothing. He shook his head as he brought the bay to the fountain to drink.

"There are three men," Surata repeated in an undervoice. "If only you'd look, you'd find them."

"Surata," Arkady said, making her name a rebuke. "When we've eaten, we can discuss this," he declared, wiping his brow with his grimy sleeve. "For the moment, I don't care." He knew as soon as he had spoken that he had gone too far; she looked as if he had struck her. "Surata, I didn't mean it that way," he protested.

"Naturally not," she said in a strained tone.

"I *didn't*." He tried to find the right explanation. "I'm worn out. That's all."

"And you don't believe me." There was a quiver in her words that shocked him. "Oh, Arkady-immai, don't you understand that the Bundhi wants to deceive you? Don't you know that he thrives on deception? He could not be more pleased, because you cannot accept he is really here, and really chasing us. We are in the place of lions." She clamped her jaw shut, her face stark with lonely terror.

"The place of lions," he repeated, remembering the mosaic he had seen on the side of the mausoleum.

"I told you that there was a place where lions walked with the sun on their backs. This is that place, I know it. You may not see the lions, but I know—*I know*—they are there."

Arkady frowned thoughtfully, watching his horse drink. "There was a tomb, back in that narrow street. There was a lion on it, with the sun on his back."

"Arkady-immai, *please*. Get us away from this place!" She reached out and fumbled for his hand. "Now."

"We need food and water, Surata, and rest. Neither you nor I can do much until we have restored ourselves." His frown deepened to a glower. "Food first, I think. Without that, we'll be too worn to go on."

"Quickly," she urged him. "And then we must find a safe place, where the Bundhi would hesitate to come."

"What place would that be?" He had not seen a church anywhere and could not bring himself to enter a mosque.

"I don't know. A place that's guarded, a place where there are men who watch such things." She was clearly at a loss, and her voice rose in desperation. "Arkady-immai, I don't know what place it would be, but I want to find it."

He looked around the marketplace. "Your Bundhi isn't going to try to attack you here, with so many people about."

"I am a slave," she reminded him. "He need only say that he is reclaiming his property."

"He would have to argue with me, and I would insist that we take it to the local magistrates. The Islamites aren't so lost

to honor that they would give away a man's slave for nothing."
As he spoke, he brought his horses's head up and started
away from the fountain, taking care to keep Surata close
to him. "Would you rather ride? I'll boost you up, if you
want."

"I don't . . . yes," she decided. "Yes. If I am on your horse,
they will see me more easily, but it will be harder for them to
reach me unnoticed." She accepted his help to mount, getting
into the saddle rather than behind it. "Do not go far, Arkady-
immai. Stay where there are many men."

He had already spotted where the grain-sellers had their
stands, and he was heading toward them through the milling
crowd. "I'll stay in the square, don't worry about that. And I
have my swords and my maul." He did not mention his cinquedea which was, as always, tucked under his belt against
his back. "If they try anything, they'll have to make a real
effort." In some part of his mind, he wished they would attack.
He longed to fight flesh and bone instead of things of light
and air that so frustrated him in that other place. It would be
satisfying to hack at a man, or to chop one of those pernicious
bamboo staves into bits.

"They are getting nearer, Arkady-immai," she warned with
an effort at calmness. "Two men, the ones who followed
me when I was sent into slavery. I . . . do not know about the
third."

"The Bundhi?" Arkady asked as he approached the nearest
grain-seller and gestured that he wished to buy oats.

"No. But a very advanced student of his, I think. He has
the feel of one who has learned much and is . . . eager." She
shifted in the saddle, as if trying to make herself less accessible
to those around her.

The merchant smiled, showing toothless gums, and held
out large, flat baskets of grain, nodding and holding up his
fingers to indicate the price, obviously prepared to haggle.

"I want three large sacks of grain," Arkady said, pointing
out what he had in mind and indicating what he was willing
to pay for them.

The merchant chuckled and made a counteroffer.

"What lies on the street to the northeast of here?" Surata asked.

Arkady glanced in that direction. "There are towers, probably another mosque." He motioned to the merchant and pointed toward the tops of the spires he had noticed.

"Ahie!" the merchant cried out and went on, pointing to the building. "Bibi-Khanym!" He then expostulated further and grinned at Arkady.

"He tells you that this is the Ulug-Beg Madrasah, here on the square, where the great man taught and worshipped. But the place where he went to study the stars is in that building, beyond the mosque." She put her hand to her forehead. "He says that all wise men come here to learn from what Ulug-Beg recorded."

"How fortunate," Arkady said, returning the merchant's grin and bowing. "What does he want for three large sacks of grain?"

"Four gold pieces. He will take half that. It is more than he usually charges, but you are a foreigner, and therefore you are expected to pay more." She cocked her head. "They are coming nearer."

"In this mess, how can you tell?" Arkady asked lightly. "Half of the Grand Turk's army could be in this marketplace and I wouldn't notice them." He held up two fingers to the merchant, and dug into his pouch to bring out the gold pieces.

The merchant smiled and nodded, holding up three fingers and launching into another tirade, this time not quite as cordial.

"He says that you are an ignorant foreigner trying to cheat him and that if he accepts so little money his family will starve. He says that you are to be forgiven because you are ignorant." Surata twisted her hands nervously. "Be swift, Arkady-immai. We should not linger."

"He'll demand the three pieces of gold," Arkady said, clinking the coins in his hand.

"Tell him this," she said and then softly recited a phrase to Arkady. "He will be offended, but he will let you have the grain for the two coins."

Dubiously Arkady repeated the unfamiliar sounds, and saw

the merchant draw back, making a sign with his fingers. He nodded several times in a deprecating way, and bowed deeply to Arkady, then began to fill one of his large sacks with oats.

"What in the name of the Saints did I say to him?" Arkady asked Surata as the merchant hastened to his work, continuing to bow in a most self-effacing manner.

"You said that you had the power to make his manhood dry up and fall off if he did not charge you a reasonable price for the grain," she answered. "It was harsh, but he would have taken half the afternoon settling on a price, just for the amusement." Her words grew swifter. "We do not have that much time, Arkady-immai. We have hardly any time at all."

"They are getting nearer?" He glared at the merchant, pointing to the next large sack. "Hurry up," he said, trusting that the merchant would get his meaning from his manner.

"Arkady-immai, look for a man, a tall man, without a turban, who carries a bamboo staff. He is near us, very near." She reached down and plucked at his sleeve. "He is walking with others, so that you will not know him."

"How would I know him, in any case?" Arkady asked, trying to soothe her.

The merchant handed Arkady the first of the three sacks of grain, lowering his head and speaking in a placating tone as he did.

"They saw you when you bought me. You might have noticed them, since they were foreigners," she said.

"*Everyone* in that town looked strange to me, Surata. I wouldn't have known one foreigner from another." He looked up at her. "Except you. You were unlike anyone I had seen, ever."

Her smile was fleeting and unhappy. "Do not let him touch you with his staff. You know what it will do to you."

He busied himself tieing the sack to the fender of his saddle. "I saw what one of those staves can do," he said softly, thinking first of the youth in the deserted village, and then of the shattered stained-glass window in that other place. "I won't let it touch me." He fiddled with the edge of his worn saddle pad while he watched out of the corner of his eye, hoping to catch some unexpected movement. "I can see no one with a bamboo staff."

"Look for men with burdens on poles. Perhaps they are water carriers, or men bringing more of the colored stones."

The merchant demanded Arkady's attention; the second sack of grain was ready.

Arkady bowed slightly as he accepted the sack, and patted his gelding as the bay nickered, his nose twitching. "There aren't any water carriers nearby," he said as he made certain there were not.

"But he *must* be close. I would not feel him so if he were not." She narrowed her eyes in a fruitless effort to pierce her darkness, then hissed with vexation. "I can tell he is coming. Do not think me crazed, Arkady-immai."

"I think you're tired and hungry and worn out, as I am." He touched her leg. "He might not be as close as you fear, Surata."

"I hope he is not," she said.

The merchant brought Arkady the third sack of oats, spat on his shadow, then held out his hand for the coins in a placating way. He grinned with his mouth while his eyes burned contempt.

"We have the grain for the horse. Now we must find something for us to eat, as well." He remembered the way the Margrave Fadey would enter a marketplace and order that half the goods there be confiscated for the use of his men. He wished he had the power to do that now, and to require that the officials of the city give him shelter and protection.

Arkady took the loop of the reins and led his horse toward the food vendors stalls, saying as he went, "You're letting your worry get ahead of your good sense, Surata." He could not deny that he was feeling less confident than he wanted to admit, and he did not know what he should do about it.

"What do you see, Arkady-immai?" she asked sharply. "Who is ahead of us?"

"Half the city of Samarkand," he replied laconically.

"Immediately in front of you, what do you see?" The anxiety was back in her voice, and she seemed to be listening to the babble more keenly than before.

"There are sellers of gourds and vegetables, and a merchant of peas and . . . lentils, I think they are, and other beans. There are six or seven men and two or three veiled women waiting to buy from him. Then there is a stall with leather goods— not tack, but pouches and wineskins and the like. There's a tentmaker setting up his stall with the help of two apprentices. Perhaps we should buy one of his tents." He chuckled at this, ambling toward the struggling men.

Surata's words cut into him. "What kind of poles does he have for his tents? Are they bamboo?"

Arkady started to dismiss her question, but a swift glance showed him that the poles were indeed bamboo. As he watched, the tentmaker unfurled an enormous length of striped cloth, and the fabric billowed in the wind, flapping toward Arkady and Surata.

The bay whinnied in alarm, tossing his head and all but pulling his reins from Arkady's hands. The ends of the loose tent snapped at his flanks and the horse reared.

In the saddle, Surata clung to the bay's mane, her hands sunk in the long hair. She shouted for Arkady, begging him to tell her what was going on.

"What the Devil . . . !" Arkady expostulated as the tent fabric wrapped around him.

"Arkady-immai!" Surata screamed, and in the next moment, she and the gelding were enveloped in the cloth.

Vadin lifted his bamboo staff and sauntered toward his catch. "Well, a fortunate coincidence, girl," he said to Surata, who stiffened at the sound of his voice.

The gelding laid back his ears, sweating with fear.

"Stay away from us!" Arkady said, trying to extricate himself from the imprisoning yards of cloth.

Vadin ignored him. "When we moved you so far to the west, we were certain that you were not going to trouble us again, girl."

"You were mistaken, weren't you?" she said, hoping that she sounded more courageous than she felt.

"Lamentably, for you." Vadin tapped the cloth with his staff. "Mayon and I have been kept very busy with you. That does not please us, and it does not please our master." Again he struck the cloth, and it grew tighter.

The two men who had been assisting Vadin stopped their work and came up to their captives. One of them nodded to Surata. "I saw you sold to this . . . moron"—he indicated Arkady with a contemptuous turn of his hand—"and assumed that would be the end of it. How did you persuade him to bring you here?"

"What are they saying?" Arkady asked, trying to make sense of their words.

"They are boasting, nothing more," Surata told him, then added to the Bundhi's men in their language. "Boasting always was the coward's way, wasn't it?"

Vadin lifted his bamboo staff toward her face. "You've already lost your eyes to one of these, girl. Say more, and you will find there are other things you can lose, as well."

Surata tossed her head but said nothing more to them, addressing Arkady instead. "I told you that two men followed me to that slave market. They are here. I do not know who the third is."

"Hara," he said unpleasantly. "You know me, Surata."

She nodded, stiff with fright. "I know you."

"What is it?" Arkady asked, hearing her dread.

"The third man is the nephew of the Bundhi, who is being trained to follow in the family tradition." She swallowed, her body shaking no matter how firm her resolve to conceal her tension.

"Not a son?" Arkady asked with some surprise.

"The Bundhi does not father children. He would have to release his seed to do so, and this is not . . . desirable for him. It is the aim of the disciples of the Left Hand Path to remain permanently excited and to withhold the fulfillment, for fear of sharing life and pleasure, which saps their strength, or so they say." She recited this in a flat tone, though her breath came quickly.

The bay pawed in agitation, his worn shoes striking sparks from the paving stones.

"My uncle awaits your visit, since you have been foolish enough to return, Surata-of-Bogar." Hara bent at the waist, then said as he straightened up, "I forgot: such courtesies are wasted on the blind, aren't they?"

Arkady did not need to have this translated. His hands tightened and he longed for the opportunity to reach for his sword. Color rose in his face, as much from shame as ire, and his blood roiled. "You craven," he said to Hara, though some of his condemnation was directed inward.

"This idiot insults me, Vadin. Castigate him," Hara said offhandedly.

"No!" Surata cried out.

Some of the merchants and buyers in the marketplace had noticed the peculiar encounter that was taking place between these diverse foreigners, and many of them gathered around, talking and pointing, most of them amused, a few guarded in their demeanor.

"Get these gawking cattle away from us," Hara added, indicating the crowd. "We must not linger here. There could be questions."

"It wouldn't matter," Mayon assured him. "They cannot understand the soldier and they will not listen to the complaints of a woman." Nevertheless, he took hold of his end of the cloth cage and pulled firmly on it. "You will have to come with us. You have no choice, either of you. If you resist, we have the staves, and we will use them. Tell him, Surata." He pointed the end of his bamboo staff directly at Arkady. "Be very sure he understands."

Surata repeated what Mayon said, adding, "They mean it, Arkadky-immai."

"Immai!" Hara jeered. "You call that fool *immai?* You've lost more than your eyesight, girl."

Arkady's face was like stone. "I don't want them to talk to you that way, Surata," he growled.

"Hara is talking about *you*," she corrected him. "He is attempting to interfere."

"What did you tell him?" Mayon demanded, poking at her through the cloth. "What was it?"

"He was afraid you were speaking against me. I told him that you were insulting him instead of me." She had better control of herself now, and she was able to speak without emotion and with a minimum of her dismay creeping into her voice. She fixed her unseeing gaze on a distant point and brought her breathing back to normal.

"Move!" Vadin ordered. "The city Guards will be here soon. I do not want to deal with them." He nudged Mayon. "The south gate. Quickly. And see that these two remain silent."

Obediently Mayon and Hara took up their positions on either side of their extensive bundle, and Hara said to Surata, "If there is any awkwardness at the gate, we will kill your soldier before we kill you. Let him know that."

Surata passed the warning on to Arkady, then told their captors, "He understands. We will not disobey you."

"That is wise of you. How much wiser you would have been to remain in the West, a slave. That way you would have lived, at least." Hara laughed derisively. "It's too late for that now."

Their passage through the narrow streets was marked by many comments and shouts. Once Mayon got into a dispute with the leader of a caravan of camels, which came to an abrupt end when Vadin lifted his bamboo staff and held it near the leader's face. The caravan leader paled and stammered in apology, then retreated to the nearest sidestreet to wait for the little party to pass.

"Where are they taking us, do you know?" Arkady asked as they passed through the gates of Samarkand.

"They haven't said," was her wary answer.

"What is your guess?" He wished he could reach her, if only to have the reassurance of their contact.

"Stop talking, you two!" Vadin shouted at them. "And you two," he went on to Mayon and Hara, "do not let them touch. You know what may happen if they do."

Surata spoke over this. "He wishes to know where we are going. So do I."

"We are going to the redoubt of the Bundhi, of course," Vadin said nastily. "What else did you expect?"

Chapter 22

That night, Arkady was tied to stakes at one side of the campground, and Surata to stakes at the other. They could hear each other, but they could not reach out with more than their voices.

"You see, we know your ruses, girl," Vadin said to her as he checked the thongs before wrapping himself in his blanket. "It was good of you to provide the horse. It saves us much trouble." He forced her hands open and rubbed the palms with salt. "I want you to stay where I leave you. Don't be upset."

"That isn't enough to stop me," she told Vadin, trying to sneer. "Salt may stop your staves, but it can't hold me."

"Then you won't mind it, will you?" He straightened up. "If you and that soldier talk, we will hear you."

"Listen, if you wish," she said, taking a little consolation from the fact that only she knew Arkady's language.

Vadin bent and grabbed the front of her clothes. "The Bundhi has said that we are not to damage you unless we must. If it

319

were not for that, I would make your brains ache for your insolence."

"Be sure you tell the Bundhi that," she responded, grateful for her defiance that kept despair at bay.

Vadin poked her in the ribs with his knuckles. "Another time, who knows? I might forget and use my staff instead of my hand, and then you would regret your manner." He sighed in anticipation. "Or that soldier—he might learn something from doing battle with my staff. What do you think, girl?"

Surata flinched as he spoke. "He is not part of this fight."

"Not at first, but you brought him into it, and there is no escape for him now." He stood over her. "There are two tigers guarding the perimeters of the camp. If you try to escape, they will catch you. I tell you this so that you will think twice before pulling out the stakes that hold you. It is wiser, believe me, to remain our prisoners than to get away from us."

Surata ground her teeth but said nothing. Her posture was defiant in spite of her bonds.

"In the morning, if we forget to feed you, remind us, won't you, girl?" He sniggered as he strolled away.

"Did he hurt you, Surata?" Arkady called out when Vadin had taken his blanket and crawled into the striped tent.

"Not seriously, Arkady-immai," she answered candidly. "I am more frightened than hurt."

"That's something . . . Surata?" He took a deep breath, then was unable to continue.

"What is it, Arkady-immai?"

"I was wrong." Saying it was painful but it was less so than he had thought it would be. "I should have listened to you. I ought to have done as you told me. I know that. But . . . there is so much that I still cannot understand, and . . . I don't listen because of it." In his mind, he recited the words he had said so often to his confessor, especially on the eve of battle, and he wondered if he had ever believed the assurances the priests had given him then.

"I know this, Arkady-immai," she said kindly but with sadness. "It pains me that you will not trust me."

"It pains me as well, Surata." He waited, then forced himself to turn his attention to more practical matters. "Do you know what they plan for us?"

"They are taking us to the Bundhi. Beyond that, I don't know."

"But you can guess, can't you?" He braced himself to hear what she would tell him next.

"At the worst—and it is the worst, Arkady-immai—he will compel us to be his creatures and give him our strength," she said, feeling her breath go cold within her. "I would far rather be dead than do that."

"Surely he can't do that to you." He was horrified at the idea, and at the same time, he could not deny his pride that she had included him in her avowal of strength. She had not shut him away from her as he feared she might.

"There are ways. He could use the staves to sap us and weaken us so that we are nothing more than walking corpses. We would not be as much use to him then, but there would still be various services that he could demand of us, and we would have to comply." She let her body go limp, trying to put her attention on her inner resources. "The Bundhi has been able to build his power, unchecked, since he killed so many of my family."

"You won't let him do that to you, Surata. You've got more resolve than that." Arkady was uncertain how she would be able to do this if the Bundhi was as puissant as Surata claimed. He thought back to the various leaders he and his troops had fought, but he could not find an example of what he was pitted against now. "Surata?" he said uncertainly.

"I am listening to you, Arkady-immai."

"How long will it take to reach the Bundhi's redoubt?" There might be a chance to escape if they had to travel any great distance.

"It is a long way off, in the mountains. It is growing late in the year, and it is . . . not likely that we will have an easy passage. The snow will come, and then we might have to wait through all the winter to resume the climb. The Bundhi would not like that, I think." She turned his question over in her mind. "The first town we will reach is Ajni. From there, we will have to climb the mountains rather than follow the river valley."

"And is there any chance the Bundhi will come down from his redoubt?"

"It's . . . possible," she said carefully. "He does not often leave there, but he . . . might. If he is determined and vengeful enough."

"Would he be likely to come beyond Ajni?" This was the crucial question as far as Arkady could think.

"I have never known him to do that," Surata said. "He does not like leaving the mountains entirely." She did not add that the House of Bogar had similar reservations—all but she were dead, and the reservation no longer had any bearing on her.

"Then we'll have to escape before we reach Ajni," Arkady decided. He lay back and stared up into the black clarity of the night, tracing patterns in the stars while he pondered their situation.

The day had been warm, but now that the sun was down, the chill breath of the mountain snows swept over him, and soon Arkady could think of little but the ache of the cold in his exhausted limbs.

For the next six days, the little party followed the Zeravšan River upstream toward Ajni. Each day they covered a little less ground as the river canyon grew narrower and steeper. Vadin insisted that they press on, reminding Mayon and Hara that the Bundhi would be unforgiving if they delayed so long that they could not reach Gora Čimtarga because the passes were blocked with winter snow.

"It must be tomorrow night," Arkady told Surata just before they fell into vitiated sleep. It was an effort to raise his voice enough for her to hear him; he was hoarse.

"You're certain?" She was as enervated as he.

"We're getting too close to Ajni. And those three are showing the strain as much as we are. If we can get out of the bonds and reach the horse before they're awake enough to fight much, there's a good chance that we can get free of the Bundhi's lieutenants without too much risk. If we don't go tomorrow night, we might not have the chance again."

She agreed. "The Bundhi will come. You're right to want to escape before Ajni. The people living beyond Ajni live in fear of the Bundhi and would not be inclined to help us, even if we are fortunate enough to succeed. Here, they might be willing to let us have food and shelter."

Arkady felt the stirrings of hope, and he stretched as much as his bonds would allow. "Get as much rest as you can. Thank God they've permitted us a blanket apiece. I think we might have frozen without them."

"It is better sleeping with you, Arkady-immai. Your arm is better than a blanket." She yawned. "I wish they'd feed us some of that roasted fowl they've been eating. Every time I think of it, my stomach gurgles like a millrace."

"What would you know of gurgling millraces, Surata?" he asked, amused by her analogy.

"You had a mill not far from your house, didn't you?" she responded, her words coming slowly as sleep came over her.

The next morning, the bay went lame, and after a brisk argument, Vadin announced that it was useless to keep the horse with them. "Without the animal there will be less to carry," he announced. "We're carrying more than two sacks of grain to feed the beast as it is, and aside from the bedding, our tent and the water sacks, there is nothing the animal is carrying that is essential to our needs. The weapons can be left behind. A man like that might be scheming how to use them, and it would be wise to have them out of his way." This last was accompanied by a self-congratulatory smirk that made Arkady long to hit him, for although he did not understand what Vadin was saying, he could grasp the intent.

"The horse *is* useless lame," Hara agreed. "And there are other beasts of burden, those with two legs."

Mayon nodded. "And the tigers are growing hungry."

"*No!*" Surata shouted. "Not the horse."

"What is it?" Arkady demanded, fearing what she would tell him. "What are they planning?"

"Your horse..." she began, then waited to hear more.

"What about my horse?" Arkady asked apprehensively. "What are those devils saying?"

"Once we get into high country," Hara remarked, "the tigers will not be able to keep pace with us, and it would be best to let them have the horse now, so that they will not be tempted to take ... something else." He gestured toward Arkady. "The Bundhi may have other uses for him, and if he has gone to the bellies of the tigers, not even his power can call the man back."

"Do not!" Surata pleaded, trying to bring her bound hands together. "You would not do that."

Vadin conceded. "It is true. It would be courting this anger of the Bundhi." He indicated the bay. "Better take off the saddle and tether him. The tigers are not far behind us, and they will want to feed soon."

Surata heard them with repugnance. "The Bundhi will be pleased with your decision, no doubt. You are striving to follow his example so well."

"Oh, not completely," Vadin said, his ghastly smile lost on Surata. "You and that servant of yours are alive and still unharmed, aren't you. Once you are in the Bundhi's hands, that will no longer be the case, Surata-of-Bogar. Think what became of your father and your uncles."

"I have not forgot them," she said stiffly.

Arkady listened to these exchanges with growing suspicions and anxiety. "What are they saying to you, Surata? What do they want?"

"They want to see us dead, destroyed. They want us obliterated. But that is for the Bundhi to do. Now, they want ... to let the tigers have your horse." This last was almost impossible for her to speak, and she had to clear her throat twice in order to get the words out. "They do not want to keep a lame animal with us, for fear it will slow us down." She had started to cry, but there were only tears; she did not sob.

"My horse? Give him to the tigers?" he repeated, furious. "It's cruel. And it's stupid. What do they plan to do with all the material he's carrying?"

"I think they intend that we should take up some of his burdens, the sacks and the tent and the water. The rest—"

"You mean my weapons?" he asked, not truly needing to hear the answer. If their positions were reversed, he would find a way to take their weapons from them.

"Yes." Her answer was almost entirely without emotion, but Arkady could hear the anguish she strove to conceal and saw her tears. He wanted more than anything to spare her from what they were enduring together and what he was afraid they would still have to endure.

Before Arkady could think of some words of comfort, Mayon shouted at them. "You! Stop that. Tell us what that barbarian is saying to you! We will not permit you to make plans against us."

"I am trying to tell him what I have heard you say," Surata said as calmly as she could. She wiped her face with the hem of her sleeve. "It is his horse you are planning to give to the tigers. He has a right to know of it."

"He has a right to know nothing," Hara shouted. "He is carrion, but for a little time more, he walks." He turned, storming off to where the gelding stood, his head down, breathing hard. "This animal is fortunate to go to such creatures as the tigers of the Bundhi. It is more of an honor than he deserves. A white bull with garlanded horns would be better, but we must make the offering that is available." He struck the bay in the withers. "This is nothing but chaff."

"What is he doing?" Arkady asked, watching the Bundhi's disciple with growing rage.

"He is going to leave the horse," Surata said, the resignation in her voice worse than her hurt.

"For the tigers?" He pulled at the thongs that held him. *"No!"* It was more a bellow than a shout. Veins stood out on his forehead and he heard the roaring of blood in his heart.

Vadin kicked him, knocking him off his feet, and indicated the bamboo staff he held. "Tell this fool, Surata-of-Bogar, that if he does such a thing again, the staff will have his eyes as one has had yours." He paused. "Tell him."

Surata repeated what she was told, adding, "He will do it,

Arkady-immai, if you give him the excuse. The Bundhi would not mind him taking your sight."

Arkady panted with the force of his emotion, but he brought himself under sufficient control to be able to speak more calmly. "I am going to kill him for this. Soon or late, I will kill him, by the Sword of Saint Michael."

"Is he making threats?" Hara asked, laughing a high, nasal sound that made Surata cringe.

"He is making vows," she answered for him, knowing that Arkady would not regard what he had promised as a threat.

"The men of the West are great fools. But you have discovered that for yourself, haven't you, Surata-of-Bogar?" Vadin asked. "Well, Mayon, it will be best to unsaddle the creature. Leave the saddle and the weapons on the ground."

"Should we save anything from it, the girths or . . . ?" Hara suggested. "The leather is not too poor and perhaps we can use it."

"If we can use it, fine, if not, leave it." Mayon was not interested in the leather. "Is there rope?"

Hara inspected the saddle—Arkady ground his teeth as he watched—and shrugged. "A few lengths, most of it worn or frayed. Our ropes are better, stronger."

"Then leave it. Take the water sacks and one of the grain sacks. The rest of their gear is . . . nothing." He spat casually, making it apparent that he regarded Arkady and Surata as little more than sacrificial animals, or prizes of the hunt. "Hurry. I do not want to waste any more time. We've lost enough as it is."

While Hara and Mayon went about the task of unsaddling the bay and going through the last of the equipment and tack, Arkady said to Surata, trying to keep his tone level and his temper under control, "Tonight, Surata, it has to be tonight. If we do not escape now, it will not be possible. They are expecting us to carry their gear as well as our own, and after the first night, we will not have the strength left to break away. Are you willing to try?"

"Oh, yes," she said gratefully. "Even if they kill us, at least our deaths will not go to add to the Bundhi's power."

"We're not going to die," Arkady told her through tight lips. "We have too much to avenge. They will pay."

"Yes, they will have their karma and it will not release them." She tried to sound satisfied with this, but there was still a longing in her voice that revealed her desire.

"The hell with karma. I want to take this out of their hides." He tossed his head, wanting to tear his way out of his bonds by will alone.

"That is wrong thinking," she said automatically. "I have wrong thinking, too. I am anxious to see them answer for all they have done. See. That is part of what they must answer for." She turned toward him in confusion. "You have done this to me, Arkady-immai. You have made me different than I was, and I . . . am not what I was."

"I am not what I was either, Surata," he said, with a complex welling of conflicting emotions that he could not describe. "Tonight."

"Tonight," she promised.

They left the bay tethered in a small hillside clearing. He raised his head, whinnying after them as they moved on, going away from him up the canyon.

"I wish I could have killed him, rather than leave him this way," Arkady said.

"Arkady-immai, they want the killing," Surata said to him as gently as she could. "It is what they seek."

Not long after, they heard a shuddering roar that echoed through the ravines, and the terrified scream of the horse. The roars grew louder, and the bay gave one last, high squeal, and then there was a sound of falling.

"God damn them, and all their issue," Arkady swore between his teeth. He had the water sacks strapped to his shoulders, and he bent under the weight of them. Listening to the distant sounds of struggle and killing, he bowed down more, as if he carried the weight of the bay as the horse had carried him for so long.

"Do you hear? The tigers are pleased!" Myron jeered, pointing to Arkady but speaking to Surata. "Tell him, Surata-of-Bogar. Let him know what we say."

Patiently, Surata translated the words. "He wishes to see you angry, Arkady-immai. It will give him power and will please him. Do not let him know that you are as . . . moved as you are."

"You're asking too much," he hissed back to her. His jaw and neck ached from the way he had been holding them.

"Then let him know just a little. Please. For both of us, and for the horse, as well. They will stop if they think that you are uncaring."

"What is he saying?" Vadin demanded, jabbing Surata with his finger. "Tell us, and no more talking with him."

Surata took the poke in her shoulder without comment. "He says that the horse was a warhorse and it was his right to die in battle, not as fodder for angry cats. He is shamed for the honor of the horse." It was close enough to the truth that Surata did not feel she was speaking against either Arkady or disobeying the orders of Vadin. "He is a soldier. He regards his horse as a soldier, too."

"That is the first sensible thing I have heard from a man from the West," Mayon observed. "Most of the time they are too concerned about their devas and other protective spirits to notice that there are those creatures around them who are worthy of their attention. I think all of them will be reborn into the bodies of asses and oxen. Tell him that for me."

This time Surata took advantage of this order to say, "If there is a way for you to need to stop earlier than usual this evening, it might give us a little advantage, so that we will not be as tired, and we can go farther tonight, when we escape."

"Right," Arkady replied. "Is that what you're supposed to tell me?"

"No, but I will attend to this." She raised her voice to their captors. "He tells me that he will sing Hosannahs—which are songs and shouts of praise—at the right hand of God while we are all in the depths of Hell."

The three disciples of the Bundhi laughed aloud at this, and Mayon said, "Does he think that all he must do is live once to earn Nirvana? Has he no knowledge of . . . but Western men do not. They prate of rewards that cannot be had on earth, they deny karma and they do not know of the ages of the world. They are all fools and liars."

"They are good fighters," Surata declared, in Arkady's defense.

"That is one of their few abilities. They make good cloth, some of them." Vadin reached over and thumped Arkady's load. "You like to fight?"

When Surata translated this latest barb, Arkady said, "No, no good soldier likes to fight. A good soldier will not enter battle unless it is necessary. That is not what they teach men when they train them to fight, but no man who has been in battle more than three times seeks it without cause unless he is mad." He paused, "Or in love with glory."

"Were you?" Surata asked, and it was a question that had occupied much of her thoughts about him for some time.

"I suppose I was, before that third battle. I was always told that retreat was worse than death, but that was before seeing what death was. After that, I did not want to have my men suffer for my . . . vanity. It wasn't even pride, just vanity." He hefted his load to a more comfortable position. "About an hour before sunset, I'll see what I can arrange. I would do it sooner, but that might get their attention too much. At that point, they will probably be glad for the chance to stop. They're carrying packs themselves."

Surata thought briefly, then said to Vadin, "Arkady-immai is worried that he is not used to this height. We have been crossing plains and lowlands for many weeks, and neither of us is used to the mountains."

"You will become used," Mayon said with great certainty. "You will learn to walk in the pure air."

"I will," she said at once. "But Arkady-immai was born on the plains of the West and he is not one who has learned to live in the mountains. He is strong, but his stamina is not as great as you might think. I do not want you to expect him to be a mountain goat."

Vadin reached over and cuffed her lightly, almost playfully.

"You may delay our arrival as long as you like, it will still come to pass and you will fall at the feet of the Bundhi and do him honor before he kills you."

Surata lifted her chin. "If that is what karma has willed for me, then it will be so, but neither you nor I can say until it has happened." She turned toward Arkady. "Be careful; they will be watching you. I have said that you are not used to the mountains. You may use this as best you can."

"I will," he assured her.

Behind them, the sky faded from blue to pink to orange, and as the sun dropped into the end of the river canyon, the air appeared to be lavendar. The gentle warmth of the afternoon gave way to the thin chill of evening.

"It should be now," Arkady muttered, alerting Surata. He deliberately let his heavy pack slide so that he could no longer keep it balanced. "God!" he shouted, getting the full attention of the three disciples of the Bundhi. "My packs!"

"You are a great fool!" Mayon upbraided him as he tried to keep the watersacks from pulling Arkady over. "Stupid and foolish!"

"Stop him from falling. If he hurts himself, he will slow us down and we will have to leave the water sacks behind." Vadin came up and railed at Arkady, showing him clenched fists and an angry, distorted face. "Ignorant foreigner. Scum. Excrement of adders."

Arkady did not know the words, but he recognized the tone well enough, and he felt an odd satisfaction at this outburst. "Tell him I have hurt my shoulder, Surata. Say that I can't carry these sacks any more today."

She did as he told her, elaborating on the injury. "His bones have been pressed too much, and the ligaments are in fever," she informed Vadin. "If you force him to go on this way, surely his bones will become inflamed."

"He has been reckless," Vadin growled. "It is not acceptable that he should have such troubles." He looked up at the sky, then pointed at Arkady. "You are fortunate that your injury came late in the day. If it were earlier, you would have to go on, no matter how much your shoulder ached, or how your bones fared."

Arkady lowered his burden carefully, moving as if he were stiff and sore.

"There is a place ahead, a clearing, level enough," called Mayon, who had gone ahead to scout on Vadin's order. Hara, who had brought up the rear, stopped walking and lifted his foot, inspecting his sandal.

"I have a broken strap on my sandal," he complained to the air. "I do not want to walk on until I have fixed it."

"This incompetent barbarian will have that task," Vadin said in disgust. "Very well. Let us go on to the clearing. Hara, take the water sacks. Surata, since he is your champion, you may carry the rest of his load, the food and the tent." He took great delight in tieing these to her shoulders.

"You shouldn't have to do that," Arkady told her in an undervoice. "It isn't right that you have such a . . . duty for me."

"It is nothing. After tonight, we won't have to carry any of these things." She was not cheerful, but her attitude was more positive than it had been that morning.

"I've been thinking about that, Surata," he said, a bit more loudly. "I don't know what we're going to do for food and shelter once we get away from these men. We might be able to take the blankets, but they have the food, and even though they haven't found the gold, what good is it when there is no one to buy food and supplies from, in any case?"

"Do not talk!" Vadin ordered, kicking out at the back of Arkady's legs. "You will know the touch of the staves soon enough, you fool."

"He wishes us to be quiet," Surata explained unnecessarily. "We will have to wait." She extended her hand so that it brushed his arm for an instant, then she grabbed her load, as if afraid of discovery.

"You two are not to walk together," Hara yelled at them and forcefully stepped between them, shoving each of them roughly.

Surata and Arkady remained silent until they reached the clearing, where Mayon waited, an attitude of satisfaction about him. "There is a spring not far up the hill. We can drink something other than the swill from the water sacks tonight."

Pleased to have the chance to rest, all three nonetheless protested that they were willing to press on until dark. Vadin finally ended their conversation and indicated to Arkady where the tent was to be pitched. "You are strong enough to do this. If you must be the cause of our stopping, then you can take care to aid us. If your shoulder and back hurt for it, so much the better."

When Surata had relayed this to Arkady, he gave a tight half-smile. "One day soon, he will regret saying this to me. And he will regret abusing you, Surata. My word on it, more than my honor."

"Hush, Arkady-immai. Do what they wish you do to. Then we will be able to have a little respite before we must flee."

"It will be night when we go," he warned her.

"For me it is always night. It makes no difference." The bitterness was back in her voice.

"I meant that there are creatures abroad at night that are not friendly, Surata, nothing more." He wanted to wrap his arms around her, put his face into the tresses of her hair, taste the sweet salt of her skin. He could not stand to leave her in the control of these three men for one hour longer, he decided, and he committed himself to exacting full price from Vadin, Mayon and Hara for all they had done.

When the tent was up, Hara had finished making a meal for his two companions. They sat and ate together, pointedly ignoring Arkady and Surata, who had been tied to trees on opposite sides of the clearing. Because of Arkady's claimed injury, he was lashed around the body rather than held by his arms, and for this he was grateful. As he watched the disciples eat, he waited for his opportunity.

"We will be underway at first light. If the barbarian's shoulder is not improved by then, he will suffer for it, and it will be more than an ache in his bones," Vadin promised before retiring into the tent for the night.

Arkady waited for the three to fall asleep, fearing to move until he heard that regularity of breathing that would guarantee a margin of safety to him and Surata while they got away from their captors. He had not yet thought of where they might go, but that was a consideration for later, when they knew they were beyond the reach of the three men.

"Arkady-immai," came her whisper, so softly that it was almost impossible to hear it over the sigh of the night wind.

"I know," he answered. "Wait a little longer, in case." He recalled one camisado he had been in when the commander of his troops had started the attack before the enemy camp was entirely asleep. Arkady's men had been in the van of the assault, and they had been met by a company of sleepy men with lances and bad tempers. He would not make that mistake again.

A little while later, Arkady twisted in the ropes that held him until he could slip his hand between himself and the tree, to reach under his belt for the cinquedea he carried. Slowly he worked the little leaf-bladed knife out of its hiding place. By the time he had the weapon free, he had skinned his knuckles, and his back felt sore from the unnatural posture he had had to maintain, but it meant little; his thoughts were triumphant.

"What are you doing?" Surata whispered.

"Getting out," he said, sawing at the ropes that held him. The fibers were tough and resisted the bite of the knife, but at last the bonds parted.

"Arkady-immai!" she exclaimed, hardly louder than before but with more hope than he had heard from her in days.

"Coming," he told her as he stepped out of the ropes. He hurried across the clearing, crouching low out of habit. His cinquedea was ready by the time he got to her side. "Hold still," he ordered her as he set to work cutting the ropes that wrapped around her wrists.

"Hurry," she said, her breath quickening in her throat.

"God, I have missed touching you," he said, feeling her closeness like wine in his veins. "It will not be enough to get away. I need more of you."

"And I of you," she said. "Don't talk now. Get us out of

here." She was straining against the ropes, her body quivering with the effort.

He pressed harder and felt the rope give way. "I'll get the other hand. It won't be long."

She fretted while he worked on her other wrist, clicking her tongue with exasperation she was trying not to express. "They are still asleep," she said, trying to assure herself as much as to give him information.

"Good," he panted. "These damned ropes must be made of iron. They're blunting my knife."

"The Bundhi makes his restraints with more than material power. You are cutting more than rope." She closed her blind eyes, her face taking on the blankness he had learned to respect. "Cut slowly," she said in a distant tone. "Cut as if you were taking meat from a roast. Long, slow, deep cuts. Think about how much you wish the Bundhi to fail at his plans."

It sounded foolish to Arkady, but he did as she told him. To his surprise, the fibers were severed more easily. It took little time to get through the bonds. "There," he said as he flung the ropes away from them as if they were the bodies of serpents.

Surata was rubbing her wrists, grimacing as she did. "My hands have no feeling and my arms are burning."

"Keep rubbing them. You'll be all right." He looked around them, peering into the darkness. "We'd better keep on the way we were going. They will expect us to try to return to Samarkand, since we do not know the way to Gora Čimtarga."

"And they believe we would not be foolish enough to go there, in any case. And we will not be, not until we have broken the Bundhi's power in that other place." Her determination was formidable, and as always, Arkady listened to her with a combination of respect and bafflement.

"Is there any way we can do that? Every time we have tried, there's been trouble." He did not mind the battle, but he knew enough now of the ruin the Bundhi could bring and did not want to fall victim to it. "Surata? How can we..."

"I will tell you, when we are gone from here." Numbly she felt for his hand. "We must look for a place to cross the river.

If the Bundhi is in Ajni, then he will be on this side of the canyon. We should be on the other. It will give us a little time."

Arkady had been watching the rise of the mountains around them and he could not help but wonder where they were to find such a place. "Is there a bridge that you know of?"

"I have heard that there is one just above the Jannur Rapids. I do not know for certain." Her confidence faltered, then reasserted itself. "We will find it, or another one."

It was not as simple for Arkady to believe this as it was for her, but he put his arm around her shoulder. "We'll find one. We'll get across."

"Is it steep? The road ahead?" They had slipped away from the clearing, going into the undergrowth that ran up from the riverbank. "*Is* there a road?"

"A narrow one," he said. "We will not stay on it. It would be too easy for those three to come after us. Anyone passing us will remember what they see and inform Vadin that we . . . If they do not see us, they will have nothing to report."

"Good," she said, lifting her hand to fend off the little branches that whipped into her face. "It is not as pleasant, but much wiser." She stumbled and caught herself before he turned to support her. "Keep on, Arkady-champion. Only, warn me if the way grows rougher."

For an answer he squeezed her fingers. He knew that their climb would be arduous, but did not want to say so.

Chapter 23

They kept on through the night and most of the day that followed, permitting themselves to rest only twice, once at a rivulet that splashed down from the peaks above them, and once at the edge of a long, narrow field where the last of a stand of soft-skinned gourds were planted.

"Take a couple with you, and so will I," Arkady recommended when they had satisfied the worst of their hunger. "With this and water, we'll be able to keep going for a while." He wanted to ask her where it was they were headed, but he hesitated, afraid that she would not have an acceptable answer.

"In a few more days, there will be little we can take from the fields. Winter is coming," she said softly.

Arkady chuckled. "Well, if we can cross the desert in summer, we can climb mountains in the winter." He tossed his head to get his hair out of his eyes. "If we encounter snow, we'll need heavier boots, but for now—" He patted her shoulder.

When he found a place where they could sleep that night,

Arkady took the precaution of piling dried brush around the little hollow in the mountainside. "This way," he explained, "we'll hear anything that approaches. They'll make enough noise to wake us and give us time to get ready for them."

"Even three of them?" Surata asked, not in doubt but in worry.

"A dozen of them," he said, bragging in spite of himself. "Yes, perhaps three," he amended in a quieter tone.

"This place, where is it?" She cocked her head, listening. "There is a stream?"

"Nearby. And the river is below. We've been following an animal path—deer or sheep by the look of the tracks—along the mountain. The drop is steep if you start downhill. If you wake in the night, don't try to go anywhere without me. You could get hurt." He stopped his work and looked at her. "It'll be night in another hour. If the Bundhi's men haven't found us by then we might get away from them. Tomorrow, we'll have to travel as far as we can." He pulled at his brigandine. "I never thought I'd miss my old one, but I do. This is heavier and it doesn't fit me as well."

Surata sighed. "After all that, a knife and a few pieces of gold is all that we have left to us."

"It isn't *that* bad," Arkady protested, taking her hand and pulling her close to him. "We're alive, we're not too hungry and we're free."

The boughs he had used to line the hollow were fragrant, and though they crackled, they were nice to lie upon. "It's going to be cold tonight," he said as he drew her close to him.

"Then we will have to warm each other," Surata answered. Arkady had intended to kiss her lightly, but as soon as he had her next to him, he knew he did not want that slow, tantalizing, expert awakening now. He had been without her too long for that.

"Arkady-champion," she breathed between kisses. "You are . . . welcome."

Never had their caresses been so fiercely gentle. All that they had done before had been in preparation for this, when

337

they could touch each other, explore each other without awkwardness or uncertainty. There was nothing that made him doubtful, nothing that broke the spell between them. They lay together on the boughs as if they were suspended between heaven and earth, each for the other the only reality.

Arkady pulled his clothing over them so they would not be too cold when they fell asleep, and smiled when Surata murmured an objection. "You, you. You keep me warm."

"Not after midnight, Surata." He could not help but smile, and he ended her protests with playful kisses, sensing that she was almost ready for him.

Thighs, groins, breasts, mouths pressed together, both as caught in the other's desire as their own. For an infinite moment they were poised apart

and once again the colors blossomed around them, seeming to fuse with them, making them part of the light.

As one they moved, slipping down ways that defied the limitations of words. There was too great an unity, too deep a closeness to want speech between them. Arkady could feel Surata as he felt his breath in his lungs. His mind experienced her blindness and the frustration it brought to her. They moved as two fish circling endlessly in a clear pool.

This was what she had meant, he realized, when she talked of yin and yang: separate, yet complete only in unity.

"Not yet, Arkady my champion," her words echoed in his mind. *"It comes closer, but we do not have it yet."*

This intrusion startled him, as if he had fallen. "Surata?"

"I am here, where you are, but you are still Arkady my champion and I am still Surata. There is another place beyond this, where you and I are fused." She paused. *"When we are as we are..."*

"The Divine Child?" He remembered all the times he had been told of the Divine Child, who came to redeem the world. Was this what Scripture had meant? Had his priest been wrong?

"Your teachings do not permit the Divine Child, Arkady my champion. You are told to worship it, not that you can

become it." She had a regretful note in her voice. "It is a pity that we must search for the Bundhi while we are as we are. If we had achieved full transcendence, then our strength would be without end and there would be little the Bundhi could do."

"We are already transcendent," he reminded her, shocked that she should be so unappreciative of what they had created between them.

"Transcendence to this other place, yes, but transcendence of self, no. When we have done that, then the Bundhi will be as easy to defeat as it is to snap a twig."

"Then teach me," he urged her, knowing that the longing he had awakened was hers as well as his own.

"My father studied for thirty years and never accomplished it," she said, her thoughts becoming unhappy. Arkady was aware that he had the same sadness within him, spurred on by his need for her and for their closeness. "For you and I to do it," she went on, "when we have had so little time—"

His thoughts broke into hers. "We have crossed hundreds of leagues together, we have nearly starved and died of thirst together, we have trusted each other when we could no longer trust ourselves, we have endured privation and loneliness and fear without turning on each other. If we can do that, then the Divine Child should not be impossible." He said it with enthusiasm, and the lights around them brightened in response. He felt their presence in the shifting lights grow more vivid.

"Of course," she agreed with a trace of amusement.

"And don't humor me; I'm not jesting. You and I have come through trials together we would not have survived alone. Isn't that what the Divine Child is meant to do?" He let his asperity color his outburst—it colored the lights surrounding them as well, and Arkady was too entranced by what he saw to be annoyed with her reluctance. "What do we have to do, Surata? Where should we go, now that we are in this other place?"

"It is wretched to be in this other place, that can be so wonderful, and have to search for such as the Bundhi. I wish we could simply ride the crest together, make this other place into anything and everything that will please us best. But *you're right, there are things we must do here that are not for our joy. I hope one day it will not be this way."* Her voice was plaintive: the bright shapes trembled like leaves with a wind passing through them.

"Where do we begin? At the castle in the marsh?" He had been hoping they might go there again, for he thought of the place fondly, seeing it as a refuge.

"No," she said slowly. *"I . . . cannot find it anymore. It is . . . gone. And if we find it again, there is no certainty it would be ours still."*

"The Bundhi?" he asked, not needing to.

"Yes." She quivered with him.

Arkady could think of nothing that would console her. *"Then it must be the bamboo redoubt?"* He did not want to return there. Even his recollections of the place made him shake with revulsion. There was so much of decay about it and so much malice in the staves . . . He forced his attention to what she was telling him.

"That could be too great a risk. The Bundhi guards himself well, and he must know by now that we have got away from his men. He will protect his fortress in this other place more rigorously than his redoubt in the daily world. As long as his redoubt in this other place stands, his redoubt on Gora Čimtarga is impregnable." Fleeting impressions of various plans slipped through her mind, hints and echos of them appearing in Arkady's thoughts.

"Would a fire in this other place burn his redoubt on Gora Čimtarga as well as the one in this other place?" It seemed to him to be the most direct means of destroying the redoubt.

"It might," she said, *"but it is not so easy to burn things here in this other place; they can turn to water or air before flames can harm them. But if we could make it burn, then it might be possible to stop the Bundhi both here and in the daily world."* She considered more alternatives. *"Water means nothing to bamboo. It only aids it to grow. The bamboo bends with the wind and cannot be uprooted. If you bury it, it springs up again through the earth. If it is cut with metal, it grows again."*

"You're convincing yourself that you cannot act," Arkady chided her. "Think what you can do, not what cannot be done."

She pondered a little while, and he enjoyed sharing her questions and her attempts to find solutions to their predicament. Finally she said, "I suppose you are right, and burning is the answer. What is this thing you have in your mind—Greek fire, you call it—that burns in water?"

"Greek fire. Where did you find that?" He sighed. "I've never seen it used or made. I have only heard of it."

"But such a thing exists?" she pursued, pressing him for more information.

"I know it is supposed to exist, which isn't quite the same thing."

They had made no alteration in the brightness around them, but still there was a change, a subtle turn of shade that gave the lights a greater brilliance.

"Still, you know of it," she asked, this time with greater determination. "You can think of it and know that water will not quench its flames?"

"I suppose so," he answered, beginning to see what she intended. "Certainly if we make Greek fire in this other place, it will not be put out by any water the Bundhi might conjure up."

"Good." She was silent again, delving through her memories, and his.

"How do you do this? I think I'm being tickled," he told her as he perceived her presence in his mind.

"I haven't words to tell you, Arkady my champion," she said, a bit wistfully. "I wish I had. I wish I had years with you, so that we could learn . . . everything together. I wish it was for joy alone that we—"

"Stop it. Time enough for that later, when we've settled things." He shared her regret, but he knew that anything that dampened morale on the eve of battle was dangerous. "The day will come. You know that and I know it, and that will have to do for now."

She took his admonition to heart. "Yes. Later we will have

all the time we want." If she sounded less certain then he, it was from her lack of fighting experience. *"When we have our . . . victory."*

"Very good," he approved.

(*"Good, so very good,"* he whispered as he took the flare of her hips in his hands.)

She was more encouraged now, and her strength grew greater as she explored his memories. "You are a valiant soldier, Arkady my champion."

"You mean that I am not as reckless as many others," he said sternly. *"Poles are noted for their recklessness. We are reputed to be brave to the point of madness."*

She responded to both the truth and the irony in what he said. "No wonder your Margrave Fadey was disappointed in you."

"He did not want prudence," Arkady observed. *"I was prudent then, but I will be less so now. Yet I will not be reckless, for that would put you in more danger than we're in now, and that is more than I am willing to do."* He felt his protectiveness answered by her own. He had never experienced such inner reinforcement as they gave each other amid the shifting motes of light.

"See how brightly we glow, Arkady my champion," she exclaimed, her delight as warm as sunshine to him.

"Is that a good thing?" he asked, teasing her kindly.

"Light on swords is a good thing to you, so this must be the same." She moved with him, making their luminosity dance and curvet through the light-filled vastness.

Arkady enjoyed each moment of what they did, and as they continued their onward motion, he hoped that this time they would not come upon the stronghold of the Bundhi too soon.

"You are as filled with our union as I am," Surata told him, her eagerness adding to his pleasure.

He wanted to give her a gallant answer, one that would be as poetic and reverent as the emotions she inspired. He tried to show her the rapture that consumed him, so that she

jerked

apart and thrown down, a bamboo staff a hand's breath from his face.

"Arkady-immai!" Surata wailed, her hands flailing as she tired to locate him in the hushed crackle of the twigs and branches.

"Do not move, Surata-of-Bogar," said the man who had separated them. At the sound of his voice, she grew still. "I have my staff with me and I will not hesitate to put it to use."

"How . . . ?" she demanded.

"My tigers tell me many things. They found you for me, and they will have their reward. Since my servants permitted you to escape, they will feed the tigers this time." The sound he made was supposed to be laughter but it was as cold as the breaking up of winter ice.

In the wan moonlight, Arkady was able to see the stranger. The man was tall, and so lean that he appeared even taller. He had little to distinguish him except his eyes, which he turned on Arkady in sudden malice; they were dark and flat as pebbles. He shook his head. "So you're the great fighter," he said.

Arkady knew from the tone of the man's voice that he was being insulted. He frowned, still badly disoriented. "Surata, is this . . . is it . . ."

"Yes," she said in a rage of defeat. "This is the Bundhi."

There had been impressions of the man before, in her memories and in the strange byways of that other place. Somehow Arkady had expected more, a larger figure, a stronger air of menace. What was most distressing about him, thought Arkady, was his normality, his ordinariness. "Tell him he is a disappointment," Arkady said, adding, "Never mind. No sense in giving him reason to fight with us now."

"Why should he fight?" Surata asked bitterly. "He has us." She faced Arkady. "He will hurt you, he wants only the least excuse. He will try to force you to fight or escape or defy him, and then he will do all that he can to destroy you."

Casually the Bundhi turned and slapped Surata with the full strength of the back of his hand. "You will no longer talk to him. You will speak to me, and if I have reason to say something to that worm, you will do it as briefly as you can. Tell him that he is not to talk to you."

"Arkady-immai," she said, her hand against her face where the Bundhi had struck her, "he has ordered us not to talk to one another. He means it."

"Right," Arkady said, wanting to add scathing words but afraid for Surata.

"Very good. You have prolonged your useless life a while and you have reduced your suffering, at least for the time being." The Bundhi came closer to Arkady, his staff almost touching his shoulder. "So white, your skin, and your hair pale as a ghost. What a creature you are." He spat, smiling. "You have no control of your body, do you? One instant outside that woman's body and you shrivel."

"Do not harm him, Bundhi!" Surata cried out.

"Do you like this untutored foreigner?" the Bundhi asked her, disbelief in his voice. "The loss of your eyes has unsettled your mind."

"This fight isn't his. He brought me here." Surata was both defiant and desperate. "You have no reason to hold him."

"He is with you, he has caused my men to behave stupidly and it amuses me to see you thus. What does it matter if this is his fight or not, when it is karma that moves him to bring you?" He reached down and grabbed her by the hair. "Tell him that you are both going to come with me."

"We're to come with him," Surata shrieked.

"Let her go!" Arkady bellowed, starting to rush at the Bundhi, hands extended.

"Tell him to stop," the Bundhi said calmly, his bamboo staff poised over her breasts.

"Stop, Arkady-immai." Her voice was low but it halted him.

"Do not doubt that I will hurt her, foreigner. For me there is merit in your pain. Tell him, Surata-of-Bogar. Tell him, too, that only Vadin will be with us; the other two are with the tigers."

Surata did as she was told, her voice almost failing her at

the end. "He is telling you the truth, Arkady-immai," she gasped.

"I know that." He remained still, feeling as cold inwardly as the icy wind off the peaks was making his naked skin.

"Dress, both of you. I will watch and listen. You may say things only if I permit it. Right now, I do not permit it. My staff is hungry, Surata-of-Bogar, and it would please me to let it devour you."

"We're supposed to get dressed, Arkady-immai," she told him.

"That's something, at least we won't freeze," Arkady said as he reached for his leggings, embarrassed by the contemptuous way the Bundhi looked at him. He pulled on the clothes with unseemly haste, wishing they had been discovered in any other situation than the one they had been in.

"Do not touch each other," the Bundhi warned Surata. "If you touch each other, you will also touch my staff. You know what its touch will do. You have the scars from its burns on your hands." He shoved Surata toward the heap of her clothes, chuckling as she stumbled and sprawled on the boughs.

"It will be light before long. Vadin will be waiting on the road, and he will follow behind us, in case you want to fall behind. Tell your foreign soldier that, Surata-of-Bogar."

She repeated what the Bundhi had said, and took a chance, adding, "We will have to find another way."

"We will," Arkady vowed. Now that he had seen the Bundhi, he was more determined than he had been in his life to defeat the foe or die in the attempt. He knew now why the Margrave had been willing to storm an unassailable fortress, why his father had felt betrayed by living beyond his battles, why there had been captains willing to lose men and lives for issues beyond honor.

In the early morning they crossed the river on a high bridge that swung and groaned with every step they took. Far below them the swirling water frothed like the jaws of a mad dog.

With the crossing of the river, they left the merchants' road behind and instead had to walk single file up paths used by shepherds and pilgrims. The rocky outcroppings offered little protection from the wind, and the few copses were limited to the places where wind and rock could not pull at them.

They travelled silently, the Bundhi leading, Surata immediately behind him and held to him with a long hempen strand that went around her waist. A few paces behind her was Arkady, and finally Vadin, his staff held high to remind Arkady that he had good reason not to fall behind. The Bundhi set a steady pace, one that demanded all the strength that the others possessed to maintain. They passed few other persons on the trail, and those they did pass stepped aside and averted their faces, showing fear more than respect in their attitude and conduct.

At night there was a little food, and two separate trees where Surata and Arkady were tied, the Bundhi and Vadin sleeping between them, Vadin serving as pillow and blanket for the Bundhi.

"Are they asleep?" Arkady whispered when the night was half over.

"I hope so," Surata answered. "I knew you would remain awake, so I forced myself not to sleep."

"How far are we from Gora Čimtarga?" he asked.

"Four days, perhaps five," she said forlornly. "They will be watching us all the time."

"As we will be watching them," Arkady said with a grim smile.

"If we once enter the redoubt on Gora Čimtarga, we will be lost."

"Then we must not enter it," Arkady said. "Before we get there, we must find a way, a reason to delay our arrival. Do you agree?"

"Yes, of course. But how?" This last was a cry of profound anguish.

"We'll find a way. What else is a champion for?" He had meant to cheer her with this quip, but to his horror, she began to weep. "Surata . . . no. Surata."

"Arkady-immai, you *are* my champion, no matter what

occurs after." She tried to reach out to him, but the bonds held her and all she could do was strive to lean away from the tree and toward him.

Vadin shifted, then was pressed firmly into a posture that could not be comfortable by the arm of the Bundhi.

"If only we could touch," Surata whispered. "Even our hands, it would be something, better than this."

"I know, I know." The admission sounded so trivial when measured against what he wanted to say that he flushed to the roots of his light brown hair and beard.

"You tell me in many ways, Arkady-immai. I know them all."

The Bundhi reached out, his hand closing around his staff, and he brought the bamboo close to him, pressing it against his palm. Although he continued to sleep, the rhythm of his breathing changed to a deeper, more passionate panting while the bamboo drew upon him, in a communion that fascinated and repelled Arkady as he watched.

"He does not use women, Arkady-immai. He is ... bound to that staff," Surata said in an undervoice. "He feeds on it as much as it feeds on him. Anything the staff devours ultimately feeds him."

"It's more than feeding," he said as he stared.

"Yes—much more."

For quite some time the Bundhi maintained his bizarre link with the staff, and when he finally moved the staff away, he slept on as if drugged, in a stupor that lasted until sunrise.

By the end of the second day, Surata was bruised from stumbles and falls; her plight gave the Bundhi malefic enjoyment, and he took pains to remind her of her blindness and helplessness.

"When we reach my redoubt, Surata-of-Bogar, you will be taken into the staff. It will not happen quickly. You will know that you are being devoured. You will embrace Siva before you die. I think I will take turns between you and your foreign soldier. I want you to hear him scream, and to feel his death when the bamboo touches you."

Arkady wanted to call to her, to tell her not to listen. He had done it once and his throat still ached from the place where the Bundhi's fingers had sunk. He was faintly queasy from the thinning air and the increasing cold, so he did his best to concentrate on walking and tried not to be goaded into action that would harm Surata as well as himself. It galled him to know that he was failing her when she had the most need of him. He wanted to pray, but none of the words made sense.

"Think what it might be like," the Bundhi exclaimed as they crested a rise in the trail, "to bring the Left Hand Path such power! You are going to give me the world, Surata-of-Bogar. Think what that will mean to those of the Right Hand Path, if there are any left other than you."

Surata did not answer, and in retaliation for silence, the Bundhi tugged on the line that held her to him, and laughed as she staggered, flinging her hands out as she fell.

"You leave an offering in blood on the stones. The tigers will like that."

From his place at the rear of the line, Vadin lifted his staff, and when he reached the place where Surata had fallen, he rested his bamboo for a moment. Arkady turned in time to see the segmented wood quiver in Vadin's hand.

That night, Surata was tied to Vadin's feet, so that any movement she might make would wake the Bundhi's servant. The Bundhi himself reclined in isolation, his head not far from the long-needled shrub where Arkady had been secured.

"If you attempt to speak, we will know it," the Bundhi said with relish. "You will be gagged and then you will be punished for disobediance." He tweaked Surata's earlobe. "Tell him."

She translated, and then was silent, her hands joined in her lap. One side of her face had turned livid from the Bundhi's blow and there were scrapes on her arms where her stumbles had taken their toll during the day. She fingered her bonds and then shook her head.

"Relish this, Surata-of-Bogar. Shortly you will enter my stronghold, and you will be mine utterly." He reached out with his staff, letting the side of the bamboo rest against Arkady's face.

Arkady felt the burn, and something worse, something that ate into him as if to reduce his skull, and all his bones, to calcined ash. That dread as much as the pain forced a loud moan from his lips. "God and Saint Michael," he swore as the Bundhi moved the bamboo away. Gingerly he raised his fingers to probe the welt that was rising on his face.

"There will be more, in time. Your face, soldier, and then the rest of you. Tell him that I will burn away his testicles with my staff, Surata-of-Bogar." The Bundhi plucked at the cords that held Arkady. "This is not too bad. This will hold him for the night."

Humiliation filled Arkady as he heard Surata repeat the Bundhi's threat. The brand on his face was bad enough—and it would be a constant reminder of his disgrace for the rest of his life—but the Bundhi's determination to make him less than a man sickened him. He wanted to purge himself of any taint of the Bundhi, though it brought him to the brink of death.

When the Bundhi's staff had been sated and the night was far advanced, Arkady made a desperate gamble: moving with deliberate care, he stretched out his arms as far as the ropes would allow. His wrists were chaffed and his fingers were numb by the time he was able to press the hemp fibers to the side of the Bundhi's staff.

At once he could feel the unearthly heat of the bamboo eat into both rope and wrists. He could smell his own flesh char, but he endured the agony until dark spots blurred his vision. Only then did he try to part the cords. It took more than three attempts to get the hemp to snap, and when finally he succeeded in breaking his restraints, he was too dizzy to do more than sit staring at his hands, corpse-pale in the moonlight.

A sound—perhaps a bird, perhaps a night-hunting animal— brought Arkady back to himself. His mind screamed at him to get away, to kill the Bundhi and Vadin, to free Surata, but his body responded sluggishly, and he was clumsy when he moved. He unwound the ropes that had held him, taking care not to let them trail on the ground or touch the Bundhi's staff. His arms trembled and ached with the effort, but he would not be rushed, particularly when he felt so awkward. When he had all the rope wound into a coil, he moved into a low crouch, wincing as his ankles and knees popped. He tottered to his feet, then crept away from the Bundhi toward the place where Vadin lay with Surata tied to his feet.

He hesitated, afraid to wake her suddenly for fear that he would also wake Vadin. The sound of his heart in his chest seemed so loud to him that he thought it was enough to rouse her.

Surata's lips moved. "Go." The word was so soft that he was not sure he had heard it until she repeated the order. "Arkady-immai, go."

Arkady shook his head. "Not without you." He kept his voice so low that he doubted he was audible.

"Go! Please." Her plea was little more than a breath, but carried all the weight of her fear and her love.

Whatever protest he might have had were lost. There was a sudden outraged shout behind him as the Bundhi reached of his staff, enraged to the point of frenzy.

Arkady turned and jumped over Vadin, who was just opening his eyes. He saw the Bundhi swing his staff toward him, and knew that if the bamboo touched him, he was lost. Peril spurred Arkady: he kicked out, aiming not for the staff but for the Bundhi himself. The toe of his boot caught the sorcerer high on the chest. He could feel bone give way under the impact. As the Bundhi howled with pain, Vadin lurched toward him, dragging Surata after him.

The Bundhi screamed his outrage, and the mountains around them echoed them back eerily. He pointed at Arkady. *"Kill him!"*

Vadin, terrified at what was happening, untied the ropes that bound him to Surata, and launched himself at Arkady. He kicked out at her to get her away from his feet so she would not hamper his movements.

"KILL HIM!" the Bundhi raved.

Vadin swung his staff at Arkady, but he ducked, then started toward the slope of the mountain.

The Bundhi rushed at him, his mouth square and foam-flecked.

Arkady ran, shoving Vadin toward the Bundhi as he went. He strove to keep his footing on the edge of the narrow path, stumbled, recovered, reached out to grab Surata's arm.

Then the staff thumped his shoulder and he, with Surata, fell over the edge of the trail, down the path of an old avalanche.

Chapter 24

They came to rest on a ledge about halfway down the gorge. Clinging together, hurt and shaken, they huddled there, afraid to move for fear of dislodging more stones and themselves.

Above them, the Bundhi's voice roared. "You shall not get away! You shall never get away!"

"You needn't tell me," Arkady whispered to Surata, holding her close to him with bleeding hands.

"He will try to reach us," she warned. She was battered, her garments torn; a cut over her lip made it difficult for her to speak.

"He won't, not without endangering himself," Arkady assured her, hoping he would be able to think of some means to get them away from the rabid man who stood shrieking at them on the trail.

"He has other means to reach us," she said, no longer held by fear. "He can find us."

"You will *die!* You will die *for me!*" the Bundhi screamed. "Hear me, Surata-of-Bogar—you will die for me, when you have served me, when your power is mine!"

"What is he saying to you?" Arkady asked as he felt her shake in his arms.

"He wants me to . . . surrender my . . . magic to him. He wishes to . . . drain me." She brought one hand to her eyes. "If I could *see*, then . . ."

"Shush," Arkady whispered. He was already taking stock of the position; he could not tell how far the old avalanche extended on either side of them, and knew that the area of slippage would provide unstable footing at best. It would be hazardous to cross the slope by day, by night it would be suicidal.

"Vadin! *Vadin!*" the Bundhi ordered. "Vadin, you let her go! You permitted her to go! You are not deserving of your staff, Vadin."

"I . . . did not think she would fall, Great Teacher, O Bundhi," Vadin bleated.

"You have carried your staff for more than two years, you accepted it from me. You took it into your hands, and still you could not keep a blind girl for me!" He was crooning to his disciple, the singsong cadences full of menace.

"She . . . is Surata-of-Bogar, O Bundhi, and not simply a girl, blind or not." Vadin cringed, backing toward the edge of the trail.

"Oh, no," the Bundhi said as his hands closed on Vadin's shoulders. "There will be no convenient fall for *you*, Vadin. I am going to reclaim the staff. You realize what that means to you." The cold laughter was magnified by the stone walls of the gorge.

Surata clung closer to Arkady.

"Is it bad?" he asked in an undervoice.

She nodded. "Very bad. If there were something we could *do* . . ."

"But what is it?" Arkady wondered, sensing her horror at what was happening on the trail above them.

"He will take back the staff, and . . . Vadin, as well. Then he will have two staves, and with that he can create a portal." She held her breath, listening to the Bundhi.

"Lie down, disciple, and accept your chastisement. Be grateful that your end serves the Left Hand Path and my goals, or it would be slower for you." He spoke softly, making a caress of his dire words. Then he called out, "Listen, Surata-of-Bogar, and know what awaits you. You hear me. You know what I can do."

Surata did not answer, but her hands tightened convulsively. "Vadin . . ." she began, but could not go on.

"Hear this, enemy and daughter of my enemy," the Bundhi cried. "The staff will claim Vadin. Hear it."

There was a scuffle on the trail and a few loose rocks cascaded down, then the thud of a falling body.

"O Bundhi," Vadin screeched, "I will prove myself worthy. I will serve you!"

"Most certainly you will," the Bundhi said, pitching his voice so that it would carry through the length of the ravine. "As you have never served me before."

What came after was a latrant howl, born of a rapturous dread.

Arkady half rose at the sound. "What *is* that?" he asked, as the hairs on his neck prickled.

The noises grew more hideous once the ululation ceased; a wet, voracious gobbling replaced it.

"The staff," Surata muttered, appalled at what the Bundhi was doing. "He . . . the Bundhi placed it in Vadin's mouth so that it could . . . consume him."

"You mean . . . *eat* him?" Arkady demanded, bile at the back of his tongue.

"Yes, and more than that. It devours more than flesh, Arkady-champion. It was Vadin's staff, so . . ." She pressed the heel of her hand to her mouth.

"Shortly I will have my portal, Surata-of-Bogar," the Bundhi shouted, mocking her. "What shall I rain down on you then? What avalanches will bury you and that soldier? Think of it, Surata-of-Bogar. Anything in that other place will come through the portal at my summons."

Quickly Surata explained what the Bundhi was determined

to do. "He could bring . . . anything."

"But can he do that?" Arkady said, unable to believe it. "How? What would give him . . . the power."

"The portal. He has two sated staves, and they can be joined, and once joined, they form a . . . doorway that will bring whatever he summons through."

"I will rain fire on you, and burning stones, Surata-of-Bogar. I will send serpents the size of oxen to crush you. I will bring every malignant spirit from every quarter of the winds to prey upon you before I let you serve me and die." He sounded delighted with his plans. He chortled in anticipation.

"What can we do?" Arkady asked, needing no translation to know that the Bundhi was determined to terrorize them.

"If we were in that other place, then we . . ." She let out a long, trembling sigh. "As it is, we can do nothing."

"What could we do in that other place?" he wondered aloud. "If the Bundhi is bringing through whatever he wishes, what good would being in that other place be?"

"We could . . . affect the summons, and what the results would be." She paused. "He will not let us die quickly. Or easily."

"If I had just *one* of my weapons—my sword, my maul, even the cinquedea, then I might be able to stop him, but . . ." He gestured to show how helpless he felt.

The Bundhi took the staff from Vadin's husk and thumped it on the ground three times. A small slide of stones and pebbles rattled down the slope, gathering momentum as it went.

"Do not let this little avalanche hurt you too much, Surata-of-Bogar. Stay conscious and afraid, for my pleasure." His laughter this time was louder, more insistent. "How sad that you will not be able to see what I will be doing. Shall I assist you? Let me describe it to you, Surata-of Bogar."

"We've got to move. He'll be peppering us with stones continuously if he thinks he can hurt us and distract us with them." He peered through the gloom, trying to discern anything that might provide a foothold for them. "I might do the same thing, if I were in his place and had an enemy below me."

"Arkady-champion!" Surata protested.

"It's a good tactic, but it has a limited use." He put his arm around her shoulder. "If we stay here, it's only a matter of time before one of those rocks does some damage. Crossing the slide is . . . risky. The Bundhi is counting on us to remain where we are."

"How great is the risk?" she asked when another flurry of stones had clattered by them.

"We're in greater jeopardy if we remain where we are," he said, not answering her question.

The Bundhi started chanting, a steady, monotonous repetition of syllables that might have been soporific in less trying circumstances. "Do you remember this, Surata-of-Bogar? Do you recall how your uncles died?"

"Find a way across the slide," Surata told Arkady.

Arkady patted her arm in agreement. "If we go down the hill, not just across, we have a better chance. There are deeper shadows upstream. It would be wiser to stay in the shadows."

"Shadows will make no difference to the Bundhi once his portal is open." She reached out for his hand. "Do not leave me, Arkady-immai."

"I won't," he said. "I only want to test the footing. If I trip, I've got a chance to catch myself, but you . . . Let me try it out."

"You should be here with me, Surata-of-Bogar, so that you could witness the opening of the portal. You could add your power to mine, you could feed my strength with your own. Do not waste your gifts on that soldier. He knows nothing. He cannot begin to understand what you are. I will reward you, I will let you share in the ruin I bring. I will spare your life until all the work is accomplished, Surata-of-Bogar, and for that, I will not make the death of your soldier too unpleasant, unless you decide that is what you want." The Bundhi was confident, giddy with the prospect of triumph.

Arkady tapped Surata on the shoulder, putting his fingers to her lips to keep her from crying out. "I think I've found a way. It will not be easy, but there is an overhang, down the hill and just beyond the slide. It will give us some protection, if there should be another avalanche." He did not want to think what would become of them if another slide of rock should trap them in that niche. "We'll have a little room to move, and after sunrise, we can try to find a way out of here."

"Yes, good," she said, shutting out the ranting promises that the Bundhi called to her.

As they were making their way to their shelter, the Bundhi began to chant again.

"Why does he do that?" Arkady whispered. The sound irritated him, intruded on his concentration and sapped his will.

"To gather power to himself," she answered. "Hurry. He will join the staves soon, and then he will begin to summon his forces. It will take him a while to bring them through, but once he begins . . ."

Arkady did not waste time in speaking. He urged Surata to a faster pace, all but carrying her the last few steps of the way. He thrust her ahead of him, under the projecting boulder, then crept in beside her. His head throbbed and he gasped, but he was able to smile. "We're still alive; that's something."

From the trail, there was a change in the Bundhi's chanting.

"He is starting to unite the staves," Surata said, not bothering to keep her voice low. "He will have his portal soon."

"The things that he calls from that other place . . . will they be like what we've seen?"

"That depends on the Bundhi. If he wants to have more destruction, he can bring it." She reached out to him. "Arkady-champion, I am sorry that I've brought you to this. I thought we would be able to have more time."

Arkady stopped her. "Wait a bit. Can't we still try? I don't know if I can, but I'm willing to try. You said yourself there isn't much we can do here, but in that other place, maybe we could . . ." He kissed her forehead, just above the faded blue mark. "Besides, if I have to die, I'd rather die that way than just hiding under a rock."

Surata held his hands tightly in hers. "If you want, we can try. Who knows?"

Rocks, some much larger than the ones that had fallen before, thundered down the slide where they had been a little while earlier.

"There will be more avalanches, Surata-of-Bogar, and they will not be rocks, but things worse that will wound you and break you to prepare you for me." The Bundhi hooted.

"Don't listen to him, Surata. He is trying to scare you. I've ordered my men to do this to the enemy, to scoff at the enemy soldier and insult them to make my men feel strong, and to harass the enemy. The Bundhi is doing the same thing to you. Listen to me, not to him." He felt oddly calm, since this was what he knew how to do. The sorcery and rituals bewildered him, but battle was another matter. "We have a chance if you will not listen to the Bundhi but to me." He took her face in his hands, looking at her with all his concentration. When he knew she was no longer paying attention to the Bundhi, he kissed her, hoping that he would respond to her once more.

"Arkady-champion, open your Centers to me." Then she wrapped her arms around him. "No, not that. Be with me, close to me, in me. The rest is nothing."

"There is ruin, Surata-of-Bogar! You will bow to it!" The Bundhi gave a long, rising howl. "You will be the last, before they are turned loose to all the world. You will aid me, you will desire the end."

"Don't listen to him, Surata," Arkady urged her. "Listen to me. I tell you that we have a chance. If we can get to that other place, we can fight him."

"And if we can't transcend, we will still defy him," Surata murmured, her hands tugging his clothes.

The ground shook and the rocks groaned and there was a sudden rushing of hot winds.

"I want you, Surata. Help me to want you." He stroked her arms, then pulled her close, unfastening her outer robe. "Let me have you."

She said nothing. Her tongue flicked over the Sixty-Four Petaled Center, then moved to the Thirty-Two Petaled Center. As he pulled out of his leggings, they shared a frisson as their flesh touched.

At the foot of the ravine, gouts of flame sprang up, multi-colored and smelling of metal and dust.

Arkady suppressed an instant of panic when he did not feel himself respond to Surata's skill. There had been other times, against the Turks, when in the first rush of combat he had been shamed to feel himself erect. He strove to recapture that thrill, to rekindle his lust as much as his desire. Then his body warmed and he drew her closer to him.

Creatures, unearthly fanged toads the size of a hound, flopped down the slide, leaving smoking slag behind them. A gibbering filled the air and a buzzing that sounded like bending metal.

"Jesus, Joseph and Mary!" Arkady yelled as one of the monsters crawled over the entrance to their hiding place.

Surata turned, moving her hands in a series of passes while she recited three harsh phrases.

The glowing creature faded, becoming a speck like a firefly as it rolled away from them.

"We are too slow, Arkady-champion," she said in despair.

"No—don't give up yet!" He laughed once, wildly. "At least let's be together." The sight of that thing had shocked him. He could fight any soldier in the world, but not something that was defeated by a collection of unknown sounds and gestures. He felt a gratifying surge in his groin and the strange, compelling tide that ran between him and Surata. The curve of her hip pressed against his as she moved over him, her mouth seeking his.

Surata kissed him deeply, her hands tweaking his nipples while he cupped her breasts in his hands. Her thighs were soft, warm, open

and the lights were more brilliant than they had ever been, as splendid as the vastness of the sky and as luminous as jewels.

("Surata?" he whispered, awed by what he felt for her.)

That other place was alive with movement, with constant shifting and rustling of unseen beings treading unimaginable byways. Sounds, excited, alarmed, echoed in the radiance.

("Arkady?" she responded, lost in him.)

Now the lights were all but tangible, and the

ground shook as something enormous and vile from the farthest reaches of that other place lumbered through the portal the Bundhi had opened. The mountainside swayed with the tread of the beast

while the glory faded to pale, mauve shades that were more like fog than light.

"*Ludicrous. Pitiful!*" *the Bundhi jeered*

sending rivers of stinking acid down the wall of the ravine, hooting derision at his enemies and

calling forth more potent manifestations of his desire for destruction. They roiled and twisted, many with little of a body about them, but with their obduracy and savagery growing steadily more powerful.

The fabric of that other place was rent with the impact of the Bundhi's summons, and the distorted evocations that came through the portal blighted the clarity that had been present there before.

"*Do not be so unwise, Surata-of-Bogar!*" *the Bundhi called from the daily world beyond the portal.* "*You have no more strength, you are weak and useless. You are nothing! Let me take your life and give it some worth in adding to my power!*"

("*Don't listen, Surata. Be with me.*")

A flood of shames rushed through the tarnished brightness, some loathsome, some ghastly, a few so foreign that they could only confuse or disorient. Nothing else responded to the call that pierced the vast distances of that other place

and echoed from the stones of the gorge.

Something gigantic, winged and smelling of sulphur emerged from the portal and hung above them, mouth gaping.

"It seeks for sustenance," the Bundhi screamed. "You can feed it as well as anything else. There are more to come. Do not fight this, Surata-of-Bogar. I have won. You are destroyed. Let me take your flesh, let me use it, and give you to the staves, to keep the portal open!"

"He hasn't won," Surata begged. "Not yet."

For once, it was Arkady who aligned their Centers of the Subtle Body. "You're letting him rattle you. Don't let that happen." He shifted his position so that they could join more deeply. Pleasure coursed through him and he felt her respond.

"Arkady-champion, more." She licked his chest and his neck, balancing so that they were both half sitting, her legs straddling his.

"If you must waste your death, then die!" the Bundhi stormed, while the ground shivered and groaned. *"Die!"*

There was the huge explosive ringing as the boulders separated from the sides of the mountains, rushing down to the river at the depths of the gorge. The sound was impossibly loud, the ground shook.

"Arkady-champion!" she screamed, clinging to him as the avalanche surged over them.

He could say nothing: he held her, taking ultimate consolation in their union. If only they might sustain that, he decided, he would not think that death and the Bundhi had cheated him of everything. "Surata!" he cried, wanting to surround himself with her and his love for her.

"Again, Arkady-champion," she encouraged him. "Please, again."

Enormous footsteps trudged down the avalanche with the stones, and something raised its complaint in a voice that mocked all the cannon in the world.

"You, Surata, only you," Arkady whispered to her.

Burning wings flapped over them. The Bundhi pranced and chanted and crowed in glee.

"Only you, Arkady-champion," she vowed, pressed to him with a strength and desire she had not known before. The current of the Subtle Bodies moved through them, more inexorable than any previous link they had experienced. Within themselves, within each other, they saw with

a Child's eyes, brightness exceeding every garden in the daily world. The Child scampered with the lights, laughing in utter joy. What had been malignant was changed as the Child came to it; what had

361

been shaped by one will adapted to the Child's wishes. Effulgent light glowed from the Child, its eyes so intense in their gaze that the shapes and colors drifted toward it to bask in its glance. It held out its hands to everything coming toward it, watching them caper. The Child ran with them, laughing, making that other place into a meadow.

Fanged and clawed shadows pursued the Child, reaching out to snare it, maws gaping, madness in their eyes.

The Child let them catch it, rolled on the grass with them, giggling, hugging the shadows, smiling while they became more and more insubstantial and finally faded away like wisps of clouds on a summer day. The Child toddled on through the meadow, watching for other shadows.

Trees grew ahead: tall, lean birches and willows; squat, green-headed oaks; massive, fuzzy pines. They were lovely and fragrant, plucking the wind like a harp. The Child ran among them, delighted with what it saw. It skipped and twirled, enchanted with all it encountered.

Strange, stinging insects swarmed around the Child, searching for targets on its fresh skin. The Child brushed them off where they settled. One of the bolder insects made straight for the Child's eyes. A small fist fended the insect off, then caught it gently and studied it where it hovered, iridescent wings glistening. The Child held out a finger for the insect to land on, but the brilliant wings flashed as the insects soared away, fleeing the Child.

The woods grew denser, the trees larger and more imposing. The Child followed the ever-narrowing path, occasionally patting the trunks of the trees in affection. Roots snarled at the base of trunks, branches dipped and made traps for the unwary; the Child bounced over them, playing with them, treating the long, tangled undulations as a puzzle, or an unraveled skein of yarn. It chortled as it followed the most complex convolutions, happily entranced by the curves and knots and gnarls the trees provided.

A keening wind arose, bending the trees, making the more flexible snap and bow before it; the larger, hardier, stolid members of the forest did not fare as well as the wind increased, breaking heavy limbs and leaving maimed trunks behind.

The Child let itself be carried by the wind, riding it as thistledown would, curvetting and dancing, making no resistance to the howling force that ravaged the forest.

The trees were gone. The their place was a broad expanse of rocks and sand, with clumps of fulvous, arid grasses. Everything that could live here did so at the price of something else that lived here. Lizards preyed upon insects and the young of borrowing rodents; the rodents preyed upon insects and the few plants that survived above the ground; snakes hunted the rodents and one another; spiders pursued insects and baby birds; scorpions snared wasps. The Child dropped to the sand near a flat rock, looking around it without alarm, knowing the place well. It got to its feet and began to walk steadily toward the first rise in the distant hills. It did not move quickly, but there was determination in its every step. Neither the hiss of snakes nor the leg-waving threats of spiders distracted it or caused it to turn in fear. High above it, three carrion birds began their ominous circle. The Child waved at them and continued to walk.

The heat grew more intense, pouring unremittingly down on the parched land, making ripples rise from the sands like unheard music.

A long way off, a spot of green appeared, like a smudge in the pale world. At first it seemed unreal, for in the heat it looked to be hovering over the ground. Then it became clear, and the oasis waited, with its panache of palms, promising water and succor from the relentless sun.

The Child walked toward the green haven, alert and curious, as much as anything. Thirst did not bother it, hunger was unknown to it, and for it, there was delight in everything. It shone like the sun as it ambled over the scorching earth.

Under the palms there were tents, most of them festooned with cording and tassels and embroidery. They stood invitingly open, some showing meals spread on sumptuous silk cloths, some revealing couches of soft pillows, some occupied by musicians and dancers, performing sweetly. The Child stood in the middle of the tents and clapped happily. It motioned the musicians and dancers to leave the tent and join it where it stood, but none of them answered the summons.

"We will not hurt you," the Child said. "But if you will come out, we can bring the food out and share it. Why should you not eat when a feast is waiting? And why should we eat and not have the cheer you provide?"

The dancers hastily closed the flaps of the tent and fell silent.

In disappointment, the Child sat on the grass in the middle of the tents and amused itself with making animal shapes with its fingers. "The Bundhi," it said to itself in sad revelation, "never shares—never shares anything."

The tent that had contained the musicians and dancers opened again and out came three armed men, each with his weapons raised. They rushed at the Child, shouting curses and obscenities, prepared to strike.

As the blows fell, the weapons melted away when they neared the Child, playing contentedly in its own luminescence. It raised its head, beaming at the enraged men. It picked up grasses and tossed them at the men, and each was transfixed with arrows.

"They need not be arrows," the Child said. "I threw grass."

The three men fell, then faded so that all that remained were heaps of clothes and weapons on the soft, green grass.

When the Child looked around again, all the tents were gone, and the oasis itself was fading. The Child sighed once and got to its feet, starting off once again toward the distant mountains, walking without fatigue or apprehension.

Thorns and brambles tore at its feet, and the rocks and pebbles yielded nothing but sharp edges. The Child never noticed, and its pace remained the same. When sudden, engulfing darkness came, the Child continued on, bearing its own light. The darkness took on a solidity, impeding the progress of the Child, but it did not falter, letting the thickness of the air hold it up through the continuing night.

The air became harder, more obdurate, until it all but imprisoned the Child, binding it as if in a cage.

("Oh, God, Surata," Arkady muttered, remembering the men hanging in cages.

("Release it, Arkady. You are held in me and can come to no harm."

("Hold me, then.")

The cloying, binding darkness grew less oppressive, then gave way to morning and a place that was eerily remote, a high plateau of very good size, but which dropped away preciptiously on all sides.

Not far away was the nest of some huge bird, with eggs waiting to hatch. Each egg was nearly as large as the Child, and there were six of them. There were signs that the chicks were about to emerge from their shells, but the parent was nowhere in sight. The Child stood by the nest, watching with interest as the first shells began to crack.

An enormous-beaked head poked out of the broken shell, already gaping for nourishment. Almost at once, there was a second chick, as demanding as the first. Both squeaked and craned their scrawny necks, desperate, ugly, hungry.

When four of the six had fought their way out of their eggs, they began to peck at one another, each trying to gain nourishment and room in the nest. The last two eggs were cracking. In unison, the first four turned on these unhatched eggs and began a steady assault on them with their beaks. From their manner and determination, the Child knew the chicks wanted to destroy the unhatched nestlings.

The Child held out its hands, hoping to separate the baby birds. The birds at once seized on it, grabbing for fingers, for face, for legs and toes, for ambiguous genitals, for any bit of flesh that might end their hunger.

As the beaks tore and snapped at the Child, it did not try to stop them; and almost at once, the huge baby birds changed. The nest was a nest no longer, but a wall of bamboo, and the beaks were the cut ends of staves, pressing the Child's body, fastening there with the determination of leeches.

"You have come to me at last," said a voice from the bamboo, a deep, gratified voice that belonged to the Bundhi.

"We never ran from you," said the Child. "We were always coming to you."

"Fool!" the Bundhi upbraided it. "What a fool you are!"

The Child sat, folding its legs with soles turned up at the knees, a contented smile on its face. It made no attempt to dislodge the staves.

"I will drain you, fools!" the Bundhi promised.

"You may try," said the Child. "But there are two of us, and we have the strength of each, as well as the strength of both together. You will be surfeited long before we are empty." Its smile became a beatific grin, and the light of it grew brighter.

More staves bent toward the Child, fastening their wooden mouths wherever there was open space on the little body. Only the Subtle Centers and the head were untouched as the staves fed and fed.

"You will be nothing! You are nothing! You are mine!" the Bundhi gloated.

"No, you are ours," the Child corrected him. "You have always given your staves your own fear for fodder. We do not fear."

"You must!" the Bundhi demanded.

"Why? Because you do?" the Child responded. "What have we to fear from you?"

"You will die!" the Bundhi thundered at the Child. "You will be nothing."

"Not even eternity endures forever," said the Child, watching as the first few staves dropped away from it, leaving nothing more than a small red mark on its skin. "They will all fade," said the Child. "Including your portal, and all that you have called through it will have to gain strength from you or vanish. You have brought too much to do your bidding—you cannot give sustenance to them all."

More than half the staves had fallen from the Child's arms and body; they lay, small, pale twigs, scattered on the plateau, light enough to be carried away on the afternoon breeze.

"They will grow again," The Bundhi promised.

"We will be here when they do," said the Child, rising from its place, nothing attached to it any longer.

The Bundhi began to chant, but he stopped almost at once. "Why don't they answer?"

"Because we fed them, not you, and they cannot hear you now," the Child said, a bit sadly. "The portal is failing."

"It cannot!" the Bundhi shrieked.

The Child put its hand on the last of the staves and watched as they shrank to little sprouts. "Your high redoubt is gone, O Bundhi."

There was no answer. Only the wind sighed over the plateau.

Slowly the Child walked to the edge of the plateau, then deliberately stepped off into

the ecstatically entwined bodies of Arkady Sól and Surata.

Epilogue

A confused old man sat beside the trail, his hands uselessly joined in his lap. He scowled at the tall young man leading the blind woman up the swath of the recent avalanches. As the two approached him, he crawled away, mewling in terror.

The sun stood high over the gorge; Arkady shaded his eyes to look up at it. "Well?" he said to Surata at last.

"Well?" she repeated.

"Where do we go now?"

She smiled. "Where would you like to go? What would you like to do?"

"I don't know," he answered after a moment. "What does a man who used to be a soldier do?"

"You ... could return to your homeland," she suggested without enthusiasm.

"And do what? I am disgraced, I have no one waiting for me. Where are you going?" There was a stronger light in his eyes. "Where are *you* going, Surata?"

She shook her head. "I don't know. Perhaps Gora Čimtarga."

At that name, the old man cried out from his hiding place.

"Gora Čimtarga? Why?" Arkady asked, looking up the narrow, rocky trail.

"It's a place to begin. It's empty. Of everything. There is no Right Hand Path or Left Hand Path there. I can make my own way." She held out her hand to him, grateful when he took her fingers in his.

"You'll never get there on your own," he pointed out.

She said nothing; tears stood in her blighted eyes.

"What will you do there?" He brushed a stray lock of hair off her face.

She shrugged. "Study."

"You need two to do it properly," he said, wishing she could see his grin. "Are you going to make me ask?" he demanded after a moment.

"Are you going to make *me?*" she countered, the tears spilling at last.

He took her into his arms, laughing though his throat was tight. "God, Surata, I was so afraid . . ."

She kissed him. "Haven't you learned yet that when you fear something, go toward it?"

He said nothing. Gently he wiped her tears from her cheeks. "Right. We go to Gora Čimtarga."

She held him more tightly. "And then?"

"Who knows? First we have to get there."

"Arkady . . ."

"Not 'immai'? Not 'champion'? Just Arkady?" he teased her kindly.

"How can I call you that when you are so many more things to me?" She was very serious now, her unseeing eyes directed at his.

"Do you think we could ever do that again?" He could not tell her what had happened to him because of their victory.

"We have accomplished it once," she pointed out. "My father and my uncles never achieved that."

"But we could," he said with growing hope.

Her smile was splendid. "Yes, it's possible, if that is what we truly want to do."

Arkady lifted her hands to his lips. "Then perhaps I should call you Child."

"Child," she said with him, making the word a pledge.

QUESTAR®

...MEANS THE BEST SCIENCE FICTION AND THE MOST ENTHRALLING FANTASY.

Like all readers, science fiction and fantasy readers are looking for a good story. Questar® has them—entertaining, enlightening stories that will take readers beyond the farthest reaches of the galaxy, and into the deepest heart of fantasy. Whether it's awesome tales of intergalactic adventure and alien contact, or wondrous and beguiling stories of magic and epic quests, Questar® will delight readers of all ages and tastes.

___**PASSAGE AT ARMS**　　　　　　(E20-006, $2.95, U.S.A.)
　　by Glen Cook　　　　　　　　(E20-007, $3.75, Canada)

A continuation of the universe Glen Cook develops in *The Starfishers Trilogy*, this is a wholly new story of an ex-officer-turned-reporter taking the almost suicidal assignment of covering an interstellar war from a tiny, front-line attack ship.

___**PANDORA'S GENES**　　　　　　(E20-004, $2.95, U.S.A.)
　　by Kathryn Lance　　　　　　　(E20-005, $3.75, Canada)

A first novel by a fresh new talent, this book combines a love triangle with a race to save humanity. In a post-holocaustal world, where technology is of the most primitive sort, a handful of scientists race against time to find a solution to the medical problem that may mean humanity's ultimate extinction.

___**THE DUSHAU TRILOGY #1: DUSHAU**　　(E20-015, $2.95, U.S.A.)
　　by Jacqueline Lichtenberg　　　　　　(E20-016, $3.75, Canada)

The Dushau see the end of a galactic civilization coming—but that's not surprising for a race of near-immortals whose living memory spans several thousand years. The newly crowned emperor of the Allegiancy wants to pin his troubles on Prince Jindigar and the Dushau, but Krinata, a plucky young woman who works with the Dushau, determines to aid their cause when she discovers the charges are false.

132